GHOST STORM

SECHIN TOWER

Siege Tower Entertainment

Published in the United States of America
By Siege Tower Entertainment, LLC, Everett, WA

ISBN 978-0-9848507-6-1

Printed in the United States of America
First Edition published 2015

Cover Photographs:
"Sturmfront auf Doppler-Radar-Schirm" (Public Domain) by Ulrich Rosemeyer
via Wikimedia Commons
"RV Thomas G. Thompson – Radar Monitor 01" (GNU Free Documentation
License/ Creative Commons Attribution-share Alike 3.0 Unported license) by
Joe Mabel via Wikimedia Commons

Mad Science Institute crest by Christopher Maddon
http://chrismaddenart.com/contact.html

Cover Layout and Design: Sechin Tower

Interior art by Christopher Martin
www.christopherlm.com/

Edited by Jane Kenealy

This is a work of fiction. Names, characters, places, and incidents either are the product of the author's imagination or are used fictitiously. Frankly, if this weren't pure fiction, we'd all be in big trouble.

No artificial intelligences were harmed in the making of this book.

WWW.SECHINTOWER.COM

To all the teachers.

Acknowledgements

First, let me express my gratitude to my Kickstarter backers, without whom the production of this book (and several other Mad Science Institute products) could never have existed:

Colleen Lang, ...the rich, Adam Kilmartin, Allia Tuttle, Argaen, Becky B, Brando Freyling, Bruce Paulson, Caitlin Jane Hughes, Chad Bowden,   Charles Spangle, Daniel Jones, Daniel W. Cisek, David Levi,   Derek "Pineapple Steak" Swoyer, Dorie McCormack, E. Mitchell, Ed Matuskey, Gabriel Garcia, Garrett Pease, Hugh and Sherri Tower, Jake Ivey, James Reed, Jeff "Freakin'" Combos, Jeff Raymond, Jeffrey Cook, Jennifer Chaffee, Jim Cook, Jordan Thole, Katherine McClintock, Katie Tower, Keith Scherer, Kennedy Thompson, Kit Wessendorf, Kristina Fox, Laura Hansen, Lauren and Nich Gray, Lee French, Lynn Lawrence, M. Craig Stockwell, Maia, Mario Dongu, Nestor Rodriguez, Nonie Skoog, Peter "Awesome Pants" Suruda, Philda Todzaniso, Rachel Barnard, Rich Harrison, Rob Steinberger, Rolanda Ward, Shawn "Groovy" Hilton, Simon "Cake or Death" Carter, Sonya Carducci Smith, Stephanie, SwordFire, Terry Neil, Thomas Zilling, Tyler and Jennifer Running Deer, Vincent Noiseux

I'll see you guys in the lab!

I also need to apologize because I failed to thank some people in previous books. Several people have contributed their imaginations and efforts to making these books what they are. If it is possible to thank these individuals enough, I certainly have not done so. What can I say: I've been a total jerk. Sorry.

Andrew Fenton fixed my Latin in the Institute's motto.

Shawn Hilton came up with the idea for disguising the doomsday machine in *Mad Science Institute* into a thrill-ride. Brilliant. And groovy.

Wes Devin instructed me in the finer points of sabotaging engines with a screwdriver, which was what I needed for *The Non-Zombie Apocalypse*.

Jason Nicholson corrected several of my misunderstandings about tornado formation. I hope I got all this right in this book!

Theresa Vasquez helped me translate "We got this elephant off the roof" and several other lines into Spanish in this book.

Jeff Raymond scienced up the science like nobody else could.

Jane Kenealy talked me out of some very stupid ideas.

Katie Tower is just plain awesome and makes me feel like I can do anything—even write a book.

And a special thanks to my proof readers: Jennifer Chaffee, Jane Kenealy, Lehuanani Pischke, Jeff Raymond, and Hugh Tower. It takes an army of eyes to combat the Typo Menace in any book this size, and I am deeply grateful for your service.

CHAPTER ZERO

Frozen rain lashed Brick's goggles as he dragged a pair of chairs across the yard—a task made much more difficult by the two old people tied up in those chairs. They squirmed a lot, and all their wailing and crying was surprisingly annoying—and surprising, considering the strips of duct tape Brick had placed across their mouths.

The weather was an even bigger problem. The cold numbed his fingers while the rain soaked through his leather chaps and denim jeans all the way to his tighty-whiteys. Then there was the crusty old snow that pulled at his feet like wet cement. Brick was twice as strong as the average man and four times as large, but here his size worked against him. A lighter person might easily have moved over the icy surface, yet each of Brick's heavy steps broke the plate of ice, dropping his boot through a foot of slush to the frozen ground beneath. To make matters worse, the white stuff didn't roll up into nice, neat snowballs in front of the chairs he was dragging. Instead, it broke loose in wedges the size of sheet cakes that added a surprising amount of weight to his burdens. By the time he was halfway across the yard, Brick felt like one of those ancient whaling ships cutting its way through icy waters on a journey to the North Pole.

"Minnesota," Brick muttered, and he meant it as a curse word. As if the weather wasn't terrible enough, he also had plenty of other bad memories of this state, none of which he really cared to dwell upon. All that mattered at the moment was getting the old farts in the chairs over to his teammates in the black trucks, just like his new boss had ordered. Then the technicians could go to work on the house, and, if all went well, they might actually blow out of the Midwest before his nose froze off.

Without warning, the old lady's chair broke and she plopped unceremoniously into the dirty snow. Brick grunted his disapproval. The way he saw it, this was her fault for wiggling around while weighing almost twice as much as her husband, whose chair remained unbroken. Too many tater-tots and hot dishes, he judged. Not enough consideration for how her bulk might affect any furniture to which she might one day be tied. Brick considered hauling her through the snow by the ankle (a suitable penalty for her inconsiderate response to being kidnapped), but he eventually rejected this notion because it would have further slowed him down. Instead, he grabbed her by the folds in her baggy Vikings sweatshirt and heaved her over his shoulder. It turned out to be easier to carry her this way than in the chair—at least, it was easier for Brick, who could have lifted a struggling donkey onto his gigantic shoulders. He wished he had taken the sack-of-potatoes approach from the start, or at least invested a few minutes in searching their house for sturdier chairs. Live and learn.

When he reached the black trucks, he set the old couple down so they would have been able to see their house if they hadn't been blindfolded. The old lady fell flat on her back and sobbed, so Brick rearranged her until she was leaning against her husband's knees. Now only her legs and bottom rested in the snow instead of her whole body, yet, he noted with contempt, she didn't even try to thank him.

Brick would have preferred to simply get rid of the old couple permanently, but the new boss had insisted that a murder investigation was not preferable at this stage of their project. As long as his paychecks cleared, Brick was happy to respond with a heartfelt "whatever." Besides, with all this frozen rain, the old people were soaking wet, so they might simply die of hypothermia and Brick would get his way after all.

The technicians in the trucks began chattering about the upcoming event. Brick adjusted his goggle straps, even though they said he wouldn't need any special eye-ware. They also said he might miss the show if he blinked, so he locked the house in a one-way staring contest.

It was a nice little upper-middle-class rambler, with a wrap-around deck, a two-car freestanding garage, and almost a city block of icicle-laden elms between them and their nearest neighbor. It even had an honest-to-goodness white picket fence encircling the front yard. Whatever these two geezers had done before retirement, they had been paid well. Brick couldn't afford a house like that, so he decided to take extra pride in what was coming next.

"Fully charged and beginning countdown," the tech's voice came through Brick's earpiece.

All the other agents and technicians hustled for cover behind the trucks. They were such goodie-goodies, always following protocol and giving each other snappy little salutes. It made Brick want to puke. He missed the good old days, back when he rode with his old gang, the Blitzkrieg Legion. The Blitzkriegers knew how to get things done, and they didn't need to act like yuppies to do it. But that was before Professor Helmholtz died and the Feds came down so hard that the Blitzkriegers had to split up and go on the lam. A few, like Brick, went to work for the new boss, and others joined different syndicates. These were sad days, having to wear a uniform and kidnap senior citizens. At least Brick enjoyed some special privileges, mostly because none of the new boss's regular operatives dared to object when he refused to wear a helmet or when he tore the sleeves off his uniform to show off his tattoos. They respected him, but some of them didn't yet fear him, so he would need to work on that.

The tech began counting down from ten, but stopped at six. "Brick," he said. "Brick, you need to get to cover."

"Go stuff yourself," Brick answered.

There was a pause. The tech may have been conferring with others via different channels, but when he resumed the count on the common channel he started again from 10. When he said "one," there was another pause, and then the world was instantly replaced by white light and a shockwave of thunder.

Just by coincidence, Brick blinked an instant before it happened and it was over before he un-blinked. Still, his retina remained burned with the afterimage of a blue-white lance of electricity blasting down from the sky. He had overheard the techs talking about how the heat-coils they had placed on the roof would keep most of the lightning's energy from being channeled into the ground. They had set it up so that the heat would ignite the gas line and flash-boil all the water in the pipes. Just as planned, this resulted in the instantaneous destruction of the house.

Brick opened his eyes in time to see chunks of roof tiles and a door flying high into the air above an expanding gray sphere of smoke. He also noted that the obnoxiously perfect white picket fence was gone, and he had only a split second to wonder where it went before he realized that pieces of it were rocketing towards him, blasted outwards by the concussive force of the exploding house. The pickets, along with other debris, speared the trucks lined up at the curb and probably knocked the glass out of the neighbors' windows two blocks away.

Three or four sharp chunks of wood also found Brick. One grazed his bald scalp, another stabbed his thigh, and a third skewered his sagging stomach. They stung painfully, but he didn't allow himself to react. The techs obviously needed a reminder of how tough he was, so he wanted to make sure they had a chance to see. After all, his former employer had implanted a special fiber mesh beneath his skin that made him bullet proof, so some chunks of wood weren't much threat.

Unfortunately, that same mesh under his skin also prevented the wooden skewers from penetrating very deeply, which resulted in the board in his thigh falling out before anyone could see it. The picket in his stomach, however, got caught in his ample folds of flab. It would have been more dramatic if it had been sticking out of his chest, but it still made a good visual.

"Brick," said the tech. "Brick, are you okay?"

"Why wouldn't I be?" he smiled grimly.

Now that he knew he had the tech's attention, he brushed the board from his belly as if he had only just noticed it. Later, when he was alone, he would have to go after all the splinters with tweezers and hydrogen peroxide—if, that is, he could reach that part of his stomach—but in the meantime, he reveled in the awe of those who had seen him shrug it off, and he knew they would whisper exaggerated stories to those who hadn't.

"Brick," another technician came over the common channel. "You are almost as terrifying as that Predecessor guy."

Almost? Brick's sense of satisfaction immediately upended into anger. *Almost!* He didn't want to be *almost* as terrifying as the most terrifying man on the planet. He wanted to *be* the most terrifying man.

He knew just who the tech was talking about, too. The Predecessor—nobody knew why he was called that—was a bony, bald-headed dude who hung around the new boss all the time. He never seemed to say or do anything, but for some reason all the men were unsettled around him. Brick felt a little uneasy in the Predecessor's presence, although he couldn't figure out why. Sure, he was tall, but Brick outweighed him by at least two hundred pounds of muscle and meanness. If not the physical size, then it must have been those cold, black eyes that made the Predecessor so creepy. Everyone assumed that he was a bodyguard, but Brick knew that wasn't so. When the boss had hired Brick, he'd specifically stated that Brick's duties might someday include putting the Predecessor out of his misery.

Just give me an excuse to get my hands on that Predecessor, Brick thought. *Then we'll see who's terrifying.*

The excavation team now took the field, rushing from the black trucks across the rubble-strewn yard to begin clearing debris away from the house's foundation. As they worked, the rain kept stinging the wound on Brick's scalp and he kept fuming. *Almost as terrifying... Almost...* If the little twerps Brick worked with forgot to be afraid, they might stop handing over their food when he glared at them, or they might begin to refuse giving up their chairs when he wanted to sit down. His immediate superiors might even find the guts to start giving him orders, and no good could come of that.

If they forgot that biggest is best, he might end up having to hurt someone to prove it. So, as a favor to all of them, he decided to grant them a clear reminder to ensure they would never again use his name and the word "almost" in the same sentence.

"Bad news," the excavation team leader's voice crackled through the earpiece. "The foundation's cracked, but not enough to finish breaking it with hammers. We'll need the C-4 to clear this."

Brick rolled his eyes. Blowing the foundation with explosives would take at least 20 more minutes to set up, and that meant more time standing around while the rain dripped off his scalp and down his jacket. Also, using high-powered, illegal explosives to clear rubble would make it more likely that the cops would be able to track them down—not that it was Brick's job to worry about such things, but it still bugged him.

Brick let out a rumble of displeasure, then marched towards the house.

"Where are you going?" one of the operatives called after him.

"Finishing your job," Brick told him as he slogged over the yard and down into the rubble that had been a house only a moment ago.

A few small fires burned despite the rain, and he found the ground was still warm from the explosion. The excavation crew stood atop mounds of cracked stone slabs. By the lights of their flashlights, Brick could see the surprise on their faces as he approached.

"This the spot?" Brick stamped a chunk of concrete with his foot.

The team leader nodded his head, fat balls of rainwater dripping from his hair.

Without a word, Brick grabbed the sledgehammer from the leader's hands, lifted it high above his head, and brought it down with a thunderous boom that bounced rain, ashes, and crewmen into the air. The blow snapped the shaft of the hammer in Brick's hands, but it also cracked the slab from one end of the foundation to the other. He grabbed another hammer and broke it, too, with a second violent swing that sprayed chunks of gray concrete all around him. The third hammer blow exposed the rebar inside the foundation.

"Saw those!" he commanded, jabbing his thick finger at the rebar.

"But..." whatever the team leader's protest might have been, he swallowed it when Brick glared at him.

The excavation team grabbed their power tools and attacked the thick steel rebar like jackals gnawing at the ribs of a wildebeest. As soon as they cut through, Brick shoved them aside and bent the bars back with his bare hands. Then he broke the fourth and final sledgehammer to obliterate the last of the concrete.

Finally, he tossed the splintered hammer handle at their feet. His hands ached from the force of the blows, but the important thing was that they were staring at him in amazement. He had single-handedly done the job of sixteen ounces of plastic explosives, and in less time than it would have taken to set up the detonator. Now they could get on with digging up whatever ancient artifact they had come to find—Brick didn't really care what it was, only that they remembered what he had done to help get to it.

Let's see the Predecessor beat that, Brick thought as he folded his arms and watched the others work.

December 13

(10 Days Before Stormageddon)

CHAPTER 1

The cold air bit hard into Dean's face and left him wondering how long it would take to die of exposure.

Probably too long, he supposed. The big down jacket he had purchased from an expensive outfitter would keep his core temperature high enough that disfiguring frostbite would set in long before hypothermia. Still, would anyone notice if he were to simply lie down atop Denise McKenzie's grave and let the snow cover him like a shroud? The cemetery groundskeeper might not find him until the storm ended, or perhaps not even until the spring thaw. Everyone would simply shrug their shoulders and assume that a California boy like him simply didn't understand how to survive in the Midwest, where the weather could kill a person in fifty different ways.

His phone buzzed, forcing him to partially surface from his morbid thoughts. It was a text from his cousin, Soap, wanting to know if he'd had a chance to review her research proposal. He had looked at it—or at least the first three sentences, which had been enough to leave him bewildered. He supposed he should respond soon, because she had a distressing tendency to conduct disastrous experiments while waiting for him to approve her other disastrous experiments. In that, she was just like most of the other students at the Mechanical Science Institute.

Dean had been in charge of the Institute for four months now, ever since McKenzie had died, yet he still felt like he didn't have a clue about how to run it. He was just a normal guy—he knew his way around a toolbox and a truck engine, but he had absolutely no knowledge of physics, chemistry, or calculus. To make things harder, the Institute wasn't structured like any school he'd ever been to. They didn't have lessons or classes, except those they took at the sponsoring university. Rather, they proposed research projects and then followed through independently, with each student giving critiques and assistance to their peers along the way. Their projects were always wild, too: aerial drone swarms, carbon-fiber body armor, and neural regeneration had all come up for review. Dean was supposed to approve or deny their proposals, but they may as well have been written in Sanskrit as far as he could understand them. Sometimes, he thought the most amazing part of his job was how the students hadn't all blown themselves to pieces conducting experiments he never should have approved in the first place.

He had stepped up to run the school after McKenzie had died, intending to clean house and make the Institute safe for the students as well as the rest of the world. He felt he needed to do it, especially because one of those students was his own cousin, but all he'd managed to accomplish during his tenure was to become entangled in academic bureaucracy. It had been foolish to expect any other result. He wasn't an academic, or a teacher, or a detective. He was actually a firefighter, and a good one, but the skills of battling blazes and extracting people from mangled cars just didn't transfer to the laboratory or the classroom. He was failing, and he knew it. Everyone else must have figured it out by now, too. If McKenzie could see him from wherever she was, then she knew it too, and that was the hardest thing for him to bear.

I'm useless here, Dean confessed silently, just as he had done every time he visited McKenzie's grave. *The best thing I can do for the Institute is to quit.*

Feet crunched through the snow behind him and he turned to see two men in dark suits. Agents O'Grady and Nash, the FBI investigators who had helped uncover Helmholtz's criminal organization, had somehow found him here in the cemetery.

As Dean watched them approach, he felt anger flare up inside him. It wasn't that he didn't like these guys, it was simply that they were intruding on his thoughts. He'd been feeling these little surges of fury quite frequently lately, usually over stupid, unimportant things. It made him want to grab the nearest person and tear him in half, but he'd always managed to hold it inside long enough to vent his wrath on barbells, a heavy bag, or some other inanimate object. He would do the same here: these agents were smart enough to recognize anger as a sign of grief, and he didn't believe they had a right to know what he was feeling. If they recognized it, they might try to console him, and he didn't want their pity, or anyone else's. He wanted to show the world he was all right. And he was all right—just so long as he could keep shoving the emotions down deep enough.

Agent Nash nodded in greeting. Despite the cold, he wore only a set of earmuffs and kept his hair trimmed so short it registered as little more than a shadow on his dark brown skin. Nash appeared surprisingly young for an FBI agent, and, for whatever reason, he was always the one to do the talking.

"2002 called," Nash said. "It wants its flip-phone back."

Dean hadn't realized he was still holding his phone. He closed it and dropped it into his pocket. "I'm trying to avoid devices that are smarter than me," he said. "It's not hard to do these days. Guess I'm not really a gizmo guy."

"Seems odd that you're in charge of Gizmo University, then," Nash said.

"I was just thinking the same thing."

As always, Agent O'Grady stood by quietly and watched. The flat expression on the older man's lined face seemed to have been stamped in steel and his wiry gray hair appeared thoroughly subdued beneath his black wool hat. Sometimes Dean wondered if the man were mute or just senile. He decided O'Grady couldn't be senile: he looked way too mean for that.

"Can I assume you two aren't here to pay your respects?" Dean asked as he started slogging his way through the snow towards the parking lot. Whatever the agents wanted with him, he didn't want to discuss it in front of McKenzie's grave.

"We need to talk to you about Helmholtz's men," Nash said.

"Helmholtz is dead," Dean blew a steaming breath out through his nose. "And if you want to talk to me, I have an office. It's got chairs and everything, which makes it a nicer place to hold conversations than out here in the middle of this blizzard. By the way, should I ask how you knew I was here?"

"You come here every Monday and Saturday, and most Wednesdays as well."

Dean glared at Nash.

"We're the FBI," the agent made an exaggerated shrug. "It's our job to know things, and this was a shorter drive for us so we decided to meet you here. Besides, up until now I didn't know if you knew how to use that phone because you haven't been returning our calls."

"You stopped returning mine first." Dean sounded petty, even to his own ears, and he knew he was allowing his anger to creep too close to the surface. Yes, his calls to the FBI had gone unanswered, but he couldn't blame them for not taking him more seriously. Back when he had first arrived at the Institute, he had sent them everything he had found that might incriminate Helmholtz in McKenzie's death. This "evidence" had included photos of dinosaur skeletons, blueprints for cybernetic implants, and recipes for weaponized diseases. Somehow, it all ended up sounding like wild stories and conspiracy theories. There was more he wanted to tell them, too, but he couldn't—not without breaking his promise to McKenzie to keep certain secrets safe within the Institute.

O'Grady folded his arms and cocked an eyebrow. Nash, perhaps taking a cue from this, cleared his throat. "It's Angela Black," Nash said. "She's requested to speak to you."

Dean stopped walking. He knew Angela Black was as crazy as a wolverine on caffeine. The last time Dean had seen her, she had shot him through the leg before trying to activate a doomsday machine that would have sent the world back to the dark ages.

"I thought Angela was in jail," Dean said.

"She is. But she's been hinting that she knows something that she's only willing to tell you."

"Why me?"

"We were hoping you could tell us. There have been a few new developments that make us want to take it seriously."

"Like what?"

Nash looked at O'Grady, then back to Dean. "Do you know any reason why Brick Stellenleiter would be back in Minnesota?"

Dean wanted to ask why on Earth the six-hundred-pound biker would return here instead of fleeing the country, but if the agents had known that, they wouldn't have been asking Dean. "I saw Brick a month and a half ago," Dean said. "We were in Arizona. I shot him."

"Really?" Nash looked surprised. "Are you saying that you killed Brick?"

"Killed him?" Dean laughed. "Bullets don't kill Brick, they just make him mad. I popped him three or four times, he threw a desk at my head, and then my memory gets real fuzzy after that."

"This is no time for jokes, Mr. Lazarchek."

Dean wasn't joking, but he supposed it wouldn't do any good to try to convince them of it. Just one more reason for them to think he was a crack-pot.

"As for Angela," Nash went on. "Do you know of anything she might want from you? Information on a research project, perhaps? Any kind of loose end that Helmholtz failed to tie off?"

"Maybe this," Dean produced a black, wrinkly rock from his jacket's inner pocket. It was about the size of a softball but shaped like an egg with a flattened bottom. He tossed it to Nash, who caught it deftly.

"What is it?" he asked.

Dean wasn't sure how to begin explaining it, or even if he should. It was some new kind of data storage device—or maybe a very old kind, since everybody agreed it had been around a long, long time even though nobody knew who created it. For some reason, McKenzie had listed this little thing as priceless among all the Institute's treasures. Dean had never believed it could be so valuable, but he had developed the habit of carrying it in his pocket for safekeeping all the same.

"We just call it 'the Egg,'" Dean said. "If you put it in the right kind of electric field, it'll project lights that show a map of how the Earth looked two hundred million years ago."

As the agent studied the Egg, Dean felt the first hints of snow in the form of jagged, icy little flakes. Since moving to Minnesota, Dean had come to realize that if it were true that Eskimos had 40 different words for snow, it was because there were at least that many different kinds. It made him long to return to California, where the types of snow were strictly limited to "none" or "emergency closure for all schools and highways."

"Nifty toy," Nash tossed the Egg back to Dean. "Too bad Professor McKenzie isn't here to explain it to us, right?"

Something inside Dean went colder than the air around him. "I need to go now," he said, and stepped onto the recently plowed parking lot.

"Wait," Nash said, with a quick glance at O'Grady. "I didn't mean to offend you. I was trying to sympathize. Maybe it'd do some good just to talk about it, don't you think?"

"Talking's pointless," Dean kept walking. In the distance, lightning suddenly blazed through the clouds. As if in response, the Egg glowed in Dean's stiff fingers.

"Thunder-snow," Nash said, looking at the distant cloud. "This is some rare weather we're having. We should probably all go indoors and wait it out."

Dean ignored him just like he ignored the weather. They had arrived at his truck, so he began the slow process of unlocking the door with fingers that felt too cold to grip his bundle of keys. He didn't mind the pain in his stiff joints. Secretly, he felt he deserved it. Nevertheless, he moved carefully, only because he didn't want to drop the keys where the agents could see him fail.

"So, Mr. Lazarchek," Nash asked hopefully. "Will you go speak with Angela?"

"No." Dean slid into his truck and placed the Egg on the passenger seat next to him.

"She might have some information—"

"She can email," Dean slammed his door and started his engine. They didn't try to stop him as he drove off into the snow.

By the time he was five minutes down the road, the snow was piling up on his windshield faster than his wipers could clear it. The roads had been freshly plowed, but the storm was intensifying so quickly that any plowing older than thirty minutes was swiftly becoming irrelevant. It wasn't until the dark clouds overhead flashed bright white that Dean finally realized he was in very real danger. People died in weather like this all the time by skidding off slick roads or getting fried by lightning. Dean wasn't sure which of those would be preferable.

Lightning flashed again, this time so bright that it made him blink. When he opened his eyes, a green man sat next to him.

Startled, Dean jerked the wheel and stomped the brakes, sending his truck into a brief but sickening spin. After one and a half full rotations, it skidded to a stop almost perpendicular to the road.

Dean now could see that his passenger was not a flesh-and-blood person, but instead some kind of pure green light, transparent enough to allow him to see through the man's green face to the snow swirling outside the truck. The ghostly passenger had a shock of curly, lightly-colored hair and a walrus-sized mustache to match. He wore an emerald necktie and a dapper jade vest that might have belonged to a banker in a cowboy movie. All the green hues gave the impression of an image on an extremely outdated computer monitor, except that this figure was three dimensional and as large as life.

Blinking again, Dean tried to convince himself it was a trick of the light. A reflection on the window, maybe. Or the afterimage of lightning on his retina. When he opened his eyes, however, the green ghost was still there.

"Who...?" Dean sputtered stupidly.

The ghost opened his mouth to speak, but the only sound was a sudden squawk of static on the radio that sounded just a bit like the word *Help*, but the rest was too garbled to make any real sense. Upon hearing this, the ghost cocked one caterpillar-like eyebrow, deposited a fat cigar into his mouth, and proceeded to exhale a series of green holographic smoke rings. He then regarded Dean with a smile that seemed somehow friendly, smug, and sad all at the same time.

At the distant rumble of thunder, the ghost faded from sight.

Dean reached out to paw the empty air like a blind man, but there was no trace of the mysterious passenger. The experience was made even stranger because Dean couldn't shake the notion that the green man's face looked familiar, like someone he had met somewhere, but he just couldn't place him.

Chapter 2

Looking at the marble bust of the Institute's co-founder, Dean suddenly slapped himself on the forehead. He had walked past this image of Mark Twain at least twice a day for the past four months every time he entered Topsy House, the one-and-only home of the Mechanical Science Institute. And yet he still hadn't recognized the great writer when he saw him.

Mark Twain! The ghost in his truck had been the spitting image of Mark Twain painted in green light. With the infamous inventor Nikola Tesla, Twain had founded the Mechanical Science Institute, along with its parent organization, Langdon University, and the town in which it was located, Bugswallow, Minnesota. Although Tesla's role was largely unknown to the general public, Twain was regarded as a kind of saint by the locals. His books were always in stock at the local bookstore and his bushy-haired image graced half a hundred portraits, statues, and storefront displays around town. Dean had heard they even had an annual celebration called Mississippi Days, which culminated in a parade featuring a young Twain in a steamboat captain's outfit waving to the onlookers from the deck of his float. Dean must be the only man within twenty miles who wouldn't have immediately recognized Mark Twain.

At least he had worked out that the mysterious green image had been projected from the Egg, even though the little rock had never done anything like that before. He knew the Egg could project a map—a very valuable map that marked off the locations of ancient geothermal stations created by the Predecessors, a prehistoric race that disappeared before the dinosaurs went extinct. This was another thing Dean had once tried to tell the FBI agents, and had been dismissed as a lunatic.

Somehow, the lightning must have triggered this new projection. Dean felt convinced of it, yet still unsettled by all the other unanswered questions. Who had recorded the image of the famous author? And, more importantly, why? Did the recording carry some kind of message, or was it just the result of someone—Tesla, perhaps—playing around with a piece of technology the way a person toys with the camera app in a new phone?

Something else nagged at Dean, too, although he didn't have the words to put it straight. The image of Twain seemed somehow aware and responsive. Those green eyes had looked right at him, studied him the way a real, living person would study a new face. And the garbled voice that came through the radio had sounded as if it were trying to speak— had it said "Help?" Maybe. Or maybe Dean was as crazy as the FBI agents probably thought he was.

He figured his best move now was to find one of the senior students and let them know what happened, even if it turned out to be nothing more than a curiosity. But when Dean stepped into the main-floor decoy lab, all thoughts of the Egg were immediately driven from his head.

The decoy lab (so called because those who worked there didn't know that there was a bigger, more terrifying lab five hundred feet below their sneakers) was, as usual, a riot of activity and unstable experiments. Energetic students argued about theories, tested inventions, hammered sheet metal, scraped sparking wires together, and tended to witches' brews bubbling inside flasks and test tubes. They were teenagers, younger than the college students they shared Langdon University with, yet typically far smarter than their older peers. Despite the Institute students' high IQs, Dean wondered if there wasn't some other missing factor in most of them. Maturity, maybe. Or even plain old common sense. Just another reason why he should hurry up and find his replacement so that he could move back to where he belonged.

Today, the red-headed McGregor twins—one boy and one girl whom most of the students called Thing 1 and Thing 2—were bickering about the best equations to represent polygons in eleven-dimensional space. Janet Cho was yelling vigorously to no one in particular about how the rats in her experiment needed less noise in the area. Mike Raskolnikov, the pudgy Russian kid Dean still worried wasn't fitting in, sat in his corner cackling madly as he tested his latest batch of home-brewed fireworks. At least this time his pyrotechnics consisted of colorful flashes rather than loud bangs, but it probably wouldn't be long before the boy combined the two.

"Raskolnikov!" Dean barked. "What did I say about fireworks indoors?"

"You wanted me to light them up?" his round cheeks pulled back in an impish grin as he lifted a burning match in one hand and a home-made Roman candle in the other.

"No," Dean said. "Do *not* light it up. Not in here."

"But everything's fireproof." Raskolnikov demonstrated by lighting the Roman candle and pointing at a wall, point blank. The colorful flashes left nothing more than charcoal smudges on the bricks. The students had quickly discovered that the walls consisted of a super high-tech material that wouldn't burn, chip, dent, or crack when exposed to anything short of a direct hit from a cruise missile. Even so, Dean had been a firefighter too long to like the idea of fireworks, especially indoors. He grabbed the Roman candle from the boy's hand and redirected it into the sink until he could drown it with enough water to put an end to its light show.

"The building might be fireproof," Dean said. "But you're not. So please hold off until we can get professional supervision. Maybe we can hire someone from the local bomb squad for you."

"Can I light stuff up outdoors, then?

"No lighting anything up right now. Period. Got it?"

Raskolnikov might have been about to nod, but Dean's attention was stolen by a sudden, thunderous *WHOMP!* sounding from the opposite end of the lab.

Dean dashed towards the noise, his imagination painting pictures of students crushed beneath gigantic robot arms. Instead, he found Collin Rosenberg, a lanky kid with a Spinal Tap t-shirt and a green, spiked Mohawk that added a full twelve inches to his height. He was typing commands into a computer attached to an immense set of sound speakers with what appeared to be telescoping cannons for woofers. Twenty feet away, inside a small cordon of yellow caution tape, several mugs rested on a coffee table and, behind them, a cardboard standee of Richard Nixon in all his presidential glory.

"What's going on?" Dean demanded.

Collin, who wore heavy earphones, didn't seem to hear. Instead, he tapped "enter" on a keyboard. One of the speaker's cannon-woofers swiveled slightly and its muzzle contracted like the iris of a menacing eye.

Dean placed a hand on Collin's shoulder, which made him jump in surprise. The boy pulled the headphones off his ears—carefully, so that the headpiece didn't crush the spikes of his green hair.

"What's up, Mister L?" said Collin, using his personal nickname for Dean. Most of the other students called him "D-Squared" because he was the Dean of Students and, by an unfortunate coincidence, also named Dean. It was better than "Double-D," as someone had initially nicknamed him.

"What's all this noise?" Dean asked.

"Oh. The noise," Collin waved his hand at the speakers. "I'm bangin' away on some targeted sonic concussion, but the 'targeted' part's proving to be a real pain in the can." He pointed to the feet of the cardboard Richard Nixon, where splatters and scrapes from broken coffee mugs ringed the floor around and behind the standee, although none had marred Tricky Dick himself.

"I think I'm dumping too much juice into it," Collin said. "I started off on power level three, but now I'm dialing the speakers down to one. Finger's crossed."

He tapped in a few more keys, hit the button, and the speakers emitted another *WHOMP!* that Dean felt in his stomach more than heard with his ears.

The coffee mugs in front of the speakers were spaced out about a foot apart from each other. When the sound blast hit them, the ones on the ends didn't budge, but the center cup flew into the air as if struck by a golf club. It sailed over Nixon's head and disappeared into the lab beyond. There was a crash, followed by a lot of yelling.

Collin looked sheepishly up at Dean. "Good thing I didn't pump it up to level—"

He didn't have time to finish his sentence before a pair of identical red-headed mathematicians stormed around the corner. One of the twins was splattered with cold coffee, and they were both demanding retribution for the whiteboard that had been broken by the flying mug. A moment later, Janet Cho joined the argument, shouting at the top of her lungs that everyone needed consider the well-being of her rats. On the other side of the lab, firecrackers boomed. Evidently, Raskolnikov had already forgotten Dean's rule against fireworks.

"Quiet! Quiet!" Dean boomed louder than the explosions. The argument paused, and all eyes turned to him. "New rule," he said. "Everybody cleans up this mess."

There was a chorus of objections as each student tried to blame everyone else.

Dean imagined what his old drill sergeant would have done in this situation, and decided it was a fine idea. "Pipe down before I make you scrub the toilets, too! I said everybody's going to clean a mess, and I meant it. But you don't have the privilege of cleaning your *own* mess. Oh, no. You have to clean someone *else's* mess. Got it?"

"But everyone else is so much more messy than we are!" said one of the twins. (Was it Thing 1? Dean couldn't remember which was which.)

"And I don't want to scrub the char marks off Raskolnikov's lab benches!" Janet shouted.

"And I don't want to clean up Janet's rat droppings!" Collin whined.

"You'll do it and you'll like it," Dean declared. "Or else—pushups!"

There was a moment of shocked silence.

"Pushups? Seriously?" said the girl twin—Dean was pretty sure she was Thing 2.

"You can't make us do pushups," Collin said. "It's a fascist repression of our rights! Besides, can't teachers get fired for that?"

"No arguments," Dean folded his arms. "It's clean ups or pushups. If you ask me, you blubbering babies could use a little more upper body strength. Besides, I'm planning on quitting long before you could get me fired."

To Dean's surprise, this elicited another moment of silence. He had to think back on what he had said before realizing he hadn't told anyone his intentions to quit the Institute. The revelation seemed to strike them with more horror than pushups.

"That's right," Dean said, his voice softening. "As soon as I can find a suitable replacement, I'm moving back home."

The stunned silence continued.

"Well," Dean sighed. "Until I'm gone, you're still going to clean up after each other, so wipe those hang-dog expressions off your faces. Now, have any of you rookies seen any of the senior students? Soap, Victor, Nikki? I need to talk to—"

"D-Squaaaaaared!" Raskolnikov howled through the lab.

Dean was ready to chew the boy out for calling him by that name, but one look at him showed that he was truly panicked.

"What's going on?" Dean demanded.

"Speed's at the door!"

Speed was their nickname for Stephanie Soto-Vasquez, the most recent admission into the Institute and a specialist in engines and aerodynamics.

"So?" Dean asked. The automatic systems at the door would detect Institute students and open up for them. Her arrival should have been no cause for panic.

"There's a guy out there with her," Raskolnikov cocked his thumb and pointed his forefinger at his temple, miming a pistol to his head. "He's got a gun, and I think he's going to shoot her!"

CHAPTER 3

"Get out here before I blow a hole in her skull!" the man at the door shouted as he pressed a chrome-plated hand cannon into Speed's ear.

Through the monitor, Dean could see them just outside the thick steel doors of Topsy House. The gunman was bundled up in a flannel shirt, a black beanie hat pulled low over his eyebrows, and a black, sleeveless vest emblazoned with the skull-in-Nazi-helmet logo of the Blitzkrieg Legion biker gang. A short, scruffy beard and wrap-around sunglasses covered most of his face, which prevented the Topsy face-recognition software from identifying him. The system had no trouble spotting his weapon, though, and it painted a red outline around the image of the man's gun on the screen, tagging it in pulsing letters:

ALERT! .357 Magnum, Smith & Wesson. 5 round capacity. Safety: N/A

The senior students had worked together to install this security measure after the last time the building had been attacked by armed intruders—an event which had happened more often than Dean was comfortable thinking about. The sensors on the door used microwave-band radar to detect the weapon and compare it to a catalogue of potential threats. Ordinarily, the doors would swing open for any Institute student even if accompanied by a guest, but they would remain firmly shut in the presence of a firearm, regardless of whether the weapon was hidden in a pocket or, as in this case, held to a hostage's head.

Dean's hand moved to the button that would open the heavy front doors.

"Wait," he heard Janet say from the far side of the entrance hall. "If he comes in here... what if he starts shooting?"

"Get back," Dean growled. "Hide in the lab, call the cops, and don't come out until I say so."

"But—"

"Do it. Now!" He watched to make sure the students retreated out of sight. Then he hit the button, and the massive doors swung silently open.

The cold hit Dean like a slap to the face, but it was a slap he needed. He felt as if he were waking up for the first time in weeks, and when he looked at the heavy revolver gripped in the man's thick, tattooed hand, he felt his heart surge and his fingers tingle. Speed squirmed in his arms, but the gunman was more than twice her size. Streaks of tears ran down the sides of her cheeks, but her eyes met Dean's with a look of grim determination and an unhealthy lack of fear. She was a typical Institute student, which meant he had to get her out of there before she did something crazy.

Dean stepped outside and allowed the doors to close behind him. The Blitzkrieger stepped back and levelled the gun at him. This gave Dean another rush of excitement and... gratitude. It seemed odd to feel grateful, but nevertheless that's what he experienced when he saw how easily he had managed to get the gun pointed away from the girl and towards him.

"You," the gunman rasped, each of his words accompanied by a white puff of breath. "I know who you are. They say you're the man who killed Helmholtz."

"They're wrong," Dean said. *But only because I didn't have a chance.*

Dean took a step forward. The Blitzkrieger responded with a step backwards, but now he redirected the gun back to the girl's head.

"Gimme what I want and nobody gets hurt," the gunman said.

"Point the gun at me." Dean showed his hands. "I'll listen as long as you keep that gun pointed at me. I'm the only danger to you here."

The Blitzkrieger hesitated, but he didn't remove the barrel from Speed's black-brown hair.

"I want a rock," the gunman rasped. "A little black one. Shaped like an egg. You know the one I mean?"

Dean knew it all right. He could feel its weight in his pocket right now.

"We call it the Egg," he said. "What do you want with it?"

"I got a buyer," the gunman smiled wickedly. "The New Boss put out the word that the Egg's worth a million bucks. And I thought to myself, if anyone knows about it, it'd be you freaks at this school."

"So you came here not knowing for sure if we had it or knew anything about it?" Dean inched closer. "You didn't think this through, did you?"

"You better hope you have it, or... or I swear to God!" Now the Blitzkrieger was angry, and the gun flew up level with Dean's eyes once again. There was something oddly reassuring to Dean about staring into the inky blackness of that barrel. One twitch of that man's finger, even an involuntary one, and Dean would be dead before he heard the boom.

He took another step closer and placed his forehead against the cold barrel.

"Shoot me," Dean said. "And you'll never find the Egg."

Uncertainty crept into the Blitzkrieger's face and he took another small step backwards. Now he was at the edge of the ice and snow that clogged the front steps, so he could retreat no farther.

"Go get it," said the gunman, a little frantic. "If you're not back out in sixty seconds, the kid gets it. For real."

"It's not inside," Dean said. This was absolutely true, since it was in his pocket. If the gunman knew that, he could shoot Dean, grab the million-dollar rock, and flee the premises in less than thirty seconds. "Tell you what," Dean offered. "I'll take you to it. All you have to do is let the girl go and take me as your hostage instead."

The gunman struggled with the decision for a moment.

"Is it close enough to drive to it?" he asked.

Dean nodded, which seemed to satisfy the gunman. Without lowering his weapon, he circled around the porch, dragging the girl with him. When he was situated behind Dean, he shoved the girl away.

"Dean?" Speed said.

"Get inside," Dean told her without looking around. "Go!"

"Enough chit-chat," the gun prodded Dean's neck. "Get moving, tough guy."

Dean moved forward as instructed, though he was envisioning the twist-and-duck motion that might allow him to disarm his opponent. This was the first move kids always asked to learn when he taught self-defense courses, but the truth was that even the best possible firearm-disarming technique required a great deal of body motion, while the gunman only had to move his finger a half-inch. It was, by definition, an act of desperation, unlikely to achieve anything except a hole in the head. Dean decided not to try it yet, not on the steps of Topsy.

The Blitzkrieger marched him out to the parking lot where a black van awaited. There were two other men in the van, both wearing Blitzkrieger cuts.

"What's going on?" the driver asked as the other two roughly pushed Dean through the sliding door. Dean recognized the driver: a weasel-faced man whose name he could never remember.

"This guy knows where it is," said the gunman.

Weasel Face grumbled his disapproval at this turn of events, but he slammed the accelerator down and the wheels spun over the fresh snow. The gunman slid into the rear bench seat and kept the pistol pointed at Dean's back while the third man climbed in after them and began binding Dean's wrists with duct tape.

The van swerved and skidded as it built up speed on the icy side road. Once it hit the nicely plowed thoroughfare, the tires gripped more firmly and the van raced towards downtown Bugswallow.

"This guy's dangerous," Weasel Face said over his shoulder. "He ain't even afraid to take a swing at Brick. I was there, man. I seen him try."

"Alright, tough guy," said the gunman. "Take us to that rock. Where we headed?"

Before Dean could answer, the van veered so sharply onto Main Street that everyone in the back was flung against the wall.

"Watch it!" the gunman yelled at the driver.

"We got company," Weasel Face said.

"Cops?"

"No. Black car. Yuppy sedan."

The left side of the van lit up in a blinding flash of light as the windows shattered inward, spraying glass at them. Fingers of electricity danced across the side wall and blackened the upholstery.

"What was that?" the third Blitzkrieger shrieked.

Dean laughed.

"What's so funny?" Demanded the gunman.

"My senior students are here," Dean said. "You guys are toast."

Chapter 4

Victor's black Lexus roared up alongside the melted gash now running along the side of the van. Dean noticed the small red pinprick of laser light dancing around inside the van. Whatever device the students were using, it was laser-guided, and it was probably about to fire again.

Dean ducked just as a blinding flash blotted out the world. When his vision cleared, he saw the wall where the red laser dot had been a moment before was now a melted hole, its scalding edges still glowing red.

Weasel Face spun the wheel hard, evidently trying to drive the Lexus off the road. The Blitzkrieger next to Dean produced a shotgun, while the gunman in the seat behind him kicked open the rear doors to get a better view of the Lexus.

The Lexus's tinted windows concealed the driver—almost certainly Victor—but both Soap and Nikki were leaning out their side windows. Nikki had poked only her head and arms out from the front passenger seat, her long dyed-platinum hair fluttering around her chocolate-colored face. She gripped some kind of bulbous weapon that looked like a high-pressure super-soaker topped by twin reservoirs of dark, sloshing liquid. From the passenger window on the opposite side of the Lexus, Soap had managed to get her entire body out the window up to her hips, holding onto the car only by her right hand. With her other hand she gripped some kind of high-tech baton that connected by a cable to a blocky, wire-festooned backpack. Her black lab coat had fully escaped the car and flapped behind her like a pennant in a hurricane. Occasionally, a wrench or a spool of wire shook free from one of the countless pockets within her jacket and bounced off into the white snowbanks to the side of the street. She was shouting something, but her words were carried away in the rush of wind and the roar of engines.

Hanging out of the car like that was dangerous, but not as dangerous as the gunman about to shoot her. Nobody threatens his cousin and gets away with it. Nobody threatens any of his students—not while Dean had an ounce of blood left in his veins. Dean could handle that pistol aimed at him, but seeing it aimed at his students for the second time that day touched off something in him, something seismic. It began in his stomach, building pressure almost instantly until something cracked inside him. On another day he might have crushed it back down, but now he decided to give himself over to it. He reached down inside himself, willingly pulling up every ounce of anger and fear and frustration until it spilled into him like water from a broken hydrant. His eyes narrowed, his teeth ground so tight he could almost hear it, and his heart shook his chest like an earthquake. All the rage and pain he had been holding inside of himself for so long exploded forth with volcanic fury, spilling through his veins and setting every nerve ending ablaze.

Though duct tape bound his wrists, Dean grabbed the nearest Blitzkrieger's shotgun and jerked its barrel towards the floor then twisted it around to point at the man with the pistol. The shotgun thundered, ripping out one of the van's side windows in a tiny tornado of glass and sparks. Barely in time, the gunman in the back ducked out of the way but almost fell out the back of the van as he did.

The Blitzkrieger with the shotgun slammed his fist in the side of Dean's head. As head-punches went, this wasn't the worst Dean had experienced. The Blitzkrieger was a fairly strong guy, but his strength was counteracted by the awkwardness of trying to hit someone sitting right beside him while wrestling for a shotgun. His knuckled grazed Dean's cheek, and the minor pain only served to redouble Dean's frenzy. In immediate response, Dean slammed his forehead into the bridge of the man's nose and was rewarded by the pop of tearing cartilage. The Blitzkrieger's grip on the shotgun weakened enough for Dean to knock the weapon free and send it skidding out of the van's open rear doors.

The chase now slalomed around a corner into the heart of scenic downtown Bugswallow, where an oncoming car blasted its horn and swerved to avoid them. The gunman in the rear seat fired once without hitting anyone, but now was taking his time to aim at Soap. Dean pushed away from his first opponent to desperately lunge at the shooter. The gunman turned to fight Dean off then abruptly stopped, gaping at something over Dean's shoulder.

Reflexively, Dean looked for whatever had startled the Blitzkrieger and saw the green ghost of Mark Twain standing behind him, regarding the fighting men with an expression of bemused curiosity. Twain clutched a fat cigar between his fingers, which he now raised in salute to Dean.

The distraction allowed just enough time for Nikki to flood the back of the van with a bath of brown, tar-like goop. The largest portion splashed over the gunman nearest the rear doors, gelling into a hard shell the instant it touched him. He grunted and swore at the mess, but he could not budge from his spot.

Soap steadied her baton-thing as best she could against the roof of the Lexus and aimed it at the rear wheel of the van. Blinking blue LEDs along the baton's side intensified, and when the lights charged up to a certain level, she unleashed a ragged, forking slash of lightning at the van. In that same instant, the Lexus skidded briefly on the wet road and her shot went wide, slicing off the left rear corner of the van's bumper and continuing onward to sear a long, black streak across the bricks of several scenic downtown storefronts.

Weasel Face either didn't understand or didn't care that his pursuers had the ability to chop his van into chunks with home-made lightning. He gunned the engine and fishtailed around a right turn so hard that he almost spun out, narrowly avoiding an oncoming car that had to slew up onto the snowy curb to avoid him.

Inside the van, the Blitzkrieger who wasn't covered in goop now tried to get his hands around Dean's throat, but the vehicle's sudden spin made him miss clumsily. Dean took the opportunity to drive his knee into his attacker's broken nose. Although he couldn't land his blow with much force, the man let out a whimper, gripped his face, and fell backwards.

Soap's gun took a few more seconds to recharge, but a few seconds amounts to an eternity in a car chase. The van raced on towards a stone bridge over a frozen river, nearly running over pair of winter shoppers. The shoppers dove to the edge of the railing, dropping all their early Christmas gifts so that the van blasted through torn packages of decorative plates and framed quilt patches.

Finally, Soap's gun let loose its lightning, and this time it caught the van's wheel right where she had aimed. Dean couldn't see it, but he heard the tire explode and felt electricity prickling his arms and scalp. Weasel

Face pulled frantically at the wheel, but the vehicle was now the plaything of its own momentum. It skidded sideways before crashing through the bridge railing and plunging through ten feet of open air. The chase ended as the van crashed into the snow banks below with a crumpling thump.

Dean struggled out of the van, still dizzy from the fall. He was lucky: the two Blitzkriegers in the back would probably need traction when they woke up. The ghost of Twain had disappeared, but Weasel Face had managed to unbuckle himself and now was limping through the snow towards Dean.

Duct tape still bound his hands, but it only took Dean a split second to develop a fight plan. He would charge in, sweep Weasel Face's legs out from under him with a swift kick, and then—

And then a flash of blue lightning ripped through the air. Weasel Face suddenly stiffened and dropped to the ground, twitching as if he had been zapped by a Taser.

Dean whirled to look up at the bridge. Soap stood in the center of the broken railing, beaming triumphantly while brushing the purple stripe of her bangs out of her eyes.

"Look at this lightning lance I found in the invention library!" She turned so that he could see the cords, cables, and blinking lights of the backpack that evidently powered her weapon. "I turned the power way, way down on this last blast so it wouldn't kill the guy. At least, I hope I did. Um, now that I think about it, would you mind checking to make sure he's still breathing?"

Dean looked down at Weasel Face. He was whimpering and attempting to roll onto his back. Alive maybe, but not going anywhere. Dean might have beaten him, or maybe Weasel Face had a hidden weapon or some other trick up his sleeve. Soap had saved him from having to find out. Just like that, the molten anger that had been burning through Dean's veins congealed back into a hard obsidian ball in his stomach.

Not only had Dean failed to protect his students, his students had now needed to protect him.

CHAPTER 5

The Bugswallow sheriff clearly would have loved to keep Dean and his students in jail for the rest of their natural lives, but the President of Langdon University, the city's largest employer, worked out some kind of back-room deal to release them in order to minimize any potential bad press. Even so, Dean didn't return to Topsy until late that night, where he found himself listening to one of Soap's unending explanations, this time concerning the intricate details of the lightning lance's design.

As she went on and on about the virtues of powerful capacitors and room-temperature superconductors, Dean found himself idly playing with a Newton's Cradle, one of those desk toys with six steel balls in a row hanging from strings. When he allowed one of the balls to swing down and knock into the others, the ball at the far end flew out while all the balls in the middle remained perfectly still.

Click, click, click, the balls at each end swung in and out, creating a steady, reassuring metronome that proved to be more engrossing than Soap's impromptu lecture. It occurred to Dean that nothing in the real world operated like a Newton's Cradle because nothing ever bounced away so cleanly after a collision. Take cars, for instance: Dean had responded to hundreds of auto accidents in his time as a firefighter, and he had seen how vehicles smash into each other and become completely entangled. People were the same way too, because whenever two lives came into contact, they became entangled, often messily. He knew that the Newton's Cradle was supposed to demonstrate some kind of physics principle, but in his experience this particular theory didn't really apply outside the lab.

"Even though this lightning lance was designed in the eighties and the blueprint specifications say it was inspired by some movie about ghost hunters, it's well worth keeping one of our antimatter reactors installed in this pack," Soap sounded like she was winding down to a conclusion. "I'm still trying to devise an experiment to test my hypothesis that the reactors draw antimatter from a parallel universe. It's the only explanation I can think of to explain how they can scale down so small. I wish Nikola Tesla had left some notes or something explaining how they operate, but I guess he wanted to take that secret to the grave."

No, she was building up to a new topic. Dean tuned her out again. When he'd first met Soap, he couldn't get a word out of her, but she'd clearly come a long way since then. When she had finally started opening up to him, the words flooded out of her. He had tried asking her questions to follow what she was saying, but everything that came out of her mouth went over his head. At least she didn't seem to mind if he did other tasks while she spoke. She didn't seem to notice him checking his email or working out with a kettlebell while she went on talking. Sometimes he wondered if he even needed to be there.

Tonight, however, he had nothing to do, and he would have been too exhausted to get anything done anyway. Looking back, he realized that his day had been a perfect microcosm of what had become a weekly cycle for him. It began with intense workouts where he would attack his weights or his heavy bag—or Blitzkriegers—with more anger in his heart than he wanted to admit. He kept telling himself that if he could push himself harder, maybe next time he would be prepared. Maybe next time he would be able to save the person he loved. Then he would push himself over the edge of exhaustion and into the valley of despair as he realized that the person he loved was already gone and, no matter how fast he sprinted or how hard he punched, he had already failed to save her. Once those dark thoughts began seeping into his mind, he would spent the rest of the week unable to do much more than stare at the wall and wonder why his lungs insisted on forcing air in and out of his body. He was nearing that state now.

"It's still totally awesome-pants when you consider how the laser fries the nitrogen in the air until it becomes a streamer of plasma," Soap, still oblivious to Dean's mood, had circled her monologue back to the lightning lance. "It's like drilling a pilot hole through a board to guide your nail, except in this case the board is air and the nail is a flow of electricity. Imagine if you could do that with real lightning! It'd be so devastating that Raskolnikov would probably laugh himself to death if he saw it."

As she spoke, she pushed the trigger button just enough for the tip of the baton to crackle with silvery sparks. She stopped abruptly and stared past Dean.

"What was that?" she asked, clearly astonished by something she had seen.

Dean turned but saw nothing. "What did you see?"

"A green guy. He looked like Mark Twain. He appeared when I pushed the button but went away as soon as I stopped."

"Oh, him," Dean said. "I think you just saw his ghost. He's been haunting me lately."

She stared at him blankly.

"I know it sounds weird," Dean said. "I've been trying to ask you about this ghost, but..." *but you never seem to pause long enough to inhale.* Instead of saying something mean, he removed the Egg from his pocket and placed it on the table. "Do me a favor. Turn on your gizmo again, just like you did a second ago. He seems to show up when there's lightning around."

With a quizzical look on her face, Soap turned a dial and pressed her finger against the button. Instantly, a green, red, and blue nimbus sprang into life around the Egg. The colors swirled and popped out into the air a few feet to the side, and then, as the reds and blues subsided, the greens coalesced into the life-sized hologram of Mark Twain. He blinked, twitched his thick mustache, and appeared to sniff the air. He nodded his head in greeting towards Dean, and then made a small, gracious bow to Soap. Finally, he moved his mouth as if speaking.

In their pockets, both Dean's and Soap's phones screeched with static.

"That's weird," Soap inspected her phone, then shrugged and set it down on the table. "I thought the Egg was made before human beings even evolved. When did someone use it to record Mark Twain? And: how?"

Dean shrugged, but he was thinking that the real question was why someone would offer a million-dollar prize to the Blitzkrieger who could find this Egg. Did it have anything to do with this apparition of Mark Twain, or did it hold some other secret? And then there was the matter of *who* wanted it. Helmholtz had known about it, but he was dead. The late Professor had run an international criminal organization, so maybe one of his underlings had now taken up the cause. Perhaps this had something to do with why Angela Black had suddenly requested to speak with Dean. Thinking about it made Dean feel even more exhausted.

"What do you think's causing our ghostly friend to appear?" he asked.

"I'll figure it out later," Soap said. "Right now, I need you to sign my research proposal."

Dean grunted in dismay. He had two official duties as Dean of Students. The first was to determine who is allowed to attend the school, and the second was to approve student research proposals. The latter, he was discovering, was a heavy burden, as much because he couldn't figure out the students any more than he could figure out their projects. If he had been given the opportunity to make up his own course of study when he was Soap's age, he certainly would have used the opportunity to slack off. The Institute students, by comparison, took their projects very seriously, and his role as supervisor seemed more about holding them back from disaster rather than pushing them forward towards discovery. Nevertheless, approving their projects only reminded Dean of how little he understood of what they wanted to do, and, consequently, of how little he belonged here.

"We have one more day before winter vacation," Dean said. "Do you really want to start a new project now?"

"Sure," she said. "I can't afford to go home over break, so I might as well find a way to amuse myself. And I've always wanted to design a jet pack." She detached her tablet from its keyboard and handed it to him. The screen displayed blueprints for what looked like a stubby-winged metal hang glider with two huge turbines positioned right over the wearer's shoulder blades.

Dean turned the tablet to the side and slid through several more pages of diagrams and formulas. "I thought we already had a jet pack."

"That's a flight pack," Soap rolled her eyes. "Electromagnetic levitation is cool if you don't want to go higher than fifty or sixty feet, but this new one should be able to launch a person almost into the stratosphere. I don't know much about aerodynamics, so that's my new learning for this project."

"Fine," Dean flipped the tablet over to the workflow software and entered his electronic signature to approve the project. "But no manned flights until it's thoroughly—and I mean *thoroughly*—tested. I mean it. I don't want to be the one to explain to your father how we had to scrape you off the sidewalk with a spatula. Also, get Stephanie to help you."

"Who's Stephanie?"

"Speed," Dean corrected, remembering the new students' tradition of using nicknames. "Her application said she was interested in any vehicle that moved faster than safety allowed. Just don't tell her about the underground lab."

"Duh," Soap said in a way that showed she was offended that he would even have to say it. Keeping the underground lab secret was probably the most iron-clad of all the unwritten rules of the Institute. It was here, hundreds of feet below Topsy House, that they kept all the really good inventions, the things that weren't supposed to exist. New students had to discover the secret elevator for themselves before they were considered full members, and many spent years madly researching in the decoy lab without ever guessing that they were missing anything.

"Sorry to interrupt," Victor arrived carrying a steel tray with a syringe and a small vial of purplish liquid. A slim, tall young man with efficiently styled blond hair and ice-blue eyes, Victor was the Institute's experimental biologist and unlicensed medical practitioner. In this role, he had diagnosed Dean with a host of new bruises and swelling in the shoulder at the site of a previous injury. After tangling with the Blitzkriegers, Dean could have ended up in much worse shape.

"Tell me again what you're injecting?" Dean asked.

Victor drew the fluid into his syringe and inspected it against the light. "This will activate the pluripotent nature of the cells surrounding the traumatized region."

"In English?" Dean asked.

"It will make your cells work like stem cells so that damaged tissue will grow anew instead of becoming scar tissue."

"Can you make it English-ier?"

"It's magic," Victor slid the needle into Dean's upper arm. "How's that feel?"

It felt like Victor was ramming a flaming softball into Dean's shoulder girdle.

"It's like walking through a bed of tulips," Dean said.

"He's being sarcastic," Soap stated authoritatively.

"Great," Victor said. "Anything else you need?"

Usually Victor was as cool as ice, but now he seemed antsy. Something was bugging him, Dean could tell.

"What's up, Victor?" Dean asked. "You leave some test tubes boiling or something?"

"I need to get back to my research," he said.

"Sorry if our little kidnapping experience got in the way of your studies," Dean said.

"I didn't mean it like that. But... as long as you're here, could you sign off on my proposal?"

Dean sighed heavily then flipped through a few screens on the tablet Victor handed to him. Unlike Soap's proposal, this one lacked meaningful diagrams, and it was full of phrases like "voxels mapped by fMRI" and "transcranial magnetic stimulation." As usual, Dean understood none of it.

"Can you explain it to me?" Dean asked. "Keep in mind that you might have to make it even simpler than what you told me about the shot."

"This experiment is only the first step, mind you. Just a simple proof of concept, but I can have it ready to go in an hour."

Dean glared at him. "Victor, don't dodge my question."

Victor inhaled deeply, apparently thinking over his words carefully. "If this works," he said cautiously, "it might be the first step in bringing people back."

"Back from where?"

"From the dead. Sort of."

Dean set down the tablet. "No way. I'm not approving any experiments with zombies."

"This isn't about reanimating bodies, it's about replicating minds," Victor said. "If you let me do this, the first person I'll recreate is Professor McKenzie."

For five full seconds, the only sound in the lab was the crackling of the Tesla coils. Then Dean picked up the tablet and signed off on the project.

If it might reincarnate his fiancé, he would gladly risk a few zombies—or anything else, for that matter.

Chapter 6

"You need to understand something," Victor said as he led Dean and Soap towards the underground lab's medical bay, where he'd been working intensely for the past hour. "Even if this ultimately works, it won't really be the deceased person—McKenzie, or anyone else—who comes back to life. It will be a collection of our memories stored in a different brain and acted out by a new body. It would be a kind of living dream of the original person. Or maybe more like a walking, talking photo album."

"I don't really understand anything you just said," Dean looked at the tablet and skimmed Victor's proposal yet again. "It says here you need a human being to experiment on. Who do you have in mind?"

"I'm hoping one of you will volunteer," Victor said. "Don't worry, I won't need to drill holes in your skull. Not today, anyway."

The three of them now entered the chemistry lab, where Nikki was swirling some brightly colored liquids in a large beaker. As she glared at Dean through her safety goggles, the temperature of the lab seemed to drop by ten degrees.

"What?" he asked her.

She pointedly turned away from him, revealing the large skull-and-crossbones insignia embroidered on the back of her pink lab coat. Whatever she was mad about, it would have to wait because they had arrived at Victor's lab bench.

"Here it is," Victor opened a small curtain to reveal several rows of large metal racks, each of which contained hundreds of circuit boards and a dizzying panoply of wires weaving them together. To Dean, it looked just like all the other complicated machines in the lab, but Soap's sharp inhale told him it was something special.

"I commissioned this computer long before you even joined the Institute, Dean," Victor said. "I spent a fortune of my own money on it. It's designed as a massively parallel, content-addressable memory retrieval system so it will work more like the human brain than a standard computer."

"You can copy someone's mind into this?" Soap asked skeptically.

"Not even close. No computer in the world can begin to replicate the 225 million billion interactions in the human brain. The best I can hope for here today is to transfer a memory cluster from one of you to this computer."

"What would that involve?" Nikki had joined them now. She stood on the other side of Soap, pointedly keeping her distance from Dean.

"It's easy work," Victor said. "All you have to do is lie in the fMRI machine for a while and think happy thoughts."

Nikki looked doubtful. Soap looked lost in other thoughts. Dean immediately decided that he should volunteer, just in case Victor had understated the danger.

Twenty minutes later, he found himself on a heavily padded stretcher as Victor backed him up towards the brain scanner. Entering the fMRI looked like sticking his head into the center of a gigantic white donut, but the tight confines made it feel more like being inside a coffin. The massive neck-brace that immobilized him from the shoulders up certainly did not add to his comfort.

"What am I supposed to do in here?" Dean asked.

"Don't move," Victor said. "Don't even speak. Just focus your mind on something. An animal, for example. Did you ever have a pet? A dog or a cat you loved especially much?"

Dean thought for a moment. "Jake, our station dog," Dean said. "He was a good pooch. Man, I miss having a dog around."

"Just think it, don't say it," Victor said. "Try to breathe shallowly, too. Picture that dog in your head as clearly as you can. Call to your mind every memory of that pet and hold them in your thoughts. Try to tune out everything else, okay?"

Dean did his best to flip back through the pages in his personal history to a time when he had first signed on as a firefighter and begun what he had assumed would be a lifelong career. Good ol' Jake had never officially been Dean's dog, but he belonged to one of the guys in the crew, which effectively meant he had belonged to everyone at the station. Jake was a Dalmatian, selected precisely because it made him the cliché fire dog. He lived up to the expectations, too: whenever the alarm went off, Jake would bark until every last firefighter had loaded up on the truck, and then he would sit at attention at the back of the garage and watch the engine roll out. Animals weren't allowed to go with them, so instead he took it as his duty to guard the station while they were away. When they returned, they always found him sitting in exactly the same place, and he wouldn't move a muscle until the engine came to a full stop and the firefighters started stepping down. Then he was all over them, snuffling around their pockets in hopes of finding a treat. Before long, everyone carried dog biscuits for him, and he probably received one from every member of the crew at least once a day. Small wonder he got fat in his old age, although it never stopped him from waiting at his post during every call.

Dean tried to hold the picture of Jake in his head, but found he couldn't fully tune out the voices of Soap, Nikki, and Victor outside the fMRI machine. It sounded like they were bickering about technical details.

"So you're going to transfer memories into a computer," Nikki said. "Then what? What's your hypothesis?"

"Simple," Victor said. "If we can transfer them in, the computer will be able to display them to us. We could eventually use this technique to quickly program robots or other machines."

"I'm worried about this computer," Soap said. "You jacked it into the main conduit from the reactor. Do you really need all that power?"

"The human brain uses less energy than the average desk lamp," Victor said. "But a computer requires massive amounts of electricity to do the same thing. Even though my machine is only designed to replicate a small portion of the brain, it still needs six million watts."

"*Six million watts*?" Soap sounded astonished. "That's enough to power the entire town of Bugswallow. The reactor has the output, but it's going to be like hitting your experimental, untested computer with a lightning bolt. Believe me: I have lots of experience overloading electrical systems."

If Victor made a response, Dean couldn't hear it. Thinking about electrical overloads made the smooth plastic walls of the fMRI machine seem to press in even closer, so Dean clamped his eyes shut and forced his thoughts back to the way Jake would dance in a little circle whenever someone held out a piece of a hotdog, or the way he always tried to sleep at Dean's feet even though there wasn't enough room in those little station-house beds for both of them.

A hissing of sparks and the unmistakable crackle of fire brought a quick end to the reminiscing. Victor shouted, there was the sound of feet shuffling quickly, and all the nearby lights flashed and went dark.

Dean grabbed the sides of the fMRI machine and yanked himself out. He managed to unclasp the straps that held him to the stretcher and struggle to a seated position in time to see a vermillion starburst erupt from one of the computer racks. Nikki had backed off and was shielding her face with her pink lab coat, while Soap dashed towards the nearest fire extinguisher.

"No!" Victor shouted. "No, no, no!" he hammered desperately at his keyboard. He was standing next to another array of circuit boards; if some had already exploded, then the ones next to his head stood a good chance of doing the same.

Dean lunged off the stretcher and dived for Victor as best he could in the billowing hospital robe and confining neck brace. He and Victor hit the ground just as the computer bank boomed and something—perhaps a chunk of an exploded battery—scudded across the room, trailing stinking, silver smoke behind it.

Soap tossed the fire extinguisher to Nikki before setting to work cutting the power. In only a moment, the flames were safely squelched, but Victor's experiment had been reduced to a blackened lump of plastic.

Victor lay on the floor, one arm across his face and both fists crunched into tight balls.

"Victor, you okay?" Dean asked. "Victor?"

"I'm not hurt," Victor mumbled. After a moment, he stood and abruptly walked away.

"Let him go," Nikki said. "This was a huge loss for him."

"This is too bad," Soap said. "I would have liked to see your memories of your dog. Want me to build you a robot dog instead?"

"No," Dean mumbled as he watched Victor go. "There's no substitute for a real dog."

Dean's fingers worked mechanically at removing his neck brace. Now that the excitement had ended, he felt the familiar disappointment crawling around inside him. Only now did he realize he had been expecting too much from this experiment, and its failure once again robbed him of hope.

If even Victor couldn't break down the barriers between life and death, then McKenzie really was gone forever.

Chapter 7

Dean lay awake in bed, watching the minutes tick by on his alarm clock. This was one of those nights when he saw her face every time he closed his eyes. She lay in front of him, eyes open and staring, just as he had found her that terrible day: her neck was turned at a gentle angle; her lips were slightly parted; her auburn hair was brushing her blue skin. In the quiet darkness of his bedroom, she seemed more vivid and solid than anything else around him.

He sat up and turned on his bedside light, determined to find some way to clear his mind. What was wrong with him? It had been months since McKenzie died, yet even on his good days he felt as empty as a dry well. Then there were the bad days, when a ton of invisible cinderblocks crushed him down until he could hardly move.

Grief is a wound, his station chief always used to say. Dean knew all about wounds and injuries. His body took care of those for him. Even without Victor's magic injections, his bruises always healed, his cuts always closed, all he had to do was wait. Yet, somehow, this grief wasn't getting better. Maybe it had become infected in some metaphorical, emotional way. Unfortunately, he knew of no such thing as an antibiotic for the soul or sutures to bind the broken pieces of his past. All he wanted was to see her again, to speak to her one last time. To tell her goodbye. If he could do that, he told himself, he might be able to move on and start recovering.

He hated being the guy who was always moping and miserable. He wanted to be whole and healthy again, but somehow he just couldn't get himself together. At least he hadn't burdened anyone else with his problem. He hadn't mentioned it or spoken about it to anyone, and he was pretty sure he hadn't let it show in his eyes to his students, either. He took pride that his grief had remained safely hidden, but he should be showing signs of recovery by now. So why did it feel so crippling?

He shook his head. Maybe he just needed a distraction. Another day without thinking about it would be another day closer to getting better, right? And, as long as he was awake, he decided he might as well do what his students did: experiment.

Heated by a massive underground antimatter reactor, Topsy house remained sweltering in the dead of winter, so Dean didn't bother putting anything over his t-shirt and boxer shorts as he rolled out of bed and made his way to the living room. He shoved his ever-present pile of paperwork to the side of his dining table and laid out the Egg and the lightning lance Soap had accidentally left in the hallway. With some fussing, he managed to prop the tip of the gun up into the air so that it wouldn't fall or start any fires, and then twisted its power dial down to minimum.

He pressed the trigger button and the tip of the lightning lance sparked and crackled. Right on cue, the green ghost of Mark Twain swirled into existence. The apparition nodded to Dean, and then peered quizzically at the television in the living room.

"Hello," Dean said. "Can you understand me? If you know what I'm saying, raise your right hand."

The ghost did just that. Then he put his cigar between his lips, and the tip glittered red like a ruby for a moment before he puffed out illusory blue smoke.

"You're not just some recording, are you?" Dean asked. "You can understand me, can't you?"

Twain nodded again, this time adding a wry smile.

"Can you speak?" Dean asked.

Twain moved his mouth. Dean's phone on the kitchen counter as well as the television in the living room squawked with irregular static.

"I think I get it," Dean said, picking up his phone. "You're trying to talk through these. Keep trying. I'll listen closely."

Twain made another attempt, but still achieved nothing more than gibberish. This time he frowned in frustration.

"I almost heard something, I think," Dean closed his eyes to concentrate on the sound. "Say it again."

The speakers squawked once more. This time it sounded like: *Garble, garble, help, garble, garble, Tes...la, garble.*

"Tesla?" Dean repeated. "Did you say something about Tesla?"

Twain placed his forefinger to his nose to indicate that this was correct. Then he uttered two more words, very slowly, and Dean understood both.

"Need... help..." The words were becoming more understandable, but each time the ghost attempted to project his voice to the speakers, the image of his body faded a little. The ghost's green eyes suddenly looked very serious. His smile was entirely gone.

"I understand," Dean said. "Or, at least, I think I do. You're saying that you need Tesla's help. Wait—you do know that Tesla is dead, right?"

"Wrong," Twain said through the speakers. The effort of these words made him fade almost beyond Dean's ability to see him in the late-night gloom.

"Tesla really is dead, I'm afraid," Dean said, feeling just a little strange about reporting obituaries to a ghost. "He died something like eighty years ago, I think. And I'm pretty sure that you—I mean, Mark Twain—died before that."

"Wrong," Twain said again.

There was a knock at Dean's door. Dean looked back at Twain, wanting to ask him more, but if a student had come knocking at this hour it was probably an emergency. He just prayed that Collin hadn't blasted his eardrums out or Raskolnikov hadn't blown himself to pieces.

Dean opened the door to find Soap. She was followed, as usual, by Rusty, her faithful dog-like robot—if you could describe a machine as dog-like when its patchwork skeleton of metal, plastic, and wires included six spidery legs and a piston-driven scorpion tail. Still, there was something vaguely canine about the shape of his boxy head, and the black domes of his eyes had a certain puppy-dog appeal.

Soap's eyes, too, looked rather puppy-dog at the moment. She stood, looking up at Dean, with thin trails of tears tracing her high cheekbones.

"Soap, what's the matter?" Dean asked. He reached out to comfort her, but she pulled away.

"You," she said. "You're the matter."

"What? What did I do?"

"Nikki told me."

Dean remembered Nikki shooting him evil looks, but he had never found out why. "I don't understand. What did Nikki tell you?"

"She said she talked to the noobs. You told them you were quitting. And you didn't even tell us."

Now it made sense. Before the whole Blitzkrieger attack, Dean had let slip that he was going to quit the Institute and go back to Los Angeles. He hadn't thought anything more of it since then, but evidently it was a bigger deal than he had assumed.

"Look, Soap," Dean said. "You guys deserve someone better than me. I'm no good at this job."

"And what am I supposed to do? I was counting on you. I had questions that only you can answer."

"I doubt that. You know I don't know anything about science."

"Not science questions. The other kind of questions. Now I've got no one to talk to."

"Ask me now. I'm right here. And even after I go back to California, you can call me anytime."

"You don't get it," she broke away and raced for the stairs. Rusty's legs pumped up and down as the robot turned in place and then obediently shot off after her.

Dean watched her go, not sure if he should follow. He had a feeling that anything he said would only make it worse—not to mention that, despite the late hour, there might be students down in the decoy lab, and he was suddenly conscious that he was still in his boxer shorts. He looked at Twain, who gazed back sympathetically.

"She's better off without me," Dean said to the ghost.

Twain narrowed his eyes and set his jaw in an expression of disagreement.

"They're all better off without me," Dean said.

Twain attempted to speak, but whatever he said was too complicated to come out of the speakers as anything more than a warbling noise. He shook his head in disappointment, though Dean couldn't be sure if it was disappointment in his inability to speak or in Dean's inability to help his students. Finally, Twain gestured for Dean to follow him.

"Where are we going?" Dean asked.

"Tesla...help..." was all the fading ghost could manage, though his beckoning seemed more urgent now. He led Dean into the kitchen but stopped abruptly at the refrigerator. He seemed as alarmed and confused by the appliance as if it he had discovered a sleeping elephant next to the stove. He pointed at it and urgently turned to Dean—then vanished completely from sight.

"Mr. Twain?" Dean peered at the spot where he had stood, but there was no sign of him. He retrieved the Egg and the lightning lance, but Twain did not reappear. He even went so far as to turn off all the lights in the residence, just in case Twain was still there but just too faint to be seen.

Nothing. The ghost was gone.

Dean guessed that Twain's battery must have drained out, and the lightning lance couldn't fill it fast enough. Maybe he would re-appear tomorrow, after a long recharge.

In the meantime, there was the refrigerator. Twain had appeared very concerned about it, and Dean was willing to bet it wasn't because of the expired carton of milk inside.

Sleep still seemed far away. Dean thought about chasing Soap, but decided there was nothing he could say to help. Instead, he decided he might as well break out his tool box and see if he could figure out what was so special about that refrigerator.

December 14

(9 Days Before Stormageddon)

Chapter 8

"Hello, Mr. Lazarchek," the grandmotherly receptionist greeted Dean brightly, just as she always did when he entered the university's administration building. He wished he could bottle her perkiness and sell it like soda pop, although he found it too sugary for his own taste.

"Hello, Mrs. Kripawsky," Dean presented the best smile he could manage. "How are you today?"

"Oh, very well, thank you," she said. "Did I tell you? My daughter just got a big promotion."

Dean struggled to keep his smile from turning into a grimace. Every time he spoke with Mrs. Kripawsky, she found some excuse to mention that her daughter was single and highly eligible.

"She's about your age," the gray-haired woman went on, nudging a framed photo of her rosy-cheeked daughter towards him. "She'll be down from The Cities this weekend. Oh, I just had a thought. Why don't you join us for dinner? We're having beef stroganoff hot dish and baked potatoes. You look like you could use a home-cooked meal."

"I really appreciate it, but I..." Dean struggled to come up with an excuse. Ever since the popular press had started spinning him as the everyday guy turned hero, he'd been getting a lot of unsolicited offers for romance. He'd refused every single one, yet there seemed to be no shortage of people like Mrs. Kripawsky who felt they knew what he needed better than he did.

"Well?" she said expectantly.

"I can't," he said. "I'm sorry. I just can't." He left it at that and walked away.

Although this was the last faculty meeting before the end of the quarter, there was no evidence of holiday cheer—or any other type of cheer—inside the meeting room. As usual, the skeletal old President Hart exhorted his department chairs to maintain academic focus (whatever that meant) right up to the start of break. Around the time Hart began his lecture on the new procedure for expense reports, Dean nodded off into an anxious, restless sleep. He dreamed he was back in high school and a teacher was yelling at him for not being prepared.

"Mr. Lazarchek, would you please answer the question?"

Dean's eyes fluttered open and he discovered that his dream had become a reality, except that instead of a single teacher, he was surrounded by a room full of professors, all of whom were looking at him expectantly.

"Mr. Lazarchek," President Hart glowered across the table. "Would you please answer? And let me remind you that your vacation doesn't start until tomorrow."

"I'm sorry, sir. Could you repeat the question?"

"The terrorist attacks in which you insist on participating. Will they continue?"

"Pardon me?" He looked around at the faces of the other professors, some of whom looked mortified while others seemed to be suppressing giggles. These teachers were behaving just like children when one of their peers got busted for texting during class.

"It's clear that you and I should carry on this conversation in private," Hart declared. "Please join me in my office immediately following this meeting. Now, for the rest of you, if there are no further questions, this completes our business today. I wish you a pleasant vacation because I'm sure all of us are looking forward to a few weeks free from dealing with young people."

Hart slapped his laptop closed and abruptly departed the conference room.

The professors collected their briefcases and donned their thick winter jackets before filing out the door. Dean remained in his seat a moment, mostly because he didn't have the energy to stand.

One of the other professors lingered in the doorway, then turned to approach Dean. "You okay?" she asked.

Dean looked up and saw that she seemed to be about Dean's age, mid-thirties, with a raw-boned face and short, honey-gold hair. He remembered that she taught something to do with ancient languages, but he didn't remember her name.

"I'm great," he answered without enthusiasm. "How are you?"

She gave him a knowing smile. "I'm not the one who looks like he's been cramming for a final exam in Alligator Wrestling 101. Is that a black eye?"

"I'm fine. I just had a minor car accident yesterday." He stood up and snatched his coat from the seat next to him. "Thanks, for your concern, Professor...?"

"Heidi. Heidi Bjelland," she shook his hand with a firm grip. "Listen, I just wanted you to know that a bunch of us are worried about you."

"Who's *a bunch of us*?"

"The department chairs," she said, gesturing around her, even though all of the department chairs had left nothing but empty chairs behind them.

"You're worried because I fell asleep just now?" Dean turned to her, not even bothering to smile.

"It's not about falling asleep, it's... well, not all of us agree with President Hart."

Dean was about to ask what President Hart expected them to agree with when the president yelled from his office.

"Mr. Lazarchek! I still need that word with you, if you haven't nodded off again."

"I should probably get in there before Skeletor decides he doesn't like me," Dean said.

Heidi laughed and slapped her hand over her mouth to cut herself off.

"I can't believe you just called him that," she said, delight dancing in her eyes.

Dean excused himself and walked through the thick, carved oak doors of Hart's office. At Hart's command, he sank into one of the oversized chairs that seemed designed to belittle their occupants.

Hart spread his bony fingers along the top of his oak desk and glared at Dean.

"I had quite a time yesterday, cleaning up after your little fiasco on the downtown streets. Reporters have been circling this town like vultures for weeks. You're lucky the press didn't hear about this latest event."

"I'm lucky I wasn't killed, sir. I was simply defending myself. The sheriff has it on record."

"I know what he has on record," Hart hissed. "I helped him write it. When will you understand that this school simply cannot afford any more of the bad press you seem intent to draw on a monthly basis?"

"It's not me—"

Hart held up his hand to silence Dean.

"A single school shooter I could handle. That's an isolated incident. But you, Mr. Lazarchek, seem determined to drive away every tuition-paying student who isn't enrolled in your Institute."

Dean was starting to get angry. He had to struggle to deaden his emotions to keep from blowing up.

"I was an unwilling victim," he said flatly.

"Can you promise that you won't be an unwilling victim again next month? And the month after?"

"Nobody can promise that," Dean let out a tense breath. He had been considering quitting, so why not give Hart the good news? "Listen, President Hart. I don't agree with your point of view, but I agree that I should step down. I'll resign."

Hart's lips pulled back to reveal his unusually large teeth, making his face look even more like a grinning skull than usual.

"Effective immediately?" Hart asked hopefully.

"As soon as I can find a replacement," Dean said.

Hart turned to his computer and clicked the mouse a few times. A moment later, the printer whirred, and Hart handed over a succinct resignation letter with Dean's name already on it.

"How long have you been waiting to give this to me?"

Hart just slid a pen toward him.

"Simply fill in the date you wish to step down. No need to give the customary two weeks' notice. The sooner the better."

Dean looked at the page. A few strokes of the pen, and he could go back to California.

"You know, Mr. Lazarchek, the new quarter will begin the first week of January. That would make a good time to transition to a new Dean."

Less than three weeks, Dean thought. It should be plenty of time to find a replacement and maybe even process a few more student applications. It wasn't like he had anything else pressing to do in the meantime.

Dean entered January First as his last day on the job, and then signed his name. He felt an immediate sting of regret. Nevertheless, he handed the paper to Hart.

Hart inspected it briefly.

"If you need candidates for your replacement, I'd be happy to suggest a few names."

"Thanks, but no thanks," Dean said as he made his way towards the door.

In the reception area, he found Heidi Bjelland waiting for him.

"You're still here?" he asked her.

"Just wanted to make sure you were okay in there."

"You know what?" Dean said. "I never thought I'd admit this, but President Hart isn't all bad. And honestly, he's right about me. So I quit."

"You quit? Really?"

"Yeah," Dean said. "Effective the first of the year. The students will return to find a new Dean of Students in my place. Smooth transition."

She studied his face for a minute.

"I know you've been through a huge loss. If you ever want to talk—"

"I don't talk," Dean said firmly.

He could feel both Heidi and Mrs. Kripawsky's eyes on his back as he left, but he didn't let it stop him.

He walked slowly across campus, allowing the frigid wind to blast against his face the whole way. After the bright morning sun, the sky had quickly fallen into a uniform gray and was currently threatening snow.

Welcome to Minnesota, Dean thought. *The other season is mosquitoes.*

Just before he turned down the little path that led to Topsy, he paused to watch a sheriff's cruiser off in the distance, inching its way along the narrow road separating the campus from Langdon's stadium. After the encounter with the Blitzkriegers last night, every law officer in the county was on high alert. Dean took it as further proof that he was no longer needed here. This town had its defenders, and they had no need for his help.

Topsy House was even better protected than the rest of the town. With white blankets of snow outlining the wrought-iron railings and the gargoyle cornice-pieces, Topsy in winter looked a little bit less like a Victorian-era haunted house than it had in the fall, but it was still a forbidding building. Beyond its stern exterior, generations of students had applied their various inventions to make Topsy more secure, and now, despite its old-timey appearance, it was a high tech bunker that would turn a colonel at Fort Knox green with envy. Topsy's walls might appear to be simple brick-and-mortar, but they were actually armored better than an aircraft carrier. Interior gates could seal rooms so tightly not even a breeze could get in. The floors could be electrified. Elevators could be gassed. Every shadowy corner could be viewed through security cameras, and the underground laboratory was so deep the kids working there might not even notice a nuclear war going on above.

So why didn't Dean feel it was safe?

As he approached the door, invisible electronics scanned his face, height, body density, and a dozen other metrics to confirm that he was, in fact, Dean Lazarchek. Then the system detected the radio frequency emitted by the big brass key in his pocket. An onlooker would have seen nothing more than the heavy, brass-and-iron plated doors simply swing open to greet him, but Dean knew that nobody could get in unless they were part of the Institute in good standing.

Within the entrance hall, he could already hear the customary student noises in the decoy lab. Outside, thunder boomed, loud enough to make him freeze for a moment. When the rational part of his brain resumed control, he paused to wonder whether this was a brand new storm or the same one he had encountered the day before circling back to vent its fury once more. Either way, Topsy was right in its path.

And soon that will be no concern of mine. The thought stirred up a miniature storm of dark emotions inside him, but he was good at ignoring such things.

CHAPTER 9

Dean found the decoy lab looking like it had hosted World Wars I, II, and III since he had left that morning. All the new students were crawling on their hands and knees, scrubbing various goops, slimes, broken glass, char-marks, and acid etchings out of every corner of their work stations.

"What happened here?" Dean asked Collin, whose green Mohawk bobbed up and down as he transferred piles of rat droppings and soiled rodent bedding from the floor to a garbage bucket.

"Nothing," Collin answered.

"Sure doesn't look like nothing." Dean looked around at the devastation. They'd even broken one of the supposedly indestructible lab tables, not to mention a whole rack of boiling flasks. "Was anyone hurt?"

"No," Collin said.

"He started it!" Janet Cho jabbed her finger at Raskolnikov.

"I did not!" Raskolnikov shouted back from the open stretch of wall where he was attempting to scrape rubber tire tracks off the linoleum floor. "She did!" he pointed at Speed.

"No, it was him!" Speed jerked her thumb at Collin.

"No, he did!" Thing 2 shouted and pointed at her twin at the same time Thing 1 pointed back at her and shouted, "No, she did!"

"Yeah, about this whole deal with us cleaning up after each other," Speed said. "As you can see, it isn't working."

"Looks to me like it's working great," Dean said with a smile.

"But it's morally wrong!" Collin said. "Some of us don't make very big messes, man. Like, all I leave behind are a few wires and some tiny spots of grease, yet I get shanghaied into scrubbing rat poop off the floor. Fascist! Totally fascist!"

"It's fair if it's your fault the cage got knocked over!" Janet shouted. "You need to be careful where you aim those speakers of yours!"

"I said I was sorry!" he shouted back.

"And he was making a mess on purpose!" Thing 2 jerked her thumb at Thing 1.

"That's because she was spreading pencil shavings all over the place and I figured if I had to do that much clean-up then so should she!"

"Okay, stop!" Dean boomed. "I am delighted that you are cleaning up for each other. That's great. Since this program has obviously been such a success, we're going to keep doing it every day until I say we stop!"

They groaned, loudly and in unison. It was the first time Dean had ever hear them agree on anything.

Let them hate me, he thought as he stepped over a pile of batteries and spark plugs. *At least this will help them like the next Dean of Students better.*

When he reached the top of the stairs, he turned to see everyone watching him. "One more thing," he announced. "There's a prospective student coming for an interview. His name is, uh," Dean rummaged through his jacket pockets until he found the notepad containing the name. "His name is Oscar DeLeon. Can I have a volunteer to show him around the lab and then bring him up to my residence?"

Raskolnikov's hand shot up in the air, but Dean didn't like the idea of a potential student getting blown to bits before he even joined the Institute. Dean looked over at the twins. Things 1 and 2 seemed responsible enough, had decent haircuts, and wouldn't give horrible first impressions. The only problem was that Dean had forgotten their real names so he couldn't figure out how to call on them without embarrassing himself.

Further proof that I'm the worst Dean of Students in history, he thought.

"Collin," he said, pretending to pick at random. "You're the tour guide today."

Collin rolled not just his eyes, but his entire head. "This is a violent oppression of my civil rights."

Dean stifled a laugh. "Hey, if the man doesn't keep you down, then all your punk rock music serves no purpose, right? While you're contemplating that, please show, uh," he glanced at his notepad again. "Show Oscar up to my residence whenever he's ready."

Dean couldn't help smiling as he left them to their cleaning. Maybe the kids he'd found so far weren't so bad after all. He might even miss some of them. Sure, they had made a mess today, but they had taken responsibility by cleaning it up, just like he had asked. If they were an odd bunch of teenagers then this was a good place to be odd. The Institute was turning out to be like the Island of Misfit Toys: those who didn't belong elsewhere could belong here.

Two steps into the residence, Dean remembered the parts from his dismantled refrigerator strewn all over the kitchen. This had been his late-night project: instead of sleeplessly tossing and turning, he had decided to figure out what the ghost of Mark Twain had been trying to tell him about the fridge. First he looked inside, but there was nothing there aside from the leftovers, a few frozen meals, and that old milk carton he really ought to have poured out a week ago. He had to strip off the fridge's inside lining and the outside paneling, all in hopes of finding some secret gizmo or message hidden inside his appliance. Ultimately, he'd disassembled the motor, the coolant system, and the whole works. It had kept his mind off dark thoughts, but it hadn't given him any new clues, and now he had a big mess to clean up and not much time before his young guest arrived.

His bachelor's housecleaning methods could be called sanitary, but not much more. Aside from the unsightly jumble of refrigerator parts in the kitchen, there were also droplet splatters on the bathroom mirror, dumbbells on the floor, and dirty dishes in the sink. He worked diligently, although by no means enthusiastically, to tidy up, and by the time he heard the knock at the door he had transformed his domicile from an unkempt pigsty into a fairly tidy pigsty.

He opened the door to find Collin with the prospective student in tow, a pudgy kid in a suit and tie with hair that looked as if his parents had made him comb it just for this occasion. The boy's smile was friendly, but his eyes darted away from Dean's in obvious shyness. His handshake was limp and moist, and he entered the residence very hesitantly, only after Dean requested him to do so. The kid's eyes lingered on the pile of refrigerator parts as he passed the kitchen, but he was too polite—or too timid—to ask. Curiosity was the most important ingredient in Institute students, and this kid had already missed his first chance to demonstrate it.

"Welcome..." Dean had planned on greeting the student by name, but suddenly he drew a blank. He decided he really should make more of an effort to learn names, even for students who weren't likely to join the Institute. "So tell me, what do you think of our lab?"

The kid cleared his throat. "Um... very nice?"

The two sat down at the dining room table and Dean logged onto his laptop and opened the student's file, which he wished he had gone through before now. On paper, this pudgy kid looked perfect—just like all the other applicants. Four-point GPA. Bilingual in English and Spanish. Plays the violin. Distinction in this. Award for that. It was unfortunate that all these students tried so hard to distinguish themselves by doing exactly the same things as everyone else. Sometimes Dean considered replacing the entire application with a single question: "why do you belong on our Island of Misfit Toys?" Answering that would certainly be more revealing of their true character than a GPA.

Dean opened the interview document and read the first line of the official script. "So, tell me..." he glanced down at the file to find the name again, "Tell me, Oscar, what makes you want to attend the Mechanical Science Institute at Langdon University?"

"I feel that the Institute will provide me with the technical foundation I need to make an impact in today's competitive, high-tech industry..." And he went on from there. And on and on, as if he were reciting some standardized interview speech. He probably was.

Boring, Dean decided, and didn't bother to type any notes on the response. He would have been more impressed if the kid had just admitted he was here for the full-ride scholarship that came with every seat at the Institute.

"Okay, Oscar, can you tell me about something unusual you've done? Perhaps a project or a hobby that doesn't show up on your application?"

That question seemed to confuse Oscar. The poor kid had probably lived his whole life for his college applications and had nothing else to talk about.

"Well, let's see," Oscar began cautiously. "I designed an augmented reality phone app to translate Spanish writing. You just hold up the phone and it displays the English words over the Spanish text."

"And why did you make this app? What was your motivation?"

Oscar nervously folded his plump fingers. Looking at those fingers, Dean couldn't help doubting a school system that allowed a child like this to receive an "A" in PE year after year. If only he'd received low grades in some classes, his higher grades would have counted for more, at least to Dean.

"The app was for a class assignment," Oscar finally managed, then gulped audibly.

And not done out of a sense of curiosity or love of the subject, Dean noted silently.

Dean's phone rang. It was Agent Nash of the FBI.

"Sorry about this," Dean said to Oscar before flipping his phone open. "Nash. I assume you're calling because you've decided to award me with some kind of medal for standing up to the big bad Blitzkriegers."

"Very funny," Nash said. "You're lucky you didn't get awarded with a coffin."

"A coffin wouldn't look as good pinned to my chest. I'd rather have a medal, preferably a big gold one with an eagle on it. See what you can do about that, okay?"

"Mr. Lazarchek, have you reconsidered speaking with Angela Black?"

"Just a sec," Dean turned to Oscar. "This won't take more than a second, I promise. Just make yourself comfortable."

Oscar smiled awkwardly, and Dean went into his bedroom and closed his door behind him.

"Okay, spill it, Nash," Dean said. "What's the rush with Angela?"

"Angela may have uncovered information that she is only willing to share with you."

"Bull. Whatever info she has, she had it before she got locked away. So why does she think it's so important all of a sudden? Or maybe I should be asking why *you* think it's so important all of a sudden. You want to let me know what's going on?"

Nash was silent for a moment. "Mr. Lazarchek, you need to leave the investigating to us."

"I would, except the Blitzkriegers don't come to your house trying to kidnap you. And Angela doesn't want to speak to you. So it looks like I'm your guy and the more you tell me, the more I can help you."

Dean heard some muffled voices on the other end of the line. Nash must have been conferring with his partner, O'Grady, about what to say next.

"We think your encounter with the Blitzkrieger yesterday was a rogue operation, not sanctioned by their leaders," Nash explained. "We do have some indication that the Blitzkrieg Legion has been on the move in Texas and possibly Oklahoma and Kansas. There was one other instance not far from your location, but they never stick around in the same area for a second attack."

"Okay, look, this week is the end of the academic quarter here. Finals and everything. It's very busy and Angela's prison is about a seven hour drive. I'll go see her next week, how about that?"

"Sooner would be better," Nash said. "If it's necessary, the FBI can compensate you for your time."

That told Dean everything he needed to know. If the Feds were willing to pay him to talk to her, then they thought something big was going on.

"Don't worry about compensating me," Dean said. "I'll leave tomorrow or the next day if I can. I'll keep you posted."

Dean ended the call and leaned back with his hands behind his head while he thought. Nash had said they were on the move: Texas, Oklahoma, Kansas, Minnesota. That meant they were heading north, through the flatland corridor between the big mountain ranges.

An idea hit Dean like a bolt. He sat up and charged out into the living room in search of his laptop, stopping short when he saw Oscar. He had completely forgotten that the kid was still there.

"Sorry," Dean said. I just need to look something up really quick." He slid the computer back to his side of the table and accessed Topsy's database.

"Um, Mr. Lazarchek?" Oscar said timidly. "Are you fighting terrorists right now?"

"Nobody's fighting terrorists here," he said. "You shouldn't believe everything they report on TV."

"I think it would be cool to fight terrorists."

Dean looked up. "It's not like that. Really, it's not."

"Okay. Whatever you say. Are we done with the interview?"

Dean regarded Oscar for a minute, and then gave him a sympathetic nod.

"How did I do? Can you tell me if I got in?"

"Look, Oscar..." Dean sighed. He preferred to send rejection letters through the mail, but it seemed cruel to keep the kid dangling when the answer was so clear. "You've got a lot going for you. You really do. But to be perfectly honest, I don't think you'd fit in here."

"You mean I'm not good enough?" Oscar's lips trembled. "What did I do wrong?"

"Nothing. Absolutely nothing. Everything you've done has been right."

"But?"

But you're not a misfit toy. "But you haven't done anything exceptional," he said.

As Oscar thought about this, he looked down at his lap. Lowering his head like that made his extra chin flare out.

"That's why I wanted to go to your school," he said quietly. "I want to go here so I can do something exceptional."

"Look, it's not you. It's not you, it's us," Dean regretted using such a cliché line, but this time he believed it was actually true. "I just think this place is too weird for you. Or you're not weird enough for it. I'm sorry."

Oscar nodded and Dean decided the least he could do was cut the awkward moment short by showing him out. As soon as he had done so, Dean rushed back to his computer and pulled up what he was looking for: the map of the Earth that had been created using the information from the Egg. It displayed all the locations of the Predecessors' geothermal stations across the world, each buried deep, deep down and built before the continents had broken apart. These facilities had remained down there, waiting in the dark, while the glaciers above had ebbed and flowed with the passing of ages. Most of the Predecessors' stations had been swallowed by the oceans or crushed by the rising and falling of mountains, but a few that were located in the middle of tectonic plates had survived. The founders of the Institute had built Topsy House on one such spot. Dean had visited another subterranean station only fifty miles north. Others, too, must have survived the long eons since their creation, and each had the potential to contain a treasure trove of the superconductor known as teslanium, the white metal that made most of the Institute's advanced technologies possible.

Dean zoomed in on the map to trace the approximate route of the Blitzkriegers, as described by Nash. Along this corridor, dots indicating the geothermal stations peppered the landscape of the Midwest. Some of the entrances would be sealed under parking lots or houses and would therefore be totally inaccessible, but there were enough others that might still be safely hidden beneath nothing but a few feet of dirt.

The Blitzkrieger who had kidnapped Dean had mentioned a new boss. Maybe this new boss was trying to raid as many of these stations as possible to get at the invaluable teslanium they contained. The thought was chilling: it meant there might be some maniac out there building a power station capable of providing more energy than all the world's nuclear reactors. If so, what would he be using it for? Surely nothing good.

All this was nothing more than a hunch, and Dean knew it. His students had taught him that ideas are cheap, but proof pays the bills. Had Nash been willing to share his list of recent Blitzkrieger sightings, Dean might have been able to predict where they would strike next. At least he had a hypothesis: if their attacks really were focused on the Predecessor station locations, then he was looking at a list of their potential targets.

Dean compiled a list of coordinates and sent them off to Nash, even though he knew Nash would probably dismiss it as more deluded conspiracy theories. It probably wouldn't help that Dean didn't want to explain *why* the Blitzkriegers might attack those spots because he feared that would bring the Institute under FBI scrutiny. Still, the authorities deserved a warning, at least so they could log it into their crime database. If that was the best he could do to help, then he would do it.

Dean froze with his hand over the keyboard. There was another way to get the information about the Blitzkrieger activity, even if Nash didn't want to tell him. Thanks to some extra-credit work by long-graduated students, the Institute had a back door into the federal law enforcement databases. If Dean could use that to see where the Blitzkriegers and their new friends had been causing problems, he might be able to figure out where they would make their next move.

The only trouble was that accessing FBI databases was a serious crime. Dean had to spend a good five seconds considering the moral ramifications before making up his mind.

It was time to commit a felony in the name of justice.

CHAPTER 10

Cursing the cold and burying his hands as deeply as possible into his armpits, Dean crunched his way across the day-old snow toward the open-air ice rink in the quadrangle at the heart of Langdon University. With each inhale, his breath created a crackling that meant his nose hairs were freezing, telling him that the temperature had dropped at least five degrees since that morning. He wouldn't have ventured out in this weather if he didn't have to, but Victor—who was moody and obsessing about his failed experiment—had said Nikki was out here playing something called "broomball" on a team with Collin, Collin's boyfriend, and several other Institute students.

Dean watched the rink as Nikki, bundled up in a thick pink coat, dashed forward across the ice, slapping at a big rubber ball with a kitchen broom. This broomball game resembled hockey, but with no special equipment of any kind, no padding or helmets, and regular shoes instead of ice skates. The lack of solid footing resulted in lots of flailing arms and spinning bodies. When one player finally managed to get the ball rolling in roughly the direction of the goal, everyone else became even more frantic and therefore more likely to slip and fall. From the looks of things, most of the players spent the majority of their time focusing on remaining upright, which meant that the best player on the ice really wasn't much better than the worst player.

Only misfit toys could come up with a game like that, Dean thought.

"Nikki," Dean called over the wall of the rink. "I need to talk to you."

"Not now," she said, her southern accent surprisingly bright on that cold afternoon. "This here's a league game and—" Suddenly, she lost her balance and had to cling to the rink wall while her feet flew around erratically beneath her.

Collin, whom Dean almost didn't recognize with his Mohawk hidden beneath a black beanie hat, managed to sweep the ball away from another player and direct it towards a boy Dean didn't recognize but guessed was Collin's boyfriend. Opposing players immediately crowded him, so he passed it on to Nikki. It slid more than rolled towards her, and two big guys from the opposing team pushed their way over the ice to pursue it. Nikki managed to regain her balance long enough to deflect the ball onward, but one of the big guys intercepted the pass. Janet Cho went after it fearlessly, her broom chopping at her opponent's legs as much as at the ball.

"Why don't you join us, D-Squared?" Raskolnikov called from where he guarded the goal.

Dean waved a polite no. He preferred his tailbone unbroken, thank you—although he could see that this was just the sort of insanity he would have enjoyed when he was their age. McKenzie might have loved it, too, because it had that rare combination of high amusement and low competitiveness that she preferred.

The game unfolded like an episode of *America's Funniest Home Videos*, complete with face-falls and one or two surprisingly skillful plays. There was no referee, but someone on the opposing team announced that time was up, and they all shook hands. The score, if there was one, went completely unmentioned.

Nikki seemed intent on ignoring Dean, but he fell in beside her as she exited the rink.

"I need a favor," he said.

"That's mighty bold of you."

"Okay, let's take a step back," Dean said. "I'm quitting. It's true—I signed my resignation letter today. You told Soap, and now she's mad about it. I guess you're mad, too."

White clouds of breath slid from between her lips, but they carried no words.

"Oh, come on," Dean said. "You have to admit, I'm terrible at this job. You deserve someone better."

"Seems like you're doin' a pretty good job to me. I think they'd agree, too," she tilted her head towards the rest of the broomball team. Janet was collecting brooms for use by the next two teams scheduled to use the rink, Raskolnikov was stamping his feet to shake off the ice and snow, and Collin was speaking animatedly with his boyfriend. Nikki's point was clear: Dean would be leaving all of them behind when he moved away.

"Okay, look, I'm sorry," Dean lifted his eyes towards the sky as they continued to walk. He couldn't see the sun, but the clouds were so bright they hurt his eyes. "Can we just forget about this for right now? I'm worried about something bigger. It looks like someone's organizing Helmholtz's men. Instead of falling into disarray, they're out there causing more problems than ever. If we don't find some answers, yesterday's attack won't be the last."

"What do you care? That's not gonna be your problem much longer, is it?"

"I made a promise, all right? I promised I would protect the Institute and its students or," Dean sniffed the cold air, "or die trying."

Nikki sighed. They were crossing over the unofficial border of campus that was guarded by the Mark Twain statue and the Humanities building. Ahead of them loomed the small forest surrounding Topsy House. All the trees were dusted white, and now a few white specks swirled through the air, though Dean wasn't sure if this was new snow falling from the sky or simply old snow carried by the breeze.

"I wouldn't ask if I didn't think it was important," Dean said. "And I wouldn't ask if there were someone better, but you're the only one who can crack into the law enforcement databases—"

"You want me to hack the Feds?" she sounded offended.

"I know it's illegal, but—"

"I don't care about that," her steely brown eyes drilled into him. "I just want to take my last exam this afternoon and then get on my plane and fly away from this God-forsaken frozen wasteland. Committin' cyber-crimes would really interfere with my schedule."

"I won't make you miss your flight."

"You're damn right you won't," she huffed. "But there's more to it. I'm a chemist, not a hacker."

"You're the best hacker we have."

"Then find someone better," she started walking faster now. "We really need a computer scientist 'round here anyway. I'm sure we have someone who's applied who could help us out."

Dean thought about what's-his-name that he interviewed an hour ago. He was a computer guy, but clearly not a good fit. "It'll take too much time to find someone. You're my only shot at this. If you can't do it, can you at least show me how?"

"Ha," she said in a tone that suggested she'd be better off trying to show a bear how to post to Instagram. "You know, I hoped you'd want me to do somethin' in my area of expertise, like paint your car with thermal-reactive pigments or make you a bulletproof t-shirt. But, no, you have to go an' ask me to hack the FBI. I'm gonna have to think it over."

Evidently, she intended to give it thought right there. Dean tagged along silently behind her, unwilling to break her concentration. They entered Topsy and went up the stairs before she finally stopped in the hallway between Dean's residence and the shower room that actually doubled as the secret elevator to the underground lab.

"I'll do it on one condition," she said. "You have to talk to Soap."

"Okay," Dean said. "About what?"

"Her boyfriend."

That was not the answer Dean was expecting. He knew Soap was dating a guy named Brett—a good guy, Dean really liked him—but Dean still didn't see how he could help. "What am I supposed to say to her?"

"It's just that she needs to talk, even though she doesn't know it."

"If she doesn't know she needs to talk, then why do you want me to talk to her? Girl talk isn't exactly my specialty."

Nikki sighed. "There are only three people in this time zone she's truly comfortable openin' up to: you, me, and Victor. She can't talk to me about this because... I'm too close to the situation. So is Victor. That leaves you."

"Not Brett?"

"That's part of her problem," Nikki said. "But I'll leave that for you and her to discuss. And I don't want her to know I said anything about it. I also don't want to know anything she confides in you. I've steered her wrong in the past, and I owe her this one."

Dean felt bewildered, but knew it was the best deal he would get.

"Okay," he opened the door to his residence and she followed him in. "Okay, I'll talk to her. Now, when you're hacking that database, I want you to use my login. Let me go find some paper to write it down for you, just in case you get caught and they trace it back."

"That's not a worry."

"You never know. The FBI is pretty good at tracking hackers, after all. I'm ready to take the fall if necessary."

"They won't track me," she said with complete confidence. "But don't worry. If it makes you feel better, I'll swear in a court of law that you did it and—hey, what's with your refrigerator?"

She pointed at the dismembered fridge in the corner of the kitchen.

Dean might have laughed if he'd felt enough energy. "The ghost of Mark Twain stood right there saying something about Tesla and pointing to the fridge. So I opened it up to see if I could find anything hidden inside."

"Are you out of your mind?" she asked pointedly.

"Maybe. The worst part is that I didn't find anything inside the refrigerator."

"Of course there was nothin' inside the fridge," she rolled her eyes. "Did you ever suppose he might not have been pointin' at the fridge, but that the fridge was in the way of whatever he was pointin' at?"

Leaning over the pile of parts, she traced her fingers around the wall. She then thumped it with her fist here and there, and in the third place she struck, the wall emitted a deep, echoing sound.

"There's somethin' back there."

Dean stood stunned for a moment before joining the inspection of the wall. There was no visible seam, but that meant only that it had been skillfully hidden. He knocked at the wall until he was sure it was hollow, and then he smashed through with the bottom of his fist. The drywall broke into chunks, which he ripped away to reveal a small alcove containing a large box made of thick wire mesh. It was heavy and dusty, but he removed it carefully and set it on the kitchen counter.

Despite the heat inside the residence, Dean felt a sudden chill along his spine.

"What's in it?" Nikki asked.

"There's only one way to find out." Dean undid the clasp and lifted the lid.

CHAPTER 11

The hinged lid of the mysterious box creaked open to reveal a stack of old books. Dean opened one and flipped through pages of hand-made drawings of what appeared to be circuit board diagrams, sketches of the human brain, and strange, dancing lizard hieroglyphs.

"Those dancing lizards—that's the language of the Predecessors," Nikki said as she set one of the volumes down and picked up another.

"Can you read it?" he asked.

"'Course not," she said. "But I recognize the signature on the bottom of the diagrams. Nikola Tesla wrote all this, which means he was probably also the one who hid these books in this wall."

Dean whistled. Tesla's lost notebooks were a find worthy of the Smithsonian. But he still wondered: after the great inventor had built an underground lab dedicated to concealing his wildest ideas, why would he have gone to the trouble of encoding these books in an ancient language and then sealing them in the wall?

Nikki sorted through the stack and found the volume marked with the number one. She opened it to an introductory section written in English, which she skimmed over.

"It looks like Tesla found some of the technology invented by the Predecessors," she said. "But he took it further than they ever did. What he's talking about here is—is a fully self-aware simulation of a human mind. An artificial intelligence that mirrors a living intelligence."

"I don't know what any of that means."

"It means we need to call Victor," she said.

"Victor's kind of grumpy right now. He's getting nowhere with that experiment of his—"

"Call him now," she set the book down sharply. "If this is what Tesla claims, then this book is a recipe for makin' an artificial intelligence. It'd be a thinking creature that's capable of as much free will and consciousness as you and me, and stored in—in one of those rocks you keep callin' an Egg."

"Inside the Egg," Dean's scalp prickled. "The image of Twain came from that Egg. That means—"

"That means our ghost wasn't a pre-recorded video of Mark Twain." She looked up at him. "We've discovered the honest-to-goodness ghost of Mark Twain, a perfect copy of his personality and memory that can make decisions on his own. And he was tryin' to give us a message from beyond the grave!"

Without another word, they gathered the books and went down to the underground laboratory to seek out the other senior students.

"The implications are incredible..." Victor muttered as he gingerly turned one of the brittle pages. "What we can accomplish with this is—it boggles the mind."

"Like what?" Dean asked. "As usual, I'm not getting it. Can you give me the bottom line?"

"Immortality," Victor looked up at him. "Imagine if you could record your whole mind into a computer. You'd potentially live forever. I can't read most of this writing, but I can understand enough to know that's what these books are describing. This process is only going to work with an Egg, though, because no computer on Earth can handle the job. We saw what happened to mine when we tried."

"So if you have an Egg you can copy yourself," Dean was struggling to imagine it. "But it wouldn't really be you in there, right? I mean, you wouldn't be leaving your body to live in the Egg, you'd just be creating a new version of yourself, right?"

"That's correct," Victor said. "Copying yourself into the Egg would be like copying a file from one computer to another. The first one doesn't go away, but now there are two versions. In this case, the original "you" would grow old and die in your physical body just like normal, and the other "you" would start a new life as a... as a..."

"As a ghost?" Dean shook his head. "Is that really a life? I mean, can we really say our glowing green Mark Twain is a full person?"

"Good point," Nikki said. "He doesn't breath, eat, move, or do anything a livin' animal does."

"We may need to redefine what we mean by 'life,'" Victor said. "It looks to me like our Mark Twain might be every bit as capable of thinking as you and I. That means it—he—is alive and conscious. And if I can figure out what these notes say, I could do the same thing for someone else—I could attempt to create a mind." Victor's far-away look drifted even farther away. "It wouldn't be easy, though. I'd need another Egg, and I'd need someone to write a lot of new software. Good thing that new computer student started today. We're going to need him."

Nikki glared at Dean. "You got us a computer scientist and then you still asked me to do your dirty work?"

"Uh," was all Dean could say. Aside from the kid he'd interviewed today, he didn't remember any computer science prospects, but he'd been through so many applications in the past month that it was entirely possible he'd forgotten all about one. "What was this kid's name again?"

"Cake," Victor said without looking up from the book.

"Excuse me?"

"His name is Cake. His nickname, anyway. I think Soap knows why, maybe. Seems like a nice guy. He went out to get some food, but I'm sure he'll be back soon."

"Wait," Dean said. "You mean this new kid, whoever he is, already found the underground laboratory? On his first day?" Dean didn't think anyone had ever done that so quickly. "You didn't tell him about this lab, did you?"

Victor slammed his book shut with an indignant bang. "Cake found out by himself. End of story. And that's good, because I'm going to need him for this experiment. I'm also going to need some peace and quiet, if you don't mind."

Victor tucked the first two volumes under his arms and headed towards the medical bay.

Nikki shook her head. "You insulted him with that question," she said. "He wouldn't have told anyone about this lab. He knows the rules, and he knows why it's so important to keep our secrets. He's been here longer than you, remember?"

Dean sighed and thought about apologizing, but then decided the best thing he could do was let Victor be alone with his work.

From the other side of the elevator, the physics lab emitted a howling roar like the rush of a jet engine.

"That's probably Soap," Nikki had to shout over the noise. "You better go find her and make sure she's not blowin' up the electrical grid again."

"What about the FBI database? I need that information."

"Don't get your boxers in a bunch. It's gonna take me a while, and you have your end of the bargain to hold up, remember? Go on, now. Go talk to Soap."

Dean found his way over to Soap's workbench where the blueprints of the jet pack she had proposed yesterday had already sprung to life in the form of an early prototype strapped to the back of a crash test dummy. The two large jet turbines on the dummy's back looked naked without their cowlings and the wings were little more than graceful skeletons, but he couldn't help marveling at how quickly she had turned her vision into reality—with the help of the Institute's mutli-material 3D printers and other fabrication machines, of course. Her assembly robot, Rusty, also must have helped, and the mechanical scorpion-dog now squatted next to her, handing her tools and equipment like the world's most precise surgical nurse. Soap had evidently found the Egg and the lightning lance where Dean had left them on her work bench, and she had set them up so that Twain could spring to green life once more. He now reclined in a metal chair as if watching her work, and he raised his cigar in salute as Dean approached.

Soap saw him, too, but didn't say anything. She hid her head into an open hatch and pulled out several wires, which she handed off to Rusty. He scuttled away on his six spidery legs to a corner where he wove the wires around spools, sorted by color, then returned to stand at the ready for his creator's next command.

"Hello," Dean said cautiously.

"Hi," Soap responded flatly.

The awkward silence stretched on while Soap tested a series of electrical junctions with her multimeter. Nearby, on the desk, the Newton's Cradle clacked weakly. Dean grabbed one of the steel spheres to stop its motion.

"Can we talk?" he asked.

"About what?"

About my leaving, Dean thought. *About your boyfriend. About the fact that there are people out there who would kill us for the technology we're hiding down here.* For some reason, the more important the topic, the more Dean hesitated to bring it up.

"How's your jet pack coming?" he copped out.

"Fine," she said.

Awkward pause.

"Decided not to tell Stephanie—I mean, Speed—about your project?"

"She's a noob," Soap shrugged. "Can't tell her about the antimatter reactors until she discovers the underground lab."

For once, she didn't chatter on about technical details or whatever else was on her mind. Nikki had said Soap only opened up like that with a few select people, and Dean began to worry that he had been dropped from that list. He looked over at Twain, whose bushy eyebrows were angled downwards in evident concentration. Dean knew the ghost wasn't physical—someone could sit down in the chair right on top of him and not feel a thing—but he could see the intelligence behind those emerald eyes and the worry on that furrowed brow. Now that Dean knew the ghost was more than just a video-game sprite projected in three dimensions, he found he had no notion of what to say to him.

"I see you got Mark Twain up and running," he observed to Soap.

Soap set down her multimeter and picked up the Egg. It now sat in a kind of modified bowl that resembled a small, upside-down crown. It consisted of a clear, glass-like material that revealed flickering blue fingers of electricity playing along a silver disk at its core. Whatever this gizmo was, it seemed to be feeding just the right amount of power at just the right frequency to keep Twain's ghost steadily energized.

"I had to use one of our antimatter reactors," Soap said, handing him the Egg and its charger. "It's one of the smaller ones, but I think Mr. Twain's worth it."

"Probably more than you know," Dean said, but he wasn't sure how to begin explaining that the ghost might actually be alive. She would find out soon enough from Victor, so Dean left it at that.

"He's getting better at talking, too," Soap said. "I think he only needs more practice. He's definitely saying something about Tesla needing our help."

"Tesla needing *our* help. I thought..." Dean now realized he'd made yet another bad assumption. He'd interpreted Twain's words to mean that Twain wanted help from Tesla without considering that it might be the other way around. Unfortunately, it still didn't explain what help he needed—or why.

"Near as I can figure," Soap said. "There's another Egg out there somewhere with Tesla's mind inside. Mr. Twain's ghost is getting some kind of thought waves or something that makes him think Tesla's in trouble."

"Is this true?" Dean looked at Twain, who nodded gravely to confirm the story.

"Well, then, let's go help him. Where is he? Where's Tesla's Egg?"

Soap shrugged. "Too far away for Mr. Twain to track him down. So we're as stuck as ever."

Dean didn't know what to make of that. He thought about it for several minutes while Soap tinkered, but he couldn't come up with any plan of action. Absentmindedly, he pulled back one of the balls of the Newton's Cradle and watched it click back and forth for a moment while he considered all the possibilities. The only good news, he decided, was that Soap was starting to open up again.

"Listen," Dean said. "I was wondering..." He stalled, thinking how much he hated conversations about romance. He hated any conversation, really. As far as he was concerned, talking never accomplished anything, but he had promised Nikki he would try it, so he pressed on. "I was just wondering how things were going with Brett."

Soap shrugged.

"Well, is he treating you okay?"

"Yeah," she said. "He's always really nice."

"But?"

"I don't know," she repeated her shrug. "It's just... I don't know. Have you ever broken up with someone? What do you do?"

"Usually I just ignore them and don't return their calls," Dean joked.

She stopped what she was doing and studied him for a long moment. "But you never wanted to do that with McKenzie, right?"

Dean felt like he'd been kicked in the stomach. McKenzie had been unlike anyone else in his life, but they had maintained an on-again-off-again relationship for years. Each time they broke up, Dean went out and did something stupid, something dangerous or life-changing. The first time they split, he dropped out of college. The second time, he joined the army. After they had broken up often enough, the craziness became normal for him, which is how he got involved in firefighting, mixed martial arts, and all his other favorite self-destructive pursuits. Each time, he eventually found his way out of his madness by clinging to the hope that they might get back together some day. Until the day he found her on the floor with her auburn hair resting against her blue skin.

"Well? Did you ever want to break up with McKenzie?" Soap asked again.

"We," he cleared his throat. "We sort of couldn't live with each other and couldn't live without each other."

"That's a contradiction," she looked puzzled.

"Tell me about it."

"Did you ever go out with anyone else?"

"Neither of us cheated, if that's what you mean. But during our breakups, we both had other dates."

"Were you ever worried that she would end up liking someone better than you?"

"All the time. There was this one d-bag—" he stopped short and looked at her. She didn't seem to have noticed his crass language, so he went on. "This guy's name was Ignacio. Ignacio Zabaleta. Math major. Mr. Suave, a real Romeo disguised as a tree-hugging hippy wannabe. God, I wanted to punch him in the face."

"What happened with him?"

"I don't know," Dean, feeling fidgety, stopped the Newton's Cradle for a moment then set it going from the other direction. "In the long run, it just gave her and me something else to fight about later."

"Hey, D-Squared!" Nikki shouted from way back at the computer pavilion.

"Sounds like she's found something," Dean said. "I better go see what."

Soap nodded slowly. Then she drew a wrench from inside of her coat a little too hastily. It snagged on another tool in a different pocket, slid from her fingers and dropped onto the computer console. The engine diagrams on screen began blinking red and a warning klaxon blared over the speakers.

"Should it be doing that?" Dean asked.

"Probably not. This might be a good time to run—"

She couldn't finish her sentence before an explosive rush of air nearly pushed them off their feet. The jet suit blasted upwards and smashed hard into the ceiling. Little bits of plastic, metal, and chunks of crash-test dummy rained down all around them.

"Now I see why you wanted only unmanned test flights," Soap said. "Probably a good idea."

CHAPTER 12

After helping with some of the cleanup of the crashed jet suit, Dean made his way back to Nikki. She had uncovered an FBI map marked with notes on suspected Blitzkrieger attacks, including the dates of the attacks.

"Most of these seem random," Nikki said. "They pop up all over the central southern states and move generally northwards, but some of the attacks happened simultaneously."

"Meaning?"

"Meaning whoever's in charge has several crews workin' at the same time. They're up to all kinds of mischief. Attackin' houses, rippin' up parking lots, all sorts of things. In Louisiana, they even blasted away half the asphalt in a busy intersection. They come in, smash up the place with explosives or heavy machinery, and then move out within minutes. Sometimes, they return a few days later, but usually not. They're not stealin' money, so nobody can figure out why they do it."

Dean's mouth felt dry because he knew why. They were after something more valuable than money: the Predecessor stations buried deep below those houses and intersections. And what were they finding down there? Gobs of teslanium, maybe enough to make antimatter reactors capable of supplying power to an entire continent—or antimatter bombs capable of erasing that same continent.

"Another weird thing," Nikki said. "A lot of times, they show up in the middle of a thunder storm, right to the spot where lightnin' hits. They swarm all over the damage before they disappear. It's like they know exactly where it's gonna strike."

Dean couldn't explain that one. Maybe this 'new boss' spent a lot of time watching the Weather Channel. If he could offer a million dollars for Twain's Egg, he must have some inside secrets.

"Thank you, Nikki," Dean said. "Can you do one more thing for me? Find our file with the map of the Predecessor stations. Can you super-impose it on the map of the Blitzkrieger attacks?"

Nikki clicked her mouse a few times and the image of the other map appeared on screen. It featured no governmental borders, just a scattering of red dots placed upon a patchwork of satellite images of North America, and each of those dots landed right on top of one of the prehistoric Predecessor geothermal stations.

"X marks the spot," Nikki said. "But who has access to the Predecessor's map?"

Dean shook his head. In truth, many of people might have access to it. Angela Black had copied it from the original information in the Egg, which meant that anyone in her former criminal network might have found it. Maybe it was time to go visit Ms. Black in prison after all.

"One thing I don't get," Dean said. "Why are they focusing on the South and the Midwest? The West Coast has just as many stations."

"Geology," Nikki said. "Remember that these stations are ancient. Beyond ancient: they're two hundred million years old. We don't understand how they survived as long as they have, even in geographically stable areas like the middle of the country. Along the Pacific Rim, they've surely been crushed long ago by continental motion and so forth."

"What about the other dots?" Dean asked. "The ones in the middle of the country that haven't been hit?"

"I bet all those are ten miles from nowhere, in empty lots, or in other places with nobody around to see the Blitzkriegers diggin' 'em up."

"But there might be some left untouched," Dean said. "Someone should go check them out."

"Sounds like you're volunteerin'."

The elevator chimed, announcing that someone new had come down to the lab. Victor, Nikki, and Soap were already down here, so it could only be the mysterious student known as Cake. Dean crossed over towards the entrance to greet the new arrival. There, he saw that the kid emerging from the elevator was none other than the same boy Dean had denied earlier today.

The chubby boy seemed as surprised to see Dean as Dean was to see him. He froze, a gigantic latte forgotten in his hand.

Dean couldn't believe it. Just that morning, he had looked the boy in the eyes and told him he didn't belong at the Institute. Now, not only had he returned, he had also found the top-secret underground laboratory, and he was bringing a tray of Caribou Coffee for everyone there.

"You." Dean pointed a finger. "What are you doing here?"

The kid's mouth opened, but no sound came out. Soap emerged from the physics wing to see what was going on.

"This is the new guy," Soap said. "The computer guy who's going to help Victor. His name is Cake."

"His name isn't Cake. It's... well, I forgot his real name, but I remember very clearly that I *denied him admission*. Fess up, Cake, or whatever your name is: how did you get down here without being a member of the Institute? How did you even know this place existed?"

Cake stared silently for a long time. Victor now emerged from the back to see what was happening, and from the look he exchanged with Soap, Dean could tell this was a surprise to him as well. Somehow, this new boy had fooled all of them.

"Tell me," Dean growled. "Now."

"I, um, I went around the security system," he said softly.

"Our security system is way too strong."

"A system's only as strong as the people who use it. I... I talked the others into opening the outer doors for me."

Dean could feel rage igniting inside him. As long as Cake hadn't been carrying a weapon, he could pass through the doors any time a full-fledged student walked with him.

"And how did you find your way down here, into this lab?"

"Um..."

"Speak up!"

"I got a password. To a computer. That someone didn't log out of."

"Who?" Dean roared. "Who was so stupid as to let you just walk in here and get a password? Did they turn their back for a moment, or did they simply hand you a computer and walk away—" Dean stopped abruptly when he realized he'd left his laptop sitting right next to the kid on his own dining room table while he'd gone into the bedroom to speak with Nash. He'd been the one who handed the keys to this hacker.

A metallic taste flooded Dean's mouth and his face felt like it was on fire. He honestly considered grabbing the kid and physically hauling him out, but he decided he couldn't justify any sort of physicality. He could, however, justify the harshest words he could muster.

"You're trespassing," Dean roared. "You lied to everybody. You stuck your nose where it didn't belong and put your sticky fingers all over property that doesn't belong to you. I don't know whether you were planning to rob us or just laugh at us, but I do know that you must think I'm the stupidest human being on the planet if that was your plan."

"I just thought—"

"Get out. Now. I don't ever want to see you in Topsy again. Got it?"

Cake opened his mouth a few times as if about to speak, but there was nothing to say. With a dejected look back at Victor and then at Soap, he shuffled towards the exit. When he arrived at the elevator doors, he turned back to them one more time. "I really enjoyed my time here," he said quietly. "For what it's worth: thank you."

As soon as he was gone, Soap ran off, crying. That was the second time in twenty four hours Dean had made her cry, and he felt a sticky sense of shame mixing in with his rage.

"Harsh," Nikki scolded. "You didn't need to treat him like that."

Dean spun around to face Nikki. "Here's what I need you to do," he barked. "Get a list of GPS coordinates for the places the Blitzkriegers have hit, and another list of the ones they might still be going after. I'm going to mail them to the FBI."

"That's going to take time—"

"Just do it," Dean made a violent slashing gesture to show the conversation was over. "And if Nash doesn't want to believe me, then maybe I can stop at a few Predecessor stations on my way to see Angela in prison. Yes, that's exactly what I'll do. You guys have your projects, and now I have mine."

DECEMBER 15

(8 DAYS BEFORE STORMAGEDDON)

CHAPTER 13

The Predecessor geothermal station was way out in the scrublands of Kansas, half an hour outside a microscopic town called Scammon and accessible only by forgotten roads and unmarked turns. The weather was a little warmer here than in Bugswallow, but the landscape was still as gray and dismal as the surface of the moon.

After driving most of the night and on through the morning, Dean was exhausted. When his GPS had taken him as close to the coordinates as he could drive, he parked next to the remnants of a lead mine which had been abandoned so long ago it now consisted of nothing but the crumbling wooden shell of an ore processing plant and the rusted skeletons of cart tracks. Although it looked like the mine hadn't been touched by human hands in decades, the ground around it was freshly tilled by numerous tire tracks. Dean was no detective, but the crisp tread patterns told him several different vehicles had stopped here, including at least two motorcycles. A line of frosted boot prints led over a hill and continued on for half a mile to a mound of dirt surrounding a freshly-dug crater. At the bottom of the excavation, the Predecessor elevator platform lay exposed to the air. If he hadn't known what it was, he might have mistaken it for a slab of granite inlaid with weather-worn carvings of dancing reptiles instead of a magnetic hover-disk that could carry him hundreds of feet underground.

The good news was that he had been right: the Blitzkriegers—or whatever they were calling themselves these days—must have been systematically unearthing and delving into these forgotten chambers. The bad news was that it looked like they had already come and gone here.

The thought of driving all this way for nothing was simply too depressing to consider, so Dean climbed down the hole to kneel on the stone elevator disk. Brushing away the dust, he studied the carvings. They had once been very intricate, but he didn't need to know what it said. If the one worked like the others he had used, he could activate it by pressing his hands into the correct locations. As he was searching for the right spots, his phone buzzed.

SOAP: And he's FUNNY too!

Soap had been texting him updates all night about their progress with the ghost of Mark Twain. She, Victor, and Nikki were convinced that this really was a living, thinking duplicate of Mark Twain's mind, copied with the help of Nikola Tesla himself, and preserved in the Egg for more than a century. The students had managed to get him speaking consistently and intelligibly through the speakers in their phones, and apparently he'd been regaling them with humorous stories ever since.

Dean's phone buzzed again.

SOAP: He told a story about a good little boy who blew himself up with dynamite. HILARIOUS! :D

If Twain was telling stories instead of coming up with more information on how to find Tesla's lost Egg, then Dean felt he could risk losing phone reception by travelling underground for a few minutes. He silenced and closed his phone, then returned his attention to the stone beneath his feet. He brushed dirt away from the surface to get a better look at the carvings. They were faded almost to the point of nonexistence, but a pair of shallow indentations resembling three-toed, reptilian footprints remained discernible to those who knew what to look for. Slipping off his glove, he placed his bare hand into the indentation. As soon as he touched the cold stone, light flashed in the gap around the disk, and suddenly he was falling.

His stomach lurched and for one nightmarish instant he thought the stone had broken beneath him and dropped him down the mineshaft. In truth, the disk remained beneath him, rushing downwards like an uncomfortably fast elevator. The rock walls whistled by as the circle of sky at the top of the shaft shrank to a speck. A thousand feet straight down, he guessed, just like the shaft leading to the reactor room below Topsy's underground laboratory.

Gradually, the elevator disk pressed up into his feet to slow his descent until it finally floated him down, out of the shaft to emerge into a large, domed room. At least, Dean assumed it was a large, domed room: both the other Predecessor geothermal stations he had seen were domed rooms lined with ornately carved pillars. Like the others, this one was pitch black so he couldn't see much, but he could feel the heat hit him like a wave. He wiped the sweat off his forehead with the back of his hand, stepped off the disk, and drew his flashlight to get a better look.

He was hoping to find some clue as to what the Blitzkrieger had come looking for. Instead, his flashlight lit up the messy remnants of someone's dinner and a scattering of crumpled beer cans. He also saw an expensive camera with a large lens mounted on a tripod. Next to the camera, a pair of sleeping pads lay on the ground.

And two men rested on those sleeping pads.

"What the—" the man on the first pad sat up with a jolt, his hand shielding his eyes from Dean's light. His head was shaved bald, but his scalp bore a skull-and-Nazi-helmet tattoo, the insignia of the Blitzkrieg Legion. A few feet away, another man rolled over to see what was going on.

"Don't move," Dean said, but they did anyway. The one in front reached for what Dean assumed was a gun, so Dean planted his hiking boot onto the back of the man's hand.

The Blitzkrieger yelped, but now the other guy began rustling around, probably looking for a weapon of his own. Dean slammed his fist hard into the first man's temple then kicked at the spot where he had been reaching. His toe connected with something metal—probably a pistol—and sent it skid over the floor into the shadows. Wasting no time, Dean leaped at the second man, aiming his flashlight at his eyes. He slammed into him bodily, driving him to the ground and straddled him. The Blitzkrieger still fumbled for a shotgun under a pile of clothes, but Dean tore it from the man's hands and then pointed it back at him.

"Who are you working for?" Dean demanded. "What are you looking for down here? Tell me!"

"I'll tell you," a gravelly voice rumbled out of the dark. It was a familiar voice—unpleasantly familiar. Dean spun the shotgun and the flashlight around, but could only see the shadowy outline of a man who loomed upwards into the darkness, higher and higher, like an avalanche in reverse. The man stepped forward into the light to reveal himself as Brick Stellenleiter.

Brick clamped one of his enormous hands around the shotgun barrels. Dean didn't mean to fire, but the jolt of the sudden grab jarred his trigger finger, and one of the two barrels exploded, point blank, into the big man's chest.

"Ouch," Brick said in a way that almost sounded sarcastic. "Did you forget that I'm bullet proof?"

Brick ripped the gun out of Dean's hands and slammed it into a pillar. The wooden butt split in half and the barrels bent to almost a ninety degree angle. Then Brick grabbed Dean's jacket and did the same to him, flinging him bodily against the wall.

A spear of pain burned through Dean's skull as his head collided with the stone. He bounced to the ground and tried to get up, but his knees wobbled so much he couldn't get his footing. Without warning, a massive weight descended onto Dean's stomach and threatened to press all the way through his body to crush his spine. He tried to cry out in pain, but he couldn't pull any air into his lungs. When he opened his eyes he saw that Brick had lowered one enormous knee onto his belly, pinning him like a bug under foot.

"What's the matter?" Brick slapped him across the face. "You ain't fightin' very hard."

Dean's vision began to narrow. He couldn't breathe, and all he could think about was that he had told McKenzie he would protect the students or die trying. Now he was going to die trying, and all he had to do was lie there and wait for the darkness to finish closing in around him. Maybe he would even see her again on the other side.

"I said *what's the matter?*" Brick slapped him again, but now both the sound of his voice and the sting of the slap felt distant. "You used to be so scrappy. Killin' you ain't fun if you don't fight back."

Dean's vision was fading quickly, to the point where he could hardly see Brick anymore. One of the other two Blitzkriegers said something about clearing out and leaving, but the meaning of the words seemed to evaporate in Dean's mind.

Brick leaned in close and whispered in Dean's ear. "You ain't the first who tried to commit suicide by fighting me," he growled. "I know all the signs, so I know what you're doing. But if you're too chicken to feed yourself a bullet, that ain't my problem. I ain't gonna kill you until you don't wanna die."

Brick might have slapped him again, but Dean couldn't feel it. All he could feel was the blackness filling him up inside, and then he was gone.

Chapter 14

When Dean came to, it was so dark he wasn't sure if his eyes were open or closed. Slowly, his memory crept back to him: Brick had knocked him unconscious in the cave and left him for dead? No, Brick had said he was leaving Dean alive, and that was much crueler.

He groped around for his flashlight but didn't find it. Then he fumbled for his phone in his pocket and flipped it open. He had no reception and its glow was miniscule in the endless shadows around him, but it was better than nothing.

By the light of the tiny screen, it looked like Brick and the other two Blitzkriegers had cleared out. All the leftover food wrappers and empty cans were still scattered across the floor, but their bedrolls and the cameras were gone. They had obviously found whatever they had come for and they weren't coming back.

Dean eventually found his way to the elevator disk and placed his hands on the indentations to activate it. It carried him to the surface, where he emerged squinting into the afternoon sky.

He walked the half-mile back to the old mining camp with its wooden buildings rotting and frozen in the cold air. His truck was gone. They must have taken it. For this, he cursed them, but he had bigger problems to worry about now, such as the threat of hypothermia. He shivered, tucked his arms under his armpits, and looked again at the tire tracks. There were lots more than when he had arrived, cutting up the thin patina of snow in every direction. He followed them into the abandoned refining shack, but it was empty. Most likely, they had parked their vehicles here to keep them sheltered and out of sight while they went down to the Progenitor station. The thin wood planks of the walls didn't offer any protection from the cold, but it did block the wind, so Dean paused inside while deciding who to call for help.

Outside, a vehicle approached slowly, its tires crunching along the frosty ground. Dean stood still, listening as two car doors opened and closed, and two men began to speak in hushed tones just outside.

Cautiously, Dean peered through a gap in the wall boards, but couldn't see anything other than the corner of a black sedan's rear bumper. Whoever was out there had stopped talking and were moving rapidly in his direction. They must have worked out that he was inside. Probably saw his footprints on the frozen ground. However they figured it out, now they were after him. Dean considered darting out through a window to escape into the scrublands, maybe hiding behind one of the scraggly trees, but any motion he made now would result in too much noise. Ambush was his only option.

The first man stepped through the door with a pistol leading the way. A quick slash of Dean's hand stripped the weapon out of the man's grip and simultaneously brought him off balance, allowing Dean to trip him and come down on top so that he sat squarely on the gunman's chest.

Dean brought up his fists, ready to pummel, but this was no Blitzkrieger: this was an African American man in a black suit.

"Agent Nash?" Dean said in surprise.

"Get off me, Lazarchek!"

Dean shifted to let him up, and Nash used this as an opportunity to thrust Dean away and to the side. With an instinct born from hours of fight training, Dean countered by using the added momentum to keep rolling, scissoring his legs to take Nash with him so that they both ended up a few feet away but back in the same position where they had started, with Dean mounted squarely on Nash's chest.

"Aren't they supposed to teach you how to fight at FBI school?" Dean couldn't resist saying.

A firm hand gripped his collar and yanked him to his feet. Dean spun and pushed back to give himself just enough time to catch a glimpse of Agent O'Grady's stern face and wiry, white hair. The instant that recognition registered in his mind, the world wheeled around Dean and the ground crashed hard into his back.

Dean's brain spun like a wobbling top. It took him several seconds to work out that he had been thrown to the ground, judo style. He tried to speak, but found he could only make little squeaking noises.

Agent O'Grady stood over him patiently, his face as unyielding as ever, but with no hint of anger. He let Nash get up and dust himself off while he kept watching Dean. For his part, Dean was content to lie there and try to remember how to breathe.

"Get up," O'Grady finally said, offering a hand to Dean. "We need to go talk."

Chapter 15

Dean half expected them to slap on handcuffs and book him on the spot. Instead, they took him into town to a little diner and bought him a burger. As they sat over steaming coffee, Dean spilled the story about his encounter with the Blitzkriegers. Not the whole thing—he skipped the part about the Predecessor station and simply let the agents believe he'd found the fugitives camping outdoors. There was no need to change the other details: getting clobbered by Brick and having his truck stolen were more likely to happen above ground, anyway.

"So, can I file a stolen vehicle report with you guys or what?" Dean asked as he chewed his hamburger. It hurt to chew—he worried that getting thrown into a stone pillar might have cracked a tooth, and he wondered if Victor's magical medicine injections could do anything for dental work. In between bites, he alternated between pressing an ice-pack to his aching jaw and then to his throbbing temple.

"You can file the report with the local sheriff later," Nash said. "What we're hoping for now is a little more explanation from you."

"Ah, I get it," Dean said. "This is the part where you threaten to throw me in jail unless I spill my guts. But I have to say, taking a guy to lunch isn't the most intimidating play you could make. Are you guys sure you're good at this?"

He was hoping to lighten the mood, but neither of the agents seemed remotely amused.

"We don't want to strong-arm you," O'Grady said.

"Not yet, anyway," Nash added. Ever since Dean had gotten the jump on him in that mining shack, the younger agent had been wearing a scowl that would have made a glass of lemon juice seem sweet by comparison. "I have told you repeatedly to keep away from this investigation," Nash growled. "And yet somehow you manage to keep finding new ways to endanger yourself as well as our case. You're making our job harder, and if our job is harder, that means the Blitzkriegers' job is easier. Don't you get that?"

O'Grady placed a hand on his partner's shoulder. "Why don't you go wash up?"

"But I—"

"Go wash up," O'Grady said in a tone that was perfectly calm and yet allowed no argument.

Nash threw his napkin on the table and stalked off to the restroom.

"Forgive my partner," O'Grady said. "He's young, and he's having a bad day."

Dean was all too happy to keep eating. His appetite had returned for the first time since yesterday, and his stomach seemed intent on making up for lost time. If it hadn't been for the pain in his jaw, he might have shoveled the whole burger into his mouth already.

"I don't think Nash likes me," Dean confided between steak-cut fries.

"Actually, he does," O'Grady said. "It was his idea to hire you as a consultant, but I told him we needed to make a show of suspicion first. I was hoping that you would rise to the bait and make an effort to prove yourself."

"Did I do that?"

O'Grady made an infinitesimal shrug. "No, you didn't. It's clear to me that you're hiding something, but it's equally clear to me that you want to take down all the remnants of Helmholtz's old empire, which means we're on the same side. That much, I remain certain of. Therefore, I've been authorized to offer you that consultant position. It's a part-time, contracted job, so it doesn't need to interfere with your responsibilities at the Institute."

Dean wiped his mouth. "I already have one job I'm not qualified for, so I doubt I'd be any more helpful with two."

"You would only have to keep doing what you've already been doing. You seem to have a knack for finding clues at your Institute that keep you right on the heels of the Blitzkriegers. All we want is for you to let us know what you find, and to help us understand it."

Dean pressed the ice pack against his jaw for a moment. He wanted to help them, but he knew he had to keep the Institute safely out of the equation. "You should probably know that I've already put in my resignation letter," he said, deciding that there was no harm in letting them know that much. "I have until the end of this month. I'll let you know everything I find out before then, but I'm not so sure I'll be able to help you understanding it since I don't understand most of it myself."

"You've already proven that your information is highly accurate. You might be interested to know that several of the locations you sent in your email have already experienced Blitzkrieger activity, which is our first chance to see a pattern in their movements. We could come look through your records for ourselves, but as long as you are in the Institute and eager to help, it would be a better use of the Bureau's resources simply to pay you to share what you find."

"I'll do what I can, but you can keep your money."

"As you wish," O'Grady made a slight nod. "However, there is one more thing I need to know, Mr. Lazarchek. How emotional are you about this case?"

Dean chewed his burger for a moment, using the time to stall. "Emotional? I don't know what you mean."

"Let me put it this way: if you had your phone in one hand and Brick's throat in the other, would you call the police, or would you squeeze?"

Dean couldn't look away from O'Grady's eyes. Brick was one of the men at the scene of McKenzie's death, and O'Grady knew it. The real question was whether Dean could let go enough to be a team player, or whether he was still out for revenge.

"I'm honestly not sure," Dean looked down at his hands. "I don't like what this is turning me into."

O'Grady reached over the table and clasped his forearm in consolation, his vice-like grip a welcome reassurance. "Don't sweat it, Mr. Lazarchek. You won't be coming close enough to any of them to have to make that decision. We're the ones who will be doing the squeezing, and, believe me, we can squeeze plenty hard."

"Yeah," Dean said. "Yeah, that's best for everyone. So, what's the next step?"

"When my partner comes back from the head, I'll give him the signal and he'll drop the bad cop routine. Then we can talk specifics."

"Why do you need to give him a signal? Now that I know what you're doing, you can just say it outright, can't you?"

"It's important for him to feel like he's in the lead on this so he can learn how it's done."

"Oh," Dean wagged his finger. "Now I get it. You're the Jedi master and he's your apprentice."

O'Grady leaned back, evidently not displeased with the comparison. "There is nothing more important than teaching, Mr. Lazarchek. We can't live forever, but our knowledge can—if we pass it along. I'm sure I don't have to tell you that, though. You're an educator, so you know it already."

Dean had been working at a school for months, but he had never thought of himself as an educator. A guy like O'Grady might have had a lot to pass on to his younger partner, but Dean didn't feel he knew anything worthwhile. It made him even sadder to think his students were stuck with him, even if only for another few weeks.

All the chewing and the talking had set his jaw throbbing, so Dean traded his burger for the ice pack again. Suddenly, he felt very tired. He might have curled up where he was and gone to sleep, except that he had the important business of figuring out how to get home without his truck.

"Hey, I don't suppose you two gentlemen are heading back to Minnesota and could give me a lift?" he asked.

"Certainly," O'Grady said.

"Really?"

"Yes. Right after we stop at the women's penitentiary. There's still the matter of Angela Black."

"Oh. Yeah. That." Dean's head suddenly throbbed and he moved the ice-pack back to the side of his eye. "You know she's crazy, right? I mean, she's fruit-bat bonkers. Whatever you're hoping she'll say, you're not going to get…"

The words faded from Dean's mouth as he caught a glimpse of a truck in the parking lot. It was big, red, and badly angled so that it took up two spots right next to the exit. It looked familiar. Very familiar.

"Is something the matter, Mr. Lazarchek?" O'Grady turned to look.

Dean rose out of his seat to get a better view. There were lots of red half-ton pickups of the same make and model, but Dean could now see the California plates clearly enough.

"That's my truck," he sat back down and began scanning faces in the diner. Whoever had stolen it was likely in the restaurant with them. It didn't take long to spot the thief, over by the front counter, about to pay for takeout. This man didn't look anything like a Blitzkrieger at the moment: he wore a thick winter jacket and a black hat pulled snugly over his head—probably to hide his tattoo. Nevertheless, Dean was certain this was one of the men he had encountered down in the Predecessor station. Judging from all the Styrofoam containers the stringy-haired teenage hostess was piling up for him, it appeared this guy was buying enough food to feed half a dorm floor, which would be just the right amount to feed Brick Stellenleiter instead.

"I think that's one of the Blitzkriegers," Dean attempted to drag his aching body out of the chair.

O'Grady placed a hand on Dean's shoulder, pressing him back down.

"Wait here," he said. "We'll handle this."

Dean didn't argue. Nash was returning just then, and with a wordless gesture O'Grady directed him towards the front counter. The two agents converged on their suspect without any further discussion. Dean couldn't hear what they said, but the Blitzkrieger listened to them, said something in response, and then suddenly flung all his Styrofoam food cartons at the agents and produced a gun to point at the hostess.

Gasps and exclamations of alarm ran through the patrons as all heads turned in their direction.

"Get back!" the man yelled as he roughly positioned his hostage between him and the agents. He backed slowly out the door while both agents followed, calling for him to release the girl.

Everything happened quickly after that. The man backed through the parking lot until he reached his truck—Dean's truck—and then flung the girl down and vaulted over the tailgate into the bed of the pickup. Another man had been waiting in the truck, and he gunned the engine and jumped the curb as soon as his buddy landed in the back. The agents drew and fired: one shot popped a tire and two others cracked the windows, but that didn't stop the thieves from blasting through the shrubs that divided the parking lot from the busy street.

Instantly, the truck was t-boned by a speeding semi. It bent up like a paperclip and skidded across the asphalt amid a spray of glass and shredded metal.

Just like that it was over. Dean's truck was now nothing but scrap metal. He sank back down in his chair and returned the ice-pack to the side of his head.

This was not turning out to be a good day.

CHAPTER 16

After what seemed like hours of paperwork and police reports, the agents finally delivered Dean to the visiting area of the federal women's penitentiary. Nash told Dean they would be watching, but they wouldn't go in with him for fear of making Angela too uncomfortable to speak freely.

God forbid the woman might feel uncomfortable, Dean thought. The last time he had seen her, she had been cackling madly atop a doomsday machine she'd designed to eradicate all of civilization. That was right before she shot him through the thigh, missing his artery by an inch. Dean wasn't eager to look the queen of crazy in the eyes again.

"You're here to see *her*?" The front office guard set Dean's paperwork down and shifted her eyes enough to show she probably wasn't supposed to talk about prisoners to a visitor. This guard was a young, husky woman. Her uniform fit like a sack and her elbows were innies rather than outies, so Dean gave her the old Lazarchek smile. He felt both gratified and cheapened when he saw her round cheeks redden.

"What's the deal with Angela?" he cajoled. "You can tell me. I'm one of the good guys."

"Well," she glanced over her shoulder one more time. "For starters, she never has visitors, not even lawyers. No phone calls, either. You're the only one who's ever wanted to see her."

"The only one?" Dean echoed.

"She's not very popular inside, either," the guard said. "The other girls, they call her *El Ángel Caído.*"

Dean's Spanish was not great, but he could piece together what that meant: The Fallen Angel.

"Why do they call her that?"

"She picked it. She insisted people call her that, and bad things happen to anyone who doesn't do what she says. Her first day here, one of the inmates tried to bully her into giving up her seat in the cafeteria. Next morning, that woman got electrocuted changing the channels on the television. Maybe it was an accident. Nobody can prove anything. But after that, everybody calls Angela whatever she wants to be called."

He thanked her and followed another guard into a room lined with tables, all of which were empty. There were no windows separating the visitors from the prisoners here, but he got a stern lecture that they were not to have any physical contact, not even a handshake. This rule was re-stated on large block-letter signs on each of the concrete walls.

After several minutes, Angela shuffled in, flanked by guards on either side. Even wearing handcuffs, an orange jumpsuit, and with her dirty-blonde hair pulled back into a ragged ponytail, she was a striking figure. Young and athletic, she moved as though she knew how to cheat the laws of physics with each step. She smiled as she walked, which started to make Dean worry that science wasn't the only thing she planned to manipulate.

"Well," she said mischievously as she sat down across from him. "Aren't you a sight for hungry eyes? Shall I see if I can reserve matrimonial visitation privileges?"

"You wish," Dean snorted. "I don't go for mass murderers."

"Mass murderer?" She put her hand to her heart in mock scandal. "First, I'm only an *attempted* mass *manslaughterer*. My lawyer tells me that's a very important difference in the eyes of the law. Second, if a few people would have died because of my experiment, then I can hardly be held responsible for their lack of fitness. Blame Darwin's laws of natural selection, not me."

"Why did you want to see me?"

"Because you're nice to look at. I'm not usually into blue-collar types, but you're such a hunk-a'-hunk-a' burnin' love that I'm prepared to make an exception."

Dean rolled his eyes. She obviously didn't have much to do with her time except sit in her cell dreaming up ways to cause trouble for everyone else.

"Whatever you want to tell me," he growled, "spit it out or I'm leaving."

"It'll cost you one kiss," she leaned forward and puckered expectantly.

Although Dean scooted himself away from her, the guard immediately stepped forward and barked "No touching!"

Dean's head throbbed again, still smarting from that morning's battle. It had already been a very long day, and he was losing his patience.

"I guess Helmholtz was pretty steamed at your failure," he said, just because he thought it might make her mad. "Is that why he abandoned you to rot in here while he boosted all his other guys out of prison?"

For a split instant, anger flashed in her eyes. He knew he'd hit near the mark.

"My former employer had no cause for complaint," she said.

"Sounds to me like your Professor dumped you. What's the matter, did he find a younger, prettier engineer?"

"How's your cousin? I hear she's really enjoying herself at Langdon."

"Don't change the subject. You screwed up, didn't you? You got fired, and you got abandoned here. So why are you afraid of turning on his former lackeys now that he's out of the picture?"

She sat back and laughed. This was not at all the reaction he had been hoping for. She was slipping free just when he thought he had her in his grasp.

"I've been interrogated by federal investigators," the mischievous grin returned to her face. "What makes you think I'll tell you something I didn't tell them?"

"I'm leaving," Dean got up.

"No, wait," she said, and for the first time she appeared to drop the crazy act. She really had something to tell him, something she thought was important. He decided to give her thirty more seconds.

"Too many ears around here," she half-whispered. "And I don't just mean your federal buddies waiting outside. Don't bother denying it—I know they brought you here, just like I know everything else that goes on within these barb-wired fences. I also know that the organization Helmholtz built up didn't die with him. He was planning to do what America used to be good at: global supremacy through superior technology. There are plenty of others willing to pick up where we left off."

"If you're just going to get all fringe-politics on me, I don't need to hear it."

"You don't get it," she shook her head. "Helmholtz had lots of capos, guys who ran different projects for him. Each capo was in charge of one aspect of the empire, usually a special weapon of some kind. Each one of them knows something the rest of the world doesn't. With Helmholtz gone, they're going to use whatever they have to their own advantage. Remember the way Helmholtz used to have the Blitzkriegers rob banks with an EMP blaster? That was just an exercise, something to keep his troops sharp before the big battle. Some of the capos have technology that makes those bank heists look like kids playing with water pistols."

Dean sat back down. She had his attention now. "What do these capos want? What are they going to do with their technology?"

"Most will go after money, of course. Others, however, will set their sights higher. Terrorism. Military conquest. Global domination. All the fun stuff. Each of them has at least one item of hardware that's a hundred years beyond what any nation on Earth is ready to defend against. That kind of power doesn't simply stay asleep when in the hands of ambitious men or women. I ought to know."

"So, tell me," Dean leaned towards her. "Tell me the names of these capos. Or at least tell me what kind of inventions they have."

She laughed lightly. "Don't you remember what I said about the ears in this room? Some of these capos know where I am and what I know, and if I say too much they have the power to... annoy me."

"You're paranoid."

"I'm not the only one with secrets that need to be kept."

He cleared his throat. She had him there: he'd been walking a fine line by holding back certain information from Nash and O'Grady, and he wasn't sure he was ready to break his promise about safeguarding Institute secrets.

"I'll tell you what you need to know," she said, "but you must pay my price. I want that kiss."

"This is ridiculous," Dean started to get up again, but she reached out with her manacled hands and grabbed two fistfuls of his shirt. The motion was so swift that it took Dean as well as the guards by surprise, allowing her enough time to pull him in close and press her lips to his.

Despite his resistance, she opened his lips with hers and used her tongue to slide something into his mouth. A small piece of paper, folded up, with corners sharp enough to jab the inside of his cheek.

"No touching!" the guard forcefully shoved them apart.

"How dare you assault me like that!" Angela trilled in mock outrage as two other guards hauled her back towards lockdown. "Guards! Take me away from this pervert! Protect my virtue from his unwanted advances!"

Dean licked his teeth, pushing the paper to the side of his cheek to keep it hidden.

After he was back in the car and O'Grady had driven many miles down the road, Dean wiped his lips as if he could erase the kiss. As he did, he slipped the small piece of wax paper from his mouth and held it down and out of sight.

"You okay back there?" Nash asked from the front seat.

"Sorry I didn't get you anything useful," Dean said.

"Don't worry about it," Nash waved his hand. "It was a long shot, I guess. Hey, you think that all her craziness is an act?"

"I don't know. Maybe."

As he spoke, Dean unfolded the paper. Angela had scratched words onto it with a ball point pen. Most of the ink was gone, but he could still read the indentations on the paper.

Buenos Aires.

Tormenta, Inc.

Steal their Egg.

Chapter 17

Dean was more than a little annoyed when the FBI agents told him they were making one more stop before returning to Minnesota, but without his own transportation he had no say in the matter. They wanted to check in at the local hospital to interview the Blitzkriegers who had stolen Dean's truck and subsequently wrecked it—and themselves—on the road outside the diner.

An armed sheriff's deputy stood outside the door to the hospital room. Dean wasn't allowed to get any closer than the nearby lobby, but from there he managed to catch a glimpse of the man in the bed. His left leg was bound up in some kind of cat's cradle of pulleys and cables. His left arm and shoulder-girdle were similarly encased in white casts and braced by a supporting rod that held his arm perpendicular to his bruised body. Much of his face was swollen and scraped, and the rest was covered with so many bandages that Dean wouldn't have been able to pick him out of a lineup.

With nothing else to do, Dean took a seat on the fake-leather couch in the lobby. In the magazine rack, he found some issues of Sports Illustrated that were at least three months out of date. He shuffled them around, looking for something that would take his mind off the present, but his head and jaw still throbbed too much to allow him to concentrate on even the puffiest of puff articles. He checked his watch, and after twenty minutes of listlessness in the lobby, he decided to ask for a new ice pack.

The receptionist smiled and said he would see what he could do (which probably meant he wasn't going to do anything), but then he froze and stared over Dean's shoulder.

Dean resisted the urge to spin around, because he could hear heavy footsteps behind him. Huge, heavy boots that thudded across the floor behind him. Only one person could have filled shoes of that size.

After the steps passed, Dean risked a quick glance over his shoulder. As he had feared, it was Brick, with the top of his craggy head almost scraping the ceiling tiles. Next to him limped the other man Dean had encountered in that Predecessor station, now with raw, purple bruises covering half his face, no doubt the trophies of his botched escape attempt in Dean's truck. They were accompanied by a third man in a sleek charcoal suit, so gray that it almost shimmered with reflected light. Dean couldn't see that man's face as he walked away, but he got a clear view of the neatly trimmed ponytail hanging behind his head.

As the three men approached the suspect's room, the deputy held out his hand. "You can't come—"

Brick grabbed him by the front of his shirt and jerked him upward, slamming his head into the fluorescent light fixture above, then smashed him sideways into the wall. The deputy's unconscious body dropped to Brick's feet while the other Blitzkrieger drew a stub-nosed pistol. The ponytail guy just folded his arms and looked quietly menacing.

Next to Dean, the receptionist yelped audibly and ducked behind the desk. Nurses appeared in doorways to see what happened. Dean looked around desperately for a weapon. There were chairs in the waiting area, but if Brick could shrug off bullets, he wasn't likely to worry about pre-fab furniture.

Brick swatted the door off its hinges, and the Blitzkrieger with the gun swung into the room, pistol first.

"Move and I blow your cop brains all over the wall!" he shouted.

Dean couldn't see Nash or O'Grady, but he didn't think they would have had time to do anything but put up their hands.

Brick squeezed through the doorway and yanked the other Blitzkrieger out of his traction apparatus. The injured man made a pathetic moan and may have gone limp, although it was hard to tell with so much of his body held in rigid casts. Ponytail guy continued to stand by with folded arms.

Dean had seen enough. He had to do something. Perhaps foolishly, he ran forward to stand in Brick's path.

Brick regarded him with a moment of slow amusement, then shifted the injured Blitzkrieger on his shoulder and threw a heavy punch at Dean's head.

Dean sidestepped, but Brick wasn't interested in continued fighting. He barreled through like a freight train, knocking Dean down as he passed, and clearing the way for the Blitzkrieger with the gun to limp down the hall right behind him.

"Torch this place!" the limping man yelled.

The ponytail guy nodded and lifted his hand, palm out towards Dean. Nash and O'Grady, no longer held at gunpoint, burst from the room. The ponytail guy spun to face them, arm still outstretched. He must have had something up his sleeve, because somehow he released a tsunami of blazing orange flame right at them.

As soon as Dean smelled the piercing tang of chemical accelerants, he knew this blaze was not kindled by natural means. Judging by the sudden and intense heat, he knew it must be a military-grade flamethrower that the man had somehow kept concealed. The real mystery was where he was hiding this weapon: it required tanks of fuel, a heavy hose, a pilot light, and heat shielding for the user. It wasn't the kind of thing one could keep inside a tailored suit without making the wearer look like Quasimodo.

This wasn't the time for overthinking things, and Dean knew it. The man was armed with a flamethrower, and even if Dean couldn't see it, people could still be killed by it. Fire alarms started blaring, but the automatic sprinklers seemed unable to wash the burning chemicals off the doorframes and the wall.

The agents had ducked back into the room to take cover from the flames, but now O'Grady popped around the corner and fired three times, deafening booms in the confined room. The man with the flame thrower stumbled backwards and dropped to the ground.

Then, slowly, he sat back up.

He grimaced and his face glistened with sweat, but there was still plenty of fight left in his eyes. He might have been wearing a bullet proof vest, but at this range the shots would have broken a few ribs and probably put him down for the count. More likely, he had the same kind of surgically-implanted armor that Brick had. The only thing worse than a human flamethrower was a human tank, and this guy seemed to be both.

The ponytail guy stood up and raised his palm again. Dean knew that one more blast could cook the agents in their room, so he turned and slammed his shoulder hard into the man's sternum. He hit with enough force to drive the man back four feet, but halfway through the fall, the ponytail guy managed to pivot and fling Dean backwards so hard the drywall shattered against his back.

Dean's vision filled with white sparks. Before they cleared from his eyes, a fist bit hard into his stomach. His lungs and intestines all sounded alarm bells of pain so loudly that they clogged the switchboard in his brain. Gasping for breath, he worked on pure instinct to duck just as a whistling right hook grazed his head and lodged deep in the wall directly behind him.

The missed punch carried the ponytail guy in so close that he was chest-to-chest with Dean for a split second. This range was good, because Dean's buddies on the LAPD had taught him to use the dirtiest tricks in extreme close quarters.

In a flash, he swept the man's jacket down over his elbows, pinning his arms to his sides, and then smashed his heel into the instep of the man's expensive brown loafers. Ponytail guy gave a yelp of pain and backed off slightly. Dean used the reprieve to snag him in a kickboxing clinch and wrench his face down while simultaneously smashing his knee up hard, over and over, bulls-eyeing the guy's nose with each strike.

Dean had intended to keep up with the knees until the guy quit struggling. Two clean hits, maybe three, should have been enough to KO a prize fighter, and Dean got in five perfect smashes in the span of three seconds. Yet the ponytail guy continued to struggle like a bucking bull and soon Dean found himself scrambling just to hang on.

Nash and O'Grady burst out of the burning room, guns up and searching for a safe line of fire. Before they could find it, Ponytail roared in anger, jerked free of Dean's grasp, and ripped through the coat that constrained his arms.

Breathless, Dean watched his opponent in cautious amazement. There was definitely something wrong with this guy. He was too strong, too tough. His face was now bloodier than a butcher's block and his nose looked like mashed up Play-Doh, but he showed no other signs of slowing down. That told Dean he was tougher than any man with a ponytail had a right to be.

The ponytail guy shoved Dean back against the wall and thrust his arm straight out, palm flat, right up to Dean's nose. This time, Dean was close enough to see a small opening in his palm and the flickering blue electric spark that must have served as a pilot light. It was inside him— built in like an ice-maker inside a refrigerator door.

Bionic weaponry or not, Dean grabbed the arm and yanked it past him. His opponent may have been unnaturally strong, but Dean weighed more and had better footing, so the arm-drag carried the ponytail guy forward so that his palm smashed against the wall just as the flame spat out of it.

A great ball of orange heat blossomed around his hand, burning Dean's back even as he slipped away. The flaming chemicals splashed back along Ponytail's arms, and as he frantically waved his burning limb the fire chewed its way towards his shoulder, faster and hotter each second. His skin blackened, but it didn't smell like charred flesh—more like melting plastic and red-hot steel.

The man's arm may have been artificial, but his expression of panic was entirely human. Fear twisted his face and an agonized shriek escaped his throat.

"Stop, drop, and roll, you idiot!" Dean tried to throw him down where he might extinguish the flames, but the man mistook this for another attack and lashed out viciously before turning to run down the hall.

Dean sprinted after him with the FBI agents close behind.

The human flamethrower trailed putrid black smoke behind him as he raced through the hospital, forcing a pair of terrified nurses to dodge out of his way. The faster he ran, the faster the flames spread, and soon his entire upper body was a bonfire. Blindly, he stumbled over an abandoned hand truck stacked with white metal cylinders, sending both him and the cylinders tumbling to the floor.

Almost too late, Dean saw the warning signs on the cylinders. Compressed oxygen: highly explosive.

"Get down!" Dean yelled, throwing himself to the linoleum and covering his head with his arms.

The shockwave that felt like it would first crush him down and then pull him apart. He found himself bouncing up several inches before slamming back down onto the floor, and then the world seemed to spin and buzz around him.

His nervous system needed a few second to reboot, after which he discovered that the blast had pushed him several feet across the tiled floor. He felt dizzy and weak, with a painful ringing in his ears. The walls nearby had been blackened and gouged by flying shrapnel from the oxygen cylinders and scraps of the ponytail guy. There wasn't much left behind at the site of the explosion, at least nothing recognizable.

Dean blinked and pulled himself up to a seated position, checking himself for injuries. His burns and bruises would be painful yet not debilitating. Slowly, his hearing returned, and he became aware of someone calling for help. He turned, still wobbly, to see Nash crouching over O'Grady, pressing his hands to his partner's chest as blood bubbled up from a hole in the older agent's sternum.

O'Grady's eyes were open, but he would see no more.

December 16

(7 Days Before Stormageddon)

CHAPTER 18

Sitting at the small table in his residence, Dean absentmindedly stirred the Cheerios in his bowl but didn't feel like eating. Yesterday, when he had almost died fighting, he felt alive. Now, he felt like he could be an extra on *The Walking Dead*.

O'Grady had lost his life, yet the Blitzkriegers and their new boss were still out there, free to continue pursuing whatever they were planning. Dean could do nothing about it except sit and watch his cereal grow soggy.

The worst part had been watching Nash as he waited for the inevitable news from the doctors. Dean had been able to read the grief in the young man's face as if it had been tattooed on his skin, and it felt strangely like looking into a mirror. It had stirred something inside Dean, something dank and poisonous, and now Dean kept seeing *her* face more often than ever. The auburn hair. The pale blue tinge on the lips. Her cold skin.

These thoughts entangled Dean's mind like creeping vines overgrowing a garden. He couldn't stop thinking about how things might have been. His mind buried itself in the past, to all the other times he had lost McKenzie. Maybe it was just because he had talked to Soap about it, but he couldn't help remembering the episode of Ignacio Zabaleta. For a time, he'd blamed Ignacio for his own breakup with McKenzie, but that clearly hadn't been the reason. Ignacio, the hippy-dippy math major who had served as McKenzie's rebound relationship, had always been too self-absorbed to be serious competition. His idea of a conversation was making sure that every sentence he uttered had something to do with himself, and he had a gift for redirecting any conversation to prove that he was more enlightened than everyone else. If you brought up the poor quality of the hamburger meat in the cafeteria, he would say "and that's why I'm a vegetarian." If you mentioned an action movie, he would point out that he had a black-belt in taekwondo, and he earned it in only two years. Did you just throw a piece of paper in the trash? Well, Ignacio always sorts his recyclables, and he even had labels on the different bins in his dorm room to make sure everyone could see how much he cared for the planet.

Now that Dean looked back on it, he knew McKenzie couldn't have been serious about Ignacio. As smart as she was, she must have seen through his pretentiousness. All Dean accomplished by reminiscing about it was to make himself want to go back in time and punch Ignacio in the face, knowing all the while that it still wouldn't make him feel any better.

The ghosts of the past hung thick around Dean that morning, and it may not have helped his mood that the Egg of Mark Twain had been left on his kitchen counter, perhaps by Soap. His kitchen was not a secure location for a rock with a million-dollar bounty, and that bothered Dean. It bothered him even more when the green ghost swirled into existence in the chair next to him, silently blowing puffs of illusory smoke that sparkled and faded above Dean's neglected Cheerios.

The ghost leaned forward and pointed a finger at Dean's phone. Obligingly, Dean turned it on, noting with detachment how slowly his fingers moved. It felt like he was at the bottom of a swimming pool and each of his motions had to push through the dark water that surrounded him.

"My deepest condolences on the loss of your friend," Twain's raspy, old-man's voice crackled through the phone's speakers. Static hissed and popped around each of his words, but his speech was now fully intelligible. Soap's diction lessons must have helped him greatly, although it seemed all the more unnerving that a man who'd been dead a hundred years was speaking to him before he'd finished his morning coffee. At least Twain was here, given a second life, which was more than could be said for Agent O'Grady.

"He was a good man," Dean mumbled. "But I hardly knew him. I've got nothing to be sad about."

Twain regarded Dean with that look of his that was equal portions knowing and pitying.

"Nothing that grieves us can be called nothing. A child's loss of a doll and a king's loss of a crown are events of the same size to their victims."

Dean looked at the ghost for a while, then back at his cereal.

"Your students missed your guidance while you were away," Twain ventured. "Especially your cousin."

"They'll be fine," Dean said. "She'll be fine."

Twain leaned back. "You're a man of few words, I see. I'm afraid I cannot sympathize with that. However, I can sympathize with your predicament."

"Are you trying to cheer me up, Mr. Twain?"

"Please call me Sam. Mark Twain is the name used by strangers. Those among my personal acquaintances know me as Sam Clemens. Now, as to the matter at hand—cheering you up—you seem like a man who could benefit from it, and manipulating emotions is the stock and trade of a writer such as me."

"Can you even feel emotions?" It came out more harshly than Dean meant it, so he softened his voice before continuing. "I don't mean to offend you, Mr. Tw—Sam—but how can a computer simulation like you possibly know how a real person feels?"

Twain leaned in, a wily glint in his glowing eyes. "I'm not so sure that I am, as you say, just a simulation. But whether or not I am a man—now that is an entirely different question. What is a man? A man is the only creature who blushes. The only creature that inflicts pain for the sake of pleasure. Perhaps the only one that experiences love and grief. I feel some of those things, and am proud not to feel others. Does that make me less of a man?"

Dean eyed him for a minute, wondering where his life had gone so far astray that he would end up discussing the nature of humanity with a green ghost while still wearing his slippers.

"If I am different from Sam Clemens," the ghost went on, "Then I still have his memories up to the year 1908 when my friend Nikola Tesla affixed a strange helmet to my head and said he could record my thoughts. The next thing I knew, I awoke sitting by you in your automobile. Yet I still feel like my old self, if that has any meaning. At the same time, I don't feel like me at all."

"I think you're confused. Is your program bugged?"

"Perhaps I'm less confused now than in what I hesitantly call my former life. I said I was proud not to feel certain things that I once did, because this has granted me clarity of vision, after a fashion. The feelings

I now lack are all those associated with the gross body. Impatience. Fear. Anger. How often are our moods tied to the needs of our flesh? I remember becoming irritable when hungry, angry when in pain, and desperate when threatened. Now those darker emotions cannot touch me because I simply do not feel hungry, angry, or fearful."

"So you're not human."

"If you define a human as a stomach and a spleen and a collection of other organs, then I suppose I lack the necessary components. What I have left, however, is everything else. I think back to the loss of my daughters, and I feel pain striking me deeply in what I shall call my soul, if I have one. Is that not a sign of humanity? New ideas occur to me, and I find myself wishing for a typewriter that I might jot down a new yarn or two. Is creativity not an act shared solely by human beings and the Divine? And I feel concern for you and for your students. Is compassion not presumed to be human as well, despite how few humans practice it? So, please believe me when I say I wish to help you, and that my first advice is to take me up on this offer. A wise man once said that one should not be ashamed to seek solace in the company of others, even if those others happened to suffer from a decidedly green hue."

"A wise man said that?"

"Yes. Me. Just now. Weren't you listening?"

Dean almost smirked. He could see that Twain was trying to draw him out of his funk, but it wouldn't work. Talking, even to the great Samuel "Mark Twain" Clemens, still seemed pointless and time-consuming.

"So you really think you're human?" Dean asked, mostly to redirect the topic away from himself. "You really think you have a soul, or whatever?"

"I certainly have a whatever. As for a soul, well, that is a matter of religion. As far as religion goes, it seems to me that the easy confidence with which I know another man's faith to be folly teaches me to suspect that the one I was raised with is likewise folly. However, my mere presence here in this..." he waved his semi-transparent green arms, "in this *form* suggests that there may be more to spirituality than I had once supposed. I stand before you—or rather sit, as the case may be—stripped of all those animal desires I mentioned. I now consist of nothing but my knowledge, imagination, and love. I am, perhaps, the best of what it is to be a human, and it only required abandoning my human form. I am now nothing if not the religious man's vision of a soul."

"Maybe we'd all be better off without bodies," Dean mused. He couldn't help thinking that if he could put his own mind into an Egg and live like a ghost, he would do it in an instant. Life would be so much easier.

"So, tell me," Twain said. "How can I help you?"

Dean stared at him for a moment, and then produced the wax paper scrap Angela had given him in prison. *Buenos Aires. Tormenta, Inc. Steal their Egg.* He held it up to let the ghost read it.

"I can't see it," Twain said. "Please, if you don't mind, hold it so that it faces my—what shall we call it? My source? My brain?"

"Your Egg," Dean said, reflecting that it really wasn't the best name now that they knew what that little rock truly did. Soap had discovered that the ghost could project his image to any point nearby, but the ghostly projection itself was blind. The Egg, however, served as a kind of eyeball and eardrum rolled into one. This had inspired a ten minute lecture from Soap about the possible photo-chemical layer coating the Egg, and even though Dean didn't give a rip about how it worked, he was glad she was once more starting to feel comfortable enough to talk to him.

Dean turned the paper so that it was only a few inches away from the Egg on its electric cradle.

"Steal their Egg?" Twain said as he read the note. "I suspect this is no breakfast order."

"You said Tesla is out there somewhere, right? Maybe it's his Egg we're talking about stealing."

"Very likely. He and I seem to share some kind of bond between our— our Eggs. I can sense some of his thoughts."

"How does that work?"

"I don't really understand it," Twain said. "The best I can describe it is that I can speak to him without words. I can sense that his thoughts are coming to me from a great distance. Most are lost in transit. I only get the sense that he's being forced to do something he doesn't want to do. I'd be able to communicate with him more clearly if only he were closer."

"How close would you need to be?"

"Within a quarter-mile, I would say. Shouting distance, as we used to call it back in my steamboat days."

Dean drummed his fingers on the table. Buenos Aires was a big place, and it was far away. It was likely that whoever had the other Egg was also the person responsible for sending Brick and his buddies all over the country to dig up the Predecessor stations. He was also probably the one offering a million dollars to any thug who could raid the Institute and steal the Egg. Whatever they were doing, they weren't going to be happy to give up their prize.

A frantic knock sounded from Dean's door. Before he could open it, Victor burst through, clutching the lab manuals they had found in Dean's wall. Victor immediately shoved a tablet at Dean with a shaking hand.

"I have a new proposal," he said breathlessly.

"You're going to propose a new project now?" Dean said. "Vacation started two days ago. You're not going to blow up another computer, are you?"

"That was misguided and unambitious. Wait until you read this."

Dean looked at the table. The entire proposal consisted of one sentence.

Bring back Professor Denise McKenzie in an Egg.

CHAPTER 19

"What the heck are we doing here?" Victor asked as he looked around the shadowy hallway that amounted to the Classics Department. Judging by the directory at the entrance to Wilson Hall and the out-of-the-way location of this office block, it looked like the entire department was nothing but an afterthought in the foreign language building. Dean wasn't even sure what "Classics" were, but he knew there was at least one person here who might be able to help him.

"We're here to make your proposal happen," Dean said. "Didn't you say that you could put McKenzie's mind into an Egg if you had the right resources?"

"I meant that I could make a sort of replica of her mind based on your memories. But I would need an Egg, like Twain's, and we don't have a spare one."

"Leave that to me," Dean said.

"And I also need a computer expert to help with some serious coding. Too bad you kicked Cake out."

"I'll get you someone for that. Now, you also said you needed a language expert to help decipher these lab manuals. That's why we're here."

"How is a Classics professor going to be able to help us?" Victor asked. "They study old cultures. I don't think they had a lot of Predecessors in ancient Rome."

"We're here to find a friend of mine," Dean said. "Don't give me that look. I have friends."

Victor muttered something under his breath and clutched the four old, leather-bound lab books closer to his chest.

Dean knocked on the door of office B14. From inside, Professor Heidi Bjelland called to invite them in.

"She sounds surprised to see us," Victor whispered.

Judging from the isolated corner in which her office lurked, Dean guessed that Classics professors might be surprised by any sort of visitor. He only hoped it was okay that he was dropping in on such short notice.

From behind a big desk jumbled with papers, Heidi rose to greet them. She wore a simple green long-sleeved shirt and jeans—a casual look that put Dean more at ease than the professional skirt-suits she typically wore during staff meetings. Behind her, shelves sagged under the burden of books piled on top of books shoved in front of other books. Cracks and flakes marked some of the book spines while others shone with glossy newness, and at least half bore yellow "used" tags from the campus book resellers. The smell of fresh books and decaying paper mingled in the air like incense. Even her computer was almost buried by books, which Dean found refreshing after living in the techno-centric Topsy House, where styluses and tablets had driven pens and paper into extinction.

"Dean," she said, pushing a lock of blond hair behind her ear. It was too short to stay put and fell back over her face almost as soon as she removed her hand. "I got your message. What's up? And who is this young man?"

"This is Victor," Dean said. "We've got a puzzle that we're hoping you might help us out with."

"Thank goodness," she said with a laugh. "I had this irrational paranoia that you wanted me to take over for you at the Institute."

Dean smiled and shook his head, but suddenly it occurred to him that she might not be such a bad candidate. He had been deleting all the résumés that President Hart had been emailing him because those candidates lacked something important, even though Dean couldn't quite put his finger on what it was. Sincerity, maybe. True, Heidi had no more background in science than he did, but she might still run the place better than he ever could. After all, she was smart, and she obviously loved books so much she'd decorated her office with them. Given his lack of time to find his replacement, he might have to revisit this idea.

Dean had a more pressing topic to discuss however, but he didn't want to come across as abrupt or demanding. He knew that asking for favors is best begun with a little unrelated small talk to put the other person in a relaxed mood. Looking around the room for a clue about something that might interest her, he spotted one patch of wall that had been reserved for a framed painting depicting a forlorn-looking man in a white robe holding a stringed instrument. This man looked back over his shoulder, down a long and dismal, underground stone staircase, to where a shadowy figure of a mournful woman returned his gaze. This painting, Dean decided, must been important to Heidi if she had put it up instead of yet another bookshelf.

"Nice painting," he said. "Who's the guy in the white bath robe?"

"It's a toga," Heidi said. "That's Orpheus. Are you familiar with the story?"

Dean shook his head.

"It's a sad tale," she said. "Orpheus traveled to the underworld to bring his dead wife back to life. He managed to cut a very unusual deal with the King of the Dead to give him a shot at getting what he wanted."

"How'd that work out for him?"

"Not so well. But I'll tell you the rest later, because I sense you didn't come here to discuss mythology. What's this puzzle you have for me?"

"It might be a major effort," he said. "If it looks like it's going to be too time-consuming, we can discuss making it worth your while."

"Stop teasing me," she favored him with a devilish grin that brought out her dimples. "What is it, already?"

"Show her the books," Dean said to Victor.

Victor still clutched the tomes to his chest.

"It's okay, Victor," Dean urged. "You scanned the pages, didn't you? You can look at your set on your computer if she borrows these. We can trust Professor Bjelland."

Victor grimaced and handed the books over.

Heidi accepted them and flipped through the first few pages.

"This looks really technical," she said. "Like someone's old blueprints. Not sure what you want me to say about them."

"Flip ahead," Dean said. "There." He stopped her on a page scrawled with the dancing lizard hieroglyphs of the Predecessors. "We need your help deciphering that writing. We've translated some of it, but only on certain topics and this book represents a whole new kettle of fish. Also, we're under some time pressure here, so we need someone who can help us quick. Someone brilliant. That's you."

She ignored his attempt at flattery as Victor handed her another stack of papers which amounted to a printout of the Predecessor dictionary of the hieroglyphics that had been deciphered. Heidi flipped back and forth, pausing here and there to read certain spots more thoroughly and frequently referencing the translations. She kept her finger on the corner of one page while she compared it to several other pages, and then pored over the printouts again.

"It's an artificial language," she finally said.

"What do you mean, 'artificial?'"

"All languages start basic sentences with the grammatical subject, but this one is structured so the verbs come first. Verb-subject-object. No natural language in all of history has ever worked that way. It's just not how the human brain is set up."

Dean had no idea what that meant, but it told him they had found the right woman for the job. He also knew she was correct about it not being a human language, though he didn't yet see how to tell her that it wasn't artificial, either.

Heidi studied him for a long moment. "Where did you get these books?"

"I found them behind my refrigerator," he said. "No, really. I did. Someone hid them there a long time ago."

"Does it have to do with the terrorists who keep attacking you?"

Dean inhaled slowly. If she was going to help with this project, she had a right to know what she was getting into. She also had a right to back out now, which is what any sane person would do.

"It's indirectly connected to the terrorists," he nodded. "There are some bad people who might want these books, if they knew they existed."

"Terrific," she said. "I'm in."

Dean was surprised that this information not only failed to scare Heidi off, it actually made her seem more interested. "I can't thank you enough," he said, standing to shake her hand. "I'll put you in touch with Victor, here, and you can collaborate with him about the science parts. I'm also arranging to find a computer guy, which I'm told you'll need."

"One more question," she said, her brown eyes flashing back to the books. "You said there's a time constraint. What's the rush? Is this some kind of treasure map?"

Dean didn't even know where to start explaining the value of what they might create. If she could translate it... if Victor could work out the technology... if—and only if—Dean could get his hands on another Egg. Those were a lot of ifs, but the payoff would be immense.

"It's all for science," he said. "If we publish, your name will be on it, I promise."

From the look on her face, Dean could see that wasn't what she was after. Victor exited the room, and Dean was about to follow.

"Wait," Heidi said. "Just one more thing. How are you doing? I mean, on a personal level."

"I'm fine," he said.

"You don't seem very happy, that's all. If you ever need to talk—"

"Thanks again for your help," he turned and left before she could ask him anything else.

Victor awaited him in the hallway. Perhaps by chance, he had found the classroom where Soap and her boyfriend Brett took Chinese every morning.

"We don't have to do this, you know," Victor said as he looked into the empty room. "Even if we find a way to bring her back, it doesn't mean we should."

"Don't give me that," Dean said. "This was your idea. You were Mr. Gung Ho about this twenty minutes ago."

"It doesn't have to be McKenzie, though," Victor said. "We could do someone else. I mean, it's—it's going to be difficult for you. I can see that now. You're going to have to do some things that might, I don't know, keep some of your wounds from closing."

"It has to be her," Dean snapped a little more forcefully than he intended. "It has to be."

Victor nodded.

"Okay," Dean removed his phone from his pocket and began scrolling through the numbers. "The second thing you needed was a computer guy. Can you work with him via email for a few days, or does he need to be in the lab with you the whole time?"

"I can work remotely. That's fine," Victor said. "Who are you calling?"

"Oscar—Cake. Whatever you want to call him."

"I thought you kicked him out. I believe you said you never wanted to see his face again."

"I might have said something like that," Dean said. "I'll admit, this is going to be embarrassing, given that he's probably already back home and I'll have to make my apologies to his parents."

"Um, wait. There's something I need to tell you."

"Hold on," Dean turned to focus on the call. "Hello, is this Mrs. DeLeon? Hi. This is Dean Lazarcheck of the Mechanical Science Institute. How are you doing this evening?"

"Really," Victor said. "There's something you should know. It's about Cake."

Dean held out a hand to shush Victor. "Mrs. DeLeon, I know you were probably disappointed when you found out that Cake—Oscar—didn't get in. But it turns out that a spot just opened up... What? What do you mean you already knew about the open spot?"

"D-Squared!" Victor said. "Cake's parents still think he's here at the Institute."

Dean placed his palm over his phone. "What do you mean they still think he's here? I sent them an email."

"Cake has their password. He deleted it before they saw it to make sure they wouldn't contradict the fake letter he sent."

Dean listened to Mrs. DeLeon's questions while he tried to process what Victor had told him.

"Well, I—I—," Dean stammered into the phone. "I just wanted to call and let you know he's doing great."

Dean hung up and then glared at Victor, feeling the anger rise inside him. "How do you know about him and the password?"

"Well..." Victor began reluctantly. "I'm actually paying for an apartment here in Bugswallow for him. See, I already sort of hired him to help me with this project."

Dean felt the heat rising to his cheeks and he had to concentrate on his breathing for a slow ten count. He'd been duped, played for a fool, and the worst part was that Cake had done it so easily. Was this really the kind of guy who should be part of the Institute? On the other hand, did Dean have any choice? Cake was already invested in the project, and it might take a long time to find someone as qualified, and even longer to bring that someone up to speed. Cake also spoke Spanish, which made him necessary for the other part of Dean's plan. This was coming down to a choice between the McKenzie project and moral considerations.

"Get Cake on the phone," Dean commanded.

Victor dialed and handed his phone over to Dean.

"Hello," Cake answered, sounding as shy as ever.

"You still want back into the Institute?" Dean said.

"What—who is this?" Cake now sounded downright terrified. "You're not Victor. Is this—is this D-Squared?"

"No, but you can call me Dean," he glanced down at the wax paper scrap Angela had slipped him. "I've got kind of an emergency and now I need you to do four things. Consider this your entrance exam. First, I need you to be honest. Period. No more sneaking around and lying and hacking. Can you do that?"

"Okay," Cake said. "White-hat only. I promise."

"Number two is, you're going to finish whatever computer stuff you're doing with Victor, but now you're going to need to do it on the road. That means video conferencing and emails and whatever else. Is that possible?"

"On the road?" His voice sounded distant. "Where am I going?"

"That depends," Dean said. "Because the third thing I need you to do is find out about something called Tormenta Incorporated and what it has to do with Argentina."

"*Tormenta* means 'storm' in Spanish," the sound of tapping keys drifted through the receiver. "Here it is. Looks like it's a company located on the outskirts of Buenos Aires. They manufacturer some kind of outdoor equipment."

Bingo, Dean thought. This kid had already dug up more information in a minute than Dean had in twenty four hours. "Okay, Cake, you now have your answer about where you're going."

"Can I just ask something?" Cake said. "Why do you want me to go to a factory in Argentina?"

"You're not going to the factory," Dean said. "You're going to stay safe in the hotel while I go to the factory. The rest of the time, you're going to be my translator and you're going to let me handle all the danger."

"Danger?" Cake gulped audibly. "I'm not really the field agent type. I'm much more of a stay-at-headquarters-and-analyze-data type."

"Book us the next flight for Buenos Aires," Dean said.

"But I—"

"In your interview, you said you wanted to join us so you could do something extraordinary. Now's your chance. If you board that plane with me, you'll be boarding as an Institute student. Oh, and when you get those plane tickets, put them on Victor's card."

CHAPTER 20

Within minutes of hanging up, Dean received an email confirming a ticket for a flight from Minneapolis to Argentina, but it wasn't until he saw Cake in the pre-boarding crowd that he was sure the boy would be joining him. Dean had mixed feelings about giving him another chance, but his programming skillset and his ability to speak Spanish made him a lifeline right now.

They didn't have time to say much to each other while boarding, and after they were seated Dean fell asleep before takeoff. That was a mistake, because as soon as the plane leveled out and the captain turned off the seatbelt sign, Dean woke up and couldn't get back to sleep. He rubbed his eyes, flexed his calves, and then accidentally bumped Cake's arm. Dean was wide in the shoulders while Cake was wide in the belly, so in theory they should have fit together like puzzle pieces, but evidently the designers of the airplane seats had taken special care to ensure that people of all shapes and sizes could feel equally cramped and uncomfortable.

Cake didn't seem to mind. He was typing furiously on his laptop, writing what looked like miles and miles of tiny programming text.

"You sure don't take long to get to sleep," Cake said without looking up from his screen.

"In the army, you learn to sleep when you can."

"In computer programming summer camp, you learn to drink caffeine instead of sleeping," he raised an oversized drink can that glittered like a disco ball. Dean shook his head but decided to skip the lecture on how unhealthy those so-called energy drinks were.

"I've been IMing Professor Bjelland," Cake said between gulps of his elixir. "She's been able to explain a lot that I didn't understand about the hieroglyph syntax. With her help, I've been able to improve the algorithm for decompressing the data represented by—"

Dean held up his hand. "Bottom-line it for me, buddy."

"The bottom line is that I should have the translation app updated and ready for testing in a day or two. Maybe three, depending on if we run into... you know...danger."

"Don't worry," Dean said. "We're just on a scouting mission. If you see any danger, I'll refund all your tuition money."

"But all Institute students have a full ride scholarship, so I didn't pay any tuition money."

"Great. Then I don't have to worry about keeping you safe." He extended a foot and bumped his carry-on bag. He didn't like stowing his bag down there, but this was a "spy kit" Soap had packed for him. She assured him that there was nothing dangerous or especially valuable in there, but he still didn't want to let it out of his sight, not even in an overhead bin.

"I found more info on that company you mentioned," Cake said. "Tormenta Incorporated manufactures a kind of button that measures air pressure and UV rays and stuff like that, and then sends all that info to your phone. It's for outdoorsmen and weather nerds."

"Great," Dean said. "Remind me next time I care about the barometric pressure. You find a connection to crime or anything?"

"Well, there's this video of the CEO's bodyguard." Cake tapped a few keys and opened a Spanish language video streaming site. The video started with what looked like someone's phone footage of night club. Right away, Dean recognized one of the men at a back table in the corner of the shot. He was uncommonly tall, with sunken eyes that peered predatorily out from his boney, bald head.

"I've seen this video before," Dean said. "That's the Predecessor. You're looking at the only known footage of the guy who killed Helmholtz."

"Really? How'd he do that?"

"Just keep watching."

Two men crossed in front of the camera and produced pistols from within their jackets. The Predecessor moved almost too quickly for the eye to register, yet his face remained as blank as ever. With a simple twist of his hand, he broke the first assassin's neck. The second one pulled his trigger twice, point blank, lighting the dark club with the bright flashes of gunfire.

The Predecessor didn't even roll back on his feet with the impact of the bullets. He simply dispatched the second gunman with grim efficiency.

"Bullet proof vest?" Cake asked.

Dean wished it were that. One of the toughest, meanest cops Dean had ever trained with had to sit out of his martial arts classes for weeks due to a chest full of broken ribs because he'd been shot while wearing a vest. Heck, even Brick had grimaced when Dean had bounced some lead off his internal body armor. This Predecessor, however, was different. From the looks of the video, he didn't even seem to notice being hit.

"What do we do if we run into this guy?" Cake asked.

Dean looked Cake in the eyes and saw anxiety. Now that Dean was getting to know the boy better, he was beginning to realize that he wasn't a weasel so much as a chicken. He probably sent that fake letter to his parents out of fear of disappointing them rather than as part of some grand scheme to get his way. It made Dean forgive him, at least a little.

"We're not going to encounter the Predecessor," Dean said.

"But what if we do?"

"We're not."

"That's the plan?" Cake asked.

"That's the plan."

And if it weren't for plans, Dean thought. *I wouldn't have anything to go awry.*

December 17

(6 Days Before Stormageddon)

CHAPTER 21

"You gonna finish your steak?" Dean gestured with his fork to Cake's mostly untouched plate. Outside of the firehouse, Dean usually observed better table manners, but the guidebooks were right: Argentina served the best beef he'd ever eaten.

After being cooped up on the plane for 12 hours, he had been afraid they wouldn't be able to find anyplace open so late, but the Buenos Aires restaurants were not only open, they were hopping. Nine at night seemed to be the national dinner hour, and even families with young children had come out to chow down. Dean had picked this restaurant simply because it had been located across the street from the hotel, but it had been turned out to be a lucky find. Aside from great steaks, it also featured a live band with a sound halfway between salsa and reggae, a refreshing mix after a day of listening to the drone of jet engines. Cake had wanted to order room service to avoid the crowds, but now that he was here, he seemed to have forgotten about his laptop as he watched the dancers.

No, Dean observed, Cake wasn't watching the dancers. He was watching one dancer in particular, a girl about Cake's age. She was short, with cute-and-spikey hair and a wide, inviting grin that made her seem like she was having the most fun of her life, right this minute. She was obviously a dance-floor veteran because each of her steps displayed energy and ease at the same time, two characteristics that can only be combined after years of practice.

"Hey, Earth to Cake," Dean snapped his fingers.

"Um, yeah, go ahead," the boy said, distantly.

"How's that brain software coming?" Dean understood that they were beginning the second phase of the project and would require another Egg in which to replicate a human mind. Dean had tuned out after the first mention of the hippocampus and the connectome (whatever those were), and just referred to the whole thing as "brain software."

"Software's fine," Cake mumbled.

"Did you read the PDFs Soap sent so you can explain to me how the spy gear works?"

"Yeah."

"Well, if you've done all your homework," Dean leaned in with a smile. "Why don't you go ask her to dance?"

Cake's head shot around like it was spring loaded. "What? I mean— what? How do you...?"

"Teenagers," Dean speared a chunk of beef. "People your age are so obvious, yet you have no idea. So get out there. What's the worst that could happen?"

"I could be deported for bad dancing."

"We'll hire a lawyer to fight against your extradition on the grounds of two left feet. You'll do fine."

"You haven't seen me dance," Cake hung his head. "Besides, just look at me. A girl like that would never want to dance with a... a fat kid like me."

Dean leaned back in his chair and chewed while he studied Cake. In the two hours since they had disembarked the plane, Cake had undergone another transformation. Gone was the tweed coat, and in its place he had donned a loose black shirt and slicked-back hair. He might have fit in as a native Argentine except that all the natives seemed as thin as guitar strings—which was utterly baffling considering the size of their steaks.

It struck Dean that Cake was a social chameleon. He wanted to fit in so badly at his old school, he had adopted the blazer and tie and tried to be just like all the other preppies at his prep academy. When he came to the Institute, he observed that everyone else had a quirk, so he had carefully selected a few quirks of his own to show off. Before buying plane tickets to Argentina, he must have researched the local styles and purchased clothes that would help him blend in. For him, it was all about camouflage, and the only possible reason was that he didn't think people would like the true Oscar DeLeon if they ever saw him.

Dean could feel this realization washing away the last of his misgivings about allowing the boy to join the Institute. Lying and hacking hadn't been the right thing to do, but he hadn't done it out of malice, and it hadn't truly hurt anyone. Maybe he wouldn't be such a bad addition to the Institute after all. Maybe the Institute could even give him a little ethical and practical guidance.

If it was time for Cake to learn a different approach, Dean could teach it to him. It was worth a shot, anyway, and it seemed like a good thing to try. Maybe that's what old O'Grady had been talking about when he said it was a privilege to pass on your knowledge.

"Okay, buddy," Dean plucked a plastic flower out of the table's centerpiece and slapped it into Cake's hand. "I'm going to give you my best play. Here's how it works: you take this flower and you go hand it to her. You say 'I'm sorry, I don't normally do this, but you're so beautiful I just needed to tell you.' Got it?"

Cake stared at the flower for a moment. "Then what?"

"Then... whatever. Maybe she invites you to dance. Maybe you walk away with nothing but a pleasant memory. I won't lie: there's no guarantee it'll work, but if you don't take the shot you'll have nothing but regrets."

"But she'll know, won't she? I mean, she'll know it's a line. It seems like it'll be pretty obvious what I'm trying to do."

"Then be obvious! Listen, sometimes it's better to stand out badly than to fit in adequately."

Cake looked at the flower, then at the girl, then at Dean, then back at the girl. Dean extended his leg under the table and nudged the boy's chair. It was enough to get him moving towards the dance floor.

Dean could feel his own heart accelerating and his fingers tightening on his armrests as he watched Cake tap the girl's shoulder and offer the flower. There was more to this pickup line than what Dean had explained. It wasn't just one of Dean's plays; it was *the* play, word-for-word what he had said to introduce himself to McKenzie back when they were both new students at a freshman-only introductory party. That summer, he had read a book about how to become a "player," and he had gone off to school thinking he would be the next campus Casanova. To his amazement, the line had actually worked like magic, only at the same time McKenzie had worked an even more powerful spell on him. They danced together all that night under the funny red and orange lighting in the school's dance hall, and what Dean had intended to be the first of many college girlfriends ended up becoming the all-consuming love of his life. He had never used the line before or since.

He couldn't tell if it was working for Cake, however, because the girl took the flower and then looked at Cake in mild confusion.

Cake paused for a beat to search her face. She continued her smile automatically but said nothing. He nodded and turned to walk back to the table.

Disappointment settled over Dean's shoulders—and then the girl took Cake's arm and pulled him back to the dance floor just as the next song came up. He was obviously unfamiliar with the music and he danced like an awkward, over-fed duckling, but the girl showed him the steps, and soon the two were laughing about it together.

Dean wanted to hop out of his seat and bellow in triumph, but then the floor lights shifted to orange and blue, making the girl's face look pale and her hair appear as auburn as McKenzie's had been. Auburn and gold.

Something shifted inside Dean. Suddenly, the memories crashed down around him with such impact that he exhaled under their weight. When he looked out at the dance floor, he saw McKenzie, but not as she had been when they first met. He saw her as he had last seen her, on the carpet, not breathing. CPR had been useless. Her lips were already cold. When he closed his eyes to escape the image, it only became more vivid.

He found himself gasping for air, and now the music acted like a vice that crushed him from all sides. He lurched out of his seat, spilling his water all over his steak. He managed to hold himself upright long enough to reach the street and collapse on a bus bench.

He fought against the tears with a berserker's fury. *No crying,* he told himself. *Don't feel it. Just choose not to feel it and it won't hurt.* His hands shook, so he clenched them into fists, but the harder he squeezed the stronger the tremor became.

The man next to him said something in Spanish. Dean didn't understand it, but assumed it was a question.

"I'm fine," Dean said. "I'm perfectly fine."

He wanted desperately to blame this reaction on jetlag or overeating or influenza. Not grief. Grief was supposed to get easier with time, wasn't it? Yet it only seemed to be growing inside him like mold, and the more he pressed it down the more it grew. It made no sense to him: emotions couldn't slice the skin or break a bone. Why, then, did they hurt so much? Why couldn't he control them?

His dropped his head between his knees, worried he might lose his steak. The man next to him got up and walked away. Dean waited like that for several minutes, watching the tremors shake his fists.

"Mr. Lazarchek?"

Dean jolted upright, thinking that Cake had come to look for him. But it wasn't Cake.

It was Agent Nash.

Even under the dim street light and against his dark skin, black circles stood out under the agent's eyes like bruises. Nash's normal buzz-cut was growing ragged at the edges and instead of his usual suit he wore jeans and a sweatshirt. He looked like hell. He looked like Dean felt.

The two gaped at each other in mutual surprise. Dean stood up, hoping to conceal his shakiness so that Nash wouldn't ask.

"If you're here," Nash said. "Then I must be in the right place to fight Blitzkriegers."

Dean extended his hand and the two shook. "Let me guess," Dean said. "You picked up on the South America connection and you've come to officially investigate?"

"Not officially," Nash tugged at his sweatshirt to illustrate that he wasn't in uniform. "I'm here for the same reason I'm guessing you're here. I'm here for revenge."

CHAPTER 22

Dean and Nash spread the map of the Tormenta Incorporated factory out as far as they could on the dash of their rented minivan.

"It's impossible," Nash shook his head. "There's no way the two of us can get in. Maybe if this were in the States, we could get a warrant and raid it, but down here..."

He didn't have to finish the sentence for Dean to understand what he meant. Aside from Argentina being far, far outside his jurisdiction, Nash had also been placed on mandatory leave following his partner's death, meaning that he wasn't even supposed to be investigating this case right now. He had come here on a hunch: as far as the FBI was concerned, he was on vacation.

"Do you still want to do this?" Dean asked. "Do you still want to go rogue, and all that?"

"Yes." Anger flashed in Nash's eyes. Dean knew that look, because he had seen it in his own face. Anger was an easy thing to feel after loss. Anger hurts less than grief.

Dean turned on a tablet and shifted through photos of the Tormenta complex.

"Where'd you get those?" Nash asked.

Dean left the question unanswered. The truth was, earlier that day, while Nash was paying a call to the embassy, Dean had planted a telescopic camera across the street from the Tormenta factory. The camera looked like a child's toy car, but it clung to a street lamp with a little magnet in its undercarriage and drove itself up to the highest point to get pictures beyond the walls. The pictures it had captured were amazingly crisp for such a tiny camera, but there wasn't much to be seen from the outside other than that it didn't much resemble a factory. If anything, the Tormenta factory looked more like a large office building, except that it had no windows and was the only new structure in the middle of an otherwise deserted industrial slum. The camera also had a clear view of the employees coming in and out of the building, and from these it had been easy to see that they used key cards and a fingerprint scanner to get through the front door.

Most importantly, that little camera had also captured the faces of all the employees as they filed in and out at what appeared to be designated shift changes. Cake had used some kind of horrifying app that matched these photos to social media posts across the net. Inside of an hour, he had a list of names, home addresses, and shopping habits for several of the workers. The terrifying part was that Cake had come up with all that information legally, using commercial software available to anyone.

"You're starting to frighten me," Nash said as Dean showed him the background on their target. "Again I ask: how did you acquire this information?"

"The less you know, the happier you'll be."

Nash took the tablet and flipped through the photos. "Just because we know about their employees doesn't mean we can get in. It's not like one of them is going to hand over a key card and then swipe his fingerprint for us."

"A system is only as secure as the people who use it," Dean quoted Cake as he continued eyeing a bar across the street. It was a little place called the Estancia Club, a high-end watering hole with expensive sports cars in the lot and a bouncer on duty at the door.

"In case you've forgotten," Nash said. "Everyone who has access to Tormenta works for the same boss who had Blitzkriegers blowing up houses all across the central United States. They're not going to just suddenly decide to turn on a guy who can do that."

"Oh, I wouldn't be so sure. Take a look at this guy. He seems like he might give us a hand." Dean pointed at a silver Porsche zipping past them to take up two spaces in the Estancia Club parking lot. From the license plate, he knew it must be Sergio Palacio, who, according to the geotag information Cake had harvested, checked in at this location almost every night at this time. Cake had also discovered Sergio's home address, that he was an avid fan of the River Plate soccer team, and that his parents lived out in the Mendoza province and owned two horses. Dean made a mental note to double-check the privacy settings on his own social sites as soon as he got the chance.

From his spy kit, Dean grabbed a device that looked like a circuit board with messy loop of copper wire and what appeared to be a phone in a plastic bag. He shoved both devices into his pockets, and before Nash could ask what he was doing, he opened the door and crossed the street.

As he approached Sergio in the parking lot outside the club, he held his guide book in front of his face. Unable to see where he was going, he bumped into his target, causing both to stumble back and stop. Sergio spat some Spanish words that were obviously insults.

"Sorry 'bout that, pardner," Dean spoke in the worst imitation of a Texas drawl he could manage. "I ain't from 'round here. Would you mind if I get your picture?" He held the phone up to Sergio's face and snapped a shot. The flash was blinding in the twilight. Sergio grabbed the phone from Dean's hand and threw it down onto the sidewalk. It landed on the sidewalk with a sharp crack as a large piece broke off and skidded away.

Sergio then pushed past Dean to go into the club, uttering more insults as he went.

Dean watched him go, and then stooped to collect the pieces of the phone. The back case had split in half and the screen was shattered beyond recognition.

Nash crossed the street to join him. "I hope that was worth your phone. What was the point of all that?"

"This wasn't my phone," Dean smiled. "It wasn't a phone at all, actually. Cake, did you get the data?"

"Yes, Mr. Lazarchek," Cake's voice sounded in the Bluetooth device in his ear. "I have all everything I need. Did you need me to translate what Sergio said? I don't want to get in trouble for swearing, though."

"I think I got the gist," Dean turned to Nash to explain what had really happened. "This broken thing that looks like a phone is really a fingerprint reader. The instant old Sergio snatched it out of my hand, it read his fingerprints and sent them back to my computer guy. He's already loaded it onto a device which, if you want the technical name, is called an electronic fingerprint thingy."

"It's called a fingerprint replicator," Cake said. "It works by reproducing the electrical capacitance in a topographical—"

Dean muted the earpiece so he didn't have to hear the explanation.

"The important thing," Dean went on, "is that it'll get us into Tormenta. Oh, along with this," he fished the copper-loop gizmo out of his pocket. "This is an RFID reader. As I understand it, this copied the magnetic signature of every card in that man's wallet. If we wanted to, we could take all his credit card numbers and go have a wild night, but we're ethical burglars so we're going to erase those. The only one we need is his employee keycard."

Nash's mouth hung open. "If we were in the United States right now, you would be in violation of so many laws I can't even count them in my head."

"Then be glad we're not on US soil," Dean said. "And be glad I'm on your side."

"I had no idea your Institute was so... dangerous."

"You need to understand something," Dean waved the fingerprint scanner and the RFID reader in front of him. "This was the easy part. We can get through Tormenta's doors, but we have no idea what's waiting inside. Or who."

Nash looked him in the eyes. "O'Grady wouldn't back down."

"You're right," Dean said. "And neither will we."

Chapter 23

Fifteen minutes after capturing the Tormenta employee's data, Dean and Nash stood at the front door of the otherwise nondescript factory. It might have passed for any mid-rent office complex in any city of the world: three stories tall, a full city block on each side, and paneled in beige aluminum siding.

"Seems awfully big for a place that builds little phone dongles," Nash observed.

Dean had been thinking the same thing. He tried peering through a window but the glass was tinted.

Here goes nothing, Dean thought as he ran the card through the reader and then placed the plastic patch of the electronic fingerprint replicator onto the scanner. The door clicked, and Dean pulled it open. Nash shook his head but followed him in.

Inside, a night guard sat at a reception desk so Dean and Nash flashed the Tormenta IDs that Cake had forged for them. Nash looked perfectly natural in the new suit they had bought for this occasion, but Dean felt as if his necktie were going to strangle him. Of course, he felt that way whenever he wore a suit, but there was something about the particular cut of these clothes that made him feel buggy. Still, Cake insisted that this was the *couture de jour* for Argentine business people. It wasn't like Dean had any other options at this point.

The guard glanced them over while Dean made sure to keep looking left to hide the side of his face with the bruises Brick had given him. As long as the guard didn't see that, he might assume that Dean was an executive who forgot his briefcase and had come back in the middle of the night to retrieve it. Hack the people, not the systems.

The guard waved them through, towards a short hallway. At the end of the hallway, they found a round, black door set in a wall that curved gently outward. Dean ran his fingers over it. It felt smooth, and both the door and the wall resembled polished black glass.

"What kind of wall is that?" Nash asked. "Is it just me, or is it bulging outwards a little?"

"Look at the corner," Dean resisted the temptation to point for fear that someone might be watching through the security camera. "The other walls don't fully connect to this curving wall. Someone just filled in the gap with a little insulating foam. I think we're about to enter a building inside a building."

The door latch sat flush against the smooth black wall, more like a car door handle than a doorknob. It opened smoothly, and they passed through into a long corridor that curved slightly as if it were an indoor race track. The metal grate of the floor clanked with each of their steps.

Dean had entered many buildings in his firefighting career and studied the layouts of even more, but he had never seen anything like this. It felt like they were walking along the bulkhead of an ocean liner, yet the ocean was miles to the East, and nothing on Earth could haul a boat this size to the shore.

Dean placed his Bluetooth receiver in his ear.

"Mark—I mean, Sam—can you hear me?"

"I can hear you," said the ghost of Sam "Mark Twain" Clemens. "I can sense that Nikola is very close. He and I have been having a little chat."

"Do you need to come out of my pocket?"

Nash shot him a look. "Who are you talking to?"

"A friend who might be able to help," Dean said, and then returned his attention to his conversation with the ghost: "Can you tell us where to find him?"

"Find who?" Nash said. "Lazarchek, there's a lot you're not telling me."

"And a lot I'm not going to tell you. Just trust me for now, would you, Nash?"

"If you two are done," Twain said. "Tesla has given me a map of this structure. I may not be able to see while I'm in your pocket, but all the same I have an excellent notion of where we are. Would you like me to manifest a map so that you can see the big picture?"

Dean would have liked that very much, but he noticed a camera in the ceiling and was afraid the guards might spot a glowing green three-dimensional map suddenly springing to life in front of them.

"Can you just tell me where to turn?" Dean asked. "That might be safer from prying eyes."

"Of course," the ghost said. "Keep heading this way and by and by you'll reach an elevator. Nik says it will take you up to the top floor. He can tell us the passcode when we get there."

They followed the ghost's instructions and wove their way deeper and deeper into the building—if it was a building. It didn't follow the usual grid pattern of hallways and offices and there were no windows or signs, although they passed several more rounded doors as they walked. Whatever this structure was, the narrow hallways, metal walls, and featureless doors made Dean feel like he was wandering around inside a flying saucer.

At one point, they encountered two of people—Dean heard them before he saw them, because they were chattering about the latest superhero movie, comparing it to the previous installments in that franchise. It took Dean a moment to realize the significance of the fact that they were speaking in English: these were not Argentines. So who were they? When the owners of the voices rounded the corner, Dean saw that one was a heavy-set man in a black Tormenta, Inc. polo shirt and Bermuda shorts. His friend was a lanky ginger woman who walked with the uneven stride of a water fowl. When they saw Dean and Nash, they nodded in a kind of submissive greeting and continued their conversation in quieter tones after they passed.

"Not what I expected," Dean whispered.

"At least they showed respect," Nash said. "It's the suits."

"Is that why the FBI issues those ugly things you wear?"

"I look better than you on my worst day."

"Given that sweatshirt you were wearing earlier, I'd say this is your worst day."

"You're right," Nash smiled. "And I still looked better than you do right now."

They followed Twain's instructions up the elevator, punched in a code on the number pad, and scanned the fake fingerprint once more. Nash folded his arms and looked annoyed, but this time he didn't ask how Dean knew what to do. They rode up to the top floor, exited into another corridor that appeared identical to the previous one, and wove their way through another series of curving passages. Finally, they emerged onto the balcony of a room that could only be compared to

Mission Control at NASA. Row upon row of computer stations filled the floor space, all lined up to face a huge screen that comprised the entire front wall. Men and women dressed in a mix of black polo shirts and baggy t-shirts occupied a handful of these computer stations, while a pair of men in suits stood at the back monitoring the progress.

"Nikola is down there," Twain said. "He's in a computer console towards the front of the room, near the base of that large screen."

Dean could see the console from where he stood. It looked like a closed metal box and was perhaps thirty feet away from where he now stood. No one seemed to be paying attention to them, so they were unlikely to get a better chance at stealing Tesla's Egg.

Nash leaned on the balcony railing, doing his best to look relaxed. He covered his phone with one hand to hide it as he snapped pictures of the control room.

"What are you going to do with those photos?" Dean asked. "I thought you weren't supposed to be investigating this case."

"If I just happen to stumble across a terrorist headquarters while on vacation, I'm sure my director will be interested in seeing my photo album," Nash said. "By the way, what do you think that big screen is for?"

"That's probably where Goldfinger tells the world he wants a billion dollars or he'll blow everybody up."

"Don't be stupid," Nash said. "Goldfinger wanted to nuke Fort Knox, not blackmail the world. Get your James Bond villains right."

"Do I detect the self-righteous anger of a fan-boy?"

Before Nash could answer, Dean turned to lead the way down the first flight of steps, hiding his smile as he went. He was glad that Nash was opening up: there was more to him than mirrored sunglasses and dark suits after all. This juvenile one-upmanship also served as a sort of coded message that he was doing well. As long as they could banter with each other, each would know that the other had not succumbed to the fear and the pressure. When the jokes stopped, they would both know the situation was truly serious.

They both tried to play it cool as they walked purposefully towards the console, but just as they arrived within arm's reach, a door opened on the far side of the control room. A tall bald man strode through the door, his oddly-shaped, bony head swiveling with animalistic alertness.

He moved with a sliding step that made him seem to glide through the bridge, almost as if he were slithering more than walking. He wore a rumpled suit with an unbuttoned collar and no tie, but there was something primal about him, as if his clothes were nothing more than camouflage. The computer operators must have picked up on this, too, because they were looking nervously at the new arrival, each of them frozen in place and fighting the instinct to flee.

Dean's heart pumped ice-water. There was no mistaking this bald man: this was the Predecessor, the man—or monster—in Cake's video who had simply absorbed half a clip of semiautomatic gunfire at point blank range without even blinking. Dean had seen this Predecessor kill with careless ease, and there would be absolutely nothing to stop him from snapping the necks of everyone in the room if that's what he wanted to do.

Dean put a hand on Nash's shoulder. "Abort," Dean whispered sharply.

"But we're within arm's reach—"

"Back the way we came," Dean hissed. "Hurry!"

Without further discussion, the two of them turned around and moved back up the stairs as quickly as they could without drawing attention. Dean glanced back to see the Predecessor still standing there, watching them with a cold, steady gaze. Those reptilian eyes seemed to strip away millennia of human development, leaving Dean to feel like nothing more than a frightened animal. In that moment, Dean's mind lost the ability to understand how any tool or weapon could help him and was left only with an overpowering instinct to climb a tree and hide.

Nash elbowed Dean to redirect his attention to the pair of suits in the corner. They, too, had spotted the intruders and now called for them to stop. Dean did his best to pretend that he didn't hear them, and as soon as he rounded the corner he broke into a run.

"Not that way," Twain said. "Three men are moving down the hall towards you from that direction."

"Come on," Dean grabbed Nash and guided him into an unfamiliar corridor.

They dashed through corridors, darted through doors, and reversed directions whenever Twain warned them of approaching guards.

"You're getting us lost," Nash said.

"Better lost than captured."

Circling back around through yet another hallway, they spotted an elevator and ran for it. Dean hit the buttons for all the floors, and then used a tiny bottle of spray paint from the spy kit to paint over the lens of the security camera.

"Now they won't know when we got off," he explained.

"You're way too good at this for a guy who hasn't seen enough James Bond movies."

Dean offered no quip or joke in response and he could feel Nash growing tense because of it. They bailed out at the second stop, where they found red emergency lights flashing at every intersection.

"They might be on to us," Dean observed.

"Yes, and they're closing in quickly," Twain said. "You're going to have to backtrack. I'll lead you to a different exit. Wait, something's happening—"

Suddenly the floor rumbled under their feet and Dean's stomach lurched. It felt like they were on a fast elevator moving up.

"What was that?" Nash asked.

"Earthquake?" Dean asked, thinking he could still feel a gentle swaying in the floor.

"I don't—" Twain seemed at an uncharacteristic loss for words. "Something... happened. I'm not sure what Nik is trying to tell me. We'll have to worry about that later. For now, just get out of there. Go!"

Dean and Nash dashed up a short flight of stairs. They rounded a corner to find two of the suit-wearing guards approaching from the other direction.

The guards yelled in what sounded like French. Dean and Nash turned and ran. Something popped behind them and electrical sparks flew from the metal wall about three feet from Dean's hand. Another arc of electricity ricocheted off the ceiling overhead.

"Stun guns," Dean said as they ran. These weapons might be non-lethal, but getting hit with fifty thousand volts would mean certain capture, and in this case capture could prove just as deadly as a bullet.

"There!" Twain shouted in his ear. "The door is just ahead! Nik says— never mind, just go!"

Dean sprinted ahead and grabbed the airplane-style turn-bar on the door, threw it back, flung it open, and—

He had to grab the threshold to keep himself from falling through. A hundred feet of open air yawned below. He found himself looking down at the glittering lights of the gradually receding Buenos Aires cityscape. Directly below, the Tormenta building's roof crumbled into itself. From their altitude, Dean could still make out chunks of roof panels falling into the black hole within, but they were swiftly rising high enough that in another moment the details would be too far away to distinguish.

"What is going on?" Nash asked desperately.

Slowly, it dawned on Dean. It seemed unimaginable, yet he could reach only one explanation: the black building-within-a-building had been some kind of aircraft. It must have been large enough to fill the entire Tormenta warehouse in which it had been hidden. Whoever designed it had built it to break through the roof and float away, though the damage to the roof below them clearly revealed that this was a one-time trick. They had just happened to stumble into this airship before its scheduled liftoff or—much more likely—whoever was in charge had given the order to take to the air expressly because of the presence of the intruders.

The guards had caught up to them now. Dean spun to face them, grabbing the first man's tie and throwing a fast right hook at his jaw. The tie was a clip-on that came loose in his hand, but the blow landed solidly, knocking the guard cold. Dean would have done the same to the other guard, but that one already held a pistol level with Dean's eye. It wasn't a stun gun, either: this was a chrome-plated semiautomatic held in a steady hand.

Dean looked back at the doorway. A jump from this height would surely be fatal, and he didn't want to leave Nash alone. He had no choice but to raise his hands in surrender.

Another pair of guards arrived from a side corridor to help search the prisoners. They took Nash's pepper-spray, Dean's pocket knife, Twain's Egg, and both men's phones. Without any further conversation, they marched Dean and Nash back to the control room and into a different elevator than the one they took before. This time they appeared to ride all the way up to the top floor.

The elevator doors slid back and Dean blinked in amazement, wondering if he'd been hit on the head hard enough to make him hallucinate. Before him, a beautiful Japanese-style garden filled the enclosed area, complete with low bamboo fences, a stone lantern, and a small, graceful house with a tiled roof and white rice-paper walls. For its small size, the space was tastefully arranged, lit dimly by lights that had been placed in a way to conceal their source yet draw the eye across the smooth stone path ahead. Overhead, the perfectly manicured cherry blossom trees partially blocked the stars that were otherwise clearly visible through the domed glass roof. Something fluttered in the branches, and Dean realized that there were birds up there, little finches or sparrows, all nestled in for the night. At the center of the small garden rested an elegant pond with a few moss-covered rocks. A short tremor of turbulence caused the water to lap at the edges of the pool, and Dean thought he also heard the swish of a fish breaking the surface.

The glass dome that encompassed the garden was perched atop an airship, and it allowed Dean his first view of the vessel which had carried them into the sky. From what he could see, the ship consisted of a flattened sphere that projected six pointed arms, each with a small turret at its tip. It looked like what would happen if Batman designed a snowflake: symmetrical and beautiful in its way, yet every inch constructed from angled, black metal panels.

Dean didn't have much time to study the ship because the guards prodded him and Nash towards the small rice-paper house, where a man in silk robes awaited them. This man stood with his back towards them, looking out past the dome into the night sky as the lights of Buenos Aires gradually retreated beneath them. His robe was pure white, so white that it seemed to glow in the dim light, and his black hair was slicked back to a neatly-trimmed line at the back of his neck.

"It certainly has been a long time, Dean," the man said, then turned and stepped forward, bringing his face out of the shadows.

Dean knew that face, but it took him a second to place it. It had been many years, and the man's jaw-line had thickened, his hair had gained a few white strands, and his forehead had taken on worry-wrinkles that hadn't been there when they had been younger.

"Ignacio?" Dean sputtered. Ignacio Zabaleta. McKenzie's d-bag, tree-hugging, hippy-wannabe, rebound boyfriend.

At least now Dean knew who the new boss was.

CHAPTER 24

"He had this with him, sir," one of the guards handed Twain's Egg to Ignacio.

"Are you attempting to monetize your assets, or shall we consider this a hostile takeover?" Ignacio asked Dean as he cradled the prize. "I expect you didn't bring this to me for the reward, but that doesn't mean there is nothing left to negotiate. Guards, take the other one to the guest quarters. We'll interview him later."

Ignacio's lackeys escorted Nash towards the elevator. He resisted at first, but it was clear he didn't have a choice in the matter. The other guards remained in position around Dean.

"Dean Lazarchek," Ignacio said with a slow nod of his head. "I must admit I'm amazed. This is like a college reunion, and you look as fit as ever. I wouldn't have thought it possible for you to have gained more muscles since those days, but here you are."

"And I wouldn't have thought you could have gained more grease in your hair, but here you are. Can we skip this garbage and get down to business?"

Ignacio cocked one of his precisely-trimmed black eyebrows in surprise. "So impatient. Can you not draw tranquility from your surroundings?"

When he phrased it 'can you not' instead of 'can't you,' Dean once again felt that old, familiar urge to punch Ignacio in the face.

"As long as you're so eager to skip the formalities," Ignacio went on. "You might as well meet my business partner." He slid back one of the rice-paper doors of the little teahouse. Inside, the Predecessor knelt at the tea table. His bony head turned and his cold eyes locked onto them. Dean, who once ran into burning buildings for a living, struggled to keep himself from running for the exit under his penetrating stare.

Smoothly, the Predecessor rose to his feet and approached. Very few people can stand up from a kneeling position with any grace, let alone anyone tall enough to bump his chin on the doorframe as he ducked through it, yet this creature-in-human-disguise seemed to uncoil with the natural fluidity of a serpent sliding out of his lair.

Dean took a reflexive step backwards. "This guy's dangerous, Ignacio. You don't know who you're dealing with here."

"He is a rational being," Ignacio bowed stiffly to his 'partner.' "He will harm no one so long as it's not in his best interest to do so. But, as he makes you uncomfortable," he turned to the Predecessor. "Would you please give us a few moments of privacy? As you can see, this man is no threat."

The Predecessor's face remained perfectly expressionless.

Ignacio gestured to his other guards. "And you as well. Allow two old college chums time to catch up, would you?"

The Predecessor paused for another minute before finally turning abruptly towards the door. Only after he moved did the guards follow.

"I meant it," Dean said as soon as the elevator departed. "That guy's more dangerous than you can imagine."

"I know all about him," Ignacio said, still calmly gazing out at the night sky.

"Did you know that he killed Helmholtz? I saw him do it. That Predecessor can do things—monstrous things. I watched him transform his body into a thousand ants and then reassemble himself later."

A bird fluttered through the dark air to land on a branch nearby. Dean jumped, startled.

"Calm yourself," Ignacio said as if he were speaking to a child. "The Predecessor is a brute, a primitive hold-over who no longer has a place in our world. He trades the technology of his ancestors without understanding its significance, thinking that I'll serve his purposes if I accept his gifts." Ignacio held up Twain's Egg. "You have also brought me a gift. I make an effort to appreciate beauty whenever I can, and I invite you to do the same. You've seen that I have real birds here in my garden. I would have had fish as well, but I feared all the sloshing and turbulence of air travel might prove unhealthy for them, so I substituted mechanical fish."

Ignacio gestured towards the water. Lights beneath the surface illuminated several fat koi, their gold and white scales flashing as they swam. They moved so naturally, Dean would never have guessed they were robots rather than real, living animals.

"Dean, my friend," Ignacio said, even though it made Dean grit his teeth every time Ignacio called him *friend*. "I had heard you took over the Institute. Good for you. I will, however, admit to being quite surprised that Denise chose you."

"No one's more surprised than me. And if you heard that, then you also heard about—about why the job was open?"

"Yes. The loss of Denise was tragic. Tragic. I regret introducing her to Helmholtz all those years ago, but who can know what course life will take?"

"You—you introduced her?"

Ignacio smiled at him patiently. "Yes, I was an Institute student. Didn't you know? If it hadn't been for me, she might never have found out about it."

Dean's mind reeled. William Helmholtz had built an international crime organization. Angela Black had invented a machine to wipe out civilization. And now Ignacio Zabaleta, who was, well, still a total jerk after all these years—he, too, had studied beneath Topsy's roof. The Institute had a clear track record of producing very unstable people. Unstable was an understatement—horrible, doomsday-driven mad scientists was more like it. And Dean had now brought in Raskolnikov with his explosives. Victor with his mystery injections. Cake with his hacking and his deceptions. And Soap with her army of heartless automatons. Was Dean unintentionally creating the next generation of dictators and terrorists?

"I hope you won't mind being forthcoming with me," Ignacio said. "In return, I'll be honest with you. It's the least I can do," he gestured for Dean to follow him inside the teahouse and offered him a seat at the extra-low table.

Dean tried kneeling at first, found it excruciating, and then was relieved to discover that the table concealed a tatami-lined hole that allowed him to sit in the fashion of his own culture, with his legs hanging down the hole the way they would hang off a chair.

Out of all the questions he might have asked at that moment, he couldn't help but start with a blunt triviality. "What's with all the Japanese stuff?"

Ignacio smirked as he set out two cups and filled them with hot water, all the while moving with the deliberate precision of a ritual. "The Japanese are a people with an appreciation for harmony and tranquility." He slid a cup of tea towards Dean. "Plus, I won't lie, I like the feeling of the silk robes. Now it is my turn for a question. How did you come to discover my little sky palace in the middle of the night, prompting me to order a takeoff long before I had planned it in order that I ensure our mysterious intruders couldn't escape?"

Dean looked at the tea but didn't touch it. The shadow of the tree branch by the door trembled gently as the silhouette of a little bird fluttered onto it. The bird paused there, ducking its head occasionally as if prompting Dean to explain himself.

"You're sure that Predecessor is gone?" Dean asked, absently watching the bird's shadow.

"I'm telling you, I have taken precautions. Brick Stellenleiter, for one. You know him?"

"Five hundred pound biker? Yeah, he and I have talked about a few different topics. Most of those topics involved which of my bones he wanted to break first. But Brick isn't going to be able to stop that Predecessor, if that's what you're counting on."

Ignacio shrugged and sipped his tea appreciatively. "He would at least slow him down, and that's all I need. My other guards are armed appropriately. Bullets won't do much, this I know, but electricity—no animal has ever developed a defense against a fifty-thousand volt shock. The Predecessor may have mastered evolution, but evolution is blind and random. So, can we put that matter behind us? You still haven't told me why you're here.

Dean said nothing.

"I don't wish to seem crass," Ignacio said. "But if you don't tell me, then I may be forced to authorize the use of drugs on your friend to ensure that I learn the truth."

"He doesn't know anything," Dean said quickly.

The silence stretched on just long enough for Dean to realize that it didn't matter what Nash knew, Ignacio's men would still hurt him to find out for sure. "Okay, fine," Dean said. "We're here for another one of those," he pointed at the Egg. "You've got one here somewhere, right?"

"I have two," Ignacio said.

"Two?" Dean leaned back, unable to hide his surprise.

If Ignacio had two Eggs, then one of them contained Tesla, and the other—Victor might finally have his chance to recreate McKenzie. It was exactly what Dean had been hoping for but hadn't dared to imagine.

"Yes, two Eggs," Ignacio confirmed. "Each aboard a different one of my sky palaces."

"Sky palaces? You have two of these ships?"

"I have three, actually," Ignacio said with undisguised pride. "We are aboard the *Tlaloc*, my flagship. We're going to rendezvous with the *Raiden* now, and the *Indra* is currently farther away, in the northern hemisphere."

"And here I thought most super villains only need one flying battle station. Compensating for something?"

"Don't be rude," Ignacio said stiffly. "And I'm not a villain. Truth be told, I would have liked to build far more sky palaces than I currently have. I had hoped to have one for every major city in the world, but a cost analysis clearly showed that it was not feasible at this time."

"Cost analysis?" Dean rolled his eyes. "Most villains sound way more cool than you do. Just saying."

"I told you, I'm not the villain here. And it doesn't matter how many sky ships I build because the real limiting factor is these," he lifted the Egg, tossing it gently in his hands. "Without this, my sky palaces can't serve their true function. Do you even know what this Egg really is?"

"It's a... I don't know. A computer of some kind, I guess."

Ignacio smirked again and took an excruciatingly slow sip of tea. Dean decided that the whole tea ceremony thing was an act, because any normal person would have drained that tiny cup on his first swig. Even dressed in phony Japanese robes, Ignacio was still the cheese-ball hippy poseur he had been in college, and his gigantic flying palaces were only the latest extensions of his ego. Some things never change.

"What you call the Egg is actually a quantum computer," Ignacio said. "Far more powerful than anything humanity has invented so far, and fundamentally different in structure. This works more like a living brain, with microscopic connections that grow, connect, and change on their own."

"And I thought it was just a lump of metal."

"Ah, but it is. It's made out of teslanium, although not even I can understand how it alters its connections or stores memory. Not yet, anyway."

"And why do you need it?"

Ignacio laughed. "You think I'm going to tell you all my plans? You watch too many James Bond movies."

"Funny," Dean said. "Someone recently told me that I didn't watch enough."

"Now it's my turn again: why did you bring it to me?"

"Good luck charm," Dean said.

Ignacio didn't seem to know that the Egg could hold a human personality, and Dean didn't see any advantage in revealing that fact. Still, he had to say something plausible before Ignacio became suspicious, so he decided to add a half-truth. "I knew someone was after it, and I thought it would be safer with me. I didn't exactly plan on getting captured, you know."

Ignacio nodded, seemingly satisfied.

"Okay, I got one for you," Dean said. "How did you end up with a fleet of flying palaces? Last time I saw you, you were just a math nerd in college." He thought he saw Ignacio's eyes twitch at the word 'nerd.' He probably didn't know that among today's teens, at least at the Institute, it was a badge of pride.

"You've been honest with me," Ignacio said. "And you've brought me a great prize, so I will tell you."

Bull, Dean thought. *You'll tell me because it's a chance to talk about yourself.*

"In truth," Ignacio said, "I developed most of my assets by leveraging my core competencies in the real estate development sector."

"You leveraged your what? In the where?"

Ignacio smiled patronizingly. "That means I made most of my money through construction companies that create buildings. You see, I developed an algorithm that better helped me estimate steel prices, weather conditions, and other factors that impacted costs. And I built green: I achieved 30 percent fewer emissions than my competitors and offered better financing. I sold solar panels for barely more than my own cost. I own several fundamental patents in wind-turbine technology. It also helped to have Helmholtz secure a few large contracts for me."

"So, basically, you were working with the mob and skimming profits."

"I shifted paradigms," Ignacio sighed, clearly demonstrating that the argument was beneath him. "Right now, I'm heavily invested in all stages of the construction industry, from the production of raw materials all the way to the workers who put the buildings together. My reach is global: I have a strong presence in the sixty largest cities of the world."

"I thought Tormenta Incorporated did something with little weather prediction gizmos."

"Tormenta is merely one of my offshoot companies, though one of particular interest to me. You might be interested to see our latest project."

He moved his hands across the table and the smooth wood grain faded into a desktop screen. Dean realized that this table was actually a gigantic tablet that had simply been displaying a set image of a tabletop the whole time they'd been having tea.

Ignacio opened a file so that Dean could see blueprints and photos of what looked like one of Soap's drone quadcopters, except that it was much larger, and the sky-blue lozenge of its body ended in a white lens. Four slender wings protruded from its body each equipped with a propeller engine. One of the animations showed these wings tilting and extending mid-air so that the drone could fly like a biplane for greater speed and range, then shift to the horizontal mode, retract the wings, and hover like a helicopter. The words "lightning-drone" flashed in dramatic, sparkling letters at the bottom of the screen.

"Nifty toy," Dean said, not particularly interested.

"The lightning-drone is no toy. This is a scientific tool, and it's also a mother-ship."

Ignacio flipped to the next set of schematics labeled "thunder-drone," which revealed the lightning-drone's lozenge-body opening up to disgorge a cloud of tiny devices, each about the size of a grape and topped with double helicopter rotors. A short promotional video followed to demonstrate how thousands of these thunder-drones could bail out of each lightning drone and spread out over a region to take microwave readings of the surrounding atmosphere.

"The invention of radar allowed us to predict weather like never before," Ignacio said, suddenly sounding very dramatic, as if he'd rehearsed this speech for a business meeting. "You're looking at the next evolution of weather forecasting technology, an amazing new vision that will make forecasts a thousand times more accurate than ever before. Radar is limited: it can either see at great distances but not deep into clouds, or it can see very short distances into clouds and fog at the expense of range. My thunder-drones will be able to spread across an entire weather system, each taking individualized readings and sending them back to the lightning-drones, which in turn relay the data to a central processor that compiles the most accurate picture of initial conditions ever possible."

"So the weatherman won't get it wrong as often," Dean said. "Big whoop."

"I think you're missing the significance."

"And I think you're missing a few brain-cells. Whatever you're up to, it's not going to work."

"I am treating you like a guest," Ignacio said with clear annoyance. "One more rude outburst and I promise that you will regret it."

"You pretend to be so civilized and, I don't know, *enlightened*," Dean rose to his feet, which was an awkward process since he began with his legs in a hole beneath the table. "If you're so in touch with your inner peace and your fancy silk pajamas, how come you've been sending your thugs all over the U.S. to dig up—"

Pain blazed across Dean's body and he tumbled to the ground. He lay there for a moment, gasping. When he tried to move, a new tidal wave of agony washed over him. Somewhere nearby, he could hear a relentless electrical clicking that pulsed in time with the throbbing pain that coursed through him.

"I've taken precautions against the Predecessor," Ignacio stood over Dean, crossing his arms smugly. "Didn't you think the same precautions would work against you? A high voltage shock locks up the muscles, scrambles the nervous system. Makes even the big, tough Dean Lazarchek as helpless as a baby."

Dean wheezed in agony and tried turning his head, but the torturous pain returned for a second round, accompanied once more by the crackling noise.

A pair of guards arrived and lifted Dean up. He felt a sting in his side and looked down to see the long wire of an electrode lodged in his abdomen. He followed the wire with his eyes and found it originated from a short, fat barrel that protruded from a large hatch that had opened in the rice-paper panel of the wall. It must have been an industrial-strength stun-gun that had remained hidden until now.

"You failed, you know," Ignacio stepped closer, and now Dean could see the small remote in his hand that obviously controlled the electric shocks. "You failed to protect Denise, and you'll always have to live with that. Guards—take him away."

Dean wanted to punch him, or at least spit in his face, but the electricity had raged through him like a wildfire and left his body a burned-out wasteland. He couldn't even lift his arm to knock the electrode out of his skin.

His head lolled to the side and he caught a glimpse of the little sparrow hopping to a new branch. Just before he lost consciousness altogether, Dean found himself wondering why that one was awake when all the other birds in the garden were asleep.

DECEMBER 18

(5 DAYS BEFORE STORMAGEDDON)

Chapter 25

Dean awoke with a buzzing in his ear and a splitting headache. Every muscle felt like a sponge that had soaked up liquid pain, and even the act of rolling over proved a complicated, agonizing process.

His body may have been weak, but for the first time he could remember, hope burned inside him. Ignacio had said he had two Eggs. If Dean could take them back to Topsy, he might be able to see McKenzie again. Of course, Ignacio's Eggs were locked up in two separate, heavily guarded flying palaces, and Dean would somehow need to steal one from each ship and escape without being gunned down as he ran. Then he would have to pray that Victor's experiment worked the way it was supposed to. All that seemed impossible, but he had overcome seemingly impossible obstacles before, and the only thing he stood to lose was his life.

As he contemplated his situation, Dean managed to struggle to a seated position. They had laid him on a small cot in the tiny room that served as his prison. Other than the bed, the room contained only a shallow closet packed with several drawers, a cramped alcove with a toilet and sink but no door, and a very small desk with a single chair. By his head, the defective speakers of a tiny alarm clock buzzed, buzzed, buzzed. The room was clean and somewhat comfortable; it was probably a cabin for a low-ranking sailor when it wasn't serving as a prison cell.

Dean sat there, thinking. Perhaps he could tell Ignacio what he planned, and Ignacio might simply loan him the Egg—after all, Ignacio once had feelings for McKenzie, too. Somehow, though, the thought of sharing filled Dean with sharp unease, probably born of some primitive, caveman impulse to protect his woman from a rival. He had always found it unpleasant to think about Ignacio and McKenzie together, right from the moment all those years ago when he'd first realized she was dating him. It had happened after their first breakup, when Dean had been harboring the hope that he and McKenzie might get back together. One day in the dorm dining hall, he sagged down into the chair in front of her, determined to talk until he found the magic words that would fix their relationship. Just as he was about to speak, Ignacio sat down next to her and took her hand, a clear gesture of possessiveness from a guy who claimed to be too pure-spirited to own anything.

Dean stared at their hands for a moment, and then raised his eyes to see her looking back at him with an unreadable expression. This was how they broke the news to him. He had been replaced. She had rebounded, and he hadn't even finished falling. In that moment, he thought about begging, or yelling, or declaring that her happiness was more important than his own. Mostly, he wanted to punch Ignacio in the nose. He ended up pushing back his chair and walking away without a word. Within the week, he had dropped out of college and joined the army.

That was many years ago, and Dean knew that reminiscing on the mistakes of the past wasn't going to help his current situation. From the cot in his little prison, he stretched his legs and rotated his ankles. It felt good to move again, so long as he didn't move too fast. Without getting up, he reached for the door handle and was unsurprised to discover it was locked tight from the outside. He eased himself back into a reclined position, thinking for a moment that he was extremely hungry. He would have loved one of those famous Argentine steaks right then, although he wasn't sure he had the strength to chew it.

His eyes drifted closed, but he couldn't get back to sleep because of the annoyingly broken alarm clock. He could ignore it when he was wide awake, but it was just loud enough to bother him when he tried to sleep. It sounded like a mosquito's buzz, except that it stuttered on and off, as though it were receiving an irregular broadcast. When he brought it close to his head to see if he could find the off-switch, he heard barely audible words contained within the buzz.

"Don't turn off..." the words were intermittent with the static. "...Dean of... help...here..."

Dean stared in surprise at the little radio. Whoever was speaking had a strange accent that sounded similar to Russian, but not quite. He pressed the alarm clock up to his ear and held his breath to listen more closely.

"You must be the Dean of Students," the accented voice said. "I am glad I found you."

"Who is this?" Dean suddenly felt energetic enough to sit back up. "Can you hear me?"

"I can hear you," the voice squeaked. "It is a pleasure to make your acquaintance. My name is Nikola Tesla."

Dean almost dropped the clock. It took his groggy brain a moment to put together that he must be speaking to the ghost of Nikola Tesla contained within an Egg somewhere. Like the ghost of Twain, Tesla must have learned to use electronic speakers to create a voice for himself.

"You're here, aren't you?" Dean asked. "You're inside an Egg in this ship?"

"Yes, I am here aboard the *Tlaloc*. I control some of the ship's functions and all of the actions of the drone fleet."

"You control them? Listen, you know Ignacio has got something bad up his sleeve, right?"

"Up his sleeve?"

"Yeah. It's an expression. It means he's hiding something."

"I am in contact with all his computer systems and records," the voice of Tesla said. "I know exactly what he is planning, and I agree that it is very, very bad. He wants to create storms that will destroy the world's largest cities."

"Storms—?" Dean considered what Ignacio had shown him about the lightning-drones and the thousands of thunder-drones each carried. Could they do more than detect weather? "I don't think I understand," Dean said. "Why would he want to destroy cities? What could he possibly get out of that?"

"He explicitly states in his records that he will destroy these cities to save the environment."

"How does destroying cities help the environment?" Dean shook his head. "What, is he going to recycle all the scraps?"

"Something like that. More likely, it has to do with the fact that he has large holdings in construction companies in each of the cities he has targeted. If he inflicts massive damage, he will gain massive profits from reconstruction."

Dean couldn't help smiling coldly. This was the Ignacio he knew: covering selfishness with the mask of altruism. "Well, Mr. Tesla, can you shut this operation down? You said you were in control of the ship, right?"

"'Control' was, perhaps, the wrong word. It would be more accurate to say that this vessel and the drone fleets it carries are in control of me. Ignacio Zabaleta has me locked in a docking station that uses my computational abilities against my will. I am essentially a slave."

"Can you at least open my door?"

"I am sorry," Tesla said. "Like you, I am a prisoner aboard this sky palace. I can only unlock your door if someone unlocks my bonds first."

"So, how do I unlock you?"

"You cannot do it from inside this cell."

Dean groaned. "You're telling me that I can't unlock you until you unlock me, and vice versa. That's not helpful."

"I have a plan, but—I am sorry. We will have to continue this discussion later. Guards are approaching your room and I do not want them to know of my existence."

The alarm clock went silent, so Dean slipped it into the pocket of his slacks just as the door opened to reveal a pair of guards. They said nothing, but gestured with their stun guns for him to get up and go with them.

Dean got the impression that this pair of guards didn't speak English. They looked Asian, perhaps Korean. All these guards came in pairs, he had noticed, and each pair seemed to have matching nationalities. It might be a sign that Ignacio had been collecting the scraps of Helmholtz's international empire.

The guards escorted him to the bridge. Nash was already there, flanked by his own pair of guards. Ignacio stood at the center of the front wall, just below the view screen, where he had evidently been delivering a bold speech. The control center was crowded with an operator behind every computer screen and pairs of suit-wearing multinationals glowering from every corner. Sergio, the guy Dean had tricked to get the security badge and fingerprint, now sat at a computer station, pointedly avoiding eye contact with Dean. Even the Predecessor lurked silently in the shadows and watched intently.

Ignacio's hair was slicked back just as it had been last night, but his silk robes had been replaced by a black suit with sleek pin striping. He wore a red tie that seemed as bright as flame and was anchored by a diamond pin, and the toes of his shiny leather shoes extended to an improbably sharp point.

"Welcome, gentlemen," Ignacio bowed slightly towards Dean and Nash. As he spoke, he gestured in such a way that made a thick gold ring flash as it reflected the lights of the control panels around him.

"I thought you might like to witness the first phase of my plan," he said. "A plan to save all of humanity—nay, to save the world itself."

"You can't save the world by killing innocent people," Dean said.

"Innocent? There are no innocent people," Ignacio gestured dramatically. He was enjoying this, Dean realized—showing off in front of his troops. He had probably brought Dean and Nash to the bridge to play devil's advocate so that he could show off his superior position in a lopsided debate.

"So-called innocent people have been contributing to the problem for decades," Ignacio declared. "Their actions are changing the climate of the Earth. If nothing is done to stop them, they will kill themselves, along with everyone else. Does that sound innocent to you?"

"If this is about climate change, there are other ways to fight it."

"Like what?" Ignacio's eyes flashed. "Like ineffective laws? Like toothless treaties for which the nations of the world have been patting themselves on the back and then promptly ignoring for the past two decades? Like solar panels and hybrid cars that barely offset the addition of all the energy-ravenous devices every household in the developed world has been recklessly accumulating? I might have hoped that you could see the bigger picture."

"Tell that to the people whose lives you're planning to destroy," Dean said.

"And you can tell it to the polar bears who are drowning as their habitat melts into the sea," behind Ignacio, the giant screen lit up with a video of a bedraggled, exhausted white bear clinging to a hunk of ice in the middle of the sea.

I have seen his mad invention, Dean thought. *And it's a PowerPoint.*

"Should I tell it to residents of Fiji, Hawaii, Vietnam?" Ignacio continued with his speech as the screen displayed flood-drenched tropical regions and photos of refugees standing in long lines with misery written large on their faces. "Those countries may be washed from the map by rising ocean levels. Perhaps you think I should tell the residents of Louisiana, Brazil, and Poland, all of which have been ravaged by floods and storms that will grow even more devastating in the coming decades? Perhaps you think we should simply pass this problem off to our children, after it's too late for them to do anything about it? That's denialism, Dean. Denialism will kill us all."

"I'm not denying—"

"No, you're not denying. And you're also not doing anything about it, except perhaps buying an energy efficient lightbulb once in a while. Well, it's time that you and the rest of the world took this problem more seriously. Did you know, Mr. Lazarchek, that the top sixty carbon-producing cities are responsible for thirty-five percent of the world's greenhouse gasses? We need to think green. We *must* think green—or we must die."

The suit-wearing guards didn't seem too impressed, but the computer operators looked like they were hanging on Ignacio's every word, and he, in turn, fed on their attention.

Dean felt anger flush his cheeks. "Why don't you tell everyone why you selected these cities?" Dean said. "Tell them how you just happen to be positioned in the construction industry in each of those cities so you'll turn huge profits by the destruction you cause. To me, when you say 'green,' I don't think you mean the color trees. I think you're talking about the color of dollar bills."

Ignacio peered intently at Dean for a moment. Dean wasn't supposed to have that information, but Ignacio clearly didn't want to ask how he knew about it for fear of appearing anything less than all-knowing in front of his subordinates.

"I assure you," Ignacio's voice was icy, "my motivations are pure."

"If that's true, then what are you sacrificing for your cause? You're not putting anything on the line, Ignacio, and that proves there's nothing behind your words except greed and arrogance."

The silence on the bridge was palpable. Dean heard one of the computer operators' sharp intake of breath. Even the security guards seemed to be leaning closer to hear how Ignacio would respond.

"If we could eliminate those cities," Ignacio spoke through the knot of tension in his jaw. "If we could simply pick up all those polluting cars and carry them away, or smash all the stores that sell potato chips shipped to them from seven thousand miles away by diesel-spewing cargo hulks—even then, it won't undo the damage human beings have inflicted on this planet, and we haven't even seen the worst of it. Someone has to take action now, or our own planet will destroy us. I will be that someone. I will save all of us, no matter what I have to destroy to do it."

Dean caught the eye of the Predecessor, who stared back at him with his blank, unnerving gaze. Why was this monster helping Ignacio? The Predecessor had tried to come up with other ways to drive humanity to extinction, or at least to bump it back to the Stone Age, just so his species could have another shot as top dogs on the planet. So what was in it for him to help Ignacio with his battle against climate change?

Dean didn't have long to think about this because Ignacio was still in theatrical mode. At a gesture from him, the large screen lit up to display the view from between two of the angular black arms of the *Tlaloc*. In the blindingly bright ocean below, sun-sparkling waves lapped at the belly of the hovering ship. Fifteen miles away, the lights of Buenos Aires twinkled along the coastline while huge, dark clouds piled up on the city like a burial mound.

"All day, my drones have been out there," Ignacio strutted in front of the gigantic window. "They've been heating the air over the city so it will combine with the on-shore flow to form thunderclouds. We've got wind-shear at higher altitudes, spinning those clouds nicely. Soon, if God allows it, the storm may bend to the ground." He turned to Dean and said, almost as an aside. "I had hoped to find more of those teslanium egg-brains, so that I could guide multiple drone fleets to strike more cities at the same time. And now, thanks to you, I have three, so I may be able to complete my work within two months, given travel time."

He set his hand proudly on a steel computer console box bolted to the floor. This was Dean's first chance to get a good look at where Tesla's Egg was kept. A metal flap closed the front of the box, sealed with a numbered keypad. Even if it hadn't been locked, Dean didn't have a chance at the smash-and-grab with all those guards and the Predecessor only a few feet away. As long as Tesla remained electronically enslaved to this ship, Dean was helpless to do anything but watch.

Ignacio gestured for the guards to take Dean and Nash to one corner of the bridge. They were no longer part of the show. Ignacio switched the display from window mode to a series of video feeds showing black funnel clouds bending their twisting fingers towards the Earth. Then he surfed through more feeds from various drones and traffic cameras that monitored buildings, traffic patterns, and the unsuspecting people in the city below. None of those people had any idea what was coming, and this seemed to energize Ignacio's continuing motivational speech.

As soon as Dean was sure that the guards were distracted by the drama of the storm on the screen, he probed a nearby keyboard with his pinky. As he suspected, the computer was locked and required a password to gain entry. He slid the alarm clock out of his pocket and pinched it between the side of his head and his shoulder to keep the speaker pressed against his ear.

He glanced around again and confirmed that no one had noticed him. All eyes remained safely turned towards the big screen.

"Okay, Mr. Tesla," Dean whispered. "I think we're ready."

CHAPTER 26

Tesla may have been enslaved to calculate the actions of millions of drones as they created a deadly storm cluster, but he still knew everything that happened on the *Tlaloc*. The crew's locations, the facing of every security camera, and each keystroke anyone typed into any computer. This included user names and passwords, even Ignacio's.

As Dean logged in with the stolen administrator credentials, Tesla began whispering instructions for opening the core code and making changes to key text. It might as well have been Greek as far as Dean understood it, but Tesla gave very specific instructions about how to access which lines of code and what to change. It was difficult to type while standing up and pinning the little alarm clock to his ear with his shoulder, but the storms and the flight of the drones provided a very welcoming distraction.

"How much more do we need to change?" Dean whispered after they had been at it for several minutes.

"This is the last change," Tesla said. "Find line 5,473,824. Erase the letters *Count N=N+1* and replace them with *Count N=0*."

"Count Enn?" Dean asked as he typed it. "He sounds like a vampire."

"Please focus. When you hit enter, this will introduce a bug that will allow me to—"

One of the guards grabbed Dean's shoulder, spinning him around. The alarm clock dropped from his ear and emitted a fatal-sounding crack when it hit the metal deck.

"What you do?" The guard demanded in deeply accented English. "Why you type?"

Several of the techs looked over at them, interested in this new type of storm brewing at the computer console. Ignacio hardly spared them a glance—this was beneath his notice at the moment.

A second guard stepped in. He looked at the screen and his hand hovered over the keyboard.

"No, don't press enter!" Dean pleaded. "I was almost done! Don't press enter!"

Gloating, the guard did just that. The moment he did, every screen in the room went dark, including the big display at the front. All the lights shut off, and the room plunged into immediate, total darkness.

Tesla was now in complete control of the ship.

Before anyone could react, Dean dropped to the ground and began crawling towards the central computer console. As he did, the moment of shocked silence gave way to noisy tumult. Someone had a flashlight and its beam waved erratically towards the ceiling, but instead of illuminating the situation it only added to the confusion. Evidently, Ignacio must have prohibited personal phones on deck, because not a single person produced one to shed light.

The metal deck rubbed Dean's bruises painfully, but crawling prevented anyone from finding him. He was well practiced at moving on the floor because it was often the only safe means of travel through a blazing house, where the heat differential between ground level and five feet above the ground could be enough to boil your blood and scorch your lungs. He could elbow his way along almost as quickly as a person could walk, although it didn't help that more than one panicking computer nerd tripped over him. Ultimately, their stumbling only produced more chaos and panic, and that worked to Dean's favor.

While Ignacio screamed for his technicians to find a light and start cracking open computer panels, Dean arrived at the central computer console, felt his way up to the top, and located the key pad. He didn't need to worry about the code; Tesla was in control of every networked electronic device, which meant he could now easily unlock his own cage. Dean felt the little door open at his touch, and inside he found the cold, hard lump that was the Egg. In a moment, he had slipped it out of its electronic nest and was back down on his belly, crawling for the elevator.

This was now the most dangerous part of the plan, because removing the Egg from the computer meant Tesla was no longer in control of the ship. In fact, without the electricity provided by the computer console, Tesla wasn't even conscious. However, he had set several of the ship's systems on timers, and Dean knew what would work and when it would work, which meant he still had the advantage.

Fifteen seconds after he had removed the Egg, Dean had crawled his way to the elevator and found the doors unlocking for him right on schedule. He slipped inside and headed up to the garden. Once there, he raced to the teahouse and located the small chest of drawers that Tesla had told him to search. Inside, he found Twain's Egg as well as the electrical charging stand Soap had designed. Dean clipped the charger onto Tesla's Egg—Twain would have to stay asleep for now, because Tesla was the one who knew how to escape the sky palace.

The garden's only exit was the elevator back down to the bridge so Dean descended back down and once more belly-crawled through the dark room, avoiding the still disoriented technicians. He moved slowly this time, avoiding contact as best he could. Ignacio and a few of his technicians had located a flashlight, and their attention was now focused solely on rebooting the systems. Nash was no longer in the control room, but Dean found him in the corridor, being led back towards his cell by a pair of guards. One of the guards held a penlight while the other prodded Nash forward with the barrel of his pistol.

They hadn't seen Dean yet, but there were two of them and one was armed. He needed a distraction to help his odds.

Almost as if responding to Dean's thoughts, a green figure materialized in front of the guards. He was tall and slender, neatly dressed in an old-fashioned jacket and vest, all of which glowed in tones of emerald and lime. His thin face was marked by sharp cheekbones, a trimmed mustache, and a high forehead, and his hair was parted precisely along the center axis of his head and slicked gracefully out to the sides in the style of an old-timey silent film star.

Dean knew this was the ghost of Tesla projected from the Egg, but the guards didn't understand what they were seeing. While they gaped, Tesla made an elegant bow, and Dean took the opportunity to strip the gun from the first man's hand and club him solidly in the jaw. Nash turned on the other and scuffled for a moment before managing to secure him in a chokehold.

Dean gave Nash a hand up from the floor.

"I see your Jiu Jitsu is improving," he said. "Somewhat, at least."

Nash wasn't amused. "Did you turn off the lights?" he demanded. "What's going on?"

"Not easy to explain right now," Dean snatched up the flashlight and the guard's gun. It was an electrical stun gun rather than a real firearm, but it would have to do. As an afterthought, he also stripped the radio earbud from one of the guards and placed it in his own.

"Tesla?" he said as he moved down the hall. "Can you use this to speak to me?"

"This will work just fine," the accented voice said through the earpiece.

"Who are you talking to?" Nash asked tensely. "Will you please tell me what's happening?"

"I have... a friend. He's running interference for us. He hacked the ship and left everything locked and dark except our escape route. Right now, we need to get moving, because the bad guys are going to regain control soon."

That seemed good enough to get Nash going, although he still didn't look satisfied. "What was that glowing green thing back there?"

"That was one of my friend's illusions. Look—here are some others."

Green lights lit up along the floor of one branch of the corridor, a visual cue projected by Tesla to show them where to go.

They dashed down a series of corridors, too quickly for Dean to remember the path in the dark. Within minutes, however, the lights overhead flickered back on. Dean stopped short and blinked as his eyes adjusted to the brightness. It could only mean that Ignacio had regained control of the *Tlaloc's* lighting, and if he'd done that he might have reclaimed other systems as well.

"Not part of the plan?" Nash asked.

"If it weren't for plans, we wouldn't have anything to go awry," Dean said. "Come on, we're almost there."

"Through the door ahead," Tesla confirmed. "When you enter, you will see a series of round openings before you. Each of you should proceed through a different opening, feet first."

Dean didn't have time to ask about what he meant by "feet first" before he and Nash burst into the room.

As Tesla had described, four porthole-like entrances faced them.

"I'm going through this hole, you go through that one," Dean pointed the way for Nash. "Follow my lead—feet first!"

Almost in unison, they gripped the bars over the portholes, swung their feet through, and dropped down a short chute towards an unknown destination.

CHAPTER 27

Dean found himself dropping into a bucket seat inside a small glass pod that granted him an almost perfectly panoramic view of the ocean. Before he could take in the view, something behind him clanked and suddenly he dropped for a moment of sickening freefall. He thought he was going to plunge into the sea, trapped inside the glass bubble that the *Tlaloc* had just flushed out. Then his chair slammed hard into his backside as he came to an abrupt, midair stop.

"Might I suggest the seatbelt?" Tesla spoke into his ear. "This pod's automatic systems kept you from crashing, but they do not guarantee a smooth ride."

As the vertigo cleared from his head, Dean numbly repositioned himself in the seat and clicked a double-shoulder restraint harness over his chest and lap. Below him, only a thin layer of glass and a twenty-foot drop separated him from the cold waves. Above him, the glass dome projected four large jets that swiveled on extension beams and blasted heated air downwards around him. Dean could hear a distant roar of the engines, but they sounded far away. The noise reduction system in that pod must be incredibly efficient.

"What kind of crazy helicopter is this?" Dean asked.

"This is no helicopter," Tesla said. "It is called a mosquito pod, a vehicle that hovers by means of those jet engines. It's powered by—"

"No time for details. Just tell me how to make it go."

"It's remarkably simple, actually. Guidance systems, proximity sensors, and engine controls are all automated by default. The foot pedal controls acceleration, and the left flight stick operates like that of an airplane. Pull back to gain altitude, push forward to descend, etcetera, etcetera."

Dean settled his hand over the control sticks and nudged the pod forward. It seemed easy enough. There was also a joystick on the right armrest, so he slid his hand over it and rested his finger on the trigger under the forward grip. "What's this one for?"

"Let's hope we don't need that one," Tesla said. "We had best start moving. They may mount a pursuit at any moment."

Dean twisted in his seat to see another mosquito pod hovering nearby. He could see Nash inside, pressing his hands against the glass with a slightly worried expression on his face.

Tesla suggested opening a radio channel to explain where he was and how to operate the pod.

"What is this thing?" Nash said as soon as they made contact.

"Relax," Dean said. "It's called a mosquito pod. It's programmed so that even I can't crash it, which means you're safe, too."

"How do you know all this?"

"A ghost told me."

"A what?"

"Never mind," Dean then gave Nash the quick run-down on how to fly the pod. As soon as he was ready, Dean floored it and his pod raced out over the waves so fast that the acceleration pressed him back into the seat. As soon as he caught his breath, he nudged the flight stick back a little to gain some altitude, just enough so that he wouldn't end up splattering himself against the sides of any cruise ships that happened to be between him and Buenos Aires.

"What's the status on the storm?" Dean asked Tesla. "Were you able to put those drones out of commission?"

"No," Tesla's voice seemed strained. "The minute I took over the *Tlaloc,* control of the drones was automatically assumed by the *Raiden.*"

"The *Raiden*?" Dean remembered Ignacio bragging about having three sky palaces in total, with two in the vicinity of Buenos Aires. "So the storm's still on. Tell me truthfully: can we stop it?"

"It may be possible," Tesla sounded like he wasn't so sure. "It would require a sacrifice."

Dean craned his neck to look over his shoulder and saw Nash a little ways behind him but keeping up. Farther back, the darkened and crippled *Tlaloc* faded into the dusk. Dean had escaped and taken two Eggs with him, but there were still millions of drones buzzing around the skies over the city, brewing up tornadoes. And Dean couldn't forget about the third Egg, the Egg that Victor could use to recreate McKenzie. He intended to find that other sky palace if it killed him.

The skies over Buenos Aires didn't look good. Inky rain and thick, greenish-black clouds consumed the horizon, and the wind was speckled with newspapers, road signs, even chunks of billboards—all swirling thirty feet or more in the air. Soon, the storm would really begin and, with it, the destruction.

He stomped his foot hard on the accelerator. The pod was already racing at maximum speed, but he still strained against his restraint harness to push harder. As he did, he dialed Cake using the mosquito pod's Bluetooth connection.

Cake sounded surprised to get a call, and there was a horrible whooshing on the line that made it difficult to hear. Dean realized that it was the sound of the wind in the streets.

"I can barely hear you over this wind," Cake had to shout into the receiver. "We're having the weirdest weather."

"Cake, listen to me," Dean shouted back. "I need you to get somewhere safe. Is there a basement or something nearby?"

He heard Cake say something in Spanish to someone on his end of the line. A woman's voice—or maybe a girl's—answered him. Dean wondered if this was the same girl from the dance floor last night.

"She says there's a laundry room in the basement of her apartment building," Cake said.

"Get there," Dean said. "Fast. Bring everyone who will come with you. When you get to the basement, close all the doors and windows, and don't show your face above ground until the fire department knocks."

He hung up to cut off any argument. Basements were the safest places, and Cake had more warning than the rest of the city. As far as Dean knew, Buenos Aires had never experienced a tornado in its entire history, which meant the people had no way of knowing what was coming or how to deal with it when it arrived.

"I have some bad news," Tesla said. "Do you see those four dots on the radar screen? I believe those are mosquito pods from the *Raiden* coming to intercept us."

"Great," Dean muttered. He strained to twist in the seat again, wishing this strange vehicle had a rear view mirror. In his squirming, he accidentally nudged the right joystick and the entire pod swiveled in response. He now no longer faced the same direction he was flying. This was disorienting at first, but as he played with the right stick he found he could swivel a full 360 degrees around and almost 180 degrees up and down. The mosquito pod was nothing more than a ball turret crowned with hover jets, which gave him an almost perfect combination of maneuverability and facing.

"Neat," Dean said as soon as he'd gotten the hang of it. "What'd you say this trigger was for?"

"I didn't say," Tesla remarked. "It activates the rail guns beneath your feet."

For a moment, Dean was pleased with the idea of being armed—a little firepower might be handy when flying towards a hostile sky palace. Then he realized that if he had rail guns, so did the four other mosquito pods that were streaking towards him right now. When he looked at the radar, he saw two other blips had now joined the chase from behind him—the remaining two pods from the *Tlaloc*, no doubt. This brought the count to six bogies versus just Dean and Nash.

A tornado ahead and enemies right on his tail. This wasn't turning out to be Dean's favorite winter break.

Dean opened the radio channel to Nash. "We've got some bad guys ahead and behind us. Split up. You go left around the city and I'll go right."

"But—"

"Just do it. I'll meet you on the other side.

Without slowing his forward momentum, Dean spun the glass sphere so that he could watch Nash's pod peel off towards the south. Satisfied, he pulled back hard on the flight stick and found that the little mosquito pod ascended rapidly. Rain lashed the glass all around him, but there seemed no chance of getting above the weather; the rising clouds seemed to go on forever

"The *Raiden* is located on the other side of the cloud formation," Tesla said. "However, we'll have to skirt the city to avoid the storms, which will take us more than fifty miles out of our way if we want to be safe."

"No time to be safe," Dean pressed forward into the winds. At least this way, he might make things more difficult for his enemies too.

"But you told Nash you were going around the city," Tesla said.

"I'm going to keep those other pods busy."

"Be careful," Tesla advised. "If you get too close to the twister—"

An aerial plume of water slammed into the mosquito pod and something bounced off the glass right at eye level—Dean could have sworn it was a fish.

"What's with all this water?" Dean demanded, but Tesla couldn't answer before a series of mid-air waterfalls struck the mosquito pod like short blasts from a fire hose. Craning his neck and swiveling the turret, Dean caught a glimpse of the bay where a huge, whirling funnel cloud had poked down into the sea and was sucking up water like a straw. A river of water shot straight up through the twister, turning the dark gray winds solid black and spouting massive plumes of the ocean into the sky. As Dean watched in amazement, the storm flung a fishing boat up over the beach where it disappeared into the tenth floor of a high-rise hotel.

Dean, unnerved, spun his pod back around to skim the road between two other high-rises. He knew that tornados lifted from beneath, which meant that all vehicles were deathtraps. His mosquito pod was probably the worst place imaginable, and the automatic crash-prevention systems wouldn't do him any good against winds strong enough to juggle freight trains.

The radar readout on his console beeped a warning: the other mosquito pods had apparently caught up to him as he had been busy maneuvering. One of them now bobbed around the high-rises, its rail guns blazing blue and red. An explosion flashed bright along a rooftop just above Dean's pod, and his engines sounded like nails in a blender for a second or two as they sucked in debris from the collateral damage.

Dean didn't want to test whether his pod could withstand a direct hit, because he was pretty sure it couldn't. As the other pod swooped in to join the first, he simultaneously yanked back on the flight stick and tilted right on the turret stick, causing the pod to dart upwards while he swiveled to face his pursuers. He squeezed the trigger and felt a slight humming in the seat as his guns kicked out a solid stream of deadly projectiles.

His shot missed the farther of the two pods by at least fifty yards, and that hadn't even been the one he was aiming at. Hitting one of them would be like bulls-eyeing a fly on the wing with a spit-wad.

"I can help," Tesla said. Suddenly, the air around Dean lit up in a dance of geometrical green lines, circles, and arrows. It looked like the head's-up display on the inside of a fighter pilot's cockpit window.

"Aim for the circle, not for the enemies," Tesla said. "I will calculate their relative movement and factor in lag, wind resistance, and the drop of the projectile. When the circle turns red, you pull the trigger."

"You can do all that?"

"It's just calculus," Tesla said simply.

"Just calculus," Dean shook his head. "You've really got to meet my cousin. You two have so much in common."

Dean twisted the control stick so that his target reticle followed the circle that Tesla painted in the air in front of him. Even with Tesla's help, it was difficult to pull the trigger at just the right moment, and when he did, he still missed because the mosquito pods were frustratingly nimble little targets that changed direction sharply and without warning. Still, so long as he remembered to wiggle the flight stick often enough to keep his own ship moving erratically, he was just as hard to hit, and they didn't have Tesla helping with their aim. On his third try, he managed to lance the engine cowling of the lead mosquito pod, forcing it to drop into a controlled spiral as its three remaining jets struggled to keep it from crashing.

Dean shifted his aim to the second mosquito pod, but its pilot was better at bobbing and weaving than the first. It zipped behind a row of apartments, then somehow reemerged dead ahead, its guns blazing electric blue in the twilight. Dean's pod rang with a grazing blow and a long crack sluiced through the glass by his right hand.

Jerking rapidly on the flight stick, Dean spun crazily as he tried to find his target again. His stomach heaved at the tumultuous motion, and by the time he got the enemy pod back in sight, he saw it sweeping around an office complex, speeding towards him with its rail guns carving the air like knives.

Suddenly, an uprooted tree flew into the enemy pod, smashing it like a fist hitting a hollowed-out egg.

Dean swore and then spun himself around to witness a massive funnel cloud fifty yards away, marching through the center of the city like Godzilla himself. It snatched up whatever was in its way—cars, street-lamps, even small buildings—and whipped them around and around before hurling the remains across the city. Lightning flashed, illuminating other funnel clouds reaching down towards the ground like the fingers of a monstrous hand.

"I thought the storm was out at sea!" Dean jerked on the controls as he felt the winds pulling him inwards.

"That one was," Tesla explained. "They often come in pairs, though the counter-clockwise ones tend to die more quickly here in the southern hemisphere."

"Just tell me how many there are!"

"Currently: six—at least. Within the next thirty minutes there could be as many as twenty."

"*Twenty*?" Dean couldn't believe that he'd heard right. Single tornadoes of this magnitude had been known to devastate entire towns, inflicting millions of dollars in damages, and claiming dozens of lives. Twenty tornadoes unleashed on a city this size... the only word Dean could think to describe the devastation was "biblical."

Four white streaks suddenly flashed through the sky, announcing that the mosquito pods from the *Raiden* had arrived.

Dean radioed Nash. "Scatter," he barked as soon as the line opened. "The other sky palace is thirty miles to the north and five hundred feet up. Meet me there."

Before Nash could respond, Dean hung up and rushed directly towards his four new enemies. He took the first one by surprise, blasting one of its engines into a gratifying eruption of scarlet flames and black smoke. Its three remaining engines sucked up most of the smoke and debris and were soon emitting sparks and smoke of their own as the pod weaved and tumbled towards the ground.

The other three pods scattered like a swarm of angry bees. Tracer rounds flashed all around as Dean jerked at his controls. He spun and dove with sickening acceleration, still managing to fire back with enough accuracy to graze the glass pod of one of his pursuers and force another to retreat to the far side of a freeway overpass.

One of them cut across in front of Dean, its stream of projectiles blasting clouds of brick dust out of a cinema. Dean spun backwards to face his attacker, lined up the targeting circles, watched it flash, and pulled the trigger. It was a perfect shot—or it would have been if he hadn't been out of ammo.

His guns clicked pathetically, and he couldn't do anything but watch as the pod he might have shot down slid out of the targeting circle and swooped around for a deadly run right at him.

Dean cursed and frantically twisted the control sticks, hoping to find some narrow streets where he might evade his pursuer. Instead, he found his mosquito pod becoming sluggish and unresponsive. He jerked his flight stick back in the other direction and was whipped through the air, faster than before but in the wrong direction.

"Be careful!" Tesla said. "We are too close to the storm!"

The world spun around Dean as buildings and dark sky swapped places over and over again. He caught sight of the huge black funnel cloud, now much closer than it had been only a few moments ago and steadily pulling him towards it no matter what direction he mashed the controls. His whole pod vibrated so violently he had to clamp his teeth together to keep them from chattering, and his stomach felt like it had turned into a bowl of sloshing water. When the winds flipped him over once more, he could see the three pursuing pods also spinning crazily through the air, just as helpless as he was. One fired a shot which he guessed might have been aimed at him, but it flew almost straight up instead.

Without warning, a whole gasoline tanker truck emerged from the black clouds, crashing down through the air like God's own nunchucks. It smashed through the middle mosquito pod, which disappeared in a cloud of vermillion fire and shattered glass. As the tanker continued its fall, the pieces of the pod were whipped away towards the vortex of the twister.

Wrestling with the controls, Dean gambled that instead of trying to push against the wind, he could move with it, build up speed, and break free at an oblique angle. He came away with more momentum than he had hoped as he hurtled towards the sidewalk, engines shrieking so loudly that they overcame the pod's noise-cancelling properties. With white knuckles, Dean rammed the controller to the other side and veered just enough to avoid slamming into a Neo-gothic building, only to have his momentum scrape him along the face of a hotel in a shower of broken white tiles and marble ornamentation. His mosquito pod limped away, its engines severely damaged and seeming to fight against his controls. If his stabilizing systems weren't working right, he knew his anti-crash systems might also fail.

As he rose just high enough to skim the roofs of the surrounding buildings, a bright flash lit his cockpit and his pod jolted forward out of control. He twisted in his seat to see what had happened: one of the enemy mosquito pods had broken free of the tornado and shot out his engine. And then, as if that wasn't bad enough, the other pod swooped in from the opposite direction and unleashed a stream of magnetic slugs that ripped one of his jet cowlings in half, blowing shrapnel through his remaining engines and punching holes in the glass all around him. He was lucky he hadn't been shredded where he sat, but his luck looked like it was about to run out.

The pod's badly damaged engines strained and swerved in their brackets, transforming what might have been a deadly plummet into merely a sickening fall. His landing gear consisted of four thin, curving "legs" that now slammed down on a flat rooftop at a bad angle. One of the landing legs buckled and the vehicle rolled to the side.

Dean, dizzy and nauseous, flung open the cockpit hatch and bailed out of the burning pod before it rolled off the ledge. The momentum jolted and banged him along the flat roof, and even his best safety-roll technique could only do so much to protect his already battered and bruised body.

He staggered to his feet as quickly as he could, but he couldn't move fast enough. One of the enemy mosquito pods barreled down on him, rail guns chewing a line of holes through the roof towards him. He dove to the side just in time, but his escape was cut short by the second mosquito pod as it rose up above the lip of the roof like the Angel of Death, its chin-gun lined up so he could see right down the barrels.

Then it exploded.

Nash's mosquito pod zoomed over the roof, flying almost straight through the burning wreck of the enemy pod as it dropped from the sky. The other pod had been flying a cross-pattern, and its turret now swiveled and fired at the new threat. Nash stopped his pod dead still to allow the other mosquito pod to overshoot the mark. Then Nash gunned down the other ship before it had a chance to adjust its aim.

Dean ran forward, gesturing Nash to open the cockpit door as soon as his pod touched down.

"I told you to go around the city!" Dean had to shout to be heard over the winds and the engines. "You never listen, do you?"

"I only listen when you're not getting your butt kicked," Nash shouted back. "So, no, I never heard you say a word."

Dean smiled, then grabbed the landing legs and held on tight.

"Where are we going?" Nash shouted.

"Up!" Dean shouted. "We've got a storm to kill!"

CHAPTER 28

The high-altitude rains lashed Dean until his clothes were saturated and his fingers were numb. He had to strap himself to the mosquito pod's landing legs with his own belt to keep the winds from ripping him off his perch, and he wondered how much longer he had before hypothermia set in. It crossed his mind that wasn't the smartest move he'd ever made—but it was still his only option.

As Nash piloted them up and away from Buenos Aires, the storm steadily pulverized the city behind them. The inky black funnels seemed to extend forever above them like some kind of magical beanstalk leading to the land of gigantic destruction. They passed a lightning-drone, its wings retracted and its engines rotated to allow it to float in the sky like a bobbing cork. The drone's lozenge-shaped body was longer than Dean was tall, making it much larger than he had imagined from the photographs and schematics Ignacio had shown him. Nash might easily have shot it down as they passed, but it would have been pointless. A thousand other mother-ship drones just like it hovered at strategic locations around the storm, and each had already released its swarm of thunder-drones. At best, shooting down one lightning-drone would have no measurable effect. Even if they could manage to destroy a significant number, they would have succeeded only in making it harder to combat the storm if they somehow managed to seize control of the fleet.

Tesla, who had survived unscathed in Dean's pocket, knew the location of the second sky palace, and explained that it would be difficult to see until they were close enough to shoot it. Its angular shape and experimental radar-cancelling technology made it nearly invisible from the ground and the active camouflage of its hull hid it from anyone approaching from the air. It was, essentially, the world's first stealth blimp, undetectable by anyone who didn't know right where to look.

As the pod approached, the tips of the *Raiden's* arms opened up like mechanical flowers, but in this case the blooms became turret guns. The mosquito pod, however, zipped right in past them and hovered so close that the sky palace's weapons couldn't swivel to track it. Nash, displaying more than a little finesse at the controls, hovered in front of the bridge's view port in the crux of two of the sky palace's arms. Anyone peering through the bridge's forward display would have been looking right down Nash's barrels.

Nash was smart enough not to cut loose with everything he had. Instead, he used his guns like a scalpel to peel away strips of the hull. He fired only very short bursts, taking his time to target the corners and the weak spots until the exterior plating dropped away and sections of the outer hull dropped off in large chunks. Through the new, gaping hole in the sky palace, Dean could see the geeks and suits inside, all scrambling for the emergency exits. Had they been at a higher elevation, Dean imagined the sudden decompression might have blown them out the new opening. Even without an explosive pressure change, though, nobody on the bridge was stupid enough to pit their pistols and stun guns against a rail gun, so by the time Nash had made the hole big enough for Dean to leap through, nobody remained to stand in his way.

First, Dean found the intercom. "We've taken control of this ship," he announced over the PA system. "We're going to blow it up in five minutes, so I suggest you find a parachute and get out."

It was a bluff, because the mosquito pod's weapons probably didn't have enough ammo left to take down the entire sky palace, but the announcement would keep Ignacio's men from rallying to retake the bridge. He knew his lie had worked after Tesla instructed him to flip on the observation cameras in the ship's belly so that he could see the jumpers bailing out, first one at a time, then in groups of twos and threes. Now the ship was his, and he was going to need it to reverse the weather conditions.

Dean found the central computer console, then grabbed a nearby fire extinguisher and bashed open the lock. Inside rested another Egg, the iridescent surface reflecting the LEDs and wires that comprised its little electronic nest.

This was it. This Egg didn't contain Tesla or Twain, which meant it could soon play home to Denise McKenzie. Dean carefully removed the electrode sleeve and drew it out, cradling it in his hands for a moment.

"Hurry," the green ghost of Tesla appeared next to him.

Dean dropped the blank Egg into his pocket, then slid Twain's Egg into the computer console and snugged the blanket of wires into position around it.

Instantly, the green ghost of Twain appeared beside the ghost of Tesla. They exchanged a very significant look that Dean couldn't read.

"I want to thank you for your hospitality," Twain popped his illusory cigar back into his mouth as he turned to Dean. "It has been a pleasure, sir, to know a man who displays such selfless concern for others. I mean that with the greatest degree of sincerity."

Dean felt like he'd missed a memo. "It sounds like you're saying goodbye."

"I am," Twain said. "And I am honored to have known you."

"Why?" Dean asked. "Where are you going? As soon as you're done with, you know," he made a twirling motion with his fingers to indicate the twister. "I'll just grab you and we'll scram together. No problem, right?"

"He doesn't know," Twain turned back to Tesla.

"Doesn't know what?" Dean echoed. "What don't I know?"

"Commanding the drones to counteract the storm," Tesla said. "He is going to need to absorb vast amounts of data, compute probabilities that defy conventional statistical analysis, and coordinate the actions of millions of drones. If he is successful, he will change the air currents and temperatures to redirect or dissipate the storms while at the same time guiding counter-rotating twisters into each other so that they will cancel each other out. It will be the equivalent of knocking one billion bullets out of the air using nothing but hand-held stones. The calculations will be intense and must be performed extremely quickly. It will overheat his Egg while it is connected to the ship's systems."

"Overheating," Dean said. "That sounds like a problem we can handle. You need me to dump water on you or something?"

"That would be like," Tesla paused to think of the proper comparison. "That would be like trying to extinguish a house fire with an eye dropper. No, I said there must be a sacrifice, and that is because for one of us the resulting heat will be terminal."

"Terminal?" Dean said. "I don't understand. What do you mean 'terminal?'"

"It will melt the synaptic structure inside the Egg," Tesla said. "It will erase whatever software has been stored on it, and that includes the personality and memories of Sam Clemens. To put it simply: it will kill him."

Dean took a step back, feeling as if he'd just been punched.

"Don't worry about me," Twain said. "I believe I shall be the second man in history to die twice. I hope Saint Peter will amend his usual policy to allow re-admittance for one of considerably lower celestial status than the first."

"Wait," Dean shook his head. "There's got to be some other way."

"It's all right," Twain said. "I will feel no pain, so please try not to be saddened. I am not afraid. Remember what I said about how I lack mortal fear?"

"I also remember you saying that you're the most important person in the world," Dean said. "Don't forget that. We can't afford to lose you."

"If you feel that way," Tesla said. "Please consider replacing his Egg with mine inside the control console so that I can be the one to make the sacrifice. I, too, lack the impulse for self-preservation, so it makes little difference to me. In fact, I think I may prefer oblivion to the loss of my friend."

"No, no," Twain scolded. "Don't listen to the man; he's given to melodrama. I've already started the job. Even now, the drones are changing their functions. I've got them pushing and pulling at the pressure zones, just as dear Nik here taught me how to do just now."

"We can exchange information much more quickly than speaking it aloud," Tesla told Dean. "I'm currently helping him with the calculations as well, but I can only give him so much assistance."

"It turns out that it's much easier to brew a tempest in a teapot than to put it back in the kettle," as Twain spoke, he flickered like an old film strip while violent streaks of red burned through his normal green hues.

"Wait," Dean said. "Wait—there's got to be some other way. Can't we just, I don't know, throw a bomb into the tornado? Wouldn't that work?"

Tesla shook his head. "We might succeed with a nuclear weapon if you happen to have one. But in that case, I think the cure would be worse than the disease."

Twain's image swiftly faded to a stiff silhouette filled with a kaleidoscopic smear of colors. It looked like he was melting, and the metal cabinet of the control console was now beginning to glow red as it heated from within.

"I can't just stand here and watch him die," Dean said frantically.

Tesla lowered his head. "Unless you can perform the calculations to create tornados of identical spin at the precise locations with the precise velocities to counter the winds of the current twisters, then the only thing you can do is to get yourself to safety."

"But Twain—Mr. Clemens—Sam," Dean pleaded with the fading ghost. "What about your story? You said you had another story to tell. It would be a gift to literature, you said."

The face of the ghost of Twain turned towards him, though it was now little more than a distorted cloud of colors.

"Every resident of that city down there also has a story to tell," Twain's voice was garbled badly and out of sync with what was left of his mouth. "They can thank me... it's all thanks to me... I was born modest... now I shall die proud..."

The last few words were nothing but a whisper of static, and then the console erupted into bright orange flames. The last hint of Mark Twain's ghost faded away.

Instinctively, Dean turned away from the image of Tesla to hide the tears he didn't want to shed.

December 20
(3 Days Before Stormageddon)

Chapter 29

Langdon University seemed like a ghost town now, and in more ways than one. The brick buildings had been interred in a shroud of snow, and all activity seemed dampened into solemn silence. The few students who remained on campus flickered like ghosts in and out of the hazy limbo between the white sky and the white ground. Dean had never seen the school during a vacation, and to him it felt as hollowed-out as he did.

Once, he tried turning on the television in an attempt to distract himself with the motion and sound, but the news kept cutting in with reports of the devastation in Argentina. Atmospheric scientists claimed the weather was a one-in-a-billion fluke and called it the Storm of the Millennium. Experts argued about whether this was the result of global climate change, but nobody seemed capable of imagining that the twisters had been artificially induced. Even if Dean had come forward to post, tweet, and blog about the truth through every media outlet he could access, nobody would have believed him. Both of Ignacio's sky palaces had disappeared after the event, and if anyone found a broken drone or a piece of a mosquito pod, they wouldn't have connected it to the storm.

Although few would ever know it, the Institute shared in Buenos Aires' tragedy. Dean may have returned with Tesla as well as a blank Egg, but any joy the students might have felt was thoroughly overshadowed by grief when they saw the charred remains of Mark Twain's Egg that Dean had dutifully retrieved from the burned-out console. Their tears were followed by a lasting melancholy that hung in the air like a cold mist. Soap created an LED lantern that flickered like a candle and placed it at the base of Twain's bust in the entry hall. Several other students soon followed her example by leaving other gifts including books, flowers, and even an ancient typewriter. They soon began planning a memorial service, though they couldn't agree whether the burned-out Egg should be buried beneath a tombstone, placed in an urn, or respectfully launched into space.

Dean, on the other hand, went about the cold business of not feeling the pain. He told himself that he hadn't known Twain all that long. The loss had been necessary. Grief wouldn't bring him back. Dean also tried to convince himself that the ghost of Mark Twain hadn't really been a person, but he couldn't make that one work: the Twain he knew might not have been a human being, but he had felt like a real person.

As the hour of the memorial service drew near, Dean decided he could not go. He said he was too busy deleting all the emails from President Hart containing candidates' résumés. Nash had also called a few times to ask questions about what they had experienced, but it sounded like his superiors weren't taking his reports very seriously. Given that all of it had happened on foreign soil and that his only proof was the mosquito pod he had flown—and that pod was now in the custody of the Argentines—the best Nash could do was write it up in such a way that he wouldn't be sent in for a psychological evaluation.

At least Cake was safe. Dean knew this because Victor and Heidi had been Skyping with him so that they could take the next step in whatever they were doing to bring McKenzie back. For Dean, the possibility of their success in that project still felt like a lottery-ticket fantasy that he didn't dare hope for but couldn't make himself forget. Soon he might be able to see her and to speak to her. And, he reminded himself, to say goodbye. He had done all this so he could say the goodbye he had never had the chance to tell her. If it hadn't been for that possibility, no matter how slim, he might never have left his room.

He checked in with Victor's team often. Too often, maybe, because Victor started being short with him, so Dean knew he had to make himself scarce in order to let them work. That was how Dean found himself outside, wandering the far corners of the university, using the stinging cold to keep his mind off everything else. This trek brought him to the eastern reaches of the grounds, near the border of the arboretum that curled around half the campus. Out there was nothing but a few outlier dorms huddled beneath their blanket of snow and an army of trees encased in exoskeletons of ice. The only student in sight trudged silently up the hill, bobbling like a small black lump of coal against the nearly pure white background. As she made her way closer, Dean realized it was Soap, wrapped in her black lab coat with her purple-striped hair protruding from beneath a black knit cap. Rusty the Robot scuttled behind her, his six insectoid legs cutting easily through the snow although he frequently slipped on the ground underneath. His segmented metal tail was thrust forward over him, and at its tip a thick metal disk blazed with a red-hot heating element.

"Hi, Soap," Dean said, stepping close enough that he could feel the warmth of Rusty's heater. It must be nice to have a robot with a portable campfire to follow you around in this weather.

"You weren't there," Soap said.

It took him a moment to figure out what she meant. He had discovered that conversations with Soap could bounce around more quickly than an electron in one of her experiments. Here, he assumed she was talking about Twain's funeral.

"Did you decide what to do with the—what was left of the Egg? Did you decide to give it a grave or what?" Dean asked.

"Viking funeral," Soap said. "Probably not a good idea on a frozen lake, but it worked in the end. Why weren't you there?"

Dean tried to smile while he thought of what to say. He couldn't do it.

"I said my goodbyes," he said. "Everything else would just be words."

"My dad always said that funerals aren't for the dead, they're for the living."

Dean nodded. It was probably true, but this topic was starting to make the too-familiar black void pull his stomach inside out. He knew he had to change the subject before he was forced to discuss his feelings.

"How are things with you and Brett?" he asked.

Immediately, Soap folded her arms, allowed her shoulders to sag, and gazed down at her shoes—or at least to where her shoes would have been if they hadn't been caked in snow.

"I don't want to talk about it," she said.

"You sound like me."

"I followed your advice, but I don't think it worked."

"Advice? What advice?"

"You told me that when you want to break up with someone, you just ignore all their calls and texts. So I did."

"Oh, Soap," he had indeed said that, but he meant it flippantly. How could he explain that he had been joking without making her feel even worse than she already did?

"At first he texted me a lot," she said. "Then he texted that if I didn't care, he didn't care either. On the last day of classes, he wouldn't sit next to me like normal, and he wouldn't even look at me. I don't think I wanted to be his girlfriend, but I really did want to be his friend. Now I messed even that up."

Dean had to look away. He knew his cousin had never had many friends, but he had seen her intense loyalty to the people who were important to her. And now, his half-hearted attempt at dark humor had cost her one of those people.

For a long, miserable moment, Dean quietly watched Rusty's heat lamp melt the snow around Soap until it created small runnels of water that slid down the sidewalk behind her.

"It's re-freezing," Dean observed.

"What?"

"The snow melted by the heat lamp. It's refreezing on the sidewalk. This hill is steep, and the next person could slip and fall badly on that ice."

She looked surprised. "But I like the heat," she said after careful consideration.

"You have to do what you think is right," Dean said.

She grimaced and watched the water trickling away. Finally, she sighed and then rubbed her hands to warm them up. "Rusty: heater off," she said.

Then she turned to Dean. "I hate doing what's right."

"We all do," Dean said. "But we're worse off if we don't."

She jammed her hands under her armpits and trudged forward a few paces. Then she stopped and turned back around with the suddenness of whatever thought had occurred to her.

"That Ignacio guy is stupid, you know," she said.

"Come again?" Dean raised his eyebrows. "Not that I'm disagreeing with you. I just wonder why you said that."

"You told me Ignacio wanted to destroy big cities because they were the major producers of greenhouse gas, right? But on a person-by-person basis, big cities have smaller carbon footprints than other places. I have no idea where he's getting his facts, but he's way off."

"I didn't know that, but I doubt he cares. I think the whole environmental angle is just marketing hype for him."

"Oh," Soap said. "Well, in that case, he isn't stupid. He's just evil."

Dean couldn't help chuckling. "Again, no arguments here."

"You know," she said, "I was reading a report on how much dust got kicked up into the stratosphere by the Argentina super-storm. If Ignacio did that to more than a dozen cities in a month, he'd block out the sun."

"That sounds bad," Dean said.

"Seriously bad. Like, Armageddon bad."

"I'll keep that in mind."

She turned to go, but stopped once more.

"You're really quitting, aren't you?" she said it so quietly, her words were almost lost in the frozen air between them.

Dean couldn't bring himself to respond aloud, so he just nodded.

She turned, shoulders hunched, and kicked through the snow. It wasn't unusual for her to forget to say goodbye—just one of her quirks—but Dean got the feeling that this time she had consciously chosen not to say the word.

He stood there, allowing the breeze to bite his nose and cheeks while the cold crept through his double layer of socks. Tiny snowflakes salted the dry wind. Dean wondered if the white-gray clouds overhead would bring much more new snow or if they had already dumped their payload. It would probably be a simple thing for a meteorologist to predict, but Dean had no way to guess what conditions would lead to what results. Soap had once tried to explain the "butterfly effect," which, as best as Dean could understand, meant that if a butterfly flapped its wings in Singapore, the chain reaction could eventually cause a hurricane in Florida. Or, it might prevent the hurricane: nobody could tell, not even after it happened. All Dean knew was that if a little butterfly could eventually cause a hurricane, the devastating shockwaves of human beings stomping their way through the world every day must be just as unpredictable yet immensely more powerful. Dean supposed that this is what people meant by the word 'Karma:' it was the accumulation of chances that add up to destiny, and nobody can see it coming even while they're the ones causing it. Humans can see direct causation when it's as simple as one little metal ball of the Newton's Cradle striking another. If there's another ball in between, however, the whole thing becomes surprising, unexplainable, and unpredictable. Separate the cause from the result by more than a few steps and you have a situation like Soap running the heating lamp and, later, someone else breaking his tail bone. Or like the average commuter dumping all that carbon into the air and, later, polar bears going extinct. Too many steps, too far away, too much time between and the whole thing leaves the realm of human understanding.

The open air might have been making Dean philosophical, because he began to wonder how he fit into the whole mess. What kind of impact was he making on the world? He'd been instrumental in limiting the damage to Buenos Aires, so maybe he had helped. Then again, Ignacio had kicked off the attack early because of him. Maybe, if he'd left it alone, someone else would have been able to stop it before it started. Or maybe Ignacio would have been able to destroy his 60 cities instead of just one. It would never be possible to know.

Icy water began to seep into Dean's hiking boots, and he realized there was nothing like wet feet to put a stop to deep thoughts. The only thing more intrusive would be the buzzing of a phone.

Right on cue, his phone buzzed with a new text.

VICTOR: We're ready. Let's bring her back.

Chapter 30

"You need to keep in mind that this won't actually be her," Victor said as he steered Dean into a padded chair that looked like it belonged in a dentist's office. Instead of being surrounded by various water picks and adjustable lamps, however, this chair was encircled by racks of computer screens showing pulsating lines and graphs. Just behind the headrest squatted a small steel table buried in a mound of wires. Somewhere in there, Dean knew, lay the Egg that would hatch McKenzie's mind.

"If we're lucky," Victor went on, "It will look like her, sound like her, and it might even be able to carry on a passable conversation using knowledge buried so deep in your head that you won't even consciously remember it yourself. Ultimately, however, she will still be a simulation, not the real thing."

"I know, I know," Dean said. *But this will still be my chance to say goodbye.*

"I just want to be clear about this," Victor began clicking ribbons of wire into circuit boards. "She's not going to be like the ghosts of Tesla or Twain, either. They were one-to-one reproductions of a full human mind. What we're doing today is taking your memories and spinning them off into the memory counterpart of a blank mind, sort of like copying all the apps from one computer to another without changing the operating systems of either. Everything you know about McKenzie will be what she knows about herself, and nothing more."

"Will she still be, you know— self-aware? Conscious?"

Victor's brow furrowed. "That would be an easy question if anyone in the world could identify what, exactly, consciousness really is. She might be. Or she might not be, but still say she is because that's what your memories will program her to say. All I can tell you is that nobody's ever done anything like this—ever. There's a good chance it might not work at all. And, to be honest, I can't guarantee that it's safe." He paused and cleared his throat. "Given all that, do you still want to continue?"

"I didn't shave my head for nothing," Dean fought the urge to run a hand over his bare scalp. He had been shorn and sterilized only moments ago to allow Victor's machines to access his brain.

Despite his bravado, Dean suddenly found his heart hammering against his ribcage. He wasn't nervous for his own safety—though the thought of someone implanting brain-probes into his skull with a big drill wasn't exactly reassuring—but what really had him worried was McKenzie. Until now, it had never occurred to him to doubt that Victor's experiment would succeed. He'd flown down to Argentina and risked his life on the assumption that this crazy idea would work. Now that he was sitting in the chair and McKenzie's fate rested in someone else's hands, he felt helpless. If the experiment failed, it would be like losing her all over again.

Against his will, Dean's thoughts flashed to the moment he found her on the floor, auburn hair resting on her blue lips. He dug his fingernails into his palms to distract himself from that memory. He didn't want thoughts of her death to interfere with her second birth.

Dean tried to get comfortable as Victor lowered a strange helmet onto his head. The helmet's inside looked a little like a metal colander, all stainless steel dotted with countless holes but with wires running through at least half of them. The outside of the helmet radiated rectangular, green computer chips that were each at least nine inches long, making the whole thing look like some kind of demented mecha-flower.

"This helmet is going to drill one-thousand twenty-eight holes in your head," Victor explained. "The good news is that each of the drills is thinner than a human hair, so you won't feel much pain."

"How much is not much?"

"Remember the part about never having done this before so nobody knows? Your guess is as good as mine. But we need to drill in there so that we can implant the thirty million nano-probes that will spread throughout your brain and then monitor the electrical activity inside your head, especially in the hippocampus region where memories are mainly stored. If all goes well, we should be able to get a pretty clear picture of what you're thinking."

"And if all doesn't go well?"

"There's always a chance of hemorrhaging and catastrophic stroke," Victor said solemnly.

"I'm not afraid," as Dean said it, he realized he was gripping the armrests so tightly that he could feel the upholstery beginning to tear under his fingertips.

He relaxed his hands in hopes that Victor wouldn't see his emotional state. "I'm ready," Dean said. "I trust you. You'll make this work: you're the smartest person I know."

"I might be the smartest if you cut Soap's brain in half first."

That made Dean laugh, just enough to relieve some of the tension. Victor lowered the helmet into place, strapped it over Dean's head and chin, and began nudging it back and forth until it was perfectly positioned. The helmet felt sticky on Dean's bare scalp, as if it were coated with honey that smeared over every inch of his head from his eyebrows to his neck.

Victor sat down at a keyboard and made himself very busy. The helmet began to itch terribly, and Dean wanted desperately to reach up and scratch his head.

"How much longer before we get started?" Dean asked. "This thing is scratchier than a wool sweater my grandmother gave me for Christmas."

Victor chuckled as he worked. "We've already started. That itching you felt was the drills, but they're done now so it should start to get better. No headaches? That's a good sign. The probes are already inside you, and we're just waiting for them to circulate into place and start broadcasting. There aren't any pain receptors inside your brain, so you won't feel a thing while we wait."

Dean's phone rang. He reached for his pocket.

"Don't move your head!" Victor lunged out of his chair and snatched Dean's phone. "It says it's Agent Nash. I can put it on speaker if you want to talk to him."

"No," Dean said. "Let it go to voicemail."

"Isn't he your FBI friend? It might be important. Maybe it's about that tornado device or something."

"That's not my problem anymore," Dean would have shaken his head if it hadn't been for the helmet.

"Okay, then," Victor shrugged and put the phone on silent. "Let's get started with the first steps."

As the nano-probes began to percolate through Dean's brain—a process that was as painless as Victor had promised—he began the stroll down memory lane. For this phase of the project, Dean had collected every photo, memento, and item that he had shared with McKenzie or that might in any way remind him of her. To this, Victor and Soap had added images they had combed from the internet and their personal collections, all to help put Dean in mind of his late fiancé. The goal was to get his brain focused on her and nothing else, to dredge up every possible memory, so that the probes could map those thoughts and send them to the Egg.

Dean began to wonder how the Egg would present McKenzie. Would she be the fresh-faced college freshman he'd first met? Or would she be the older, wiser, cool-as-a-cucumber college professor she had become? People change over the years, and Dean had known her for almost half her life and had observed her in different situations and in different moods. However, his perceptions had always been colored by his own needs and expectations. Would the Egg stick with one version of her, or would it change her around, perhaps starting off as a young girl that aged as the real Denise McKenzie had aged? What would happen when her "ghost" became older than she had ever been—would it start over from the beginning or freeze her in time forever?

After an hour, the majority of the nano-probes had found their assigned locations and were sending back their signals. Now that they had a baseline for Dean's memories and the way his brain organized them, Victor injected him with something that he said would help him concentrate, essentially putting Dean into a highly suggestible state so that he could focus on McKenzie and nothing else. Dean wasn't so sure the injection worked, because he didn't feel like he had gained any mental focus. He simply wandered back through his memories, all out of order with one leading to the next by some irrelevant connection, and saw them as if they were playing out in front of him.

He recalled the first time he'd seen McKenzie at that freshman party, when he'd strutted up and used the line he'd memorized from his book of pick-up lines. The two ended up staying awake all night, talking about their families and their home towns, and he'd realized how different the world could be from what he'd always assumed. She seemed so much smarter than he was, and her family was so much wealthier than his, and her humor was as fast and sharp as an arrow. She was out of his league, he knew, and he assumed that she kept speaking to him only out of curiosity or kindness. When he thought they'd been alone for a mere hour or two, he saw the Eastern horizon burning with the Californian dawn and realized they had been talking all night. They had to part then—each had to go to class in the morning, not to mention that they needed to unpack and take care of all the other details of settling into a new life on campus. But just as they were saying their goodbyes, she grabbed him by the collar of his t-shirt and gave him a quick kiss. It was brief, but electric. It was enough to send him floating back to his dorm room feeling like he was living in the clouds.

They went on together like that, each day seeming to magnify the private gravity that drew them towards each other. He felt a passion like he'd never known, and she said the same. They studied together, ate together, pissed off each other's roommates together. Dean had to laugh at those memories. He knew her friends called him "the Neanderthal" behind his back. His friends called her "Dean's nerdfriend," and mocked her ignorance of all things related to sports. She never failed to come to his games and always listened politely when he talked about training routines or game-day tactics, but he knew it wasn't interesting to her. Whenever he tried showing off his athletic ability she would inevitably cheer "go, sportsball!" He never quite figured out if she was making fun of him for his sporting interests or of herself as an alien in that world. It became a code of theirs, used so often that the phrase "go, sportsball!" transformed into a kind of compromise, a way of showing that she cared about him but not about his hobby. To be fair, she spent far more time sitting at his games than he did in her study halls or watching the documentaries she enjoyed. Maybe he should have developed a funny little phrase of his own. Better yet, he could have paid more attention to her interests, but he never managed to do so.

Given their unlikely relationship, his teammates mocked him for being whipped and said it was throwing off his game. In retrospect, Dean knew this was nothing more than the idle social bluster common to all adolescent boys, but at that time he felt a powerful urge to prove them wrong. He started being more assertive in his relationship with McKenzie and made little shows of rejecting interest in live theater, botany, and all the other things she wanted to share. She said he could be a professor if he found the right topic and applied himself, but he didn't want that: he just wanted football, parties, and her.

Years later, she admitted she was being too controlling, and he knew too that he had been foolish, but after that first year their differences had begun to gnaw at the ties that bound them. Half way through their sophomore year, she sat him down to discuss the direction of their relationship, but he had changed the subject. He was never any good at talking things out, he said. They started fighting more often. Then they began griping to their friends. Eventually, they agreed to split. Two weeks after that, he saw her with Ignacio in the cafeteria, and that was the beginning of the end of his college career.

Without his wishing for it, Dean's memory flashed once again to another ending, the final ending: the moment he found her on the floor of his home, her auburn hair draped over her blue skin. Her eyes seemed so empty as she stared off into eternity. Something about that emptiness sucked him in and he'd never found his way out since.

Somewhere outside his head, he heard a medical monitor beep faster. Victor's voice floating in from far, far away, saying something about being concerned. But, at that moment, none of those things were real to Dean. McKenzie was the only reality. He forced his mind to other times, happier times.

They broke up, but they didn't stay broken. Those early splits set the pattern for them: sometimes they'd be apart for months, sometimes days, sometimes years. When they were together, life blazed with joy. When they separated, they each had time to grow. It got easier as they got older. He found what he was good at while she achieved her scholarly goals. All the teenage garbage about identity and peer judgment fell away into the nothingness it had always been, and they progressed towards the summer of their lives, their times together grew longer and the separations grew shorter. Dean never thought of himself as very smart, but even he could see the pattern: it would only be a matter of time before they stayed together permanently. He accepted it as surely as spring following winter. The final problem was nothing more than the fact that he didn't want to leave Los Angeles, and she didn't want to leave what he assumed was a cushy teaching position (though a few months of working in a school had taught him that teaching was never cushy). It was down to logistics, nothing more.

Then she appeared one day saying she was being followed, that she needed his help. He didn't want to remember that day, but Victor had told him not to omit any memory. He'd given her a ring with a little diamond. His grandmother's. He remembered McKenzie's face rush through a dozen expressions when she saw it. One of those, clearly, had been fear. Fear—of a final commitment to him, or of what was to come? Had she known what they would do to her? Of course not: she couldn't have known that within a few hours he'd find her there on the floor. Later, at the morgue, all he'd wanted to do was talk to her one more time, but instead had to face a world with nothing left of her but memories.

"Dean," Victor shook his arm. "Dean, wake up."

He blinked his eyes open, not realized he'd fallen asleep. No, sleep wasn't the right word, because he hadn't been dreaming, he'd been remembering. He hadn't even been aware that Victor had removed the brain-scan helmet, but now he could feel a cool draft along his bare scalp. He was about to ask Victor how many more times he would need to come back and put that helmet on before he could say his long-awaited goodbye—and then he saw her.

She stood by his chair, smiling down at him. She was cast almost entirely in shimmering green light and yet she looked exactly the way he'd remembered her. Subtle sparks of auburn light flowed along her emerald hair. And her eyes—the jade of those holographic eyes were the exact color they had been when she was alive.

"Hello," he said.

"Hello," she said back.

CHAPTER 31

"How many students do we have now?" McKenzie asked as she accompanied Dean through the decoy lab.

Dean couldn't keep himself from staring at her. True, she was green and slightly transparent, but it looked just like her, including the way her shoulder-length hair curled at the ends and how the sharp line of her jaw turned elegantly atop her long neck. When she was being wry, she smiled only with the left side of her mouth, which was just as he remembered her. When she walked, she moved so smoothly that she didn't bob her head—he had never noticed that before, yet it made him aware that this is exactly how she had always walked. How much more was there that he had failed to observe in the past? This time, he decided, he wouldn't allow the opportunity to slip away.

"Hey, Earth to Dean," she waved a hand in front of his face to snap him out of his daze. "How many students?"

"We're up to ten," Dean said, hoping she wouldn't be too disappointed by the low number.

"I can't wait to meet them." She stopped to study the branching pathways and swinging doors of Janet's rat maze. "I'm sure this place has changed a lot since I've been gone."

Of course, she wouldn't know how it had changed, because Dean hadn't seen it while the original McKenzie was still alive for comparison. Dean allowed himself to think that, given time, she could watch the lab change for herself and perhaps it would help her become her own person again. Perhaps not the same as the old McKenzie, but a brand new version. The thought that the world once again had a Professor Denise McKenzie, in any form, made Dean want to grab a microphone and sing karaoke at the top of his lungs.

"And what about my garden up on the roof?" she spun to walk backwards for a moment. She was as energetic and eager to explore her surroundings as he remembered her. It was easy to forget that she was just a computerized sprite.

"Oh, never mind," she said. "This is the middle of December, isn't it? It'll all be snowed over right now."

"If you want, we can work on it when it thaws," Dean said. "You just tell me where to dig. I'll be the hands, you be the brain. Just like old times."

Victor shot a worrying glance at Dean, and then cleared his throat. "Professor McKenzie," Victor said. "I'd like to ask you a question. Would you say that working in the garden is a goal of yours? Something you would choose to do if you didn't have to?"

"It seems like what I should do." She smiled and walked ahead of them to inspect the bank of 3D Printers.

"Another question for you, Professor," Victor scribbled notes as he spoke. "If the people don't like her robots, Soap will pack them up in boxes. What will Soap pack up in boxes?"

"Her robots," McKenzie said, seeming a little mystified by the question but more interested in the chemistry experiment Raskolnikov had left bubbling on the lab bench.

Dean pulled Victor aside. "What's with the weird questions?" he asked.

"According to the technical rules of grammar, I just said that Soap would pack the people into boxes, but no human being would make that assumption."

"Maybe they don't know Soap very well," Dean said. "But why did you ask it?"

"It's called a Turing test," Victor said. "I'm trying to see if I can detect a difference between her and a regular human based on her answers. A simple computer program would likely stick to the strict rules of grammar."

"So she got that one right," Dean smirked. "What about the garden thing? What was that question about?"

"If she picks her own goals and comes up with her own plans to achieve them, that would be one more sign of self-awareness. It would mean she's making her own decisions instead of following a pre-determined program."

Dean thought about this for a second. "Well, is she passing the test? Is she self-aware, like a person?"

"Too early to tell. I doubt it, but I haven't been able to rule it out yet. Either way, this has a lot of implications for brain science."

This was good enough for Dean. He returned to McKenzie's side and together they discovered Raskolnikov elbow-deep in something that looked suspiciously like a ballistic missile.

"This is another of our newest students," Dean told her. "Raskolnikov is our resident firebug. What are you working on, Ras?"

The boy spun, startled, looking back and forth between them in some combination of confusion and guilt. Then, as if putting on a mask, he offered a cherubic smile and stepped aside to reveal stacks of long metal tubes with red, pointed nose cones.

"Those look a lot like things that go boom," Dean said.

"Yeah, there may be some booming involved," Raskolnikov admitted. "Not quite military grade, but they'll light things up for sure."

"Ras. What did I tell you about explosives?"

"You said not inside."

"And?"

"And not outside, either." He spread his hands in a sort of pleading gesture. "But, D-Squared, I need to work on the guidance systems. I don't think I could hit anything smaller than a barn right now."

"And that's supposed to be reassuring?" Dean was in such a good mood, he couldn't bring himself to push the issue. When he looked over at McKenzie, he saw that she was laughing silently.

"There's an old farmhouse out east on 330th," Raskolnikov said. "It's just falling apart in some guy's field. Can I go light that up?"

"Only if you want to spend the next few years in jail," Dean said. "How about you test your guidance systems on missiles without the warheads?"

Raskolnikov looked genuinely befuddled. "I guess I could. But it wouldn't be as fun."

After they had resumed the tour, McKenzie leaned in close to Dean. "You make a good Dean of Students," she said.

He had to stop walking and stared at her. She'd said he made a good Dean—yet if her entire existence stemmed from his mind and his memories, then she should have shared his opinions, too. In his opinion, he was terrible at this job. If she disagreed, where had that thought come from?

"What?" Mckenzie said. "You're looking at me like I have lobsters crawling out my ears. What gives?"

"It's just—it's just amazing to hear you say that." Dean wanted to look back to see if Victor was taking notes, but he couldn't pull his eyes away. He had a sudden impulse to hold McKenzie's hand, but knew that his fingers would pass through hers. He was, however, carrying her Egg in its charger, so he gave that a little squeeze.

McKenzie led the way to the entrance hall where she studied the statue of Tesla briefly. Then she asked Dean to hold her Egg close to the photographs so that she could look closely at all the portraits of past Deans of Students.

"Photographs are harder for me to see than three dimensional objects," she said as Dean moved the Egg from one picture to the next. "Something about the photoreceptors on the surface of the Egg. They don't do as well with objects that don't move around. Oh, there's my picture. What a rotten photo! I hate that hairstyle. Don't know what I was thinking. Hey, where's your photo?"

She pointed to the picture frame, the one that should have held the photo of Dean Lazarchek but actually contained a picture of a pigeon.

Before he could tell her he'd never had one taken because he hadn't expected to be around that long, Topsy's front doors slid open and blasted the entrance hallway with a gust of Arctic air. Soap rushed in, kicking a thick pack of snow off her shoes. Rusty quickly followed her, his tail-tip carrying Tesla's Egg in a sort of electronic howdah. Behind them, the ghost of Tesla slid effortlessly out of the snow, his legs cycling as if he were walking although his feet never quite touched the ground.

"Guess what!" Soap exclaimed. "Professor Tesla is going to help me test my hypothesis about the antimatter—hey! You're bald!" She pointed at Dean's scalp. "I don't like it. And is this—is this McKenzie? Victor—you did it!"

"A qualified success," Victor said.

"You took Tesla out in public?" Dean said. "We can't let people see him."

"No big deal," Soap shrugged, snow dropping from her black coat as she did. "People have seen us do weirder stuff than this."

Dean was about to object when McKenzie spoke up. "I agree with Soap," she said. "It's not like we're handing over reactors to North Korea. Professor Tesla and I aren't anything but a flashy light show."

"You're more than that," Dean said, considering that she had yet again displayed an opinion that hadn't come from him.

"Hey, Dean," Soap said excitedly. "I hear you have thirty million nano-probes in your brain."

"Yeah, but it hasn't messed with me at all, banana snorkel toothpaste."

Soap looked confused but McKenzie laughed. It sounded like music to Dean.

"He's fine," Victor explained to Soap. "He's just joking. The nano-probes don't seem to have harmed him in any way."

"Oh, well, in that case," Soap jerked her thumb at the other ghost in the room. "Professor Tesla and I were also talking about a new way for you to interface with the jet suit. If we build it, will you give it a try?"

"The jet suit?" McKenzie looked at Dean. "That sounds dangerous."

"That's why I won't let her fly it," Dean said. "Frankly, I'm not so keen on ending up like that crash test dummy of yours, either. There are still bits of him lodged in the lab ceiling." A week ago, he would have volunteered to be the Institute test pilot and secretly hoped for a suicide flight, but today he didn't feel like taking risks.

"We can reasonably eliminate all danger," Tesla said. "All we need to do is establish a wireless connection between your brain and our machine."

"Isn't this guy the best professor ever?" Soap beamed.

"Fine," Dean said. "I just want a guarantee that I won't get splattered all over some building. I'll trust you as long as Professor Tesla oversees the project."

McKenzie nodded, and Dean knew he'd made the right call.

"Professor McKenzie," Victor asked. "I want to go back to the goal-setting inquiry. Can you tell me what you'd do if you wanted to rob a bank?"

She looked at him in bewilderment. "Why would I want to do that?"

"I don't think I like these questions," Dean said.

"It's just a mental exercise," Victor said. "Well, Professor? What would you do?"

"I really have no interest in robbing banks."

"I see." Victor jotted down more notes on his tablet. "May I ask what you want right now?"

"Right now? At this moment?" She looked at Dean. "I don't know. I just want to be here, in Topsy, with Dean and all my—his—students."

"Do you want to stay alive?" Victor asked. "Like, what if I were about to smash your Egg with a hammer. Would you try to stop me if you could?"

"Whoa, there," Dean placed a hand on Victor's shoulder and moved him back. "I think we're done with the questions now."

"It's for science," Victor said.

"Well, science is starting to sound pretty threatening." Dean looked over at McKenzie, but she didn't seem disturbed about it. "Listen, Victor, I think you should give us some time. Just her and me, okay?"

"But I—"

"Just her and me," he carried the Egg out of the room. "McKenzie and I need to catch up."

They left him in the decoy lab and returned to the residence where they fell into a long conversation. Dean wouldn't have thought it possible to talk for so long with the ghost of McKenzie, considering that everything she knew had come from something he knew. Yet they sat on the couch for hours catching up. Victor's memory probe must have gone incredibly deep, because she recalled things from their shared past that his conscious mind had completely forgotten. She named people who had lived in their dorm that he hadn't thought about in years, and she even insisted that when she first came out to visit him in California he was driving an old hatchback Subaru despite the fact that he felt certain he already had his red pickup by that point. They looked it up in an old photo and she was right.

Interestingly, she lacked any knowledge that didn't directly relate to her. Dean had to recount his whole adventure in Argentina, and she was as surprised as he had been to learn that it was none other than Ignacio Zabaleta, her former boyfriend, who had raided the Predecessor stations and used the teslanium to build several sky palaces and a weather machine.

"What did you ever see in that guy, anyway?" Dean asked as he sat back on the couch with a freshly microwaved mug of hot chocolate. Suddenly, he became self-conscious of drinking in front of her when she couldn't physically touch food. He pretended that it was too hot and set it down.

"I'll be honest about Ignacio," she said. "He was a rebound relationship. That's the pattern, right? We broke up from time to time and dated other people. But we always came back together eventually."

"Granite," he said, which was an old joke they had shared for years. It had begun with the phrase "I'll take that for granted," but they had shortened it to one word and mutated it until 'granted' became "granite." It was the kind of thing that wasn't funny to anyone except the two of them.

"Does it make you uncomfortable that I dated Ignacio?" she asked without warning.

"I can't blame you," he said. "I had lots of rebound girls." Then he added teasingly: "I mean *lots*. And they were all hot, too."

She threw a pillow at him—it was nothing more than the green image of a ghost pillow, yet it was realistic enough that he flinched. He tossed a couch cushion back at her, and it passed harmlessly through her and landed on the floor. At that moment, he would have given anything to be able to touch her shoulder.

"Spiderface," she said, another of their old jokes. This one meant that he was cutting his nose to spite his face.

"How am I a spiderface?" he asked. "At least none of my rebound relationships ever tried to use carbon footprints as a justification for mass murder."

He had to explain that one to her, because he hadn't mentioned Ignacio's supposed environmentalist motivations, or how this pretense really covered up profiteering in the construction industry. This led Dean into an attempt to explain how the sky palaces carried thousands of lightning drones, and each lightning-drone contained thousands of tiny thunder-drones. He didn't do a good job clarifying how it worked, but she seemed to follow along well enough.

"They change the weather with microwave emissions or something," he said, then found himself in the midst of a vast yawn. He glanced at his watch and found it was much, much later than he might have guessed.

"You need your sleep," she said. "Off to bed with you. Besides, it'll be nice not to have to listen to you badmouth my dear ex-boyfriend anymore."

He threw another pillow through her. "Okay, I'm going, I'm going. But I don't think I can sleep as long as I know you're around. I don't want to say good night. How do you end a date with a ghost?"

"Well, I can't grab you by the shirt and kiss you like the first time we stayed up all night talking," she said. "Instead, I'm going to shut myself off for eight hours so you can rest easy knowing you won't be missing a minute of my awesomeness."

"Well, that doesn't sound like much fun."

"Goodnight, Dean," she smiled gently. "I'll see you in the morning. Or the afternoon, as the case may be."

With that, she disappeared. It was abrupt, without so much as a pop or a puff of smoke.

He sat staring at the spot on the couch where she had been. Eventually, he got up, brushed his teeth, and checked his phone once before turning in. Agent Nash had left another message for him. Apparently, the military hadn't had any luck tracking Ignacio's sky palaces.

Not my problem anymore. Dean shut his phone off and lay down. For the first time in months, he slept soundly.

DECEMBER 21

(2 DAYS BEFORE STORMAGEDDON)

Chapter 32

"You can't defeat me," Soap glared at Dean with steely eyes as she whisked her broom back and forth over the ice. "This game is about physics. It's about angles of impact and friction coefficients. I can conceive of every possible interaction and—and—" She shuffled her feet as she spoke, and one went a little too far out to the side. This led to her flailing her arms before plopping onto her backside with an indignant grunt.

Dean stepped forward and simply nudged the ball around her. Raskolnikov charged in from the other side of the rink and made a kamikaze dive for the ball—his trademark move, and by now, utterly predictable. Dean knocked the ball into the wall and picked it up again on the rebound while Raskolnikov skidded past on his belly, waving his broom wildly but ineffectively. With both members of the opposing team floundering on the ice, Dean took his time and carefully pushed the ball towards the goal.

"Yes!" Collin shouted. "My team rules!" He opened his coat to reveal a set of ultra-lightweight speakers he'd sewn into the inside of his jacket, which now blasted Queen's *We Are the Champions.*

"Go, sportsball!" McKenzie cheered from the sidelines. Dean had set her Egg on the corner post of the outdoor rink so that she could see what was happening, but she was projecting her ghostly image outside of the rink walls like any normal spectator.

"We're playing broomball, not sportsball," Soap said to McKenzie. "I've never even heard of sportsball. What kind of game is that?"

"She calls everything sportsball," Dean explained. "It's her way of saying she doesn't care."

"It all looks the same to me," McKenzie said. "But just because I don't care about sportsball doesn't mean I don't care about you."

Beside McKenzie's ghost, Rusty had risen up on two of his legs so he could observe the rink through his glassy black eyes. Maybe he was filming the game or tracking it with radar, but he didn't move his head or react in any way to the events of the game. Dean looked at the two of them next to each other—ghost and robot—and decided that even Victor would have to admit that McKenzie was much more than a machine.

Collin returned the ball to the center line and set up for another round. Dean was starting to understand the appeal of broomball, and for a brief, sparkling moment the thought of outdoor sports in the middle of a Minnesota winter almost didn't seem crazy. All he had to do was try not to think about how his bald head felt so much colder than it used to, even when covered by a black wool cap.

"How about all three of you against me?" Dean proposed. "That might be a fair match."

"Yes!" shouted Soap.

"No!" shouted Collin.

"How about the other side swaps out a player and I join up?" Professor Heidi Bjelland declared boldly.

Dean was surprised to see her and realized she must have approached the rink while he had been concentrating on playing. She was dressed in a sleek white outfit that might have been an extra-thick track suit. She had a white hat pulled down over her ears, but not far enough to prevent her honey-colored hair from sneaking out to hang over her eyes. She looked flushed and out of breath. Judging by the trail of footprints she'd left behind her in the fresh snow, she had been out for an afternoon run.

"Are you sure you want to join us?" Dean asked her. "This sport leaves bruises."

"And blood bounces on ice," she said with bravado. "Unless you're too chicken?"

That made Dean smile. "Black hats versus white hats," he said, pointing from his hat to Soap's.

"My hat's green," Raskolnikov observed.

"Close enough," Heidi said. "You're on my team, buddy. The human sound-track can provide color commentary."

"Righteous!" Collin immediately played himself out to the sounds of German death metal.

The two new teams repositioned themselves with Dean and Heidi at the center of the rink, the ball between them. As soon as Collin shouted to begin, their brooms clacked and scuffled against each other. Dean managed to power the ball past Heidi, but she stayed right on him, harrying him so persistently that he had no choice but to pass to Soap.

Soap saw it coming, wound up for a big swing, and drilled it right towards the goal. It would have hit the net dead center, except that Raskolnikov stood directly in the way. For no good reason, he dove onto the ice, swinging his broom but missing completely. His momentum carried him face-first into the ball, and he hit it hard enough to send it skidding back down towards the other end of the rink.

Heidi slid in behind the ball, nudging it side to side to prevent Soap from getting close. Dean backpedaled to get between her and the goal. He swished his broom rapidly, ready to block either left or right, but instead she lowered her broom and shoved the ball forward with the bottom of the bristles, knocking it right between his legs. Before he could turn, she darted around him, hit the wall with her shoulder and shoved herself back towards the center of the ice. Dean spun around too fast and his feet might have flown out from under him if he hadn't managed to grab the rink wall. With a powerful yank that almost pulled the wall down, he managed to get himself upright and moving in the correct direction just in time to see Heidi sweep the ball into the goal, then turn around with her arms held high in a champion's stance.

Collin blasted *She's a Maniac*.

"Go, sportsball!" McKenzie called.

Dean found himself laughing. "Nice work, Bjelland," he said. "Let me guess: you were on the broomball team in a Siberian prison for twelve years. It's the only possible way you could be this good."

"You don't teach in Minnesota for most of your tenured career and not learn a thing or two about walking on ice," she winked. "That, and all the fish steroids they fed me in Siberia. What's the score, anyway?"

"Depends on how you count," Soap said. "We keep changing teams."

"Hey, wow, blood really does bounce on ice!" Raskolnikov climbed shakily to his feet, gently cupping his nose with his hand as a red streamer drizzled through his fingers.

Dean slid over to him as quickly as he could manage. The boy's nose didn't look broken, but it was bleeding enough to make a mess. He instructed Raskolnikov to pinch it and tilt his head forward.

"Where's the first aid kit?" Dean asked.

He was answered by silence from all the players.

"I've got some hand sanitizer," Soap began plucking small bottles from various pockets of her coat.

"No thanks," Dean said. "He can't exactly snort hand sanitizer. Ras, all you need is some applied pressure and a little clean-up. Let me take you over to the commons, you can wash your face, and I'll buy you some hot chocolate."

"How about a moga ladd-eh?" Ras said, which was as close as he could pronounce 'mocha latte' with a pinched nose.

"I'll go with you," Heidi glanced over at the green image of McKenzie. "I want to talk to you about the experiment, anyway. You two seem to be... doing just fine."

Dean had an impulse to grab the Egg and take it with him, but something in Heidi's voice read like a challenge. He suddenly felt the needed to show that he wasn't getting too clingy with a hologram. Instead, he told Soap to look out for the Egg. She nodded, scooped it up in her mittened hands, and clicked it into the charging dock she'd installed in Rusty's tail.

The Student Commons were only a few hundred yards away, and the going became much easier as soon as they made it to the plowed sidewalk. Raskolnikov was doing fine: his nosebleed had probably stopped by the time they exited the rink. Nevertheless, Dean told him to keep pinching his nose and bowing his head, just to be safe.

The weather was warming up noticeably. Dean must have been acclimatizing to the Minnesota, because he used feel that 32° and -32° both rated as 'way-too-freaking-cold' on the thermometer of his perception. Now, however, he could discern that his cheekbones didn't feel like icicles and the insides of his nose didn't freeze with each inhale, all of which marked a distinct warming trend. It might have had to do with the dense, dark clouds overhead that had grown much thicker during the time they had been playing broomball. These clouds were dark enough to threaten rain, which meant it was probably good that the game had ended when it did.

"As you could see back there," Dean said to Heidi, "The experiment with McKenzie was a complete success. Victor tells me he never would have been able to decipher all that information about the Egg without your translations. I can't thank you enough for that."

She said nothing as she grabbed the big brass handle to open the door to the Student commons. Raskolnikov scurried off to the restroom, and Dean and Heidi went to the snack bar to order hot drinks. As they waited for their order, Dean pulled off his hat.

"Your head!" Heidi said.

Dean ran his cold fingers over his naked scalp. "My sacrifice in the name of science. You like it?"

"It makes you look tough," she said. "Like Mr. Clean."

"Mr. Clean?" He laughed. "That's me, all right: tough on dirt. Also, aside from the fun of a good, old-fashioned brain probing, I'm going to save tons of money on shampoo. You should give it a try."

"Actually, I did shave my head once," she said, unconsciously tousling her short yellow locks.

"No way," Dean said. "Bald? You?"

"This was back in college. It was a soccer team thing."

"I want pictures," Dean said.

She smirked in a way that said he would need a court order before she released the photographic evidence.

They collected their drinks and sat down by one of the big bay windows. From where he sat, Dean couldn't see the ice rink or the students he had left back there, but he could see most of the classroom buildings that ringed the quad. Everything was dusted over with a layer of pristine new snow. With so few students on campus, the only thing that moved was some little creature that buzzed past the window so quickly Dean couldn't see what it was. A hummingbird, maybe. Briefly, he wondered why the humming bird hadn't flown south for the winter.

Dean's phone buzzed again. With a sigh, he read the text.

NASH: We really need to talk about Zabaleta. Please call ASAP!

Dean folded up his phone and turned to look back out the window. It was too nice a day to worry about things that weren't his responsibility any more.

"It's nice to see you like this," Heidi said.

"Like what?"

"Happy. Playful. Until today, I wasn't sure you knew how to smile," she quickly sipped whatever vanilla concoction she had ordered.

"Yeah, well, I'm just glad the experiment turned out okay." Dean took a gulp of coffee. He took it black, because anything more fancy seemed too girly to him.

"I'm worried, though," Heidi said. "I'm not sure the experiment turned out the way you think it did."

"What do you mean? McKenzie's here, and she's better than we thought possible. Victor pulled off a miracle of science, and you helped bigtime."

"It's not the science part I'm worried about. It's the psychological part."

He looked at her intensely, deliberately stretching the moment into awkwardness.

"Okay, sorry," she said. "It's none of my business."

"Never stopped you before. So, go on. Now that you brought it up, you have to explain it."

She sighed. "You remember that day you came to my office? You asked about a painting on my wall."

"Yeah, I remember. It was a creepy picture of a guy in his underwear with a harp and a bunch of ghosts chasing him."

"It wasn't his underwear and it wasn't a harp. It was a toga and a lyre."

"I remember now. You promised you'd tell me the story later. I'm going to guess that later is now?"

"That's a picture of Orpheus, the demigod of music and a man who was passionately, madly devoted to his true love, right up until she died."

"That was a fun story. Thanks, Professor."

"That's only the beginning. He was so torn up by his loss that he roamed the Earth, so the story goes, until he found the gates of the underworld, where the spirits of the dead go to live in eternal gloom. He traveled down to find Hades, the King of the Dead, and he played music so beautiful that Hades told Orpheus he could take his wife back to the world of the living."

"I still don't see your point," Dean turned to look out the window.

"Hades made one condition," Heidi went on. "He said that she would follow Orpheus out of the underworld and back to the land of the living, but if Orpheus looked back to see her on the way she would return to live forever among the dead."

"So of course he did. Look back, I mean. Right?"

"He couldn't help it. It was doubt that drove him to it. His wife was nothing more than a spirit so her footfalls made no sound, and Orpheus had no way of knowing whether she was really behind him or not. Then, in one moment of inattention, one careless second, he glanced over his shoulder, and in that instant he lost her forever."

"I see what you're saying," Dean tapped the table impatiently. "You're trying to tell me that I'm Orpheus and that I can never really bring McKenzie back to life."

"If the toga fits," she shrugged. "Then again, maybe she's been good therapy for you, judging by the fact that you're not growling and depressed and falling asleep during meetings anymore."

"But?"

"But nothing. Except, okay, maybe just one small 'but.' I just don't want you to look back one day and be surprised that it's not actually her, that she's really gone. I don't want you ending up like Orpheus."

"How did he end up? Sad and alone, I'm guessing."

"Yes. And then a gang of women tore him limb from limb and threw his head into the ocean."

"Yeah, okay, I'll do my best to avoid that one." Dean tried to make a joke of it, but it fell flat.

He wished that Raskolnikov would hurry up and get here and give Dean an easy excuse to change the topic. Instead, Dean turned to look out the window once more. The little creature that had been zipping over the snow-covered walkway, now flashed past the window in the other direction, flying like a dart above what would become a flower bed whenever the sun found its way back to the Midwest. After another few seconds, the little creature zipped back again, almost along the exact path as before.

Dean still couldn't see what the creature was, but he now recognized that it was a lot smaller than a humming bird. A dragon-fly perhaps, or maybe a gigantic, gray bee. Were there such things as gray bees? Were there any insects that could fly around in sub-freezing weather?

"Excuse me," Dean got up and went for the door.

"Dean," Heidi said. "I'm sorry. I didn't mean to—"

He stepped out in the cold just in time for the little gray thing to shoot past him again. Now he could hear a hissing as it went by, and saw that it left a puff of steam and shallow trench in the snow behind it.

As quickly as he could, he whipped off his jacket and flung it like a net into the buzzing thing's path. It darted sideways too quickly to be captured, but the maneuver slowed it down enough to allow Dean to get a better look.

It was small and plastic, hardly bigger than a grape, with dual rotors whirling at its top.

A thunder-drone, just like the ones Ignacio had used to create the tornado cluster in Buenos Aires. It could only mean that Ignacio had sent it here, probably accompanied by a million others just like it.

As soon as he realized that, Dean heard a distant howl of jet engines coming down from the dark clouds.

Mosquito pods—heading right for Topsy.

Chapter 33

Dean cursed himself for a fool—he should have known Ignacio would come for Tesla and McKenzie. Without those Eggs, the weather machine wouldn't work, and Ignacio wasn't one to give up easily.

McKenzie's Egg was out with Soap. It would be safe as long as Ignacio's men didn't know where to find it. Tesla, on the other hand, was still inside Topsy, so Dean sprinted in that direction. He heard Heidi call out behind him, but he didn't have time to explain. Instead, he fumbled with his phone as he ran, dialing Victor.

"Hello?" Victor sounded groggy.

"You at Topsy?" Dean demanded.

"No, I'm at home. Haven't slept in a week."

Dean cursed and slapped the phone shut. Without Victor, nobody would be on hand to operate the defensive systems. The only things protecting the Egg were Topsy's front doors. Granted, the building was specially designed to withstand anything short of a dynamite blast, but Ignacio was an alum and would have known that. He might have a way to hack the electronic lock—or he might simply use dynamite.

Dean pushed himself to run faster, but the deep snow slowed him down until his legs felt like lead. Then, as if someone had turned on a faucet, rain spilled from the sky in a violent torrent. His jeans became drenched and tightened around his thighs like steel bands. His jacket guzzled in the water and weighed him down until he felt like he was wading through a swamp.

Thunder rolled, and Dean could see the first snakes of white lightning slithering through the black mountain of clouds that seemed to be growing straight up from Topsy's roof. He had expected to see four mosquito pods blazing away at the front door with their rail guns. Instead, he counted only two pods, both up on the rooftop garden, and their pilots working outside to set up some kind of machine on a tripod.

Only two, Dean thought. Mosquito pods came in sets of four, leading him to wonder where the other two pods might be. Perhaps, with a little luck, these were the only ones Ignacio had salvaged after his defeat over Buenos Aires.

Each pilot wore an assault rifle slung over his shoulders, but they were engrossed in whatever they were doing and hadn't seen Dean. Without further thought, he dashed from the tree line towards the door. He hadn't take two steps before the men up on the roof turned and covered their ears. A split second later, a blinding flash and a massive noise hit Dean like a fist, almost knocking him off his feet. His ears rang and he had to blink the spots out of his vision. Whatever they had used, it wasn't dynamite, but it looked like it would do the job all the same.

Now the thugs up on the roof had spotted him and wasted no time unslinging their rifles. Still a little shaken, Dean madly dove for the building's overhang while bullets made small white geysers in the snow behind him.

As soon as he was under the eaves, the front doors obligingly swung open for him. He raced through the entrance hallway, his mind scrambling to predict their next move. He had to assume that whatever explosive they'd used had successfully opened up the door to his residence, which meant they were inside his living room right now. Their disadvantage was that they couldn't know where to find the Egg. They might start their search by ransacking his room, but Ignacio was smart, so he would have been more likely to order his men to get to the underground lab as quickly as possible in order to seize control of the building's systems. Once they held the underground lab, they could search the rest of the building at their leisure.

That gave Dean a chance to get to Tesla's Egg first. But where was it? He couldn't remember where he had last seen it. If it was down in the underground lab, Ignacio's men would likely get to it before he could, but he might be able to ambush them on their way back up. But wait—he remembered that the students had worked out a sharing schedule for Professor Tesla. Soap had him yesterday, and tomorrow would be Raskolnikov's turn—Dean remembered that because he was dreading Tesla helping perfect the guidance systems for those rockets. Victor was sleeping at home, Janet had said she didn't need a turn, and Speed had complained about having to wait until next week, so today Tesla must have been assigned to... Collin.

Dean veered towards Collin's work station. Sure enough, Tesla's Egg sat on the counter, its charging dock glowing softly beneath it. Dean grabbed it just as he heard a shout from the stairway. Gunfire ripped through the flasks and beakers behind him. He leaped sideways and pressed his back against a freezer unit, then listened to the gunmen on the stairs shouting back and forth in some language he didn't recognize.

Dean's phone made a kind of whisper as Tesla's ghost tried to tell him something.

"What?" Dean said as soon as he had the earpiece in place. He had to turn up the volume because his ears were ringing from the noise of the guns.

"I said they have some kind of selective hearing guard," Tesla said. "It protects their ears from the sound of their guns but not their speech. This is nice for me, because they are speaking Serbian, my native language."

"What are they saying?" Dean gritted his teeth as another volley of bullets slammed into the freezer behind him. "Are they saying anything useful?"

"Yes," Tesla said. "The first man said: 'you go left while I pin him down.' The other man grunted. The grunt is not a word in Serbian, but I take the meaning to be an agreement with the first man."

Dean grimaced. Ignacio's men were executing basic gun-fighting strategy: if Dean moved, the first gunman would fill him with holes. If he stayed put, the second guy would circle around until he had a clear shot. Either way, Dean was destined for an unwanted lead injection if he didn't figure out a way to change the game.

As if the situation weren't bad enough already, the door to the entrance hall opened and Raskolnikov bounced blithely through, utterly unaware of what was going on.

"D-Squared?" he called. "Where'd you go—"

Dean sprinted from his hiding spot and dragged Raskolnikov to the floor. It knocked the wind out of the boy, but this was still kinder treatment than he would have received from the bullets that quickly followed. This left them in a more vulnerable location than Dean's previous cover, with only a few flasks and a lab bench between them and the gunmen.

Raskolnikov's eyes widened in surprise, but Dean shushed him. The fact that the gunmen didn't quite know where they were was the only reason they were still alive.

"They can locate us," Tesla said. "Rather, they can locate me. From their discussion, I gather that they have some kind of device that can track me, much as my dear friend Sam tracked me inside the *Tlaloc*."

So that was it, then—Dean had no escape. He couldn't leave the Egg behind, but to carry it was death.

Dean tossed the Egg up and down in his hand a few times to test its weight. "Tesla, I've been meaning to ask—how fragile are you?"

"If you are referring to the physical stone you are holding, I should survive a reasonable impact," the ghost said. "But please do not strike me with a sledgehammer."

"Wouldn't dream of it." Dean flung the stone out across the floor so that it bounced between table legs like a pinball until finally coming to rest near Collin's massive bank of speakers.

"Ouch!" Tesla exclaimed indignantly.

Both gunmen, alerted by the sound of the stone, instinctively fired in that direction.

"Stay here!" Dean barked at Raskolnikov, then sprinted for new cover, hoping that either he or the Egg would draw attention away from the boy. The bark of the assault rifles told him it had worked, and bullets chewed through the desk around his new hiding place.

"Tesla!" Dean shouted between gun bursts. "Distract them!"

"How?"

"They don't know you're a ghost, right?"

It was all Dean had time to say before another volley smashed through the cabinets above him, raining glass shards and wood chips down onto him.

Then it stopped, and there were some surprised-sounding Serbian words from back in the lab. The green ghost of Tesla had appeared.

Dean risked a glance. The image of the ghost wandered out into the middle of the laboratory and waved his arms. He was greeted by several rounds of gunfire, followed by a burst of harsh shouts.

"They say not to waste more bullets on the glowing image of Nikola Tesla," the ghost said through Dean's earpiece. "Oh, how flattering—they recognize me! I knew I could rely on my fellow Serbians. Such intelligent, gracious people."

"Keep in mind that these particular Serbians are the bad guys in this scenario," Dean muttered. "Can you see where they are? Can you tell me where they're going?"

"One has taken a position behind some tables and in front of a large set of speakers. The other is behind a—oh, he just moved. He is now behind the cooking station."

Dean knew the cooking station was only two aisles over from where he now hid. He was trapped like a fox in a hole, and it was only a matter of time before they dug him out.

"Wait a minute," Dean said. "You said the first guy was in front of those speakers?"

"Correct."

"And you can use your electromagnetic magic to activate machinery, right?"

"I have a limited ability to influence electronics. Speakers and other machines that operate with simple magnets are especially easy for me—"

"I need you to crank those speakers up to full volume."

The ghost paused for a second. "They go up to eleven," he said. "Why would someone use a scale that peaks at a prime number?"

Another volley of bullets exploded around Dean.

"Pump up the volume!" he shouted. "Now! Now!"

There was a moment's delay, then the air in the warehouse rippled with a rising pitch coming from the speakers. Dean took this as a cue to plug his ears.

The thunderclap from Collin's special concussion woofers blasted everything nearby into the air. This was followed by a short series of follow-up crashes and a shattering sound across the room.

"You should have seen that!" the ghost said, a hint of laughter in his voice. "The gentleman in front of the speakers was flung bodily through the laboratory and collided with a cabinet of glassware. Most spectacular!"

"Is he out?" Dean demanded. "Just tell me if he's going to shoot me or not!"

"He is most decidedly no longer a threat."

"Where's the other guy?"

"He has not moved. He seems confused. Wait—he is moving now. Behind the centrifuge cart. He is peering along the sights of his rifle, covering an arc of approximately 45 degrees—"

"What direction is he facing?"

"Thirteen degrees west of magnetic north."

Dean had to think about that for a second, but worked out that the gunman wasn't facing the right direction. "Keep telling me where he's looking," Dean instructed as he slipped behind a bank of microscopes. He moved obliquely around and behind where Tesla said the gunman had positioned himself.

"He's moving again," the ghost said. "I think he's following your noise."

"Facing?"

"West. East. Now west again. He is moving past you. At this moment, he is on the other side of the shelving unit behind which you are hiding."

Dean shoved hard at the shelf. It tore free of its bolts and fell in a tremendous rain of glassware that might have been considered deafening if it had not followed Collin's booming speakers. As it crashed down, Dean drove his shoulder into it with all his strength to slam it like a bolder into his enemy. The gunman managed to get clear of the worst of the impact—he must have had the reflexes of a cat—but he couldn't dodge both the shelf and Dean at the same time. Dean seized the carry-bar atop the rifle with one hand and gripped the stock with the other. With a swift upper-cutting motion, he swung the butt up into the man's chin, felt the sharp reverberation of cracking teeth and saw the man's eyes glaze over. Dean yanked the weapon away and aimed it back at its owner, but this was clearly unnecessary. The man was out cold.

"Impressive," Tesla said.

"Ras!" Dean yelled. "Ras, you okay?"

The boy shouted that he was all right, so Dean busied himself securing his enemies before they woke up. He found a roll of duct tape by Collin's sound equipment and had the two gunmen hog-tied in under a minute. Then he dashed up the stairs to his residence.

A blast of cold air hit him as soon as he opened the door. The exit to the rooftop garden—the glass door that was actually not glass but really incredibly strong, transparent carbon nano-tubes—hadn't been blown open so much as melted away. The door was brown and burned and the edges had been peeled back into four scorched sections like mutated pizza slices.

Dean stepped through the melted gap. Out on the rooftop garden, the two mosquito pods squatted, their engines still casting up white steam amid the dark rainfall, but there were no more enemies nearby. Dean peered around the sky and saw two more of the pods zipping away to the east. Their trajectory took them towards a blurry, white slash in the sky.

That blurry patch had to be one of Ignacio's sky palaces hiding behind its active camouflage. Dean almost jumped into one of the abandoned pods and went after it, but he didn't like his odds in a two-against-one dogfight. Not only that, the sky palace was almost impossible to see even while he was looking right at it, and, unlike in Buenos Aires, they would be ready for him.

"Raskolnikov!" he shouted as loud as he could without taking his eyes off the blurry spot in the sky. "Ras! Get up here—now!"

A moment later the boy trotted through the door.

"What's going on?" Raskolnikov asked.

"Those rockets you were working on. Go get them."

"Why? What're we going to do?"

"We're doing what you do best. We're going to light 'em up."

CHAPTER 34

Raskolnikov retreated downstairs to gather his equipment while Dean kept watch on the sky palace. Its remained nothing more than a faded smudge against the gray backdrop of clouds, and more than once he had to wonder if he was still looking at the right spot—or if he'd ever seen it at all. Gradually, he realized that it was getting larger, coming his way, although it was so well camouflaged that it had to arrive almost directly above Topsy before he could be sure.

The wind picked up and the rain intensified, so Dean stepped back inside the burned-out doorway of the residence. The airship was close enough now that he could feel the ominous vibration of its engines in the air. Were they coming to board their enemies, like a ship full of pirates? If so, how many men would Dean need to repel?

The other two mosquito pods zipped out from behind the blur in the sky and streaked forward towards him, raking the sides of the building with rail-gun fire. The noise of the impact was thunderous, but the walls held strong—whatever they had used to cut through the rooftop door, it had been something more than a rail gun.

Rasknolikov burst back into the residence, his arms full of his homemade missiles. He tripped on the corner of the carpet and the rockets clattered to the floor, bumping and slamming into each other as they rolled. One of them bounced off of Dean's foot and came to a stop with its "High Explosives!" warning label facing him.

"Be careful!" Dean said. "We don't want anything to go boom—"

The building shook with a humongous roar that drowned out all other sound. Instinctively, Dean squatted down and covered his ears until it was over. Then he risked a glance outside to see the turrets blazing with blue sparks and red flames. In that instant, Topsy shook with another tooth-rattling, ear-splitting series of impacts. One corner of the rooftop garden erupted into a red, dusty cloud as the brick façade disintegrated under the fusillade. Nearby grass, snow, and rows of dormant rose bushes exploded, launching tiny chunks of wood and brick to ricochet off what remained of the safety glass of the rooftop door.

They weren't planning to board Topsy, Dean realized. They were planning to level it.

"Don't worry!" Raskolnikov shouted loud enough to be heard through ringing ears. "They'll never break Topsy with that level of firepower. Believe me, I've tried!"

That didn't sound reassuring. Still, the guns were rapid-fire weapons, and Dean knew from his army days that rapid-fire usually meant anti-aircraft or anti-personnel, not bunker-busting.

"MECHANICAL SCIENCE INSTITUTE," a voice thundered from a loudspeaker somewhere on the sky palace. "YOU HAVE TEN SECONDS TO SURRENDER THE EGG OR BE DESTROYED."

Dean gritted his teeth and considered is options. Hand over Professor Tesla and leave the world's cities to the mercy of a pompous madman, or allow them to keep shooting at Topsy until they hit something vital?

"You said your guidance system couldn't hit anything smaller than a barn," Dean said to Raskolnikov. "That floating ship of fools looks about as big as a barn to me. Ready for some target practice?"

A huge grin crept across Raskonlikov's face. "Cover your ears," he said, and placed the first missile in a metal launching rack, then stepped back, ducked, and pressed a button on his phone.

The sheer force of the blastoff crushed Dean against the wall. For an instant, he thought it had exploded where it stood. It had actually only scorched away the carpet clear down to the floorboards, overturned his coffee table, and shattered his television. Patches of flame still crept along the couch and chewed at the corners of his picture frames. But when Dean looked out the window, he saw the crimson streak of exhaust curving upward over Topsy's garden and then exploding in a great, golden ball of fire at the dead center of the blurry patch in the sky.

In the wake of the impact, the sky palace's active camouflage sputtered and flashed a kaleidoscope of mismatched images before shorting out entirely. Now, the ship's angular black hull stood perfectly visible against the white backdrop of clouds. It rocked with the force of the impact, tilted far enough for two of its star-point tips to dip below the tree line next to Topsy amid a flurry of ripping branches and spraying snow.

"Direct hit!" Raskolnikov whooped as he loaded another rocket.

Some of the sky palace's gun turrets fired again, but they were disorganized now, the gunners seemingly unable to aim properly. Two of the turrets swiveled wildly at the sky, perhaps mistakenly searching for whatever had hit them. Another turret locked onto Topsy and unleashed a sustained rain of projectiles at the rooftop, cutting down the snow-capped bushes and tearing the landed mosquito pods into chunks.

"Ras!" Dean called. "Hit 'em again!"

The boy did, quicker this time, and before the palace had stabilized itself from the first impact, the second rocket slammed into its underbelly. Dean watched as the massive vehicle lurched backwards, shedding a huge chunk of its hull onto Topsy's back lawn. The turrets went silent and the palace began to climb higher in the air, limping off to the west in evident retreat.

They were hurt, but they weren't beaten yet. A hatch opened beneath the palace and three bodies dropped into the air below. Dean's stomach lurched as he watched them plummet, but instead of hitting the ground as he had feared, they slowed in midair, then sprang back up again and flew in his direction. Flight packs—Dean recognized them more from the way they moved than from the actual shape of the objects strapped to the troopers' shoulders.

"Keep firing!" Dean instructed Raskolnikov, then ran out onto the roof.

The flight pack troopers swooped towards him, close enough now for Dean to see that they were dressed head-to-toe in black leather and wearing motorcycle helmets with reflective visors.

The rail guns had ripped open the garden shed, scattering tools all around. Dean scooped up the nearest one, a broken sledge hammer, and tested its weight in his hands. The head of the hammer had been snapped off, but the shaft was still heavy and thick. He swung it like a baseball bat into the helmet of the first flight pack trooper to come within reach. The blow landed with a homerun crack, and because the flight pack kept the man essentially weightless, he sailed clear off the roof and into the arboretum, limp and unconscious.

The second man landed behind Dean and grabbed his arms, while a third seized him and the hammer shaft from the side. He struggled with them, sweeping his feet against theirs in an attempt to trip them, but their flight packs kept them upright no matter what Dean did.

During the struggle, the man in back slid his arm around Dean's throat and clamped down with a chokehold. Dean lunged backward as hard as he could, but only managed to slide himself and his attacker a few feet across the snow. He could see Raskolnikov standing inside the residence next to his rocket, wide-eyed and unsure of what to do. If he fired the missile, it could knock Dean off the roof or even kill him outright as it passed. But if he didn't fire it, the sky palace might sail away to safety, and the troopers might kill Dean anyway.

"Fire!" Dean tried to shout, but the chokehold cut off his words along with his circulation. He planted his boot in the center of the second man's chest and shoved off, giving himself just enough space to seize his choker's elbow and attempted to flip him over his shoulder. He should have been able to execute the move easily, but once again the flight pack prevented it. He might as well have been trying to judo-throw a brick wall. Next, Dean tried twisting ferociously to drive his elbows into his attacker's ribs. This was a desperation move and shouldn't have worked, yet it managed to free his neck long enough to take one breath in and then shout back at Raskolnikov.

"Fire! Fire!"

The man behind Dean abandoned the chokehold and threw him down, and then both troopers were on him again, pounding at him with their fists and boots. But not for long, because Raskolnikov had apparently decided that if he didn't fire the rocket, Dean wasn't going to survive much longer anyway.

The missile ripped past them, flinging all three men through the air like candy from a ruptured piñata. One of the troopers flew clear off the roof and ended up hovering twenty feet away from Topsy. The other was knocked back hard into a wall. Dean skidded face first through the snow before managing to roll to a stop. By the time he climbed back to his feet, the second trooper had already regained his equilibrium and rushed back at him. Dean caught the man as he approached, spinning to use his own momentum against him.

These flight packs were excellent for frictionless speed, but now Dean's ability to plant his feet on the ground meant he had the advantage. The other man could do little but scrape his toes on the snow while Dean dug in and charged forward. Placing one hand under the chin of the attacker's helmet, Dean slammed him into the brick wall with a freight train's momentum. He felt the man weaken, his helmet barely protecting him from a clean knockout.

Dean spun to hurl this trooper at the other one. The collision wasn't enough to do much harm, but it did tangle the two up for a moment, and Dean used the distraction to leap back through the hole in the window into the residence.

Raskolnikov rolled another missile into the launching just as Dean reached him.

"Give me the button," Dean took the phone and held his thumb over the trigger, ready to fire the minute either of the flight-pack troopers appeared in the doorway. Launching a missile at a human being would be like swatting a fly with a speeding car, which is why Dean had seized the trigger. If these missiles were going to kill someone, Dean wanted it on his conscience, not on his student's.

Outside, the sky palace sank into the arboretum like a broken galleon going under the waves. Flames spurted from half a dozen gashes in its angular black hull, and its slow descent belied its massive bulk. Three seconds after the sky palace disappeared into the trees, an echoing boom rolled out of the arboretum and a plume of blue smoke rose above the trees.

The flight-pack troopers hovered like nervous hummingbirds as they watched the palace sink. Then, without a word to each other, they leaped off the roof and bounded away.

"We did it!" Dean slapped Raskolnikov on the back. "We won!"

The boy looked too stunned to talk, but to Dean, the victory was clear: they had shot down the sky palace, driven off Ignacio's men, and saved Tesla's Egg.

Dean's ears still rang from the gunfire and rocket explosions, and he envied whatever decibel-dampener Ignacio's men had been using to protect their hearing from the sounds of their own rifles. After a moment of working his jaw and popping his ears, he could hear his phone ringing.

He guessed it must be Nash and tried to think of how to answer the phone with some dry, cool quip. Maybe something along the lines of, "I would have called you sooner, but I had some things up in the air."

But when he took out his phone, he saw that it was Soap's number, and that she'd called six times while he'd been fighting. When he flipped his phone open, she didn't wait for him to say hello.

"They got her," she sobbed.

"What? Soap, slow down. Tell me what you mean."

"They got her. They had guns and I couldn't stop them, and now they have her."

"Who?"

"They got her Egg! They took Professor McKenzie!"

DECEMBER 22

(1 DAY BEFORE STORMAGEDDON)

CHAPTER 35

"Looks like it was a vicious attack," Nash said, each syllable emerging from his mouth as a cloud of steam in the cold air. They were tromping through the arboretum towards the crash site of the sky palace, and Dean's mood was growing fouler and fouler with each step.

"I saw the wreckage," Nash went on. "You're lucky you survived."

"I don't feel so lucky," Dean mumbled. One of the Eggs was gone, Topsy House had been severely damaged, and he'd spent the better part of the last twenty-four hours answering stupid questions from investigators representing every federal agency he had ever heard of and a few he hadn't. He hadn't even met with President Hart yet, so the worst was still to come. The whole situation seemed like a joke compared to the gnawing realization that McKenzie had been stolen. She had come back to him so briefly, and now Ignacio had taken her from him, just like when they were in college. Dean felt as helpless and as foolish now as he had back then.

Nash led Dean through the secure perimeter surrounding the crash site in the arboretum. This, Dean noted, was the second military barricade Langdon University had seen this year, and they had only just finished the first academic quarter.

A half a mile farther into the forest, they had to stop at yet another checkpoint. All these checkpoints were absolutely worthless, Dean mused darkly. Ignacio's men had already escaped in their flight packs and mosquito pods, right after hitting the "panic button" that erased all their hard drives and blew up most of the valuable components on board. Then the Institute students had swept through the wreckage and stripped out every remaining ounce of teslanium and removed the antimatter reactor. They had done all that and were back at Topsy enjoying hot chocolate and marshmallows before the sheriff had located the wreck and set up the first line of yellow tape.

Dean hadn't visited the crash site yet, but he wasn't surprised by what he saw. It looked like a dropped pie: all bent up, with globs of broken equipment hanging out of the holes in its hull. It had dug a short, but deep trench through the forest when it had crashed, either knocking the trees out of the ground by their roots or else impaling itself on them. Without its active camo, the painted name of the ship was clearly visible on the crumpled hull: the *Indra*. So this was Ignacio's third sky palace, different from the two Dean had encountered above Buenos Aires.

"We're going to be extremely thorough," Nash gestured to the agents in blue FBI jackets who swarmed all over the downed airship like ants on a bear's carcass. They had taken measurements, set up grids of string on the ground, photographed evidence, and packed away pieces to send to their various laboratories. For all that, Nash didn't sound satisfied. "We've found no sign of Ignacio, though. He either wasn't aboard this ship or he had already escaped long before we arrived. Still, there are people in the pentagon who are very interested in this thing."

"The kid who built the rockets," Dean said. "Mike Raskolnikov. He's not going to face a trial or anything?"

"I wouldn't worry," Nash stepped up to a small refreshment table and filled two Styrofoam cups from an insulated coffee dispenser. "I think the Department of Defense is more likely to recruit him than we are to prosecute him. I understand he didn't use any illegal components. Just imagine what he'll be able to create when they provide him with a full military lab."

"I'd rather not imagine that." Dean refused the coffee that Nash offered. A warm beverage might have been nice, but he couldn't bear to bring his hands out of his pockets and into the sub-freezing air. It startled him how much the temperature could drop in a single day, and swaddling himself with every layer of flannel in his closet had only left him feeling like an overstuffed lumberjack.

Nash, by comparison, seemed fine in this weather. He wore only a blue FBI jacket, a furry hat with earflaps, and a fashionable pair of leather gloves, yet he appeared downright comfortable, even happy to be there. It made Dean angry to think that anyone could be happy right then.

"You know, Dean, some of my superiors think you know more than you're telling us."

Dean just grunted.

"Actually, they asked me to work closely with you. They said I know you better than anyone, so I should keep tabs on the Institute."

"So now you're going to spy on us?"

"No spying," Nash seemed surprised. "It would just be a chance to work together."

Dean's look was icier than the air temperature.

"That offer to work as a consultant is still on the table," Nash said. "For you and for your students. My bosses, some of them are starting to see your value. They want you on the payroll. And your students—maybe they could earn extra credit for helping us. I'm sure we can work something out, right?"

"Are you going to water-board me if I don't agree?"

"Dean, it's not like that. I swear."

Dean wasn't convinced. This was why McKenzie—the original, living McKenzie—had made Dean promise not to let go of the Institute's secrets. Once these agencies got their hooks in, it would be only a matter of time before the students got yanked away to some sterile research facility surrounded by cranky old scientists and suspicious security guards. All of these kids had such bright futures. Each of them had the potential to truly change the world, for better or worse. Dean just wanted to make sure they could choose for themselves.

There was nothing more for him to say, and nothing more he wanted to hear from Nash, so Dean turned his back on the wrecked sky palace and began walking back towards Topsy.

"Hey, what's wrong with you?" Nash hurried to catch up to him. "Listen to me. I'm trying to be nice here, but you're not making it easy. I've seen you during a crisis, Dean. I swear to God, you enjoy trying to get yourself killed. And then the rest of the time you act like some kind of emo sad-sack. So what is it? What's your problem—are you bi-polar, or just deranged?"

"I'll talk to my shrink and keep you posted," He kept walking, and Nash gave up and let him go. Dean didn't know if the guards at the checkpoint would shoot him if he tried to exit the cordon without permission, but it turned out that they only wanted to run a metal-detector wand over him and then return the phone he had surrendered on the way in.

When he arrived back at Topsy, Soap was the only student in the decoy lab. She and Rusty were working on some kind of drone bodies at the 3D printers. Her eyes never came away from her work, but the muscles in her cheeks were bunched into knots and her eyebrows were angled so far down that she looked like she was going to drill holes through the machine with her fiery gaze.

"You look angry," Dean said.

"Of course I'm angry," she said without looking up. "They attacked my friends. They attacked you."

"They attacked you, too," Dean said. "Held you up at gunpoint to steal the Egg, right?"

She went on as if she hadn't heard him. "They broke into my house and stole important things."

Dean noted that she said 'my house' instead of 'our laboratory,' but he wasn't going to point that out. "Just promise me something," he said. "Promise you won't do anything stupid, okay?"

Soap ground her teeth. "I figured out what gear they used to cut through the rooftop door."

"Are you trying to change the subject?"

"No, I'm not trying. It just happened. What they did was to put some metal strips on the door so it could get super-heated. Then they hit those strips with lightning."

"Lightning?" Dean thought about it for a second. "Wouldn't lightning have to go sideways to hit a door? And—how did they even know where it would strike?"

"They knew, because they made it happen. They used a laser to create a plasma channel through the cloud, kind of like my lightning lance but with the real thing. The laser probably came from a drone flying up above the cloud. I'm guessing that's why they call them lightning drones. They either angled the laser from up high or used another laser at a ninety-degree angle to channel the lightning bolt right into the door."

"That's pretty elaborate," Dean said.

Soap shrugged, not seeming impressed.

"Well, if he wanted to really mess us up, why didn't Ignacio just create a tornado?" Dean asked. "He had the drones. He could have hit us with a super storm worse than Buenos Aires."

"I thought that would be obvious," Soap said. "It's too cold to create tornadoes here right now. Here's another unrelated thing you should know: Nikki's coming back."

"From Georgia?" Dean asked. "In the middle of winter break?"

"She's as pissed as I am. She says somebody's gotta do something about it."

"Yeah, the FBI," Dean said. "The Department of Homeland Security. The United States Air Force. Those are the people who are going to do something about it, not you or Nikki or me—got it?"

Soap reached for a bundle of wires and began untangling them with the speed and deftness of a Rubik's Cube champion.

"Soap," Dean said. "Acknowledge me, please. This is not for you or anyone else from the Institute to get involved with, and even if we wanted to we have no way to follow them. Ignacio is out of our reach, okay?"

She gave a grunt that sounded somewhat affirmative, but then added: "Even if the military beats Ignacio, they'll impound Professor McKenzie's Egg. They'll put her and everything else on his ship into a big warehouse right next to the Ark of the Covenant. If you leave it to them, you'll never see her again. You know that, right?"

She had just spoken the fears that had been gnawing at him since the attack. Dean was suddenly glad that Soap wasn't making eye contact, because that way he didn't have to hide his dismay.

Alone and in silence, he left Soap to her work and climbed the stairs to his residence. A rush of cold air met him at the door. He had covered the gaping hole with a tarp and boards, but this did little to keep out the Minnesota winter.

You'll never see her again. The words echoed inside him. *You'll never see her again.*

Dean opened his recently reassembled refrigerator and found it as empty as always. He didn't even have a can of beer or a slice of leftover pizza. Instead, he dug a teakettle out of the cupboard and began filling it with water from the tap.

"Ignacio's weather device could destroy the world."

Surprised by the words, Dean dropped the teakettle in the sink, splashing water everywhere. He had assumed he was alone in his apartment, but now the ghost of Tesla materialized right beside him.

Dean slowly mopped up the water with a dishcloth but left the pot empty on the counter. Only after he finished did he turn and speak to the ghost. "Come again?" he prompted.

"I've been analyzing the effects of the storms in Argentina," Tesla said. "Soap's calculations were correct: the storms lifted an immense amount of debris into the stratosphere. In time, it will spread out and fall back down to Earth, but if Ignacio uses his drones frequently enough he may plunge all of us into the equivalent of a nuclear winter."

"That's got nothing to do with me."

"On the contrary," Tesla said. "It will affect everyone on the planet. Crops will die. Food shortages will lead to mass famine. Violent winter storms will shut down all transportation for weeks at a time. I was so alarmed by these discoveries that I had Collin send my findings to several professors of atmospheric science. Nine out of ten confirmed that this is a possibility."

"But only a possibility," Dean set the empty pot down on the stove and folded his arms. "Look, I don't want to sound insensitive, but the world's got a lot of problems that I can't do anything about. This is one of them."

"On the contrary," Tesla said. "I can predict the location of Ignacio's next attack."

Dean stared at him for a long moment. If he could predict where to find Ignacio, he could also predict where to find McKenzie's Egg.

"I'm listening," Dean said.

"Well," Tesla made a sound as if clearing his throat. "From my time serving as Ignacio's computer, I know which sixty cities he is targeting."

"So? I already told Nash all about that. Sixty cities is a lot of ground to cover. And if the Air Force can't see those sky palaces coming, there's not much they can do to stop them."

"But consider this," Tesla said. "Ignacio's drones cannot create tornados anywhere at any time. He requires certain pre-existing weather conditions. That's why yesterday he attacked us with his men, not his storms: the conditions weren't right."

"And how does that help us?"

"All I need is an accurate weather report for all the potential target regions, and in this age weather information is freely and widely available. I'm amazed at what can be done with radar and satellites—although I wish I could have helped develop these fields, because they would have come even further with my help. Nevertheless, I have already identified the most likely two or three spots for Ignacio to appear within the next twenty-four hours."

Dean studied Tesla's face. Of course, he was a simulation projected by a quantum computer so it might have been silly to try to read his expressions, but he seemed as honest and open as ever.

"Where's he going to be?" Dean asked.

"If we presume that Ignacio is going for maximum destruction, there is one clear target at this time. Southern California."

Dean stared at him. *California—home!*

Despite his sudden urge to go find Ignacio, Dean couldn't see how. Even if Tesla was right, how would Dean get halfway across the United States in time? And what would he do with Ignacio even if he did catch up to him?

He shook his head, then placed the teapot back on the stove. If he got in his truck right now, he still couldn't drive all the way to California in time. An airplane would probably be detoured by the storm Dean wanted to fly into. No normal means of travel could get him there, but he was standing above a warehouse full of mad science inventions—and he thought he knew just what he needed.

Dean walked out to the balcony overlooking the decoy lab. He couldn't see Soap, but the reflected light of her arc welder still splashed brightly along the racks of tools so he knew she was there.

"Soap," he yelled.

There was a short pause and the welder stopped flashing.

"Yeah?" she called back.

"How fast can that jet suit be ready? I think it's time it gets test-piloted."

December 23

(Stormageddon)

Chapter 36

Dean swooped in low, cut his engines, and stalled himself out only a few feet above ground so that he could slide to a graceful stop on the golden sands of the southern Californian desert. At least, that was his plan. In reality, he came in too fast, skidded through the dirt until the friction jerked his feet out from under him, and ended up sprawling face down in the dirt.

For a machine that was literally supposed to read his mind, the jet suit was proving as difficult to pilot as it was uncomfortable to wear. Fortunately, Nikki had created the suit out of high-impact ballistic armor to protect him from any minor collisions. It had probably saved his life during the long flight from Minnesota when he hit a flock of ducks. (Sadly, it hadn't helped the ducks.) Of course, Dean had asked how tough this armor was—specifically, could it stop a bullet? Nikki's response was simple: "you're not Iron Man."

After he had come to a complete stop, Dean grunted and shifted his arms, creating dust angels in the desert as he attempted to rise to his knees. With a heavy set of jets and a long pair of wings directly behind his shoulder blades, he was about as nimble as an overturned turtle.

"I thought this thing was supposed to respond to my thoughts," Dean grumbled aloud.

"It does, in a way," Tesla's voice came through the speakers in the helmet. "It recognizes the pre-set electrical patterns in your brain and equates them to different behaviors of the suit. Do you need me to go over the technical details once more?"

Dean had heard enough already. Tesla and Soap had programmed the suit to respond to signals from the nano-probes that had remained in his brain after the memory probe that led to the creation of McKenzie's ghost. To make it work with the jet pack, Victor had placed his brain-scan helmet back on Dean's head and had him imagine himself performing certain actions which Soap and Tesla had then linked to the jet suit's functions. If, for example, he pictured himself dipping his shoulders to one side, the flaps on the wings would work in such a way that he would bank in that direction. Tilting his head down or up would make him dive or ascend. Flexing his buttocks made him go faster, while flexing his ankles cut the throttle. Some of the procedures were more intuitive than others, and all of them took a fair bit of practice to get the suit to respond when he wanted it to and in the way he expected. Fortunately, he'd had the whole trip from Minnesota to practice—there was no in-flight movie, after all. Obviously, he still needed to drill the landing technique.

"Any sign of drones?" he asked as he worked his way up from his knees to his feet.

"Not yet," Tesla said. "Judging by the cold front coming down from the north, Ignacio would be using them much closer to the city. If he's here at all."

"If he's here?" Dean repeated. And if he weren't here, then Dean had done nothing more than prove that flying coach on a commercial airline was only the second least comfortable way to travel.

Once he had climbed to his feet, he quickly patted himself down to ensure that everything was still in operational condition, giving extra attention to the pocket containing Tesla's Egg. It was a reinforced pouch on the side of his thigh, bulky with extra padding and securely fastened by a Velcro strap and a row of clips. He found everything to be in order, but given that the Egg was probably more valuable than Dean's own life, he wanted to leave nothing to chance.

After completing his self-inspection, Dean surveyed the wide desert and found himself less happy to be back home than he had expected. Without the air-cooling action of the wind rushing through the suit's ventilation ports, the desert sun threatened to char-broil him where he stood—and this was only California's winter. It was a mere 66 degrees here, downright cold by Californian standards but strikingly uncomfortable to him now. Evidently, he had been living in the northern hinterlands for so long he'd grown unaccustomed to nice weather.

He turned to face a suburb that sprang up from the desert so abruptly it seemed as if someone had set down a gigantic pop-up book and opened it to reveal miles of white-stucco walls and red tile roofs. In the hazy distance, a pair of gigantic wind turbines spun lazily, and beyond that a highway snaked through the hills towards the coast.

Dean plodded towards a nearby gas station, wobbling a little as his wings snapped down behind him. His throat felt raw and dry, yet his bladder was dangerously full. It seemed unfair to have too much water and too little at the same time, but that was the reality. Every inch of him was stiff and sore, too. His neck was the worst because he'd had to hyperextend it throughout the journey to see where he was going. Superheroes made it look easy to fly around with their bodies parallel to the ground and their heads pulled back at ninety degrees to their shoulders, but real human beings simply weren't designed to hold that posture for any length of time.

As he walked, Dean attempted to wipe the film of dirt from his visor with his thick gloves, but all he did was smear the grime around. It prevented him from seeing the town ahead clearly, but at least the GPS display on the inside of his helmet offered a clear readout. Palmdale, California. Just a few dozen miles north of Los Angeles (as the rocket-man flies), and absolutely as far as Dean could go without a bathroom break.

"You're not going to fly this last distance?" Tesla asked. "We are almost there."

"I need a pit stop before I blow out a tire," Dean said.

"I'm confused. You have wings, not tires."

"Sports metaphor," Dean said. "You and my cousin really are peas in a pod."

"Garden metaphor?" Tesla asked.

Dean left it at that.

After holding himself rigid for so many hours, it felt good to move his arms and legs freely, or at least as freely as he could under the weight of the suit. In the good-old-days, he'd worn a hundred pounds of gear into burning buildings, but this suit felt much less well balanced and with every step his heals bumped against the lower edge of the folded wings. He was grateful when he made it to the asphalt because that presented easier going than the dusty desert. There were no sidewalks, so he was stuck with walking along the shoulder as cars whizzed by at speeds much greater than the posted limit. The drivers and passengers craned their neck to ogle his strange getup, but they still didn't slow down. Dean smirked. It was starting to feel like home.

It took him ten minutes to waddle to the gas station. Before he could go into the little restroom, he had to clearly imagine playing patty-cake—a safety precaution designed to keep him from accidentally removing his suit while five miles above the ground. He didn't need to actually move his hands to go through the imaginary motions, he only needed to picture himself going through the motions and his suit clasps automatically released. First, the helmet disengaged. Then his gloves popped off and his wing assembly dropped from his shoulders. If he continued long enough he would end up wearing nothing but his underwear, but he didn't need to go that far in public.

When he emerged from the bathroom, he selected an extra-large bottle of water from the soda refrigerator, then worked on retrieving his wallet from beneath the thick ballistic padding of his outer pants. The suit was so bulky and puffy that he kept accidentally bumping candy off a shelf by his elbow.

"So, what are you filming?" the store clerk asked.

"Filming?" Dean repeated, a little confused.

"Yeah, what's the movie?" the clerk used his chin to point to the heavy wings propped up against a rack of potato chips. "Are you rebooting the Rocketeer or something?"

"Um, sure. The Rocketeer." Dean plopped a few dollar bills on the counter, then took a heavy, almost desperate swig of the water.

"Okay, well, no offense, but you don't look anything like him. I mean, the Rocketeer has style. He's iconic. Your costume's too puffy. You look like, I don't know..."

"The Michelin Man?" Dean offered, and accidentally bumped another shelf with his elbow as he took a large gulp.

"Yeah. The Michelin Man. So, when you see the producers of your film, you tell them they got it all wrong, Okay? As a matter of fact, tell them they need to start coming up with original ideas, for once. Nothing's coming out of Hollywood these days except reboots and sequels, and it's all because those producers don't have the brain cells to think up anything new."

"Thanks for the editorial."

"They've obviously lost their sense of costume design, too. I mean, no offense, but you look awful. Hey, can I take your picture?"

"You want my picture?"

"Sure," the clerk produced his phone. "My Twitter followers are going to freak if I post some early shots from the set."

"Sure, why not," Dean set the empty water bottle on the counter. It wasn't like he could stop the guy from taking the pictures. "Just let me get my helmet on. I'm just the stunt-man, you know. Nobody wants to see my face. Matter of fact, come out to the street and I'll let you take a video of some special effects."

Dean struggled to connect the wings back into place, then worked on getting the gloves and the helmet correctly attached. Once he had all of it in place, he walked out to the parking lot where he paused for a dramatic moment while the clerk aimed his phone.

For the launch sequence, Soap had wanted Dean to imagine doing the Dougie, but Dean hadn't known what that was. Instead, he had chosen to do the Macarena, a dance apparently utterly unknown to Soap's generation but indelibly burned into Dean's muscle-memory from countless bad renditions at weddings.

With an all-too clear mental playback of the bouncing, pulsating music, he imagined himself moving his hands from his hips to his chest.

The heavy brace pressed into the back of his helmet, protecting his head from whiplash.

Then he imagined lifting his arms behind his head, and the wings flipped out perpendicular to the ground. He stumbled backwards a few paces with the shift in weight, but it didn't stop his imaginary hip gyrations from continuing in time with the music.

As soon as his hips kicked in, the antimatter-fueled jets blazed to life and hurled him forward. In a moment, his body snapped up parallel with the wings and then he was fully airborne.

He circled back over the convenience store to give the clerk one more photo op, then aimed himself more-or-less south, towards a stretch of mountains that, from his elevation, looked like crinkled brown construction paper. Just beyond those rocks, Los Angeles sprawled all the way to the sea. He couldn't see the city just yet, but he could see a massive continent of black clouds smothering the entire region. Lightning flashed back and forth among the conglomeration of thunderheads, illuminating the anvil-shaped clouds from within.

"The chances that all those clouds formed naturally are next to nil," Tesla said.

Dean didn't say anything. This storm meant that Ignacio was here, somewhere, and Dean needed to track him down before the City of Angels became the new Tornado Alley.

CHAPTER 37

Ignacio's drones were there, all right, buzzing like swarms of flies above the swimming pools that polka-dotted the landscape. Tesla was able to follow the thunder-drones' transmissions up to the lightning-drones hovering high above. From there, he traced the laser pulses of information they exchanged with the sky palace seventeen miles away.

After Tesla had pinpointed Ignacio's ship, it was Dean's turn to take care of the details. Before he could get close, the full complement of mosquito pods buzzed out to intercept him, so he had to veer off and try to ditch them over the city. Although no tornado had touched down yet, he soon discovered that the increasing winds had already begun spinning debris up to alarming heights, including a license plate that whirled through the air like a ninja star and collided with his shoulder. Even with his armor, it hit him as hard as a fastball. Without the suit it would have surely sliced his arm like deli meat, and it proved that he didn't want to be out in the open by the time the storm reached its peak.

The mosquito pods may have been far more maneuverable than Dean, but the jet suit more than made up for it with raw speed. Dean banked, dived, and corkscrewed away from them so fast that he kept having to circle back towards them just to make sure they didn't give up and head back to the sky palace. The pod pilots occasionally squeezed off a stream of metal slugs from their rail guns, but the shots never even came close.

Finally, Dean spun a wide circle above the Griffiths Observatory. This, he decided, was as far as he needed to lead them. He rocketed right back past them with such acceleration that his spine threatened to telescope in on itself. He might have blacked out, but his jet suit's pants automatically tighten around his legs to squeeze the blood from his extremities up towards his head to compensate for the g-forces pushing it back. Even with this help, silver stars smeared across his vision and his head swam. That kind of acceleration was uncomfortable and dangerous, but at least it had allowed him to leave the pods so far behind he could board the sky palace without their interference.

He was rapidly closing the distance when a bright flash ripped horizontally through the clouds. In the same instant, Dean hit a wall of pure noise, a shockwave so intense that it left him dazed and half-dreaming that he had been struck from the air by a titanic flyswatter. It had knocked him out of connection with the world, even with his own body, as if all sensations had been blasted out of him by the pure force of—of whatever it was that had hit him.

His perceptions came back to him one at a time, beginning with a lurching feeling in his stomach as he fell and followed by the recognition that his suit was still squeezing his legs. Next, he became aware of the tug of his arms as the wind dragged them out into a spread-eagle position. When his head finally cleared, he realized he was tumbling through the air, as limp as a rag doll.

"Dean!" Tesla called to him from what seemed like a hundred miles away. "Dean! You must wake up!"

"Wha-what hit us?" Dean mumbled, discovering that his mouth was somewhat numb. He fought back a wave of nausea and the accompanying fear of vomiting inside his own helmet, then managed to straighten his limbs and get his jets pointed in the right direction to level out his flight.

"Lightning," Tesla answered. "Not a direct hit, but too close for comfort. There's a good chance it was a lightning-drone, using its laser to guide the cloud's ionized electricity at you. I can't be sure, but it suggests there are other drones in this area ready to do the same. I recommend that you fly in an erratic pattern to make yourself more difficult to target."

An erratic pattern, Dean thought. *As if I could fly straight right now even if I tried.*

He pulled up, weaving and wobbling so wildly that if he'd been driving a car he would have been pulled over. A moment later, the clouds let rip with another flash and boom behind him—terrifyingly close, but not close enough to harm him. A few seconds later, another flash split the sky off to his right. Erratic flying, he decided, was a good idea. Meanwhile, Tesla had triangulated the position of the sky palace and displayed a green circle on the inside of Dean's helmet to show him the way. As he drew closer, the hazy patch of sky outlined by the circle resolved itself into an indistinct silhouette of swooping star-arms and a sloping hull. It was enough to navigate, but no matter how close Dean got, the sky palace never looked like anything more than a patch of sky someone had cut out and pasted over a nearly identical patch of sky.

On his first flyby, he saw the small lump on the top that must have been Ignacio's rooftop garden, protruding from the back of the hull like a Plexiglas bug's eye. He swooped in towards it, thankful that the turrets couldn't angle low enough to shoot him while he was so close.

Dean attempted to land by stalling himself out and found it was actually easier than on the ground. Here, he could start lower and swoop higher to bleed off all that extra speed. Nevertheless, when he touched down on the ship's topside, his legs rolled out from under him and he ended up tumbling and bouncing like a high-speed crazy-ball in his padded suit. He might have simply fallen off the far side of the ship if he hadn't collided with the Plexiglas dome.

Holding on as best he could amid the high winds, he unclipped an earthquake grenade from his belt. He clamped it onto the dome and watched as it zeroed in on the exact vibration frequency that would rip open the glass to which it was attached. Sinewaves on the grenade's screen twisting like a nest of snakes. As they writhed, they came closer and closer together until they finally merged in a perfect rhythmic dance. Dean had to let go and back away before the dome shattered. A few shards of Plexiglass blew outwards with the cabin's depressurization and bounced off his ballistic plates. He lost his footing, teetered on the edge, and the next thing he knew he was in freefall once more.

This time, his brain knew what to do: immediately, he imagined placing his hands behind his head and began gyrating, Macarena style. For split second, all he felt was the instinctual panic at falling. Every test pilot, he was sure, had that moment of doubt about their equipment, and it didn't matter if it was a button, a lever, or an imaginary dance. Gambling one's life on untested machinery was not something Dean enjoyed.

"Hey, Macarena!" he yelled the last lyric out loud and moved from imagining the dance to physically acting it out.

Power surged through the jets, yanking him upwards to safety as he uttered a swift prayer of thanks.

He flew back towards the dome, swooping to a stop just as he had before. This time, he managed to keep his balance as his feet skidded towards what was left of the dome. The earthquake grenade had reduced it to a ragged ring of sharp shards like the teeth of a lamprey. Dean mentally commanded the wings to snap closed behind him, then used his momentum to angle himself towards the hole, and hopped up at the last moment to avoid the jagged glass—a trick he might not have accomplished if it hadn't been for his recent practice slipping around in the broom ball rink.

He landed on his back, safely if not gracefully. The wind whipped Plexiglas shards around the inside of the dome, but not violently enough to pierce his suit. Dean was just grateful he had something solid beneath his feet. All those high-speed maneuvers felt like they were tearing his limbs off. He promised whatever deities might be listening that if he lived long enough to kiss solid ground then he would never, ever strap jets to his back on again.

He lifted his head and looked around the dome to see that this was no Japanese garden. Rather, it was a flat observation deck with a polished black floor and a row of leather bucket seats ringing the outer edge. It looked like the kind of place one might find on a high-class passenger train, where tourists could lounge with their binoculars and day packs and watch the scenery chugging by. Clearly, he was not aboard the *Tlaloc*, which meant it could only be the *Raiden*, the same sky palace Nash had shot up with the mosquito pod back in Buenos Aires. Obviously, Ignacio had fully repaired it and put back into action.

A quick check beneath the observation seats revealed that the earthquake grenade was nowhere to be found—it must have tumbled off the ship as soon as it had broken the dome. Dean proceeded to the elevator and wasn't entirely surprised when nothing happened.

"They've locked us out," Tesla said. "But I'll show you how to rewire it."

Under Tesla's guidance, Dean removed his helmet and gloves, then pried open a panel down by the floor and began yanking out wires. He had no tools, and Tesla seemed shocked when he stripped one of the wires with his teeth.

"That's very dangerous," the ghost said. "You could chip a tooth."

"We need this done fast. If you have a better idea, I'd love to hear it."

"You could have used a glass shard to strip that wire."

Dean paused, feeling more than a little foolish. Without a word, he found a shard of Plexiglas and scraped off the end of another wire. The broken plastic wasn't quite as sharp as glass, so he ended up taking away almost as much of the copper innards as the insulating material. Once he had exposed enough of the wires, Tesla explained where to reconnect them and Dean tapped them together. They sparked dramatically, and he felt the thrum of the approaching elevator almost immediately.

"What do we need to do when we get to the bridge?" Dean asked as he stepped into the elevator.

"Insert me into the central console. I should be able to assume control of the drone fleet and begin to reverse the process of the storm, if it is not too late already."

"Won't that—" Dean wanted to say 'won't that kill you,' but for some reason he couldn't speak those words. "Won't that do to you what it did to Twain?"

"It will certainly destroy me," Tesla said bluntly. "But none of that will matter if you die first."

Dean was just about to ask what that meant when the elevator doors opened. The bridge was lit only in dim red emergency lights and the blue glow monitors, but it was still enough to reveal a half-dozen of Ignacio's suit-wearing security guards with their weapons pointed right at him. But what worried Dean most was the man who towered behind them.

"Glad I didn't bother to snuff you last time we met," Brick growled. "It's gonna be way more fun killing you now."

Chapter 38

All six guards fired their stun guns in almost perfect unison, and Dean braced himself for the crackling, searing pain. It never came. Blue sparks danced around each contact point, and nothing more. Soap, it seemed, had insulated the jet suit well.

Dean decided his best play was a direct charge out of the elevator. The heavy suit added to his momentum, allowing him to smash through the guards like a bowling ball. He shoulder-blocked one into two others, sending the lot flailing into the computer consoles behind them. Then he whirled on the remaining guards, smashing at them with his heavy gloves. Moving in the suit slowed him down and taxed his muscles, but each of his blows landed like a club. They fought back with punches Dean couldn't even feel through his impact plating. He knocked one down as another performed some kind of fancy, but embarrassingly ineffective spin-kick. Dean slammed the guy while he still had one foot in the air, but as he did, another guard circled around behind and drove the butt of a fire extinguisher into the back of his helmet. Dean whirled, mashing his elbow into the nose of the guy with the fire extinguisher and sending him sprawling to the ground next to his two friends.

With only half the guards still on their feet, Dean began to think he just might win this fight. Then a pair of enormous hands closed over his shoulders and flung him across the room.

Computer monitors flashed around him as he spun through the air, and he caught a glimpse of the face of a very startled technician, mouth agape, evidently too afraid to leave his station during the fight. Dean flew for what felt like minutes even though it couldn't have been more than a second or two, until he finally thudded into the bulkhead. Even for a suit designed to withstand hitting a flock of ducks at half the speed of sound, this was a bone-jarring impact.

It took him as long to get to his feet as it did for Brick to lumber across the bridge, and when they met they fought like old-fashioned pugilists with their feet planted firmly on the ground, too slow-moving to bother dodging or rolling with the punches. Brick's blows hurt, but Dean's helmet kept him safe from a knockout, and the ballistic suit prevented the gargantuan fists from breaking any bones. Brick was also protected, though he kept his armor hidden beneath the skin, and if Dean's club-handed wallops hurt the big man, he didn't show any sign of it. Brick also had the annoying, but effective habit of thrusting his huge belly forward while leaning his head back as he fought. This was an unusual stance, but, combined with Brick's height advantage, it prevented Dean from landing a solid punch anywhere on the giant's head. Dean shifted to body blows, hoping to drive his fists up and into Brick's side to maybe bust a rib—anything to force a grimace out of him, at least—but it didn't pay off. Ordinarily, cracking a floating rib would be almost as easy as breaking an egg inside a carton, but with all of Brick's mass it was like that egg had been safely sealed inside a refrigerator, and that refrigerator had been rolled up inside a carpet.

As they pounded away at each other, Dean glanced past the giant to see that all the guards had retreated over by the room's exit to watch the fight. One of them was smiling, either because he was relieved he was no longer involved or else simply happy to watch Brick clobber Dean (or maybe the other way around).

After a good thirty seconds of relentless pummeling between the two immovable objects, Dean could feel his punches slowing down as his muscles protested with both fiery pain and slow, creeping exhaustion. The jet suit might have been able to absorb Brick's blows all day, but Dean couldn't keep dishing them out. Brick, perhaps feeling the same way, was the first to break the stalemate. He enveloped Dean's faceplate with his enormous hand and drove it backwards with a sudden freight-train charge to slam him hard into the steel bulkhead. Dean's head rang like a gong. He tried to twist away, but found escape impossible as Brick blasted his head into the wall again and again. A crack snaked across Dean's visor, and the third time Brick slammed him, the visor shattered, forcing Dean to squint as chunks of glass washed backwards over his face.

Dean tried to regain his footing, slapped Brick's arms away, but the giant plowed forward again and the two became locked together in a kind of sumo stance as each tried to wrench the other off his feet. This wasn't good news: now that the giant had figured out to seize and throw rather than cudgel and pummel, it was only a matter of time before Dean went down beneath the avalanche of Brick's weight.

"The difference between you and me," Brick said, his face so close that his sour breath splashed through the gaping fracture in Dean's helmet. "My armor don't come off, but I can rip yours open, piece by piece."

"Nah," Dean shot back. "The difference between you and me is, I know the Macarena."

Brick's heavy brow pulled upward in an almost comically exaggerated expression of confusion, and Dean used that moment to run himself through the imaginary steps of the dance. As he did, his wings flipped up and the turbines roared to life. Those jets were designed to propel a large man like Dean through the air with an acceleration just shy of lethal. Actually, they contained the power to accelerate him faster, but they were designed to measure their own thrust balanced against his drag, and then automatically held back enough to keep from flattening Dean's brain into the back of his skull. Even with Brick's weight, the jets still managed to launch them both across the control room, splitting a computer console in half and flinging technicians out of their path as they flew. Together, they hit the wall at the back of the bridge like a wrecking ball. The impact felt like a car crash, but Dean had Brick's huge and pliable body to serve as an airbag. Brick, on the other hand, had no such protection from the cold, hard steel.

At the moment of impact, amid the sharp sound of rending metal, the safety features of the jets cut the thrust, but their momentum carried them through a Brick-sized hole that had opened in the wall. They skidded a short distance to a stop inside a small, irregularly shaped box of a room. Dean may have blacked out for a moment, but when he sat up he saw Brick lying next to him. The giant's eyes were fluttering, and his arms and legs were spread out limply while the enormous mound of his stomach jiggled in time with the vibrations of the ship's engines.

A rush of air whistled through the broken gap in Dean's helmet. He pulled himself to his feet, shaken but intact, and stumbled a little to his right. He thought his difficulty in finding his footing might indicate a head injury, but then the small mountain of Brick's unconscious body slid a few inches across the floor in the same direction.

"You burst one of the helium chambers," Tesla said in his ear. "As the gas escapes, the ship is going to list a little to port."

"Is the gas—" Dean was startled to hear that his voice had become high-pitched and squeaky, like a cartoon rodent. "Is it poisonous?"

"Helium? Of course not. It's a noble gas, but it does have the amusing effect of allowing your vocal cords to vibrate more quickly, which is why your voice has increased in pitch."

Dean stepped back through the ragged hole into the bulkhead and onto the bridge. He found the guards waiting for them so he stared them down for a moment. He didn't feel he had much fight left, but they didn't know that. They'd been battered, bruised, and knocked toothless, and then they'd seen him defeat their giant. When Dean took one step in their direction, they scattered like a flock of pigeons. The remaining technicians raced out the door behind them, leaving Dean all alone on the bridge.

The deck had a noticeable tilt to it now, and Dean had to step carefully to keep himself upright. He paused at the control panel and made the mistake of glancing at one of the screens. It was a video feed, evidently from one of the drones out in the field, displaying the unsteady image of a tornado ripping through a neighborhood. The storm first stripped the palm leaves off all the trees, and then it grabbed an SUV from the sidewalk and tossed it through the air. The vehicle crashed all the way through one house and lodged itself in the bay window of another. The angry vortex proceeded to blast through windows, peel shingles from roofs, and finally crumple a house into splinters. It was like watching the footsteps of an invisible giant mercilessly stomping on everything in its path. For three seconds, Dean stood transfixed by the destruction, and in that time the tornado consumed two more homes before rising up into the air to leave a third untouched, and then slamming back down to pulp another one across the street.

Dean looked up to the other monitors. Most displayed empty, wind-blown streets puddled with unaccustomed rain. One feed tracked a tornado as it gutted an office park, slamming cars together in the parking lot and spinning all the broken glass high into the air. Another screen showed a twister ripping through downtown Beverly Hills, tearing expensive dresses out of storefronts and sucking them up towards heaven as if it were the Fashion Rapture. Yet another tornado ate its way through a big amusement park, yanking roller coasters right off their tracks. The winds blew plush mice and ducks out from the souvenir stands and flung them around, smashing them against the brightly painted walls of the gigantic rides. Then a woman in a princess costume sailed by the camera, her perfectly made-up face twisted in a scream Dean couldn't hear but would never forget.

He had to shut his eyes and look away. To be pulled through the air like that, flying almost as fast as his jet suit yet with no sense of control, knowing the whole time that when you finally connect with the Earth you will be smashed to pieces—it was too horrible to imagine. Los Angeles was more populated than Buenos Aires, which meant the casualty count would be higher. This city also had no warning sirens, no storm shelters, and, while their building codes included the most advanced earthquake countermeasures, their homes and offices were poorly prepared to resist killer storms like these.

His throat emitted a strangled noise without his being aware of it. He was witnessing the random, widespread destruction of his home. Maybe Los Angeles wasn't his current legal residence, but, dammit, this was the place he knew best in all the world. He recognized the streets, the buildings, the cityscape—and watching it get torn to pieces filled him with a gut-level dread he hadn't experienced in Argentina. It was as if the tornado had reached his chest and ripped him up from the inside.

All this, and he knew the storms would only get worse. Within sixty minutes, there would be ten times as many funnel clouds causing ten times the devastation. Two hours from now, Los Angeles would be a scarred wasteland. He didn't have the luxury of weeping or contemplating the horror, not while there was still something he could do.

He grabbed the fire extinguisher one of the guards had hit him with and used it to bash at the little keypad lock that protected the central computer console. Once he got it open, he took a quick glance inside: McKenzie's Egg wasn't in there. That was a setback, but he'd have to worry about it later.

He shoved Tesla's Egg inside the empty console and slid the mesh of wires and cables into place around it.

"Bad news," Tesla said a moment after the hookup. "We have the wrong sky palace."

"The wrong—?" Dean shook his head. "How many palaces does Ignacio have cruising around up here?"

"Two. The other is the *Tlaloc*, and it assumed control of the storm drones as soon as you landed here. This sky palace, the *Raiden*, is currently locked out of the drone network. However, I have been able to discover the coordinates of the *Tlaloc*. They're right—oh dear."

The deck rattled violently and a boom echoed from all around them.

"Turn on the screen!" Dean yelled at Tesla just as the ship bucked and thundered again. "Turn it on!"

The front screen sprang to life, peppered by static and dead pixels but still displaying the vivid green-black sky outside. Ignacio's flagship, the *Tlaloc*, rose into view, its turrets blazing fire at the *Raiden*.

"Perhaps you should feel flattered that Ignacio would shoot down one of his own sky palaces simply because you are aboard it," Tesla suggested.

Dean didn't care. When you're aboard a balloon that's being popped, flattery isn't much compensation.

CHAPTER 39

Onscreen, the *Tlaloc*'s rail guns flashed once more and the *Raiden*'s bridge shuddered with the impact of another volley.

Dean grabbed Tesla's Egg out of the control console and slid it back into his leg pouch. The ship rocked again, even more violently this time, and then tilted wildly down towards its starboard side. Dean flailed his arms and managed to grab onto a rack containing two flight packs to keep himself upright.

He looked back over his shoulder to see the *Tlaloc*, looming larger than ever on the monitor just before the screen shorted out in a shower of sparks.

"Uh, what?" rumbled a voice that sounded deeper than the rail gun fire. Brick peered out from the gap of the bulkhead, one hand holding onto the ragged metal for balance and the other pressed against his lumpy forehead.

"Your boss is shooting us down," Dean said. "You better bail out, if you know what's good for you."

Then Dean turned his attention back to his own escape. He let go of the rack of flight packs and stumbled over the shifting deck to the elevator. He swung himself inside and was relieved to find that the buttons were still illuminated, meaning it was still receiving power.

Brick staggering towards him, hand outstretched in what might have been a pleading gesture, or it might have been a threat of strangulation.

"This car's full," Dean said as he jabbed the button to make the doors slide shut.

He left Brick below and, a moment later, he emerged onto the observation deck where the wind howled around him. He put the helmet back on, but the gaping crack Brick had put into the visor seemed to direct the wind right into his eyes.

Suddenly, it occurred to him that it had been a full minute or more since the *Tlaloc* had fired on them. Had they given up? Were they convinced that the *Raiden* was as good as sunk?

With the deck spinning beneath him, Dean struggled out to the edge of the broken dome. He could see the *Tlaloc* now, and its guns weren't flashing. Instead, it was slowly floating up and away towards the heart of the city.

Dean was confused about why they would be retreating. Then he looked behind him and saw that one of the funnel clouds was reaching down for him out of the roiling black sky.

Almost instinctively now, Dean imagined the steps of the Macarena and launched himself into open air. Even with the jets pushing him onward, hitting the wall of wind outside bounced him first sharply to the right and then forward. Nearly blinded by the air streaming through his visor, he could see only enough of the storm to know that its currents were carrying him towards the retreating *Tlaloc*, so he goosed up the jet power and went with it.

Either they hadn't noticed Dean coming or they weren't bothering to aim for such an impossibly small target, allowing him to freely swoop up and land on the top of the ship. The gale-force winds, however, pushed him down, knocking his helmet against the metal hull and then nearly sweeping him over the side. He quickly contracted his wings to reduce his drag, then looked up to see the air currents carrying the *Raiden* almost directly overhead, spinning it like a top as it went. Chunks of the damaged sky palace broke off and spiraled away, either sailing out to rain down on the city below or else falling in towards the swirling vortex of the pre-tornado.

One object, however, didn't seem to be following the usual physics of falling. At first, it appeared as only an indistinct lump in the sky. It floated towards the *Talaloc* and even picked up a little speed as it came, and soon Dean could make out arms and legs, and he knew it was a person. When it got a little closer still, he saw that the person's head resembled a lumpy plug atop thick, rocky shoulders while the belly dangled like a mid-air avalanche. It could only be one person.

Brick Stellenleiter.

"You've got to be kidding me," Dean muttered, though his words were carried away by the wind.

Brick sailed in, his arms folded over his chest and a flight pack strapped to each bicep like gigantic water-wings. One flight pack might not have been enough to support Brick's massive body, but the double-pack arrangement seemed sufficient to carry him safely towards the *Tlaloc*.

The big man landed with a reverberating thump. Dean braced himself for another fight, but Brick's face was crumpled up in a mask of fear. Those flight packs would stay magnetically locked into position on the back of the ship, and it didn't look like he was about to let them go to come after Dean.

The battered *Raiden*, meanwhile, had lost its buoyancy while picking up momentum. It spun a Frisbee's curving path downwards and angled out over the studios and towards the hills, where it lost three of its arms as it ricocheted off the cliffs. The winds drove it into the rocky slope until it hit what might be the most famous hillside in the world: the one marked by gigantic letters that spelled HOLLYWOOD. The ship cut through the white letters like a buzzsaw, snapping cables and sending panels cascading down the hill in a spectacle that would have made any disaster movie director choke with envy. Finally, the sky palace came to a rest in a cloud of dust, half buried in the cliff face. Many of its hull panels had been ripped off and flotsam leaked from its amputated arms, but, amazingly, it was still recognizable and fairly intact. Dean had to hand it to Ignacio: he knew how to make a tough ship.

As the *Tlaloc* put some distance between it and the crashed *Raiden*, the storm winds intensified until they threatened to yank Dean from his perch. He had to get inside before he lost his footing, but this time he had no earthquake grenade to break the top dome or a friendly mosquito pod to blast an opening for him.

"Tesla!" he shouted against the wind.

He got no response.

"Tesla! Can you hear me? I can't hear you—I think my helmet speakers broke when I landed. Say something if you can hear me!"

Dean's only answer were little hisses and pops of static. If they were meant to be words, they weren't coming through. He was about to give up when he suddenly saw a bright green figure spring into existence above him. It was Tesla, standing perfectly comfortably on the hull. He body was nothing but bent light so the wind didn't bother him, but even so it felt strange to see him there without so much as a hair out of place while Dean and Brick had to struggle to keep from being blown off.

Tesla's mouth moved and the helmet speakers crackled, proving they were broken.

"Tesla!" Dean shouted again. "I can't hear you, but I need a way into this ship! Can you show me how to get in?"

It didn't take the green ghost long to figure out what to do. Wordlessly, he transformed the image of his body into a blinking green arrow that pointed over the edge of the sky palace.

To keep from being blown off, Dean had to crawl on his belly to follow the arrow. He couldn't use his jets without blasting off the sky palace, which would only put him back to square one. Instead, he had to inch along, searching for handholds as best he could. He envied the ability of Brick's flight packs to anchor to metal objects, but he wasn't about to go ask to borrow one.

After a few agonizing minutes, Dean reached the spot Tesla had indicated and peered over the edge to see four mosquito pods clamped to the side of the ship. He dangled his legs down over the side, dropped down onto one of the pods, and nestled himself comfortably (relatively speaking) between the four jet cowlings atop one of the pods. Although the pod rattled and swayed beneath him, the big engines blocked most of the wind, giving him a moment's rest.

Now Tesla's image transformed again, becoming a little diagram of Dean squatted between the jets. The image zoomed in on Dean's upper body and a compartment between his jets unfolded into a scrolling catalogue of parts. Tesla was demonstrating how to remove his wing pack and extract the reactor.

Dean wasn't crazy about taking off those wings. If he slipped or if a sudden gust knocked him off, it would be a long, long way down with nothing to do but say his prayers. Still, Tesla had a plan for getting him inside, and it would be much safer in there, with or without wings. Reluctantly, Dean removed his gloves, clipped them into their magnetic slots on his belt, and then struggled out of the shoulder assembly. The whole pod wiggled and bounced as he worked, and he tried not to think about the possibility of knocking it free from the mother ship.

Following Tesla's visual cues, Dean opened a hatch between the two jets and carefully removed the antimatter reactor, a grooved cylinder about the size of a half-gallon carton of milk. It was surprisingly heavy and a little warm to the touch, but Dean found Tesla's instructions easy enough to follow and soon managed to open it up and reverse a few wires. Finally, he jammed the reactor snugly under one of the engine struts at the top of the cab, just as instructed.

"Okay, now what?" he asked loudly.

In response, Tesla's green lights became red numbers, counting backwards from 10.

Nervously, Dean looked back at the reactor. It was already glowing red-hot.

He's set the thing to blow, Dean realized. He had no idea how big an explosion that reactor could make, but he was sure he didn't want to be sitting on top of it when it went off. In a rush of fear, he jumped up for the roof and was immediately carried much higher than he had intended by the wind at his back. He slammed down six feet away, managing to catch the edge of the star-arm with the tips of his fingers. He tightened his grip until the sharp corner of the hull plate bit into his palms, and then he began wondering if he was far enough away from the reactor to survive. He was no physicist, but he had spent enough time listening to Soap's babble to know that antimatter was potentially more explosive than a nuclear bomb. Still, Tesla wouldn't have instructed him to blow up this ship, especially with himself on board. Dean just had to trust the ghost and hold on for dear life.

Whatever Tesla had made Dean do to the reactor, it didn't result in an outright explosion. From where Dean lay, he could see it blaze red and then white as it heated. The heat soon spread to the mosquito pod's jet struts and the whole thing burned with such intense energy that Dean had to shut his eyes. When he opened them again, the reactor was gone, the metal was cooling, and the wind whistled around a gaping hole in the top of the mosquito pod. The reactor had completely melted away the upper apparatus, opening his entrance while also allowing the four jets to tumble away through the air. Unfortunately, Dean's wing pack, which had been resting in between the jets, had also been lost. The wings wouldn't have done him any good without the reactor, but he suddenly felt as vulnerable as a bug on a windshield without them.

He crept back towards the wrecked pod, his hands and arms aching murderously as he pulled himself across the metal plates of the fuselage. It felt like the longest six yards of his life, and then he had to begin worming his way in through the burned-out hole, head first. It smelled like scorched plastic, but at least the edges were already quite cool, thanks to the blowing winds. The hole was barely big enough for him to fit through, and one of his gloves was scraped off his belt and tumbled away as he worked his way inside. The reactor had burned and ruined the pod's bucket seat and melted one of the joysticks into an ugly lump, but the access hatch was open enough to allow him to force his bulky shoulders and even bulkier suit through to safety.

Straining like a baby emerging from the womb, he slid onto the floor of the hangar bay. For a long moment, he lay on the metal deck, unable to do anything but breathe. He hadn't plummeted to his death, and that was something to be thankful for. On the down side, his arms felt like jelly—if you made the jelly out of lighter fluid and then set it on fire. He tried to take a deep breath and found that his ribs felt like they were wrapped in steel bands. His legs had been so battered and pinched by his flight suit, he was sure they were one big bruise from his toes all the way to his thighs. He had been less exhausted after battling a five-alarm blaze all night... and he still had to figure out some way to beat Ignacio and all his men, seize control of the drone fleet, and kill the storms before he could call it a day.

Dean could hear the wind howling through the open porthole to the mosquito pod behind him, which was probably why he didn't hear the four guards approach. One of them, a lean blond guy with sallow cheekbones and a black eye, drew a pistol from his jacket holster. Not a stun gun, but a real, pop-a-cap-in-your-brain nine millimeter, probably loaded with dum-dum ammunition to make it less likely to pierce the walls of the pressurized aircraft and more likely to shred internal organs.

The guard pressed the pistol against Dean's head sideways, the way street thugs do in movies.

"Let's go, Bee-atch," the guard said. "I'd kill you here, but the Boss says he wants to snuff you himself."

Chapter 40

There wasn't much Dean could do aside from allowing the guards to roughly shove him towards the bridge. He wasn't going to punch his way out of this one, not while he was almost too exhausted to lift his arms. And even if he'd still had both of his club-like gloves and his thick helmet to protect him, the jet suit wasn't bullet proof, so the guy with the gun had all the power.

Dean arrived to find a very busy bridge. Technicians hammered away at every keyboard, and all the screens blazed with technical readouts and streaming video. Constant chatter filled the air, but the voices were low and the sentences clipped and disciplined. These were carefully trained women and men passing along only critical information about the atmospheric assault on the city below. This was now a war room, and Ignacio stood at its beating heart, barking bold commands and making grandiose, sweeping gestures to accentuate his orders.

"Dean, you've become a real impediment to my vision," Ignacio said, his eyes still moving from monitor to monitor. Immediately after speaking, he pointed to something on one of the screens, probably just to show Dean that he had better things to do than to bother with the guy who had crashed two thirds of his fleet.

"Ignacio, for the love of God, you need to stop this," Dean said. "You don't understand what you're doing."

"I'm doing what's necessary."

"No, it's worse than that. If you keep this up, you're going to send us into an ice age."

That made Ignacio stop and give Dean his full attention. "What are you talking about?"

"I know a guy who ran some calculations. We had ten scientists crunch the numbers, in fact. Nine of them agreed. These tornadoes will send so much dust up into the stratosphere that it'll block out the sun."

"Nonsense," Ignacio snapped. "Don't waste my time with—"

"Don't you see?" Dean said. "You're being used. That bald guy—that Predecessor—he's turned you into his puppet. He set you up with the technology and the materials for you to do exactly what you're doing. He *wants* you to create global climate change without even knowing you're doing it."

Ignacio, along with every one of the technicians in the room, turned to look towards a shadowy corner of the bridge. Dean followed their eye line to see the lanky, bald Predecessor watching them from the shadows. He had been there throughout the operation, and every human being had been very aware of his presence. If they were nervous about him, then this was a weak spot in Ignacio's iron-clad authority.

"Don't let him manipulate you," Dean pressed his advantage. "Don't you see? He wants to use you to change the climate, to put human beings out of their element. Maybe even drive us into extinction, if he can. He tried to get Helmholtz to do that, and now he's tricked you into doing the same thing. If you succeed, you'll be responsible for the downfall of the entire human race. And if you fail, that guy's going to dispose of you—"

The door behind Dean slid open to admit two more guards followed by Brick, whose arms were folded across his chest and his fingers crammed under his armpits. His blue lips were pulled back in a particularly unhappy snarl, and he was clearly fighting the urge to shiver in case others might observe his weakness.

"*Jefe,*" said one of the guards with Brick. "*Nos tomó mucho tiempo para sacar este elefante del techo.*"

"*Gracias,*" Ignacio replied. "*Sus esfuerzos serán reconocidos en su próxima revisión del desempeño.*" Then Ignacio turned to Brick and spoke in English. "You look cold, and I know you've been working beyond your contract to support our agenda. Why don't you go up to the garden room and warm up. You can use the sauna if you like."

Brick's frown turned up slightly at the corners, and he strode to the elevator with a look-at-me-I'm-the-boss's-favorite swagger.

As soon as Brick had departed, Ignacio turned back to Dean. "Now, you said you had nine scientists—how did you say it?—'crunching the numbers?' Did they take into account that the border between the troposphere and the stratosphere constantly shifts elevation? I'm sure you don't even understand why that's important."

"No, I don't understand what you just said," Dean said. "But I do understand that it's nine to two, including you. Nine to two say it could disrupt our global environment—"

"No," Ignacio slashed his hand through the air to cut Dean off. "It's not your turn to speak. It's my turn. And I don't care how many others disagree with me. Numbers don't decide the truth: I do. Now, Dean, you've proven yourself too great a liability for too long. I'm going to have to liquidate you."

He made a gesture for the guards to take Dean out to the hallway, where, presumably, it would be easier to mop up blood.

"McKenzie!" Dean called. "McKenzie! Do you hear me?"

"I'm sorry," Ignacio said. "Invoking her name won't move me to pity, if that's what you're thinking. The truth is, she just didn't mean to me what she meant to you."

"No," Dean said, struggling as they pulled him towards the door. "McKenzie, if you can hear me, get out here!"

A green shaft of light sprang up in the center of the bridge, right next to the central computer consol. As it resolved itself into the ghost of McKenzie, Ignacio took a step back. The technicians stared in amazement. The guards maintained their grip on Dean, but they, too, gawked at the sudden appearance of the mystery woman. Even the Predecessor looked at her.

"I admit that I'm impressed," Ignacio moved around McKenzie slowly, appraising her as she looked back at him. "Is this projection coming from the Egg? I didn't even know they could do that."

"McKenzie," Dean called to her. "Can you help me? Can you do something? Sabotage the weather drones, crash this ship—anything?"

"But I thought I was dating Ignacio now," she spoke through the bridge speakers. "Isn't that the way things work? You and I break up from time to time and go out with other people?"

Dean felt like she'd slugged him with a rock. Yes, that was the exact course their relationship had run in the past, and she only had his memories to draw upon for comparison.

"No, listen, it's not like that now," Dean pleaded. "If you don't help me, more people are going to die. Lots more people, me included. I need you to, I don't know, fight your programming or something!"

Ignacio laughed. "Fight her programming? What do you think this is, an episode of Doctor Who?"

"McKenzie," Dean looked at her. "I need you, baby. Please."

She bit her lip and looked confused. "I'm sorry, Dean," she finally said. "I can't do that for you."

"There, you see?" Ignacio said triumphantly. "I don't know what kind of sick program you installed on this Egg, but I'm going to erase it as soon as we're done with Los Angeles. And now, Dean, you're overdue for your destiny. Take him away, please."

"No!" Dean shouted. He made one last attempt to pull away from the guards, but there were too many of them, and his suit offered many handholds for easy restraint.

He looked to McKenzie, and she looked back at him with a pleasant half smile on her face as if nothing important were going on. Dean stopped struggling against his captors, but he couldn't stop staring at the ghost.

Then, all the lights on the bridge went out. Absolutely all of them, even the computer monitors. After a moment of breathless surprise, Ignacio swore viciously and said "Not again!"

As if in answer to him, the main screen flared to life to show Soap with her usual black lab coat and the purple stripe running down the long side of her asymmetrical haircut. She also wore an eye patch with a cheesy skull-and-crossbones symbol that looked like it might have been a child's birthday party prize.

"Avast, ye scuppering lubber-dogs and prepare to be boarded!" Soap declared as she waved a flimsy plastic cutlass. Then she leaned closer to camera, lifted the eye patch and added, "Hi, Dean! Did I sound like a pirate just there, or what?"

CHAPTER 41

"Who—who the hell are you?" Ignacio raged at Soap's face on the screen.

"Wouldn't you like to know?" she shot back. "All I'm going to say is that you shot up my school and now you've kidnapped my cousin." She paused a second. "I guess I just gave away who I was, didn't I?"

Ignacio turned to his technicians. "Get her off the screen."

The nearest technician shook her head. "Controls are dead. We're locked out. Nothing's responding."

"I don't want excuses!" Ignacio roared. "I'm firing the next person to make excuses instead of progress—and then I'm personally going to shoot that person!"

The technician hunched forward and tapped at the dead keyboard in a pathetic ploy to appear busy.

Dean looked up at the screen. Soap's camera was angled up so the churning black and green clouds served as her backdrop. At the bottom edge, however, Dean could see palm fronds waving in a strong wind and the tip of a red pointed roof that he immediately recognized as the famous TCL Chinese Theater.

Somehow, she had come here, to Los Angeles. Despite all his efforts at keeping her out of this ugly business, Soap had placed herself in the path of the storms almost as quickly as he had. (He had been flying a jet suit—how had she covered so much distance in the same time?) She had lied to him and disobeyed him, and now she had found her way to the center of Ignacio's bull's-eye.

Dean might have expected himself to feel angry about it, but he just couldn't gather the energy for such an extreme emotion. Whatever Soap had done, he was guilty of the exact same thing, and she was in a much better position than he was. All he could do was acknowledge the absurdity of how everything was turning out. Somehow, his acceptance planted the seed of a giggle in his stomach. Before he knew it, that giggle swiftly bloomed into raucous laughter that echoed all around the bridge.

"What?" Ignacio demanded. "What do you think is so funny?" The anger on his face seeming to glow like an ember in the gloom, and it made Dean laugh even harder.

His laughter wasn't really about humor. It was more of a psychological release, the emotional equivalent of loosening the pressure valve on a boiler. His mind was as spent as his body, and now he found he couldn't take anything seriously, not his students and his cousin being here in LA, or the guard with the gun standing behind him, or even Ignacio's red face pressing close to his. All he could picture in his mind was the Newton's Cradle, the stupid ball-clicking desk toy that transferred energy from one side to the other. *Click, click, click*, over and over again with no visible motion connecting the moving parts.

"You can't see the connections, can you, Ignacio?" Dean laughed. "To you, this is just as random and unpredictable as the weather. You had no way to predict that when you attacked our school, you knocked one ball into the next, and now it's swinging back to hit you."

"You're insane," Ignacio said.

"That's backwards," Dean said. "Usually, it's the good guy who says that to the bad guy,"

"I am the good guy," Ignacio insisted.

"Ahem!" Soap's voice boomed through the loudspeakers. "Remember me? I'm the one in charge of everything right now. So, here's the scoop, Mr. Stormy-pants. My hunter-killer drones are better than yours. Like, way better. I just had them break the antenna array on your ship and install my own, which is how I'm broadcasting to you, by the way. Next, I'm going to have them destroy your entire drone fleet, right after they're done cutting through your hull and messing with all your systems."

Ignacio let out a long, inhuman sound that might have started as an angry roar but ended up sounding more like a frustrated gurgle. He shoved one of the technicians out of his chair and hammered furiously at the keyboard, but got no more results than anyone else. Then he flung himself at the central computer console, ripped it open, and started rearranging circuit boards inside.

Dean could see McKenzie's Egg inside that console, and he stopped laughing.

"My drones also borked your generators," Soap said. "That's why you have no power, and now they're busy poking holes in your helium tanks, so your ship's going down. Hard. Right in the middle of the tornado storms you created. How much did you spend on this hunk of bolts, anyway? 'Cause your ride's about to get totaled."

Without warning, the deck lurched under their feet. Ignacio turned to the screen and made a dramatic show of spitting at Soap. Then he seemed to remember himself and slicked back his hair as he took a long, slow breath. Every technician and guard watched him the way a beaten dog watches its drunken master on a rampage.

Ignacio saw them looking at him and yanked McKenzie's Egg out of the central console. As soon as he did, the green image of McKenzie winked out of existence. Then he stalked over to Dean.

"Give me the gun," he demanded of the guard. "I'm going to shoot Dean in the face. I'm going to do it myself, and she can watch!" He pointed back at Soap's image on the screen.

"Wait, no!" Soap said, flipping up her pirate eye-patch. "That's not part of my plan!"

Dean didn't need a plan to respond to that. He was content to improvise.

Ignacio held out his hand like a surgeon expecting a scalpel. It took the guard a moment to figure out what he wanted and then, hesitantly, he placed his weapon in his boss's palm. In the instant after one man's fingers opened and before the other man's closed, Dean snapped out a quick kick, knocking the pistol out of their hands and sending it skidding across the floor into the shadows.

Ignacio stared into the darkness where the gun had disappeared, his breath whistling in and out of his nose.

"You can't," he seethed. "You can't..."

"Just did, you big hippy sap," Dean grinned. "What're you going to do about it?"

Ignacio punched Dean in the head. It was a weak blow that thudded into the thick of Dean's skull and probably hurt Ignacio's hand more than Dean's head. Even so, this was enough to give the message to the guards: pummeling time had begun. The two men pinning Dean's arms wrenched him backwards to hold him tight while the third came around swinging.

Dean wasn't about to sit there and take it. Even without the jet suit, he would have outweighed the heaviest of them by at least fifty pounds of pure muscle. With the suit, even as tired as he was, he could buck like a mule. He shoved first to the left, and when he felt them pushing back, he reversed directions and slammed all his weight to the right, driving the guard on that side all the way to the wall.

The guard's arm bent into the wall with a loud crunch that almost certainly indicated a fractured bone. Dean knew it would take an incredibly determined fighter to keep going after that, and he knew this guy didn't qualify because he yowled in pain and sank to the floor holding his wounded arm.

Two more guards remained, but Ignacio had already given up and bolted for the elevator to his garden. As if that weren't bad enough for his employees' morale, at that same moment a pinprick of white flames burst through the port-side bulkhead and moved in a counterclockwise arc around the wall. When the flames had completed a full circle, a disk cut from the wall fell to the floor with a clank.

Through this new hole, one of Soap's drones buzzed onto the bridge like a fat, lazy insect. It was about the size of a human head and painted with an exaggerated animal face like those found on World War II fighter planes, complete with fiery red eyes and a snarling mouth full of sharp teeth. Its blocky body projected four struts, each with a softly whirring helicopter rotor, and its chin carried a small turret that spurted the bright blue flames of an acetylene cutting torch.

The drone floated slowly into the room, turning slightly as if watching everyone with its painted red eyes. As it drifted closer to one technician, he panicked and fled to the exit, causing all the other technicians to leap from their seats and stampede right after him. They pushed and shoved the guards out of their way, until the guards, too, took the opportunity to disappear into the crowd as they raced for the escape hatches.

Now it was just Dean, alone on the bridge with the picture of Soap up on the screen.

"You're in big trouble, young lady," Dean said. "I mean it. Double-secret probation."

"Double what?" she asked innocently.

"Never mind. And I'm not going to ask the obvious, stupid question about why you're here. Did the others come, too?"

"Most of them. Victor. Nikki. Collin. Speed, too. She's cool."

"How did you guys get here so fast?"

"Victor rented a private jet."

"A private..." Dean's voice trailed off. For once, Dean wished Victor would waste his family fortune on ridiculous cars with gold hubcaps instead of enabling deadly science side-projects.

"Never mind any of that," Dean said. "Soap, can you really use your robots to take out Ignacio's drones?"

"Well..." Soap's face was suddenly grave. "I was kind of bluffing back there. Nikki said I should bluff."

"Bluffing about what?"

"Don't get me wrong, my drones really are awesome. The thing is, I don't have very many. Five, to be exact. Ignacio has millions, so it would probably take me a month just to make a noticeable impact."

Dean closed his eyes to think. They couldn't take out Ignacio's drone fleet, and even if they could, it wouldn't be soon enough to stop the storms from ripping L.A. to pieces. Dean needed to find a way to take control of the drones, the way he had controlled them in Buenos Aires. But that had destroyed an Egg and killed Mark Twain's ghost. If he did this it again, he would have to sacrifice Tesla... or McKenzie.

"Soap, can you get this broadcaster working again? Can we take control of Ignacio's fleet?"

"Sorry, I accidentally shredded their communication cluster, pretty much. It would take a long time to fix."

This time it was Dean's turn to end the conversation abruptly. He dashed towards the elevator that ran up to the garden. Ignacio was now Dean's best hope—he was the only one who might be able to repair the equipment on this ship. Ignacio might not be favorable to the idea of working against his own storms, but Dean was reasonably confident that Ignacio might come to see things differently after getting punched in the face a few times.

The elevator doors were wide open and the car was still in place. Dean hadn't been able to watch where Ignacio had fled, but he realized that without power to the elevator, it wasn't going to carry anyone anywhere. So where had he gone? Dean might have been fooled by the disappearing act if he hadn't been trained in elevator operation and rescue. He raised his hands to the ceiling and found the emergency escape trap door. He pressed it open and stepped away just in case Ignacio was waiting in ambush. He wasn't, so Dean stripped himself of the flight suit down to the waist, thereby lightening his gear by about twenty pounds, and hoisted himself up on top of the elevator car.

The elevator shaft was short—it only served two floors—but it contained an access ladder. Dean scaled the rungs as quickly as he could and found the doors on the next level already open. Inside, a riot of birds screeched in alarm, but Dean could hear Ignacio's voice amidst the racket.

"The palace isn't falling that quickly," Ignacio said. "You'll survive the landing. I guarantee it."

"Then how come you're bailing out?" The low rumble could only be Brick's voice.

"I'm not bailing out, I'm going to finish—"

Dean took that moment to step through the door. He had hoped to see Ignacio jump at the sight of him, at least a little. Instead, he and Brick were facing away from him. Ignacio glanced around, saw Dean, but then turned to continue looking towards the far side of the dome. If Ignacio and Brick seemed so unconcerned about Dean, it could only mean that there was a greater threat in the garden, and it didn't take Dean long to see what it was.

The Predecessor loomed in the shadows of the little Japanese-style teahouse, watching Ignacio with pale eyes that seemed to shimmer in the gray light. He stood calmly, with one hand behind his back, the other flexing his fingers in a slow, patient, I'm-going-to-kill-you gesture.

Whatever twisted, animal logic was playing out inside the Predecessor's bald head, it was bad news for Dean and probably everyone else in that room.

CHAPTER 42

"How'd he get in here?" Brick jabbed a bratwurst-sized finger at the Predecessor.

The question went unanswered. Dean didn't dare to guess, but he had once seen the Predecessor transform himself into a string of ants, march through a barrier, and then reassemble his human form on the other side. Two hundred million years of genetic manipulation on his own body meant nothing would be off-limits to the Predecessor.

Ignacio, however, had a few tricks of his own, and the Predecessor was standing right next to the electrodes hidden in the teahouse. Dean remembered clearly how well they had worked on him and hoped they could do the same to the Predecessor.

"I've got a little surprise for you, my friend," Ignacio said as he drew a small remote from his pocket. "It runs on its own batteries so it doesn't matter if the rest of the ship has lost power. Risk management is important in my business, after all."

With a smug grin, Ignacio pressed the button.

Nothing happened.

He pressed it again, and then again. The birds overhead continued to screech, and there was no flash or crackle to startle them into silence.

The Predecessor revealed the hand he had been hiding behind his back. Lightning burned the sky above them, perfectly timed to reveal that he held a broken metal prong, the head of the electric stun gun Ignacio had hidden inside the wall.

"How—how did you know?" Ignacio stammered.

The Predecessor didn't speak, but a single bird fluttered to his shoulder and hopped sideways up to his neck. It paused there, pressing into him as if nuzzling, but there was something unnatural about its motion. Slowly, its feathers popped off one by one and its little body sank into the Predecessor's skin like a scrap of bread sinking into water. Soon, it looked like a deformed growth on his neck, with a crooked wing sticking out at an odd angle and a little bird foot occasionally twitching as it gradually merged with his neck.

That bird had been the spy, Dean realized. It had been a piece of the Predecessor's body that he had left here, hidden among the other birds, for the single purpose of listening in on Ignacio's schemes. Ignacio and the Predecessor had evidently been playing a deadly game of chess with each other all along, and Ignacio was now in check.

Dean knew the smart thing to do would be to sprint for the elevator shaft and hope the Predecessor would be too busy slaughtering Ignacio to worry about chasing him. But then again, the Predecessor might track him down like a bloodhound. And the storms would be free to rage on. If Dean didn't find some way to pull Ignacio out of the fire, a whole city would burn with him.

A quick glance around the garden revealed that the best weapon was a little stone Japanese lantern, about two feet tall. Dean wrenched it from its spot as the Predecessor slid towards the three of them with graceful, unhurried steps.

Ignacio had one last line of defense, however, and he wasn't about to forget it.

"Stop him!" he commanded Brick. Then, like any other corrupt CEO, he turned and ran from the trouble.

Brick, either ignorant of what this Predecessor really was or—more likely—supremely overconfident, stomped out to the center of the garden to cover Ignacio's retreat. For a second, Dean believed that maybe, just maybe, Brick might be able to win. Yes, the Predecessor was millions of years old, but he was an animal, and ultimately the smaller animal in this fight. How could those long, snaking limbs really overpower Brick's massive body? How could he pierce all that armor Brick carried under his skin?

Just to be sure, Dean rushed in to help, the stone lantern unwieldy but reassuringly heavy in his hands.

Brick was still a few paces ahead, thundering forward like a rhino claiming his territory. He seized the Predecessor by the shoulders and lifted him into the air in preparation for a body slam. Another bolt of lightning bathed the struggle in a brilliant blue-white strobe. If it hadn't flashed at that exact moment, Dean might not have seen that the Predecessor's index finger now ended in a curving, translucent spike. His nail had become a sharp snake's fang, and it glistened at the point with some kind of thick fluid.

The Predecessor scraped Brick's arm with the elongated fingernail, a quick gesture performed with the precision and detachment of a surgeon's opening cut. It left a wound no more than two inches in length and barely deep enough to draw blood. It was nothing more than a scratch, but the finger-fang didn't have to go deep to deliver its venom. Brick howled in pain, sank to his knees, and grasped the curving red line that ran down his bicep. The Predecessor landed lightly on his feet and the fang-like nail slid back into his finger like a silent switchblade.

Dean took the opportunity to swing the lantern hard against the side of the Predecessor's head. The impact shattered his makeshift weapon into jagged chunks and sent a shockwave of pain through Dean's hand. Any normal human being would have needed a CT scan and a few days in the hospital after being bashed in the temple by twenty pounds of concrete, but the Predecessor took only one step backwards. One, single step. And then he turned his attention to Dean.

Dean didn't even see the blow coming. All he knew was that everything suddenly seemed to fly backwards around him and it only stopped when he crashed to the ground. Hard. Then the pain caught up to him: his ribs throbbed, his shoulder blazed with pain, and his vision filled with pulsing white streaks of pure agony. Slowly, as if seeing through a fog, he became aware that the Predecessor was striding towards him.

Dean tried to roll to his feet, but when he put weight on his left arm he felt lances of fire skewering his upper shoulder girdle. It was his clavicle bone. He knew it because he had broken it once before.

"You busted the same shoulder," he panted. "The same damn shoulder as last time we met."

Dean looked up at the Predecessor and gasped. The creature was undergoing some kind of bodily transformation: his jaw had lengthened and his lips pulled back to reveal a row of scimitar teeth. He was now bent forward at the waste as his hindquarters sprouted two extra sets of legs, thin enough that they might have looked insectoid except that they were covered in pebbled reptilian skin. His forearms split down the middle so that each of his arms ended in two hands, and all his fingers now sprouted claw-fangs just like the one that had put Brick down.

Dean fell backwards in surprise, forgetting the pain in his shoulder as his mind struggled to take in the Predecessor's new appearance. He had always known that this was a monster masquerading in the shape of a person, and now he had to wonder if this was the thing's true form—or if it even had a true form.

The Predecessor looked towards the elevator shaft, evidently weighing whether to chase after Ignacio now or kill Dean first. Then his reptilian eyes flicked back to fix on Dean. Brick lay helpless nearby, his lips blue, his body shuddering slightly with each agonized breath. The big man could be of no help, so it was just Dean, alone, against a monster that was faster and stronger than any human being. He hadn't been able to beat this creature with his best sucker-punch. Now, with a broken clavicle, he didn't stand a chance.

Shakily, Dean rose to his feet and looked the creature in its yellow eyes. It might have been about to kill him, but at least he could show that he wasn't afraid, right to the very end.

The Predecessor lunged forward—and stopped short as the deck bucked violently under their feet. The ship groaned with the sound of bending metal and a shockwave knocked Dean to the floor. A jolt of pain shot from his broken shoulder all the way down to his fingers and back up again. His vision blurred for an instant but cleared just in time for him to throw his good arm over his head to protect against the shards of Plexiglas that rained down from the breaking dome overhead. The Predecessor bounded backwards, landing ten feet away and almost—almost!—losing his balance. He dropped down on his mutated fingers and reptilian toes, coiled like a nightmarish panther ready to spring. His new posture made him seem less human than ever, and the snarl on his grotesque lips showed that he wanted to kill whatever had shaken the ship.

The ground, Dean realized. *We were falling and hit the ground.*

The birds shrieked deafeningly as they swirled out through the shattered dome. The deck tilted downwards as the ship settled, and water drained in a steady stream from the koi pond. Occasionally, the draining water carried one of the robotic fish that flapped its tail automatically as it slid towards the far side of the room.

Dean clamped his injured arm to his side and tried to stand, which he found nearly impossible on the wet, sloping floor.

The Predecessor straightened out to walk on his four hind legs, pacing cautiously towards Dean once more.

A red dot flashed on the floor directly in the Predecessor's path. It was a laser point, like a cat's toy, but larger by a full inch in diameter. The crimson spot danced around in erratic circles, criss-crossing the Predecessor's head several times. Finally, it reached a shaky sort of focus right in front of him and remained there.

The Predecessor obviously didn't understand that this dot was the end point of a beam originating high above. He reached down to scoop it up off the floor, sliding what now passed for his hand underneath the dot so that it now appeared in his palm.

He sniffed the dot, peered closely at it, and finally licked it with a long, snaking tongue.

Without warning, the Predecessor's head snapped towards the edge of the shattered dome. A moment later Soap sailed in, an electromagnetic flight pack on her back. Her elaborate techno-goggles covered her eyes and her purple and black hair played freely in the wind. She carried her phone in her right hand, and from the way her thumb flew over its surface Dean knew exactly what app she was running: she had control of some drone up in the sky and was steering it to keep its targeting laser aimed right onto the Predecessor.

And Soap wasn't alone. The Predecessor's head swiveled left to right, sensing each new student a moment before they rode in on their own flight packs. Victor arrived next in his trim white lab coat and polo shirt, followed by Nikki in a bright pink coat that fluttered and snapped in the wind. Then came Collin with his green Mohawk, and Speed in a red-and-black Italian-style motorcycle jacket. They touched down lightly to form a circle around the Predecessor, and all of them held lightning lances with targeting lasers dancing on the monster's chest.

The Predecessor looked around at them, then down to the red dots skittering across his body. He still cupped the large laser dot in his hand—or what had once been his hand and now looked more like the spike-tipped tentacle of some deep-sea monstrosity.

"You are weak," the Predecessor spoke with a voice that reverberated throughout the garden. He sounded as if he were speaking through several throats at once, and none of these voices were entirely human. His words came out as a nightmare chorus, a sound that boiled up from nowhere and everywhere at the same time. "You are easy prey," he uttered. "Your weapons do not even hurt me."

"Nope," Soap said. "But this is going to kick your ass."

She pressed the button on her phone. The big red dot pulsed in the Predecessor's hand, growing wider for an instant. Then the world went searing white and shook with a deafening explosion.

The light had flashed so quickly Dean couldn't blink fast enough to protect his eyes, yet it left no trace save a white slash on his vision. Gradually, the white mark faded to red and then yellow, and after a full three seconds he could finally see the blackened patch of artificial lawn where the Predecessor had stood a moment before.

"Vaporized!" Soap yelled in triumph. "Fifty thousand degrees—even a Predecessor can't come back from that one!"

Dean worked to stand up, bracing himself at the intersection between the sloping floor and the wall. He failed to keep his feet out of the water that had drained from of the koi pond, but at least he managed not to jar his broken shoulder too badly. Several patiently flapping robot fish also occupied that corner, as well as Brick, whose enormous belly and blocky head rose above the small pool like a volcanic island.

Dean bent down over Brick and found that he was wheezing raggedly. He may have been a giant, but a king cobra's venom could take down an elephant, and whatever the Predecessor had used could have been even more lethal.

"Only a scratch..." Brick whispered, reaching for the mark on his forearm where the Predecessor had nicked him with his finger-fang. It seemed like such a small wound, even now that the edges were burning red with inflation and the center had taken on a deathly blue pallor.

"Don't speak," Dean said. "Save your strength.

Brick ignored him. "A scratch. But I'm... bullet proof... This ain't fair. Just ain't fair..."

His breathing then stopped altogether, and his gigantic body settled in on itself like a tire with a fast leak.

"What happened to him?" Victor knelt down in the water next to Brick.

"Snake venom," Dean said, not sure how to be any more accurate than that.

Soap crowded in next, and when she saw Brick, her eyes glazed over with tears. That was something Dean would never stop wondering about her: for all the violent power she commended through her robots and lightning lances, she never felt hatred for anyone, not even this big, cruel giant. Her tears reminded Dean that Brick had always proven to be a brave and loyal soldier to his employer. Maybe he deserved some respect for that, despite everything else.

A sudden buzzing outside drew their attention to a mosquito pod zipping away through the stormy sky.

Dean narrowed his eyes as he watched it fly off. It had to be Ignacio in that pod: no one else remained on the ship to pilot it.

Collin fired a blast from his lightning lance out through the broken dome, but Ignacio's pod was already far out of range.

"Where's he goin' to, anyway?" Nikki asked. "Just runnin' off with his tail between his legs, I guess."

"Maybe not," Soap said. "He might be going to the other sky palace. He has the codes so that he can shift control of the drones back over there and keep boosting the storms."

"And he's got McKenzie's Egg," Dean grimaced as he said it.

"Can he do that?" Collin asked. "Can he get that other ship running? I thought it got wrecked worse than one of Pete Townshend's guitars."

"He's got a better chance there than here," Soap shrugged. "If I was him, I'd at least give it a try."

Dean moved to the edge of the garden dome. They had landed in the middle of a suburb, where white stucco houses and red tile roofs were all ringed in by a witch's brew of clouds. From where he stood, Dean could count at least a dozen black funnel clouds in the distance, all clawing their way towards the Earth. If Ignacio could make this storm even worse, he had to be stopped. And Dean still had Tesla's egg, which meant he had a chance to do something about it.

"We can't catch him with these flight packs," Speed said. "That flying jet bubble thing looked like it moves about six times as fast as we can. How's your rocket suit doing?"

"Fubared," is what Dean meant to say. Most of the word came out, but the syllables were severely hampered by an involuntary wince of pain as his broken shoulder shifted in its socket. Suddenly he felt woozy and a little dizzy.

"Let me look at that shoulder," Victor cradled Dean's arm and ran his fingers lightly over the injured spot. He managed to do it in a way that wasn't quite excruciating.

"Get me a sling," Dean told Victor.

"You need a full cast," Victor said. "You also need some sedatives, and then a course of my stem-cell activator injections."

"No time," Dean forced his eyes to focus through the pain. "I'm going after him. Alone. Right now."

And I'm coming back with McKenzie, he added silently to himself. *Or else I'm not coming back at all.*

CHAPTER 43

The students tried to argue, but Dean remained adamant that he and he alone could pursue Ignacio. Only one functioning mosquito pod remained aboard the *Tlaloc*, and it wasn't big enough to carry a housecat on the pilot's lap, let alone a group of overeager young techno-wizards. Furthermore, he needed to get Ignacio to cooperate. He didn't know how he was going to do that, but none of them knew Ignacio the way he did so none of them had a chance of talking sense into the man. There wasn't much they could do to stop Dean, so the students let him go while they stayed to strip the crashed sky palace of its teslanium and antimatter reactors.

It took no more than a few minutes to load himself into the remaining mosquito pod and skim out towards the hills. Soon he could see what was left of the Hollywood sign and the *Raiden* wedged in the cliff next to it. The once-menacing ship now sagged at a dangerous angle, almost perpendicular to the ground, with burst hull plates hanging loose from their scaffolding. It was lucky that the docking procedure for the mosquito pod was automatic because no human hand could have guided it in at that angle, especially with the wind gusting up the hillside and threatening to knock the pod around like a ping-pong ball.

When the hatch finally clicked open and Dean's seat spun around to allow him to exit, he crawled through sideways to board the darkened and badly tilted ship. He was as careful as he could be with his injured shoulder, but he still bumped it on the side of the hatch which paralyzed him with pain. He lay there for a time, clutching his shoulder and pressing his cheek to the cool metal of the deck floor. A little drool may have escaped his mouth—he wasn't sure about that, but he was beyond caring anyway. This was the danger time: he had burned through all the adrenaline his body could make, and now the agony of all his injuries and the exhaustion of all his labors worked together to grip him like hands that threatened to drag him down into oblivion.

The thought occurred that he could simply lie there. He was safe, at least for the moment, and the floor felt surprisingly comfortable. No one could blame him if he just passed out. Sleep might have taken him right there if not for the howling of the wind outside.

He forced his eyes open. He couldn't allow himself to rest. Not while the storms were out there, ripping the city to pieces. And not while McKenzie was so close. Now he clung to those two ideas: his home and his love. If he let them go now, after all he'd been through, then there would be nothing left of him. Dying meant he would have no future, but losing his home and his love would mean he had no past, and that thought wouldn't let him stay down.

He rose to his feet and staggered into the hallway and then paused. He had a crazy idea, and after a good thirty seconds of deliberation, he decided he might not live long enough to regret it. The emergency pod release lever was concealed next to the docking portals. Dean undid the locking clasp and found the lever surprisingly easy to throw. With a clank, the hatch opening slid shut and the pod dropped away to tumble down the hillside. Dean repeated the procedure with the pod Ignacio had flown.

There were no other pods: now it was just the two of them, Ignacio and Dean, trapped inside this ship together.

Now Dean had to find the man and reason with him. Moving through the *Raiden* was doubly difficult because the angle of the ship had turned all the corridors nearly sideways, forcing him to walk on the curving wall while the floor decking ran beside his head. Darkness proved to be another obstacle, because he had to grope blindly in search of doorways in what had once been a wall yet now served as the ceiling. It was like a carnival funhouse, but without the fun.

"Tesla," Dean said. "Can you give me some light?"

Tesla's Egg was still in his pocket, and now the faint image of the ghost sprang into being in front of him.

"Without light, I'm as blind as you are," Tesla's voice came through the hallway PA speakers, no louder than a whisper and more than a little garbled. "I may be even blinder, considering that my low-light vision seems to be worse than yours."

Tesla's glow didn't extend more than a few inches, but it was better than nothing. The two worked in silence through the difficult angles of the corridors and bent corridors.

Eventually, Dean found the bridge door; it was already open and could just manage to peer through it. There, at the very bottom of the bridge, Ignacio sat with folded legs, typing away at a keyboard in his lap. The left half of his face was cast in a blue light from a monitor he had set up on the floor next to him, while the other half of his face was bathed in green from the ghost of McKenzie standing to his right.

"Eastern sector 431?" he asked her in a coldly hurried tone.

"Winds at 210 miles per hour," she answered. "Curvature of one degree per 0.8 meters. Pressure differential 80 percent."

"Raise heat 2 degrees, and find me 3 more points of humidity. That pressure differential needs to be at least 300 percent by the next—"

Dean swung his leg over the oddly angled doorway and dropped into the room.

"Ignacio," he called, but that was all he had time to say before Ignacio threw the keyboard off his lap and produced a gun. It looked identical to the one the guard had back on the *Tlaloc*. Either he had retrieved it before he fled or else he had another stashed aboard this sky palace.

Ignacio evidently had no intention to discuss anything, because he began squeezing the trigger as fast as he could even before he finished rising to his feet. For the span of about five seconds, the bridge thundered with the gunfire as bullets sparked off the walls and computer terminals. Dean dove sideways towards a cluster of broken swivel chairs and desks, hitting hard against the uneven surface and gritting his teeth against yet another jolt of pain in his shoulder.

"Go, sportsball!" he heard McKenzie cheer through the bridge's sound system, her voice magnified to be audible even over the ringing in Dean's ears.

Heck of a time to start playing ironic cheerleader, Dean thought as he hid amid a jumble of chairs.

As the pain in his shoulder became more manageable, he became aware of a new stinging sensation in his calf. When he looked down, he could see that he'd been shot. The jet suit bore a hole so small that it would have been invisible in the dim light had it not been for the wet, black stain that spread along the fabric as he watched.

The pain was quickly amplifying now, working its way up from a sting to a grinding throb. Dean knew that there was no such thing as a trivial gunshot wound: In the split second when the bullet hit, the supersonic shockwave had stretched the muscle and skin around the injury like a balloon, ripping and pulling everything out of place. It would be a long time before he'd be able to play broomball again.

He ran his fingers along his shin and muttered a quick prayer of thanks that the bone hadn't been broken. On the downside, he could find no exit wound, which meant the bullet was still inside him. Every time he so much as twitched his toes, his calf muscle would slide over that jagged hunk of lead and slice themselves up even worse. And if the slug wiggled its way to the artery, he would bleed out long before he could receive medical help.

There was nothing he could do about it now. He stood on his one good leg and raised his good arm in the air to show surrender. In the movies, action heroes exchange witty lines in the middle of gunfire, but in real life, spoken communication is nearly impossible for several minutes after that kind of noise in an enclosed space.

Dean remained standing, awkwardly, and dropped his hands down to his sides. Ignacio kept the gun pointed right at him.

"We need to talk," Dean said.

Ignacio didn't react. The green ghost of McKenzie looked back and forth between the two of them, a pleasant smile on her face. She looked as if they were all about to sit down for brunch.

Dean worked his way out from behind the clutter of chairs, hopping on his good leg. Ignacio said something not quite loud enough for Dean to hear yet, but clear enough to express the threat that he would shoot again.

"You can't fire," Dean said as loudly as he could. "You panicked, and people who panic waste all their ammo. I'm ready to bet my life that's exactly what you did."

The pause lingered long enough for the ringing in his ears to mostly subside.

"I didn't panic. I just don't need this anymore." Ignacio tossed the empty gun away, the hint of a pout on his face.

"I only want to talk," Dean said. "You need to stop the storms. Stop them now, before it's too late."

"It's the only way," Ignacio's eyes flicked down towards Dean's injured leg. Whether or not he could see the trail of dark blood behind him, it was clear he knew Dean had been hurt. "You can't stop me, Dean. Look at you: you can hardly even stand up. With your arm in a sling and that hole in your leg, you're weaker than a kitten."

"This is only the second worst I've ever been shot," Dean tried to sound strong as he hopped forward. This would have been the perfect time to cash in on all that practice at not showing weakness, but his leg betrayed him. On his third hop, he came down slightly off balance on the curving floor and he instinctively set the toes of his bad leg onto the ground to compensate. The moment he did, a bolt of pain shot through him and his mind played the horrible mental image of his calf muscle pulling apart like a frayed rope. He fell on his good shoulder, but the jolt still made the broken ends of his clavicle grind together.

"I'd say you've overextended your business model," Ignacio gloated.

Dean gasped air until he could speak again. "The atmosphere," he said. "You're going to send us into nuclear winter. It's a fact—"

"Oh, you can shut up about your facts," Ignacio picked up his fallen keyboard and began typing, although he kept watch on Dean while he worked. "I'm the one with the power to do something about it, so I'm the one who gets to decide what the facts are."

"The fact is," Dean rose shakily to his hands and knees—or, at least, to one hand and one knee. "If you keep this storm going, it's going to kill you."

"Ha!" Ignacio said flatly.

"I mean it," Dean looked him in the eye. "You're stuck here in the path of your own tornadoes. I ejected the mosquito pods; I doubt there's a single flight pack left on this ship after the crew bailed out—hell, Brick took two packs just for himself. Climbing down that cliff would be suicide, especially in this weather. Face it: it's just you and me, trapped in here until we can come to an agreement."

"You can't stop me," Ignacio held the keyboard up, his finger hovering over the enter button. "It's an automated program. As soon as I press this, the drones are on their own and there's no going back."

"Use your head, Ignacio. You're not safely parked on the outskirts any more. You're right in the middle of it. If you don't start reversing these storms, it's only a matter of time before the wind scoops us off the side of this cliff and spreads tiny pieces of us all over the county. I'm not asking you for some kind of grand gesture. I'm not asking you for a brilliant plan. All I'm asking is that you not kill yourself, because now whatever you do to this city, you're going to do to yourself, too."

Ignacio's face went slack for a moment, but his finger still floated over the activation key. Outside, the wind roared and hammered at the warped hull of the sky palace.

Dean limped closer, now a comfortable conversational distance from Ignacio. He thought about making a grab for the keyboard, but in his condition he wasn't sure he could move fast enough. The agony of his leg burned relentlessly, as did his shoulder. He felt lightheaded, either from blood loss or the raw pain of his injuries, or probably both. Here they were, parked right on top of the Hollywood sign, and he was having to break another of the time-honored movie-hero traditions, the one where the good guy gets hurt, then miraculously bounces back, fully recovered after only a few minutes. Dean was no movie hero, and his injuries were going to continue to get worse until he either died or underwent surgery.

"I see our predicament," Ignacio's shoulders slouched with an exaggerated resignation. "It's my life or my project. You once said I was a flake, didn't you Dean?"

More than once, Dean thought. *And words much worse than "flake."*

"Yes, there's no point in denying it," Ignacio went on. "You said I was a flake, a person who doesn't truly believe in what he says. You were convinced that everything I did was some kind of show, put on for the gratification of my ego and my bank account. As you pointed out, I was risking nothing for my ideals. Well, now it's different. Now I have to lay down my own life if I wish to implement my dream. So I thank you, Dean. I really mean it. You've forced me to risk something. You've given me the chance to prove what I'm really made of."

With a small flourish, Ignacio clicked the button.

Dean's right hook caught Ignacio on the point of the jaw with an immensely satisfying *THUNK!* But his satisfaction was cut short as his left leg gave out from under him and he tumbled down to land right next to Ignacio.

Dean's head swam through oceans of red and white anguish. When his eyes finally focused, he looked over to see Ignacio out cold, his lips pulled back in a slack grin and a trickle of drool escaping between two missing teeth. He didn't look so slick any more but, to be fair, neither did Dean.

The monitor on the floor scrolled through columns of numbers in a continuous blur of calculus.

"McKenzie!" Dean croaked as he tried to sit up. "McKenzie! Can you stop this storm?"

"Yes, of course," she said.

"Even though Ignacio locked the drones into autopilot?"

"That's not an issue," she said. "He's a great mathematician, but not the best programmer. However, it will take me some time to counteract the tornadoes. Also, the process will cause me to overheat and die. I'll begin right away."

"Hold on," Dean managed to get back up on his one good foot. He opened the control console, saw McKenzie's Egg inside its nest of wires, and drew Tesla's Egg from his pocket. In the darkness, it was limned in a pale rainbow and seemed incredibly heavy in his hand.

"Tesla," Dean said. "Can you stop it?"

"Yes," Professor Tesla's green form sprang into existence in front of Dean. "But it will destroy me just as surely as it would destroy McKenzie. So you must decide—which of us is it going to be?"

CHAPTER 44

Dean looked from the ghost of McKenzie to the ghost of Tesla, then up to the open control console. Her Egg rested inside, but it would only take a second to swap it for the other one. If he did, Tesla would die. If he didn't, McKenzie would die. And if they did nothing, thousands of innocent people would die.

"If you place me inside the console," Tesla said. "I shall not hesitate to follow the example of my noble friend Sam Clemens."

"But the kids—they love you," Dean didn't want to see Soap's face when she found out that her idol had been lost forever. "We'd never be able to find a better professor for the Institute, living or dead. And—and you're alive. Aren't you?"

Somewhere along the way, Dean had lost track of whether he was speaking to Tesla or McKenzie. His statement and his question could have applied to either.

"Perhaps I am alive," Tesla said. "Or perhaps I am simply programmed to feel alive. I have always believed that all human behavior is simply a response to stimuli, yet that is no reason to choose me over her. If indeed you are correct and she has the capability to think for herself, then she is a new kind of creature, not exactly like me, but certainly with an equal claim to life. If you are wrong, however, then she's the logical choice to sacrifice."

"How do I know?" Dean closed his eyes and allowed his dizziness to wash over him. "How do I know?"

"The Turning test," McKenzie said. "It's the only test of consciousness we have."

"Indeed," Tesla confirmed. "If she can pass for a person, then she deserves to be treated like a person. As you are the only certifiable person in this room, Dean, this is a test only you can conduct. Please decide swiftly."

Tesla didn't have to say what was at stake. Every moment Dean delayed, lightning burned through houses and winds ripped open buildings.

"McKenzie," he said.

"Yes, Dean," she answered with a lightness that might have been more fitting for a sunny day at the beach.

"When Ignacio shot at me and I dove for cover, you shouted 'go sportsball.' Why?"

"Is this question part of the test?" she asked.

"Just tell me why. I need to know why you said it."

"Well, I shouted 'go sportsball' because you were running and jumping," she said simply. "It's what I say when you run and jump."

Dean nodded, feeling the tears sting his eyes. What she had said was true: whenever he took to the football field or the baseball diamond, the original McKenzie had always shouted her ironic, teasing cheer. This ghostly version of her did the same except that now she lacked the frame of reference to distinguish between a ballgame and a gunfight.

In the instant of his realization, Dean's loss flooded through him just as strongly as it had on the day he found her body. He couldn't pull his eyes away from the ghost, but he couldn't help looking right through her shimmering, translucent form to the Egg in the console behind her. She was a spirit, a shade, assembled from nothing but the passing footprints of the woman he had loved. Now, finally, he could understand what Heidi had been telling him about the myth of Orpheus and how looking back meant losing her forever. The story wasn't just ancient mumbo-jumbo; it spoke of something that happened everywhere, in every culture, to everyone who had ever lost someone and tried to permanently stop themselves from moving into the future in order to cling to the memory of the past. They might not know they're doing it, but they can't go on like that because human beings simply aren't made to stop living their lives. Stopping is the opposite of living: living people have to set the Newton's Cradle of the world in motion and then swing with whatever happens, good or bad. Maybe people can't always see how the ripples of their actions ultimately spread around the world, but nobody gets a choice about whether or not they make an impact. The only choice is what kind of impact to make.

"Do it," Dean whispered to McKenzie. "Stop the storm."

Speaking those words felt like performing heart surgery on himself. He looked at her ghostly form, desperately determined to memorize every detail of her face. All he could think about was that the green of her holographic body was identical to the green her eyes had been in life. Or where they? Maybe his recollection had been blurred by the new version of her. Maybe his memory had already transformed the real McKenzie into something she had never been.

"I have begun," she said, and her glowing form began to flicker with scarlet starbursts. "I will not be here much longer."

"Does it—does it hurt?" he asked.

"No," she said with a smile. "But from the look on your face, I'm afraid it's hurting you."

Dean turned away to hide his pain. Part of him hunted desperately for an escape from this conversation. This impulse told him that if he could ignore it, it wouldn't be true. If he said it, he would feel it, and once he started feeling he wasn't sure he knew how to stop feeling it.

He took two limping steps towards the door. Then he stopped, realizing she would never hear anything he left unsaid. He had learned that lesson the first time she died.

Slowly, deliberately, he turned back to face her. The computer console was glowing red with the heat of McKenzie's calculations. This had made Mark Twain's image glitch and jitter, though its primary effect on McKenzie was to discolor her ghostly body. Her skin had lost its green luster and faded to blue, while her hair had taken on the reddish tinge of the fire that was burning her up. She now looked more like the real McKenzie than ever—the real McKenzie at the moment of her real death.

Unlike Orpheus, Dean chose to look at her. He knew it wouldn't make any difference. She was gone, had always been gone, and would never exist again except in the ways that she had shaped the world she had left behind. She couldn't change ever again, but he could, and he owed it to her to do so.

"Every day you were alive, I said that I loved you," he whispered. "Every day—even if I only said it in my heart. I've said it every day since you've been gone, and I'll say it over and over for the rest of my life whether you can hear it or not. But there's one thing I never said, something I should have told you. But I didn't, because I was a coward."

She smiled at him. Blue light swirled around her cheeks and spilled out into the air around her.

"The thing I never said to you," Dean couldn't bring his voice above a whisper. "The thing I needed to say was... Goodbye. Goodbye, McKenzie. Goodbye."

He moved close to her, and they reached out to embrace. His arms enveloped empty air and hers passed through him. He leaned in to kiss her, his lips touching nothing but insubstantial light. He could feel her warmth, the warmth of the flames that now burst from the console behind her. For one slender moment it was like she really was there. Then her bright colors faded into a cloud of muted hues that surrounded him briefly before disappearing into nothingness.

"Goodbye," he whispered to the empty air.

DECEMBER 25

(WINTER VACATION)

CHAPTER 45

Dean awoke in his bedroom at the residence in Topsy House. From where he lay, he could see through the window to watch fat white flakes drifting down and clinging to everything they touched. On his bed, so many blankets lay upon him that he almost longed to be outside in that cold. When he tried to pull the covers away he found his left arm wrapped in a plastic spider-web cast that looked like it had been made in a 3D printer. He could feel that his right leg was thickly bandaged, too.

"Are you awake?" the speakers of Dean's clock-radio spoke with the familiar Serbian-accented voice. An instant later, Tesla's green ghost materialized sitting in the bedside chair.

"I'm awake," Dean confirmed. "Awake, despite my best efforts. What day is it?"

"You didn't miss much time," Tesla said. "It's December 25th."

"Christmas Day," Dean said. He looked over at his translucent nursemaid and saw a bouquet of bright flowers next to him. The red petals next to the green ghost made a festive combination, and Dean wondered if Tesla represented the ghost of Christmas past, present or future. In this case, Dean decided, all three.

"So," Dean said. "You drew the short straw and had to sit by my bed until I woke up? That doesn't sound very exciting."

"I was the logical choice," Tesla said. "I could maintain the vigil because I do not need to sleep, and, furthermore, I would not bother you with a physical presence. Now, the others have asked me to let them know when you awoke. May I tell them they can come in?"

"Yes," Dean said. Then: "No, wait. What happened? I mean, I remember talking to McKenzie, getting her to do the anti-storm function of the drone fleet. I remember that, but then..."

Tesla smiled gently. "You wandered the bridge for a time, and then you slipped into a stupor. You kept mumbling something about Newton wearing a toga. Blood loss, I expect. You're lucky to be alive. The injury to your calf was rather bad, but, fortunately, it was less than an hour before our students arrived, and Victor tended to you and pronounced that you would make a full recovery."

Of all that information, Dean found it most interesting that Tesla had described the Institute gang as 'our' students.

"Lucky the kids found me before the cops did," Dean mused. "I guess the cops seized the *Raiden* and the *Tlaloc*?"

"The emergency response personnel in Los Angeles had much to occupy their attention," Tesla went on. "Our students had plenty of time to get you to safety as well as strip all the advanced technologies out of both sky palaces. All that material is now safely down in the underground lab, where it belongs. As a result, the Institute has far more antimatter reactors than ever before, and enough teslanium to build ten Wardenclyffe Towers."

"And Ignacio? What happened to him?"

"We left Ignacio to be arrested and stand trial for his crimes."

Dean grunted.

"You seem dissatisfied," Tesla said. "Do you think we should have dealt with Ignacio more harshly?"

"I don't know," Dean sighed. "I was wrong about him, you know. He had the will to fight for something important, and it's got me thinking that maybe our students should work on environmental projects more often. Maybe the world would be a better place if everyone took action like Ignacio did—except focused on creation instead of destruction. How much damage did those storms end up doing, anyway?"

"They were devastating," Tesla said gravely. "But they would have been exponentially worse if McKenzie had not ended them when she did. Now, my friend, I have one question for you, if I may. A scientific question."

Dean raised his eyebrows. What could Tesla, one of the greatest scientific minds in history, want to know from a meat-head like Dean?

"I am curious how you reached your decision," Tesla said. "That is, the decision between McKenzie and me. You asked her one question to determine whether she was alive or simply a mindless program. Why didn't you ask me any questions?"

"I didn't have to ask you anything," Dean let his head settle back down on the pillow. "Remember when we landed on top of the *Tlaloc*?

I'd already used my earthquake grenade to get into the *Raiden*, but you figured out another way to break in."

"It was a simple matter of assessing our available resources and determining the system's weak point," Tesla shrugged. "It was a shame to sacrifice the engines from your jet suit, but under the circumstances I saw no alternative."

"That's just it," Dean said. "You made a judgment call, and it was a good one. Maybe some other time you'll make a bad call, but the point is you had judgment to use."

"It was easy when I knew every inch of the sky palace, thanks to having served as its central computer for some time. And I invented the antimatter reactor, so it was even more familiar to me."

"But I'm willing to bet that nowhere in that ship's manual did it say anything about breaking in by melting a hole in a mosquito pod. And you probably never before considered rigging up an antimatter reactor to overheat without actually going thermonuclear. That was a creative solution—and you developed it on your own."

Tesla seemed to ponder this for a moment. "The ability to select goals and develop novel approaches to achieve those goals. Yes, I think that is as good a criteria for consciousness as any. You have created an effective test."

"Too bad most human beings wouldn't pass," Dean could feel a wry smirk creeping across his face. "Maybe if they could, we could solve global warming."

"Maybe if they could, we would have even greater problems," Tesla said. "You seem to be feeling somewhat better. May I invite the others in now?"

"Sure," Dean said. He expected that the "others" would include Victor and Soap, so he was surprised by the mob of people who stormed his bedroom. The first three all wore the customary lab coats of senior students: Soap in black, Victor in white, and Nikki in bubblegum pink. Then came the new students, Mike "Firebug" Raskolnikov, Janet Cho, Stephanie "Speed" Soto-Vasquez, and finally Collin Rosenberg, whose green Mohawk was as pointy as ever.

"You guys didn't have to stay here with me," Dean said. "This is vacation time. You should be home with your families."

"You're family," Soap said.

"And not just her family," Collin pointed to Soap, then to Dean. "You're family for all of us now, so here we are."

"Thing 1 and Thing 2 wanted to be here, too," Nikki said. "They just couldn't get their parents to buy 'em the airfare from Maine two days after they got home. But they all send their regards. And Cake is still down in Buenos Aires. He says he's takin' dance lessons—that boy didn't look like much of a dancer to me, but that's what he said."

Dean laughed a full belly-whoop, and it felt good. "Don't worry about Cake," he said. "Something tells me he has a very good dance instructor."

"Check it," Collin stepped forward. "You even got a card. I think it's from your FBI friend."

Dean saw that the card was, indeed, from Agent Nash, but it wasn't a sympathy card—it was the first check for his work as a consultant. The handwritten note explained that EMS had been on high alert in Los Angeles before the tornadoes hit, thanks to Dean's warning. The devastation was terrible, but the foreknowledge had saved countless lives.

Dean set the check aside, already having decided he would donate it to the Red Cross to help the disaster victims he hadn't been able to save.

"We have an important request," Soap popped up on the side of the bed. "We decided that we want you to stay. It's unanimous, and that includes Tesla."

The green ghost, who was quietly hovering in the corner, nodded in confirmation.

"Look, it's not that easy," Dean held out his hand apologetically. "It's too late now even if I changed my mind. I already tendered my letter of resignation to President Hart. My last day was the end of the quarter, and I need to name my successor by January first or else he gets to pick for me."

"You said you get to pick your successor?" Nikki asked.

"Yeah," Dean said. "Know anyone qualified?"

"Yes, sir, I do," she said with a sly grin. "Name yourself. You'll be your own successor."

Dean had to think about that one. Hart would be furious, but it sounded like there would be no way to close that loophole, given the bylaws governing Langdon University and the Mechanical Science Institute.

"Maybe now we'll finally get a picture of you hanging with the other Deans of Students in the entrance hall," Speed said. "It's about time, you know. I hate waiting for stuff like that."

"Yeah!" Raskolnikov said. "And if you're technically coming back for another term, does that mean we can call you D-Cubed instead of D-Squared?"

"Ha ha ha: no." Dean said flatly.

Victor stepped forward, and Dean now saw that the side of his face was darkened by a fresh scar. It seemed that the students had run into more trouble in Los Angeles than they had mentioned.

"We know you've been wanting to leave for a while now," Victor said. "But all of us agree that you're pretty much the best Dean ever."

The room was filled with yesses.

"Plus," Soap said. "We know you wanted to be a firefighter in Los Angeles again. Now that you've saved the entire city, wouldn't it be anticlimactic to go back to saving just one building at a time?"

"Well, I—"

"Don't say a thing yet," Nikki cut him off. "It's your choice, of course, and that's why you should let us decide for you. So we got you a passel of presents in hopes of convincing you to stay here and keep puttin' out *our* fires."

Another round of agreement from the crowd.

"First," Nikki handed him a large cardboard box. "Every full-rankin' member of the Institute has a lab coat, so here's yours."

Dean struggled to open the box with his one good arm until Speed impatiently yanked the lid off for him. Inside, he found a heavy, insulated jacket, like a firefighter's but long enough to cover his shins. It was neon yellow with thick, silver reflective stripes.

"I made it myself," Nikki said. "It's heat resistant, fireproof, and knife-proof. It might even stop a bullet—theoretically, if it had more padding. Plus, I put your symbol on the back."

"I didn't think I had a symbol," Dean said, but she turned it around for him to see the large, triangular fire hazard warning symbol sewn from reflective fabric. Below, also in reflective lettering, she had embroidered the words "Mean Dean."

"Wow," he said. "I can honestly say that this is the most hideous garment that's ever touched my heart. Thank you. If I ever wear a lab coat, this will be it."

"Wait, there's one more thing," Soap said. "Professor Bjelland!"

Heidi entered the room, smiling, with a fuzzy yellow puppy squirming in her arms. She dropped the puppy unceremoniously onto Dean's chest. Suddenly all he could see was a manic tongue giving him puppy kisses.

"It's a golden retriever," Heidi explained. "Soap says you missed having a station dog, so she asked me to help find one. We looked, but there wasn't a Dalmatian puppy available within driving range. I hope this one will be just as good."

Dean ruffled the fur on the puppy's back, which made it wiggle its tiny tail furiously and run excited circles around the bed.

"He's perfect," Dean said. "He'll make a great station dog."

"But the puppy lives here in Topsy!" Soap almost shouted. "If you want him, you have to live here, too! That's the deal!"

"Okay, okay!" Dean sighed. "You guys win! I'll stay on board here, at least until the end of the school year."

"Did you here that, everybody?" Nikki said. "He's staying forever! Three cheers for the Dean who's so nice they named him twice! D-Squared!"

Dean tried to protest, but his words were drowned out by chants of "D-Squared!"

"All right! All right!" Victor finally shushed them. "Let's take the party outside. My patient needs rest."

Reluctantly, they filed out of Dean's room, noisily discussing whether dinner should be pizza or Chinese or both. Nikki collected Tesla's Egg as she left, and Heidi squeezed Dean's toe in a take-care-of-yourself gesture before she followed them out. Soap was the last to go, and she scooped up the puppy to take with her.

"You can leave the puppy, Soap," Dean said. "And I want to talk to you for a second. In private."

"Okay," she said. "Am I in trouble?"

"Actually," he said. "I wanted to apologize to you."

"Apologize?" She looked stunned. "For what?"

"I gave you bad advice. About your boyfriend, Brett."

"Oh. Yeah," she hung her head. "He and I haven't spoken in weeks, so—I don't know."

"He's ashamed." Dean said. "But he doesn't want to talk about it. You need to go to him, explain yourself, and explain what he means to you—and what he doesn't mean. Keep it short, because he'll be uncomfortable, and it might take him some time to open up. Don't push him to answer you right away, but keep reminding him that you want to hear it. He'll open up when he's ready. Guys are like that. We're just afraid."

"Of what?"

"We're afraid of being afraid."

She studied him for a moment. "That kind of puts some things in perspective," she said. "But that makes it tough for me, because I'm not the best at picking up on feelings and all that stuff. Does the same apply to you? The part about being afraid and not talking, I mean?"

Dean was quiet for a long moment as the puppy playfully nipped at his hand. "Yeah," he said. "Yeah, it does. But I think maybe I should start being more open about things."

"Is it harder with stronger feelings? Like, does it hurt more to talk about McKenzie?"

Thinking about her felt like a knife in his heart. But nothing he could do would change the fact that McKenzie was the past. Soap was the future. Soap, and all the other students at the Institute.

"Dean?" she asked. "Are you crying?"

His first impulse was to deny it. Instead, he chose to be brave.

"Yes," he said, and he didn't try to hide his tears.

"Tears means you're sad, right?" she asked.

"I'm sad and happy," he said.

"That doesn't make sense," she frowned.

"No," he admitted. "No, it doesn't make any sense at all. But it's how I feel."

The puppy climbed onto his neck and excitedly licked the tears away while Dean let himself cry and laugh at the same time.

About the Author

Sechin Tower is a writer, game designer, and teacher. He lives in the Seattle, Washington area with his beautiful wife and noisy cat. In his spare time, he prepares for the zombie apocalypse by running obstacle courses and playing way too many video games.

Also by Sechin Tower

Three Weeks Before Doomsday

Mad Science Institute

The Non-Zombie Apocalypse

A Note from the Author:

Thank you for purchasing and reading this novel. I hope you had as much fun reading it as I had writing it!

Please consider taking a little extra time to leave feedback where you purchased this book. Your review and your opinion will help others find this book and it really does matter—both to other readers as well as to me.

If you have questions, comments, or suggestions, please contact me through my website SechinTower.com, on twitter @SechinTower, or on Facebook/MadScienceInstitute. I would love to hear from you!

CPSIA information can be obtained
at www.ICGtesting.com
Printed in the USA
LVOW12s0357291216
519080LV00001B/23/P